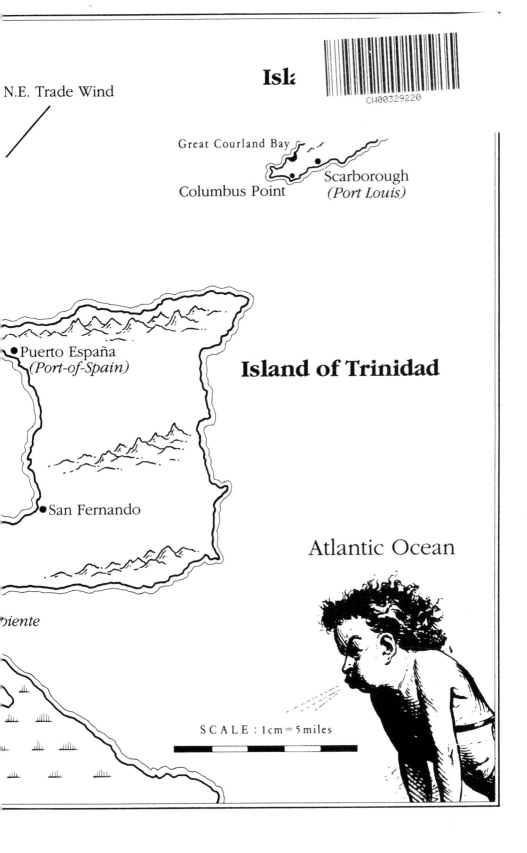

N.E. Trade Wind

Isl

Great Courland Bay

Columbus Point

Scarborough
(Port Louis)

•Puerto España
(Port-of-Spain)

Island of Trinidad

•San Fernando

Atlantic Ocean

)iente

S C A L E : 1 cm = 5 miles

THE QUIET STRANGER

being the Life and Times of a Scottish Merchant, known to the World as Richard Mason, who was born in the Island of Tobago in the Year 1767, and who died in the Island of Trinidad in the Year 1849

"— this commonplace, quiet stranger — how had he become involved in the web of horror?"

Jane Eyre
CHARLOTTE BRONTE

"Richard Mason is a sly man and he will tell you a lot of nancy stories, which is what we call lies here —"

Wide Sargasso Sea
JEAN RHYS

THE
QUIET STRANGER

a novel by ROBBIE KYDD

MAINSTREAM
PUBLISHING

Copyright © Robbie Kydd, 1991

First published in Great Britain in 1991 by
MAINSTREAM PUBLISHING COMPANY
(EDINBURGH) LTD
7 Albany Street
Edinburgh EH1 3UG
ISBN 1 85158 300 9 (cloth)

The publisher acknowledges subsidy of the Scottish Arts Council
towards the publication of this volume.

British Library Cataloguing in Publication Data
Kydd, Robbie
  The Quiet Stranger
  I. Title
  823.914 [F]

ISBN 1–85158–300–9

Both design and map by James Hutcheson
Typeset in 11/13 Caslon by Selectmove Ltd, London
Printed in Great Britain by Mackays of Chatham, Chatham

This book is dedicated
with love and gratitude
to my wife of thirty years
NORA CHERRIE
a true Trinidadian, without whose
knowledge and help I could not even
have started it

Notes, Acknowledgments and a Glossary will be
found at the end of this book

CHAPTER I

A memorable Day during my Childhood at Braemore Estate, Island of Tobago;
I am involved in Misdemeanours but am rescued from the Consequences; I find a
Friend; and after Dark a Horseman arrives and departs without dismounting

"Hai-hai-hai! Giddy-up there! Giddy-up! Giddy-up!" shouted my sister
Antoinetta as she rode one of the hogs round the yard of our little rough-
hewn estate house. "Hai-hai-hai!"

The hog was a slow dusty gravid sow of the small breed then common
in Tobago; she was not at all happy to be used as a mount and was grunting
in protest, but could find no means of escape from her tormentor.

The time was late afternoon. The year was 1773 — of that I am
certain, for reasons which I shall recount later — and I was therefore six
years of age, while Antoinetta would have owned proudly to nine years. I
was watching my sister with considerable trepidation, for such behaviour
was liable to provoke my father's wrath, which rarely confined itself to
Antoinetta and her sins but spread inexorably outward to encompass me
and my shortcomings both moral and physical. My sister was already in
disgrace for a previous misdemeanour and had been forbidden to ride her
pony as a punishment, so that Father would be enraged to a degree which
I did not like to contemplate.

Antoinetta's cavortings upon the sow were also being witnessed by a
small crowd of Negro children, consisting of those who were too sickly or
too young to perform even such easy tasks as weeding the provision-garden
or sweeping the yard. Some of them were backing away toward the tall
pigeon-pea plants where they were wont to hide when danger, or what
they fancied to be danger, threatened; others stood with their fingers in
their mouths, gazing wide-eyed at Mamzelle's antics.

My young brother Henri, of three years, was present too; he was lying on a blanket near to me on our rudimentary galerie so that I could keep an eye on him. As usual, he did not seem able to observe much, or to hear much, even the rumpus which was going on so near to him, and his head moved ceaselessly from side to side. His round pale face was without expression, his eyes vacant, and his mouth so loose that it could not fail to dribble; every so often he made a meaningless babbling noise.

I knew, as I watched Antoinetta and the waddling sow, that yet another pair of eyes was observing the scene. Projecting into the yard there was a hut, even rougher-hewn than the main house against which it leaned, and through a chink between its horizontal planks would be visible the whites of those eyes, if I cared to look for them.

My sister's yells, and her behaviour, became more and more outrageous; indeed, close on daemonic. Even after a lifetime I do not seem to have garnered the words to describe them, although I have been emboldened to write them down as exactly as I can by reading Miss Austen's description of Catherine Morland's behaviour in the first three pages of *Northanger Abbey*, a novel which has recently reached me from London. Antoinetta was, like Catherine, "noisy and wild"; she too "hated confinement and cleanliness"; and she certainly preferred "riding on horse-back and running about the country to books." Whether her subsequent life-story bore any resemblance to that of Miss Austen's heroine my readers will discover for themselves if they care to persevere with these my memoirs.

Impatient of restraint, Antoinetta (or Tony, as she preferred to be called) had thrown away her hat, tied up her hated long black hair into an untidy knot on the top of her head, kicked off her confining shoes and stockings and (I am scarce able to write the words) tucked the skirt of her dress into her drawers. Thus attired, she was able to sit astride the hog and grip its sides fiercely with her boyish nether limbs in bareback horseman fashion, her dark brows knitted and her teeth showing whitely in a face burned to an uncomely brown by too much exposure to the sun. For reins Tony held one of the creature's hair-fringed ears and for a whip she had broken off a piece of green bamboo. Round and round the yard they went, the sow complaining with soft grunts and whistles and still hopefully seeking an escape, while Tony's yells rose to screams as she tried to lash the poor brute into a canter, a gait which her gravid condition made impossible.

Tony's excitement must have communicated itself to the little Negroes for one or two of the bolder ones ventured away from the pigeon-peas into the open and followed her, performing silent little pantomimes of horse-riding. However, when the grunting sow and its Amazon rider wheeled round and approached them they scampered off without a sound. (Father was in the habit of saying that Silence was a Negro-child's best friend, a lesson which they seemed to learn very early in their lives.)

My readers may be wondering at the lack of an adult presence that permitted such pranks as Tony's. I have to inform them that Braemore Estate was not at that time large or prosperous and that we could not afford Negro house-servants (at prices of up to £100 a head for prime trained examples) in anything like the numbers we owned later. On that afternoon Father was out in the cane overseeing the overseers and their gangs; Maman was dozing on her bed befuddled with brandy, her French novel fallen on to her breast; Matti, our house-keeper and cook and part of Maman's *dot* (in which she was valued at £120) was still in the garden with her assistants, digging ground provisions and picking dasheen-bush for dinner; and the two ancient Negresses (valued at £5 each) and their two or three heavily *enceinte* field-hand *macommères*, who were supposed to keep an eye upon us as well as upon the Negro infants, were sleeping as soundly as they always did at this time of the afternoon. Thus Tony was at liberty to act as her nature dictated while I acted in accordance with mine — that is, I observed keenly with all my senses and stored my observations away in a memory that is proving to be exceptionally retentive and capacious as I explore its distant recesses for the purpose of writing my Life and Times. The one serious defect in my memory is that whilst it is clear about persons and events it is not always clear about the order in which the events happened.

On that afternoon Tony's nature drove her to new heights of unpredictability; tiring of the slowness of the sow, she leapt lithely off its back, ran across the yard and up the steps to where I was peering through the crude wooden railing of the galerie.

"Come on! Be doing something, instead of just watching me all the time!" she cried, seizing me around the waist and, although I was even then heavier than she was, lifting me off my feet and carrying me down the steps. Once on the dusty earth of the yard she set off in pursuit of the hog, which was waddling hopefully toward its usual shady resting-place near the pile of cocoa-nuts which were to be opened for its dinner. The poor creature was no match for Tony's speed, even hampered as she was by my impotently struggling form. In what seemed like no time at all I was astride the beast's scurfy back, holding on to its ears and inhaling its sickly odours, while Tony held me upright with one hand and used her bamboo freely with the other.

I decided that enough was enough, opened my mouth and bawled. Henri must have heard me, for he whimpered and then wailed in sympathy. Our two house-dogs emerged from under the house, barking excitedly and straining at their ropes, inducing the torpid group of fowls to wake up and run about squawking. In the midst of this uproar Tony suddenly loosed her hold on me and stood stock-still with her hand to her ear. Then, with incredible speed, she let down her hair and her skirt and ran to the makeshift gate in the yard fence, screaming: "It is Papa on Hector! I can hear him coming! Papa! Papa!"

At this the dogs became hysterical and Henri's wail increased in volume. The sow, quite oblivious of the mounting hubbub, stopped in her tracks and flopped over on to her side, taking me with her and trapping one of my legs under her great soft belly. I was shocked into silence; I was not in pain, but I could not move. In seconds, or so it seemed, Father arrived and hastily dismounted from Hector.

"I was seeing what you were up to!" he shouted, striding across the yard toward me. His choleric face seemed even redder than usual under the brim of his enormous hat. He bent down and seized me by the ankle of my free leg, pulled me out from under the sow and lifted me off the ground so that I hung upside down. I knew that his whip was raised to thrash me when a deep African voice came from the galerie.

"Massieu!" called Matti, rocking the now pacified Henri in her arms.

With a muttered Gaelic oath Father stood me on my feet but continued to hold me by my shirt-collar. He raised his whip and held it high while he and Matti stared at each other for what seemed to me like an eternity. Although Father's grip on my collar was nearly choking me and fear of his whip gnawed at my vitals, yet my powers of observation did not diminish — rather to the contrary, for I could see the hog settling herself beside her beloved pile of cocoa-nuts; I could smell the leather of Father's boots and breeches and whip; I could see three distinct processions of ants pursuing their business in the dust of the yard; I could hear the Trade Wind rustling its unremitting rustle in the cocoa-nut palms; I could see the sun dipping behind the trees of the forest; I could hear the muted sounds and snatches of song from the Negroes' downwind quarters, signalling that they were resuming their dimly-lit domestic lives after spending all the daylight hours in the labour which was to recoup our family fortunes; I was aware, I am almost certain, of the whites of that ever-vigilant pair of eyes watching me from between the planks of Matti's lean-to; and finally, I could certainly see what Tony was up to.

She had run to Hector as soon as Father had dismounted and signalled imperiously to Jéhu, the young Negro who acted as a part-time groom and who was now holding the huge horse's head. She was ordering him to lift her into the saddle; he hesitated and she stamped her foot at him without a word. After a quick glance at Father's back, and another at Matti, Jéhu bent down, gripped Tony by her ankle and effortlessly hoisted her into the saddle. When he refused to hand her the reins a silent struggle was waged, with both protagonists eyeing Father, until Jéhu managed to edge Hector out of the yard towards his stable, a direction the horse was only too willing to take.

Meanwhile the other silent struggle, the one between Father and Matti, was still in progress. It seemed to me that Matti was forbidding Father to thrash me, but she did not speak. (Indeed, if I may digress, she rarely spoke, and her silence hid some power, derived perhaps from the Dark Continent whence she had been brought in chains. Yet she was no commonplace Obeah-woman such as terrorizes the common run of Negroes; no purveyor of potions and spells and empty bottles and bundles of egg-shells and feathers. My words are but inadequate puffs of air, mere useless fly-specks upon paper, to convey her numinous quality. In my dotage I can admit to this ledger in which I write, although not to any living person save one, that I loved and feared that black African slave-woman more than I loved and feared my parents — her "Yea" and "Nay" were my Right and Wrong and remain so to this day.)

I know not how long Father and Matti would have remained locked in mute conflict for the battle of wills was ended suddenly and dramatically by Tony trotting Hector back into the yard and then, as she approached Father and myself, jerking at his reins to make him rear. Father instantly pushed me to the ground amongst the ants and reached for Hector's head.

"Run, Dickie!" shouted Tony from the saddle, "Hide under the house! Quick!"

I hastened to make my way crabwise on all fours — running has never come naturally to me — away from the trampling hooves and across the dust and ant-processions of the yard to the space under the house. There, amongst the roughly squared baulks of timber awaiting the enlargement of the house, was a refuge which Tony and I fondly imagined was known only to ourselves and the dogs. Of humans, only small children could reach it, but lizards, cockroaches, ants of all colours, and snakes were our constant companions there — we regarded them all as friends to be treated with respect. I wormed my way in, sat down on one of the empty boxes which were the only furnishings and listened — how hard I listened!

Father and Tony were arguing loudly as they took Hector back to his stable; Maman was crooning to Henri — Matti always passed him back to her as soon as he was pacified; Matti and her assistants were moving

11

about in the outside kitchen and murmuring to each other. Then Father's man Martin came into the house carrying water for Father's bath and was reproved by Maman for letting the water slop over. Martin's twin sister Milly began to lay the two tables for dinner — I could hear the chink of silver and glass. From the lean-to came no sound at all — Betsy, Matti's wraith-like daughter, and the owner of the peering eyes, must have been hugging her best friend Silence to her.

In the day-time my refuge was well enough lit but night was now approaching rapidly and my fear of the dark began to war with my fear of Father and his whip. I heard Maman call out to Martin to light the lamps and hoped that a comforting ray might penetrate the ill-fitting floor-boards, but little light came, for the refuge was directly under the chamber which I shared with Henri and no one was likely to light a lamp there just yet. Then, through the horizontal gap between two of the baulks I saw a glimmer of light from the open door of the kitchen; Matti must have lit at least two candles there. I could see her shadow moving about and that was enough to relieve my fear of the dark, but my dread of Father was shortly revived when I heard him and Tony returning from the stable, talking quietly. I knew before I could distinguish Father's words that he and Tony had made up their quarrel — it was easy for him to forgive madcap courage, especially upon a horse.

"Indeed and indeed, Antonia, you are a bold girl," he was saying, "and, yes, you may be riding Cassandra tomorrow." He raised his voice as he approached the galerie steps and asked: "But where is that blasted boy?"

"He will be hiding under the house," answered Tony, "and feared to come out."

Father bent down and shouted to me: "I do not understand at all why a son of mine would be riding a hog when he is not man enough to ride a pony. If that sow loses her litter, sir, I will be having your hide!"

Terror held my lips shut and I answered not.

"There will be no dinner for you and you will be going straight to bed when you come out. Do you understand me, Richard?"

Again I could not answer.

"You will be having enough of the dark in there in five minutes. Come, Antonia."

I stayed in that dark place for a great deal longer than five minutes, still afraid to face Father but not unwilling to prove that he was wrong about my fear of the dark. All was quiet for a while as Father disrobed for his bath and I dared to let myself dream dreams of lonely islands and empty forest glades and far Highland hill-tops and other quiet places to which, when I

12

was a little older, I would escape. My dreams did not last long, however, for Tony had crept to the point on the galerie nearest to my hiding-place and had put her head through the railing. She was intent on tormenting me.

"Ha-ha-ha!" she cried, "I am having my dinner and Dickie is having none!"

I refused to be provoked; I knew from long experience that keeping quiet was the best answer to Tony in this mood. She tried again, singing this time.

Ha-ha-ha! Hee-hee-hee!
Someone will be hungry,
And it won't be me!

"Silence! In the Name!" Father's voice leapt over the partition walls, rose to the tree-trunk rafters, and lost itself amongst our roof of thatch. ("My parents would die of shame," I had heard Maman complain, "if they knew that their *fille* was living in a thatched hut." Father had promised, testily, that he would buy shingles or tiles just as soon as he had produced and sold enough hogsheads of sugar and puncheons of rum. Even at my tender age I had begun to wonder if there were enough sugar and rum in the whole world to buy the things which Father promised to Maman.)

Tony crept away and I would no doubt have lost myself in dreams again had not hunger supervened. All the sounds and smells which reached me from the kitchen spoke of the imminence of dinner. There came the soft clink of wooden spoon upon iron pot; the rasp of a knife being whetted; the thud-thud of something being pounded in a mortar; and a mixture of delectable odours. Milly, I could hear, had finished her slow laying of my parents' table with silver and crystal and porcelain and was now laying the children's table at the end of the galerie nearest the kitchen. (Milly was housemaid, nursemaid to Henri, or kitchen-maid as need dictated, but was exceedingly slow at her tasks. She and Martin were not slaves, but Charaibe foundlings, and so stupid that they did not know that they were free and could have asked for wages.)

There was a scrape of chair-legs as Father and Maman sat down, followed quickly by some confusion as Henri was tied into his high-chair to be spoon-fed while Tony argued that since I was not to have dinner she should sit in my place at the head of the little table. There was a moment or two of silence, which was Father saying Grace in a mumble, and then his much louder ritual of complaints about the food.

13

"Madame," — rarely did he address Maman as "Madeleine" in public — "I have had enough altogether of pork and fowl and turtle and *le calalou* and these tasteless ground provisions."

"Jonas, you know it is all we have," sighed Maman.

"I will be having mutton and salt-beef and flour for bread if I have to go to Scarborough myself to fetch them."

"But there is no ship due for months; and anyway the last food we bought in Scarborough was bad. We had to feed it to the hogs. You must learn to like Créole food."

From the children's table came Tony's voice, much clearer and louder than Father's, and unashamedly aping him.

"Milly! Take this away! It is nigger food. It might as well be salt-fish! I want beef and fresh bread."

"Eat your dinner, Mamzelle."

"No, I will not! Take it away!"

"I fetch Matti, Mamzelle."

"Fetch her! I dare you!"

There followed a silence, during which my hunger pains grew sharper and sharper as the aromas of the despised roast pork and *calalou* (rich with cocoa-nut milk and crab-meat) distended my nostrils and brought water to my mouth. In the stillness I could hear the firm sound of Matti's bare feet ascending to the galerie; a deeper silence followed and I guessed that she was staring down Tony and daring her not to eat. (There was nothing dramatic about Matti's stance on these occasions; she merely stood with her feet apart, her kerchiefed head erect, her massy lips turned down, and her hands loosely crossed in front of her. Her power needed no trappings.)

My attention was distracted from these happenings above my head by a faint scratching noise very close to me. At first I thought it was one of the dogs, but then I noticed that it was coming from the direction of the lean-to and the kitchen, where there were no dogs. I turned my head and heard a faint whisper, unfamiliar and almost ghostly.

"Master Dickie! Master Dickie!"

Between two of the baulks of timber on the side of the refuge whence the voice was coming there was a gap of perhaps a handspan; through it I could now see the flame of a tiny cocoa-nut oil lamp. I gasped in amazement as a plate appeared in the gap, followed closely by the aromas of dinner which had been so tantalizing me.

"Master Dickie!" came the whisper again and I perceived that whoever was handing me the plate was dazzled by the flame of the lamp and could not see me, just as I could not see him or her.

"I am here," I whispered back.

14

"Take the plate, if you please."

I put my hand into the gap and took the plate from a pair of small black hands, which could only have belonged to Betsy.

"Now take your spoon, if you please."

I took the spoon; it was my very own horn spoon, the one with a silver shield and a silver thistle on the handle which Father had brought from Scotland, mysterious Scotland.

"Now take the lamp, please."

This was not so easy. In the dark I had to find a level place upon which to lay down the brimming plate where it could not be reached by the cockroaches which were swarming over my feet; I had no antipathy toward them, but did not propose to share my dinner. When I had succeeded I took the little half cocoa-nut and placed it firmly where its light would shew me the plate.

"My mother say," came another slow, most carefully enunciated and now less than ghostly whisper, "that you are to eat very quickly, give me back the plate and spoon, and not tell anyone you have had your dinner."

I was torn between my hunger and my astonishment at all these speeches in English from Betsy; I had only rarely heard her speak more than two words before, and those in patois. She was usually as silent as her mother and I only saw her when she appeared to sweep a floor or run a message.

I should explain that our family used three languages: we spoke English with Father and his overseers (although they often spoke to each other in incomprehensible Gaelic); we spoke metropolitan French with Maman; and we spoke St. Domingue patois with the Negroes, for most of them had been brought from that Island. How then had Betsy learned to speak English? At my age I did not ask this question, but I guessed much later that Matti had encouraged her daughter to eavesdrop as often as she could in order to learn the language of the all-powerful Master.

I did not allow my astonishment at Betsy's command of English to keep me long from my dinner. After a quick glance through the gap to confirm that the lamp was still reflected in her liquid eyes, I seized my spoon and started to eat, delighted to find that there were delicious pieces of boiled plantain and crab-meat amongst the chopped-up roast pork and ground provisions, all swimming in *le calalou*. I have never understood why Father objected to this kind of dinner. When I had finished I handed the plate and spoon back to Betsy through the gap.

"Messi beaucoup!" I said, patois coming naturally since I was talking to a servant.

15

"My mother say I am to speak only English to you when no one else can hear us," said Betsy slowly; then, speaking more rapidly, she added: "Would you like some jumbie-beads?"

"Are they magic?" I asked, for I had heard talk about them and knew that Betsy, like most other Negro children, wore a string of them around her ankle.

"Do not be a silly goose," she answered, using one of Tony's phrases, "these are for playing games with."

"But I thought you wore them to protect you from spirits," I objected, "I thought they were Obeah."

"I wear a string of them because they are pretty. These others are for you to play with." She handed me a little piece of rough linen cloth tied into a bag. I could feel the slippery seeds inside; I opened the bag and tipped them into my palm and held them close to the lamp's flame and wondered at the marvellous sheen of the lacquer-like black-and-scarlet shells.

"Count them," said Betsy.

"Un, deux, trois, quat — " I began.

"One, two, three, four — " interrupted Betsy.

"Why must we speak English?" I asked.

"I shall not always be a slave; that is what my mother say." She broke into the quietest of giggles. "Dickie ride a hog! Dickie upside down! Dickie sent to bed!"

"You saw?"

"I saw everything. I am glad you were not licked. Give me the lamp, if you please."

I passed the lamp to her and she disappeared, leaving me with the joyful sensation that I had been teased by someone to whom teasing could be an expression of affection. If Tony had said those words they would have been cruel taunts. In the dark I passed the jumbie-beads from hand to hand, counting and re-counting them and feeling their smoothness with reverence.

(I lay down my pen and reach across my desk for Father's silver snuff-box with the stag's head embossed upon it. I open it and there they are — one hundred and thirty-seven jumbie-beads. I count them, in thirteen groups of ten and one of seven; all are present. I know that they were given to me by Betsy, but whether they are the ones which she gave to me on that memorable night I could not say. An old man's facile tears fill my eyes. I shall be scolded if I am found weeping thus.)

I think I would have continued to count those precious beads for a long time had I not become aware of ominous sensations in the soles of my feet, which were planted upon the hard earth. In a moment I recognized them as the vibrations from the hooves of a horse being galloped furiously toward our house. I was hesitating whether to call out the news to Father when Tony and the dogs forestalled me.

"Papa!" shrieked Tony, as the dogs barked madly, "There is a horse coming at a full gallop! On the road from Scarborough!"

"Stations! Ring the bell!" shouted Father, and I could hear nothing but confusion. Someone rang the estate bell, all the lights were blown out, there were hurried footsteps all over the house, the dogs became hysterical, and I was prey to all sorts of terror, for my "station" under Father's "Standing Orders" for emergencies was under my bed and there was no possibility of my reaching it now, for all the doors and jalousies would be shut and fastened. I could only sit and tremble while the galloping horse breasted the hill. (Our house had been sited on a hill for easy defence, Father used to boast, like a castle in Scotland.)

The moon was high and bright and the rider's eyes must have been well accustomed to the dim light for he rode straight up to the darkened house and reined in his horse.

"Which wey tae Courland Bay?" he cried in a broad Scotch accent, "In the Name o' Goad, gie me a bearing!"

"Is yourself informing me that the French have landed at Scarborough?" asked Father in a calm, almost phlegmatic, voice.

"There's nae word o' the French. Direct me to Great Courland Bay, I beg of you, sir!"

"There would not be Negroes in revolt, would there?"

"Na, na! A'thing's peacefu'."

"In that case, I am warning you that my musket, though no weapon for a gentleman, is loaded and yourself is in my sights. Moreover, my friend, it is liable to fire without warning, for my right hand bears an ancient wound and cannot be controlling the trigger as it should. Are you alone?"

"I assure you, on the level, that I am alone."

"And who is yourself?"

"A fellow-Christian taken aback in this damned forest. Oblige me, sir, with a bearing to Great Courland Bay."

Even my six-year-old ears noticed that our visitor's accent varied as wildly as his manner, much as Father's speech did, depending upon his temper and to whom he was speaking.

"And what would be your hurry, fellow-Christian?"

"Ah, Mr. Mason, sir, I recognize your voice. Pray oblige me, for if this is Braemore, I am far off course."

"Indeed and indeed, you are describing your situation with great exactitude, but yourself has still not told me who you are and what your hurry is."

"I am Captain Paul of the ship *Betsy*, presently anchored at Scarborough. I have met you on the quay, sir."

"Ah, Captain Paul, is it? A very good evening to you, Captain. And as to the hurry you were going to inform me about?"

"I hae urgent letters fir the Falmooth packet and she's due oot o' Courland Bay at the keek o' day."

"Well, well. I must be accepting your word on that. Fergus!"

"Fergus is here!" cried the overseer of that name from his station in the shadows.

"Light a flambeau and shew the captain the very quickest road to Courland Bay."

"Och, that is good of you," said the Captain, "but I am still in the devil of a fix — could ye no pay me the siller ye owe me for provisions?"

"I am not in the habit," replied Father with even greater calm, "of opening my house at this time of night to pay my debts, especially when they are owed for bad provisions. Your butter was rancid, your salt-beef tainted, your potatoes rotten and your oatmeal full of weevils. I have not been eating a proper meal in months."

"Ah, Mr. Mason, these things are sent tae try us. You are a man of honour, I know, and will pay Archie Stewart what you owe me."

Father did not answer and a heavy silence filled the darkness. Then a sudden blaze of flickering light intimated that Fergus had arrived with his flambeau; it made my refuge seem even blacker.

"Ach, to the Devil!" shouted Captain Paul, leaving me uncertain whether he was consigning Father to the Horned One or proposing to visit Him on his own behalf. I was straining to hear his horse's hooves as he departed when a small strong hand grasped my arm — Tony had crept up on me without my hearing her.

"If you move quickly," she whispered urgently, "you will be under your bed before the lamps are lit again. Then Papa will find you in the right place."

There followed the most terrifying part of the whole day. I knew that Tony must have had the temerity to unbar an outside door, contrary to Father's most strictly enforced Standing Order. If he caught us re-entering through that door, there was no knowing what his rage might lead him to do. I might suffer more than a thrashing, if that were possible. He was as unpredictable as Tony when roused.

Tony, needless to say, had no intention of letting my terror hinder her plan; she pushed, pulled and cajoled me until we were through that unbarred door. While she was gingerly replacing the stout bar I crept on all fours to the door of my room, meeting no one on the way. I prayed that the hinge would not creak, opened the door just wide enough for me to enter, slipped through, and closed the door again with the utmost care. Then, still on all fours, I very promptly joined the po-cham under my bed; I was still clutching my little bag of jumbie-beads.

I waited for disaster, but nothing happened. Father did not come to find me, nor did he inquire about me, being confident, no doubt, that his womenfolk would see to my welfare. Instead, he called his overseers — five of them without Fergus — and very audibly conferred with them about the likelihood of a squad of militiamen, or perchance an irate husband with a posse of armed friends, arriving in pursuit of the Captain, but no one came. In half-an-hour or so Fergus returned with the news that he had put the Captain on the right road without further incident, and Father declared the end of the emergency. Lamps and candles were lit again, I could hear the servants returning to their tasks and Maman saying a succession of Hail Mary's in front of her picture of the Virgin.

(Although Captain Paul will not appear again in my story, his hurried stop at Braemore is important in that enables me to be certain that these events took place in the year 1773, a year which was constantly referred to by Father and everyone else in Tobago as the one in which the notorious adventurer, slave-trader, murderer, pirate, rebel, Freemason, intriguer, philanderer and dishonest trader Captain John Paul disappeared from the Island in mysterious circumstances, after running through and killing an honest local seaman whom he had goaded into mutiny. It transpired that he left behind him, not creditors as is usual when villains decamp, but many debtors such as Father; which aspect of his abscondence lent substance to the view that he had committed other, though hardly more dastardly, crimes. That, in extremity, he had tried to dun Father for the paltry sum of £15 is hardly surprising; there was not then, or indeed ever, enough money in the world to satiate the cupidity of "Rear-Admiral" John Paul Jones, nor was there an ocean wide enough to accommodate his naval ambitions.)

And what of my little friend Betsy, my readers may ask, where was she during these alarms? I am ashamed to write that I know not. Perhaps I was too young to overcome my numbing fears and wonder where she was, what she was doing, and whether she was afraid too. Lying under my bed, it was Matti's step for which I was listening and no other. I knew that she must have been caring for Henri throughout Captain Paul's visit, otherwise he would have raised his idiot voice at some awkward moment. How I longed for her to come, so that I might take refuge in her ample linsey skirts, or better still, in her arms!

(It was Matti alone who could assuage my fears: she alone who could quieten Henri when he wept his hopeless snuffling laments for his idiot condition, and still his dreadful rocking; she alone who could offer wordless comfort to Maman when she mourned for her lost youth and beauty and for the four children whom they had nursed together through the fatal wasting fevers brought on by the dreadful deceitful climate of Tobago — yes, my readers, three fine active straight-limbed boys and an adorable fair little girl had succumbed one by one, leaving behind the three of us, each as unsatisfactory as the other two in our different ways; it was Matti alone who could moderate the rages which consumed Father and Tony — whether they loved her I know not, but they both feared her, Father more than Tony.)

When Matti eventually arrived, carrying the sleeping Henri, I was cowering in a pool of my own making, despite the proximity of the po-cham. Matti put Henri to his bed, then undressed me, washed me, put on my nightshirt and put me to my bed, where I discovered that I was still holding on to my bag of beads; perhaps they were a representation of the friendship I had been promised and did not want to lose.

The very fact that Matti put me to my bed would have made this day memorable, for she did so only on special occasions, for example, when Henri or I (or both of us) needed the kind of reassurance which only she could give before we would consent to sleep. I remember clearly winding my arms round her neck and kissing her black cheeks with childish passion while the safety of her arms surrounded me; then she laid me down and kneaded the base of my neck with her strong hand. When I was close to sleep she put her finger to my lips for a moment, stood up, and walked noiselessly from the room. She did not say "goodnight", for she never did.

CHAPTER II

*Maman commences my Education and I share it surreptitiously; Father despairs
of making a Man of me; my Turpitude is discovered and I am punished*

Father's "Standing Orders" and his other preparations for the defence of
Braemore were not required again for many years. Although I often took
pains to overhear him and his overseers and occasional visitors arguing
vehemently for and against the rebellion in the American Colonies and
lamenting how it was interrupting the sugar trade and preventing Father
from amassing the quick fortune which he so ardently desired, yet to
me, as a small boy, the actions of King George, Lord North and the
Rebels did not seem to bear directly on my life in Tobago. In fact, the
Island was experiencing a period of such peace and tranquillity as was
possible in that era when the production of sugar and Negro slavery went
hand-in-hand. The further childhood memories which I am about to recount
are therefore of domestic events at Braemore, without irruption from the
outside world.

Early one morning, not long after the incidents described in the last
chapter, my life took one of its few turns for the better. Father had left
for the fields as usual and Tony, Henri and I had finished our breakfast
when Matti arrived to supervize Milly clearing our table; she insisted that
it be thoroughly wiped down and dried. Then she went through to the
dining-room and produced from a cupboard books and pencils and paper,
all brand new. She brought them out on to the galerie and proceeded to lay
them out on our table with particular care.

"What are they for?" I asked.

Matti motioned me to sit at the table, which I was only too happy to
do, for I was fascinated by the unfamiliar objects and full of the notion that

21

they were to afford me pleasure of the quiet indoor kind which I preferred. Tony, however, had other sentiments.

"I have had lessons before. I am off!" cried she, and ran along the galerie with the plain intention of escaping down the steps. To her, of course, there were few, if any, quiet indoor pleasures — the out-of-doors with its heat and dust and horses was her natural element and it was calling to her.

"Mamzelle Toinette!" called Matti, stopping Tony in her tracks. They locked eyes and Tony walked slowly back to the table and sat down on the edge of her chair.

"You can make me sit here," she muttered, "but you cannot make me do stupid lessons. I want to be galloping Cassandra before it gets too hot."

Matti did not deign to answer; instead, she made her stately barefoot way through the house to Maman's chamber, entered without knocking and closed the door. Matti going to Maman at this hour meant that there was serious business on hand, for ordinarily Maman's maid Sara would have gone to take away her breakfast tray and help her to dress. I slid quietly off my chair and followed Matti.

"You will be catching it," whispered Tony venomously, "you little spy."

I took no notice, for I was already overhearing what Maman was saying in the high-pitched and childish patois which she often used when she was alone with Matti.

"They ready, are they?" she asked in a complaining and petulant voice. "Oh dear. Oh no. Oh, be a darling and pour me another cup of coffee; no, me no finish that papaya, it no properly ripe, and me no want anything else. Oh Matti, let me finish my coffee. Why we no afford governess? Me no said my rosary yet. Me no good at being teacher — remember what happened with the others. Oh dear. Pass me my *peignoir*, then. No, me *no* dress."

I scuttled away in time and was sitting on my chair when Maman appeared, *en déshabillé* and as pale as if she had risen from a bed of sickness. She sat down and started the lesson by allocating to Tony and myself our reading-books and copy-books and pencils. She then explained that we were to learn to read and write in both English and French; she had thought that French alone would have been quite sufficient, but our Papa said that he had learned three languages before he was eight and that neither of us appeared to be stupid, whatever our other shortcomings.

I was avidly listening to Maman, but Tony was still on the edge of her chair and fidgetting as only she could. However, Matti appeared on her way back to the kitchen and stopped beside us; she was carrying Maman's breakfast tray, with its silver coffee-pot and sugar basin, its Sèvres cup and saucer and plate, and its barely touched papaya. She stared at Tony until that

22

termagant had stopped fidgetting and had sat up straight; then she went on her way to the kitchen.

We had hardly opened our *livres* for our first reading lesson in French when Henri, who had been rocking quietly on his day-time blanket upon the floor, commenced to howl in unearthly fashion.

"Ah! Ah!" shouted he at the top of his voice. "Ah-bab-bab-bab-bab — "

"Matti!" wailed Maman, "see to that child for me now. How can I possibly teach these others when he is making that noise?"

Matti appeared very quickly, picked up Henri and his blanket and took him away to her lean-to, where he quietened down. (Although we did not know it at the time, thus began Henri's move out of the main house to where he could most conveniently be cared for by Matti and Milly, and later by Betsy.)

Maman, despite her protestations that she was "no good at being teacher", was in fact an excellent one — that is, after she had overcome her morning lassitude and before she had drunk her third brandy. It gives me great pleasure to commend her thus, for she had few other accomplishments or achievements to her credit. She had a fund of simple poems and songs and stories, most in French but many in English, and she could read aloud more advanced stories with enough dramatic emphasis to engage even the restless Tony. She also had ways of making even the most repetitive arithmetical tables and writing exercises interesting to me, if not to Tony. With me she could be firm enough at times, as when I reverted to patois during French lessons, or wanted to use my jumbie-beads to assist me with my sums.

Under Maman's tuition I made a good start — nay, an excellent start! — and was soon reading appropriate excerpts, writing whole words in my copy-book, and chanting my arithmetical tables in both French and English. My previously empty days were filled with pleasurable activity.

Tony's education proceeded on very different lines, for she had neither the patience nor the will to learn. My readers may wonder, as I have, whether being required to learn to read and write in two languages at once was overtaxing to her mental powers, but her command of spoken English, French and patois was far superior to mine and suggests that her mental capacity was perfectly adequate. She was, moreover, the first in our family to be entirely at home in the unbelievably corrupt and degraded form of English which was first used to communicate with the Negroes and which has now spread across the British West Indies like the plague; I have vowed, perhaps rashly, that it shall never proceed from my pen. Tony could berate and wound, or tease and raise a laugh, or sing a song, in any of the four tongues and with equal facility. Moreover, if a song took her fancy, one hearing was enough for her to memorize it, no matter how many stanzas it contained, or how difficult the melody. She had a fine strong contralto voice and nothing delighted her more than to shock our parents, or some priest visiting Maman, or a strait-laced Presbyterian come on business, by singing the latest topical (and, I need hardly add, scandalous) Negro song which she had heard in the cane, swaying her body the while and moving her limbs in time with the barbaric rhythm.

Within a month or two I was so far ahead of Tony in the formal subjects that she became ever more restless and abusive to me. She would wait until I was half-way through writing a word and then shake the table so that my pencil made a wild arabesque across the page; when I protested, she would call me a *cochon* and a *macommère*-man and other even less savoury names. Maman could not control her at all and Matti had to remove her to the kitchen and sit her at a corner of the table; there she muttered and cursed and wasted precious paper on scurrilous drawings. It was not until Father took a hand and suggested that she draw horses that Tony was able to sit quietly and truly work at something without wasting paper. Maman tried hard to encourage Tony in this lady-like pursuit by providing landscape sketches as backgrounds for the horses, but Tony's interest in her drawing was never more than short-lived and after an hour she would be hankering after real horses again.

In addition to Tony's misbehaviour there was another, although lesser, distraction to my studies. Since the episode of the contraband dinner I had been watching Betsy as she moved about her simple duties in the house, or ran outside to talk to Jéhu, the young groom who was a special friend of hers. (According to Tony, who knew him well, Jéhu was more than a friend of Betsy's, he was her brother. I did not know whether to believe her and was too diffident to ask Matti about it.) I was hoping for a sign from Betsy that she still nursed friendly feelings for me, but she gave none. Yet every morning, as soon as lessons started, I was aware of her eyes gazing through a slit in the lean-to wall only a few inches above the galerie floor; they continued to gaze all morning, as if their owner were eavesdropping as hard as she could. Only when Henri whimpered and threatened to wail did her eyes disappear for a while; then, when Henri was quiet again, they would re-appear. Often I could not help looking at that slit when my eyes should have been on my book.

My afternoons were free of lessons, unless I chose to read my story-book to myself, or to recite my tables to the desert air. On the particular afternoon I am about to describe Maman was falling asleep half-way through a brandy; Tony had cantered off upon Cassandra to join her Papa, as she did every day now; and Henri was rocking his whole body and making low muttering

24

noises in the manner which preceded his afternoon sleep. I decided, for no reason that I can remember, to visit the hidey-hole under the house. I had no sooner sat down on one of the upturned boxes than a ghostly whisper reached my ears.

"Master Dickie!"

This time Betsy only had to say it once; I turned my head to the gap through which that memorable dinner had been passed and there was Betsy's face, illumined from below by the sunlight reflected from the white dust of the yard. Her eyes were dancing.

"May I come into your housie?" she asked, speaking so precisely and slowly that I thought she had been rehearsing her little speech. (As time went on I learned that speaking thus was natural to her.)

"Someone will see you," I warned, thinking that she would have to run all the way around the house to enter by the same route as I had.

"But I have made a new door to your housie, just here," she said, pointing to the ground.

I looked down and saw that some of the smaller pieces of wood had been moved and some dirt scraped away to form a low opening; I squatted on the floor, bent my head down as far as it would go, and saw Betsy's face at the other end of a short tunnel.

"May I enter?" she asked.

"Oh yes please!" I answered.

She wriggled through without difficulty, stood up and dusted down her dress with dainty gestures; she then looked slowly around her, plainly taking in everything.

"I could sweep the floor for you," she said, and I saw for the first time that the secret little place was truly in need of a good clean-up.

"I have no broom," I said.

In a flash Betsy was out through her tunnel and back again with a well-worn *cocier* broom. I had to stand on one of the "chairs" and watch while she bent down and with one hand behind her back swept away the layers of wood-shavings, dead leaves, cockroach carcases and other débris which covered the floor. The dust which she raised made me cough and sneeze.

"Oh!" she whispered, "someone will hear if you sneeze like that! I will fetch water."

She scrambled out through her tunnel and since she was gone for a little while this is perhaps the moment for me to describe the unlikely fellow-conspirator who is to be of no little importance to my story. Betsy's skin was as warmly and indelibly black as her mother's, her hair as crisped and her features as boldly sculped in the African manner, with full black lips and heavy-lidded eyes. In public and to any white person (other than myself and occasionally Tony) those features were immobile, those lips turned down, and those eyes inexpressibly dull; if she spoke a word, it was in mumbled patois, without a trace of Maman's metropolitan French. Betsy's limbs were thin and bony and her feet, which were never encumbered with shoes, were remarkably broad, with widely splayed toes; the soles were grey-white and covered with horny skin. Her hands, in contrast, were slim, with elegantly tapering fingers; they were black on the back but the palms were like the soles of her feet, a strange pallid white with black etched into all the creases. In short, there was nothing in her appearance to please an observer accustomed to laud the fine nostrils, the rosebud lips, the milky skins and the wispy golden or chestnut or raven tresses of European beauties.

It is unlikely that such an observer would have troubled to notice that Betsy's mother made very sure that her person was always clean, her skin kept moist with cocoa-nut oil and her clothing neatly patched and spotless. Matti took the greatest of care, in particular, with Betsy's kerchief, which she tied in a special knot over her head.

If any of my readers are moved by prejudice, malice, or even envy, to doubt whether any true friendship could possibly have arisen between such disparate persons as Betsy and myself, may I respectfully suggest that they throw this book down now, if they have not already done so, or return it undamaged to the circulating library and trouble their heads no more about it? To those who are yet willing to continue reading, however uncertain they may be about my veracity, I should reiterate that we were children and therefore only barely conscious of the differences between our stations and our races. Moreover, as children we needed playmates as we needed air to breathe, and we did not have much choice. Neither the fierce tomboy Tony nor poor Henri were truly agreeable companions for me, although I loved them both to some extent; nor was either of them a likely playmate for Betsy. There were no other Negro children available, for only Betsy, as the daughter of the housekeeper, was allowed in the house. The swarming Mulatto children of Father's six Scottish overseers were for some reason thoroughly objectionable to him and he liked to pretend that they did not exist. Furthermore, because Maman was a Roman Catholic, because Father's attitude to religion was equivocal at best, and because we had been in possession of our land before the British occupation of Tobago, we were regarded with suspicion by the other estate-owners, who were mostly Scottish Presbyterians and all, right up to Governor Melville himself, staunchly anti-Catholic and anti-French. The few who had uprooted their wives and families from Scotland and transported them to the Island seemed unwilling to bring them to meet us when they made business or duty calls. My readers will understand from all this that I rarely met other boys or girls, let alone had the opportunity to play with them, and that the legendary Créole hospitality had not yet reached the shores of Tobago.

Perhaps I should add that in 1773 Tobago was a place of strangers, having been a British Colony for only ten years. Prior to 1763 it had been for many years "deserta", one of the neutral islands ostensibly set aside by Britain and France as homes for the Charaibes, the only sugar-estate having been "Braemore" which had been illegally cleared by Father and the overseers and Negroes whom he had brought from St. Domingue. Everyone, whether Scottish, English, Irish, French or African, was a newcomer and a stranger to everyone else. Even straight-haired, copper-skinned Martin and Milly, who were natives of the Island, no longer belonged to anyone, for their relatives had been exterminated by disease, or rum, or an inter-tribal war, or one of the punitive expeditions mounted against the Charaibes by the British and French in turn. Their survival was due to a whim of Maman's; they had been found wandering in the bush near the burned-out ruins of a Charaibe village and she had insisted on bringing them to Braemore as household pets. In this she had been aided and abetted by Matti, who had thought that the tiny twins might afford some comfort to Maman, then grieving over the loss of the first two of my brothers to die. In this Matti was disappointed, and I am sure that a brace of baby monkeys would have been more efficacious than the two little dullards.

In such a place, then, where all were strangers, I had to find a friend where I could.

To return to my story: the friend whom I had found (or who had found me) returned to our "housie" with a calabash full of water which she passed to me through the slit. Once through herself she sprinkled the floor, flicking the water off the ends of her fingers in a manner which I found fascinating. When she was sure that all the dust was laid, she found a safe resting-place for her calabash and sat down. She looked around again and I could see that she was still not satisfied.

"We need a table," she said,

I was amazed that Tony and I had played there so often without perceiving the need for something so obvious. Now Betsy and I searched around and found a short piece of smooth plank; we dragged it between us to the housie, already "ours" by right of occupation. We managed to fix the plank firmly, cat-a-corner and almost level, and drew up our "chairs". We were contemplating our "table" proudly when I was struck by a doubt.

"What are we going to use the table for?" I asked.

Betsy had produced a rag and was wiping down the table with water from her calabash, reaching across in front of me so as to leave not one corner dusty. I had not been so close to her before. Her little person smelled of well-washed linen recently dried in the sun and of warm cocoa-nut oil. (To me, these are still the scent and aroma of true friendship.) When she had finished her wiping she turned her head away shyly.

"We could play at lessons," she said in a voice even quieter than a whisper. "You could be teacher and I could be your *élève* — your pupil, I mean."

I was dumbfounded at such a prospect of delight.

"I want to read and write and do sums as goodly as you," added Betsy, still not looking at me.

"As *well* as me, you mean," I said, accepting the role of teacher without hesitation and, unless I flatter myself, without presumption. "But you cannot speak French, only patois."

Betsy turned to face me.

"*Je parle français bien, moi!*" she said, imitating Maman almost perfectly. "*Comme cette île atroce m'ennuye! Paris me manque tant! Paris en avril — au printemps!*"

She lay back and fanned herself languidly and I laughed, whereupon she sat up straight.

"We should not be laughing," she admonished. "Will you not fetch your books so that we can start playing at lessons now?"

"What if someone sees me?" I asked. Conspiracy seemed to be second nature to us; we certainly did not have to learn to conduct all our conversations in low whispers.

"Why should you not play with your books down here?" argued Betsy. "Nobody knows that I am here with you."

"Not even your mother?"

"Of course my mother knows," answered Betsy, "you silly goose!"

We looked each other in the eyes while the implications of that statement became clear to me.

"If you will fetch your things," urged Betsy, "I will bring the papers and the pencil which my mother is keeping for me."

Matti's approval was all the reassurance that I needed. I hurried to fetch my books, papers and pencil and when I returned with them Betsy was already seated at the table with *her* papers and *her* pencil. We were soon engrossed in writing the letters *a b c d e* and so on, if my memory is correct; I certainly read out a story to Betsy, pointing out the words as I went along. If she had not been an extraordinarily apt pupil I doubt if I would now be writing my Life and Times in this ledger.

Betsy's papers would be laughable today, when one can purchase an excellent exercise-book for a halfpenny in any stationery shop in Frederick Street. They consisted of every scrap which had been discarded in the house for months, if not years; some, I could swear, had been washed and dried and smoothed with a flat-iron. Betsy's pencil was a stub of not an inch long which had been fitted into a six-inch length of bamboo cane. (A slate and a slate-pencil would have answered her need better, but no trader had then thought of bringing these amenities of civilization to the shores of Tobago, and my parents had not troubled to order them from Edinburgh.)

In this manner I started the long, exciting and successful "game" of sharing my education with Betsy. Matti made sure, by her allocation of Betsy's duties, that we could meet every afternoon except, of course, on Sundays, when the law forbade work in the fields and Father and Tony were at home. We would have a precious hour, or two, or sometimes even three. In the early days I used to wonder how it was that Betsy had early intimation of possible discovery and would gather up her papers and vanish; later I learned to hear and "read" Matti's messages, tapped out almost inaudibly upon a hollow bamboo with a slit in one side.

Betsy's education was not a matter of steady day-to-day progress; as children, without a teacher actually present to guide and control us, we could not apply ourselves consistently to such a grave business. We would break off to tell each other childish stories and even more childish jokes; or to draw strange pictures (for neither of us had Tony's talent for drawing); or to play ever more intricate games with our jumbie-beads which, as I recall, we used as a kind of currency. Sometimes, if there had been a heavy shower, Betsy would bring a ball of clay from a special place which she knew of and we would make a whole menagerie of animals unknown to science, with pieces of stick for legs and small stones for eyes. I could not understand how it was that Betsy's hands stayed clean on these occasions, whilst I was covered in clay to the elbows.

"Oh dear me," she would tease, "Dickie is a dirty little boy. Show me your hands. What have you been up to?" Then she would dip her rag into her calabash and scrub away until I was clean; she would even scrape under my finger-nails with a pointed stick. Finally, she would dismiss me with the words: "You may let Madame see you now!"

Frequently Betsy would enliven our breaks from lessons with news from the cane-fields and the Negro-houses — news which I could have heard from no other source — about births, and about what the Negroes call "making babies", and about deaths; news about Negroes being landed from Africa and bought and flogged and sold; news from all over Tobago and from Grenada and beyond; and all conveyed to me with the detail and conviction of a born observer, listener and reporter.

I am now convinced that Betsy's artless yet artful prattle provided me with up to half my education and that therefore I am in debt to her as much as she is in debt to me. From her I acquired a knowledge of estate life as seen from the Negroes' side which was denied to most white men and women, a knowledge from which I have profitted throughout my life.

Perhaps the most extraordinary interruptions to our afternoon schooling were our quarrels. We would disagree over the pronunciation of a word which we had found in a story-book but which we had never heard spoken.

"It is *beer*," I would announce, never having heard a "bear" mentioned in conversation, since no such animal was to be found in Tobago.

"No it is not," Betsy would maintain obdurately. "The proper way to say it is *bare*." The argument would then develop into a quarrel; I would declare that I was the teacher and therefore must be right, while she would aver boldly that teachers could be wrong.

Often we would find ourselves at odds over a debt-of-honour in jumbie-beads.

"You owe me twenty," Betsy would announce.

"But nine and four and six add up to nineteen," I would argue, "and anyway you owe me two from yesterday, so it is seventeen I owe you."

(I need not continue with paltry details such as these. I am sure my readers can supply examples of grounds for childish quarrels from their own memories of childhood, or from observing their own offspring.)

When these quarrels between Betsy and myself grew so fierce that we either had to raise our voices or engage in fisticuffs, we had no choice but to do battle — we dared not be heard, for Maman, poor Maman, though ordinarily the most placid of mortals, was very bad-tempered when wakened in the afternoon. (Sara and Martin and Milly all knew what was going on, of course, but were too much under Matti's thumb to be any danger to our secret.) Betsy, with her mouth firmly closed, would rain blows upon me with her hard little fists whilst I, my mouth closed also, tried to counter her attacks by pinning her down by her stick-like arms and using my much greater weight. At least once she succeeded in giving me a black eye; and once I pushed her pettishly and knocked her head so hard against the unyielding lumber wall of our housie that a huge lump appeared, with an effusion of blood which stained her kerchief; yet it did not occur to either of us to cry out or to inform upon the other — if my readers ask why I did not use my position as the young Master to have Betsy punished for insolence and worse, I can only reply that I knew for a certainty that I had only one friend in the world and that I was unlikely to find another if I lost her — an unendurable prospect.

We both invented accidents to account for our injuries. My parents, and even Tony, believed these inventions but Matti's silence, as she applied compresses made of soothing leaves, withheld both belief and disbelief.

It was Betsy's determination that her accomplishments should not be inferior to mine through lack of industry on her part that changed the playful game of "lessons" into something which became more serious and drove us back after all these distractions to our makeshift table and our books. She rapidly equalled me in reading and arithmetic, whilst in writing she excelled me — her hand was neater than mine and had an elegant elaboration to the loops to which I could not aspire. Betsy's spoken French, however, never lost its tinge of patois, since she could not recite for Maman in the way I could and have her mistakes corrected. Her spoken English shared with mine and Tony's a residue of the Scottish Highland lilt which we learned from Father and his overseers, and which puzzles people to this day.

All the while, whether pursuing our studies or playing or quarrelling, Betsy and I were constantly aware that our secret life was under threat of discovery by the unpredictable ones — Father and Tony. We knew also that our hidey-hole would be demolished as soon as Father decided to rebuild the house on more convenient and commodious lines, as he was promising Maman from day to day. However, the American rebellion continued to interfere with legitimate trade and the house remained as it was. Although Betsy and I banished these dangers from the front of our minds, in the manner which I have observed to be common amongst children, I am sure that they added spice and sweetness to our companionship, as well as lending steel to Betsy's resolve that she should learn as much as possible in whatever time was to be available to her.

I do not wish to give the impression that Father had altogether given up trying to make a man of me, for once when Tony was cajoling him to excuse her from lessons so that she could have the whole day to enjoy the excitements of the sugar-harvest, he turned upon me in a fury.

"It is you, boy," he shouted, "who should be asking to go to the fields. You are the oldest son and will be inheriting all this — " he swept his arm towards what, to him, was a fine prospect of cane-fields — "and maybe a glen or two back home, if justice is done. You have a fine quiet garron and you will be riding it *now*!"

I dared not tell Father that I hated the dull uniform green of the cane-pieces and would much rather gaze at the prospect in the opposite direction, where the wild uncleared forested hills were dotted with the brilliant colours of the poui and flamboyante trees, so Jéhu was called and I was sat willy-nilly upon a torpid Créole pony which was supposed to be mine and taken outside where I had to endure the attentions of myriads of flies attracted by the pony, and where the sun penetrated my hat and beat upon my shoulders and made me feel sick. Jéhu led the pony slowly past the Negro-houses and I was forced to smell salt-fish and sweat and dirt and see miserable dun-coloured clothes hung out to dry; then on to the fields where the Negro men and boys momentarily straightened their backs from cutting the cane and looked at me without seeming to see me, while the Negresses, young and old, smiled at the young Massa with smiles which I did not understand but could not believe to be friendly.

As if that were not enough unpleasantness, Father then had Jéhu lead me past the sugar-houses, where even more flies were to be found, swarming round the cattle pulling the cane-carts and turning the sugar-mills. I was choked by the smoke of burning *bagasse* from the boiler fires, by the fumes of boiling sugar, and by the sickening stink of molasses draining from the cooling sugar in the curing-house. Then further on was I carried, while Jéhu looked up at me with a baffling expression, to the rum-sheds, where the fermenting-vats and the stills gave off vapours so vile-smelling and abhorrent to me that I became faint and threatened to fall out of the saddle. Jéhu then had to support me homeward while Father loudly cursed his misfortune in having sons like myself and Henri.

How happy I was to return to the cool shadiness of the house, which was, of course, sited to windward of the effluvia generated by sugar and rum and salt-fish and sweating field-Negroes! Here the gentle Trade Wind carried only the scents of the ocean and the forest, wafting them softly through the jalousies and mingling them with the homely scents emanating from the dark beeswaxed floors and furniture and from the savoury meals being cooked by Matti over fragrant coal-pots. No matter how ill-constructed and rickety the building, its interior was the home I loved in my childish way; here I could watch the tiny humming-birds sipping from the flowers of the papaya-tree which grew close up against the galerie, and the little yellow sucriers flying in to raid the sugar-bowl, and the other nameless small black birds stalking about the floor and the tables stealing crumbs. Here too, at night, I could watch the fire-flies and tell myself stories about who they were and where they were going. Best of all, here was the quiet which radiated from Matti and enfolded Maman and Henri and myself and Betsy; the quiet which sometimes soothed even Father and Tony, quarrelling as they so often were as they approached the house.

In despair of an active son, after several experiences of the kind I have just delineated, Father acceded more and more to Tony's importunacy and took her with him to the cane in the mornings as well as the afternoons, so that at twelve years of age Tony had learned more about sugar production than any grown woman in Tobago, and even the overseers would listen to her views with respect. Cassandra was exchanged for a larger and livelier horse — its name escapes me — and Miss Tony became a scandal to our Presbyterian neighbours, dressed as she was in a boy's wide-brimmed straw hat, boy's shirt and boots. Although Maman and Matti were successful in persuading her to wear a seemly skirt, Father's attempts to have her ride side-saddle were half-hearted and therefore unsuccessful — any lady's saddle upon which Tony sat quickly and mysteriously galled the horse.

To the scandal of Tony's attire was added the scandal of her behaviour every year at Camboulay (or "*Cannes-brûler*") — the annual occasion when the dead lower leaves of the standing cane are put to the torch in order to clear the way for the cane-cutters, to rid the field of poisonous snakes, and to make the juice run more freely when put to the mill. Even as a tiny girl, I had been told, she would demand imperiously that she be allowed to attend and when she was a little older she would be badgering Father before they left the house to accord her the privilege of touching off the conflagration. I did not see her with my own eyes, of course, but I heard reports from Betsy and others about how she screamed and sang and danced with unseemly jubilation as the flames licked and roared through the cane-rows and the smoke stained the sky. When she was older still she would gallop her horse up and down, her voice clearly heard above the hullabaloo and making the general excitement even more feverish — then, as I knew from my own observation, she would return to the house redolent of smoke, march straight to her chamber and, without taking off her boots, fling herself upon her bed and fall instantly asleep.

As Father grew used to having Tony with him, willing to help in any way which involved riding a horse, and especially delighted when asked to gallop across country with an urgent message, he stopped taunting me with my cowardice and lack of manly spirit and seemed to accept Maman's assurance that I was talented in other ways and liable to be a credit to the family later on.

Tony, however, carried on taunting me except when Father was present — it was as though her daemon had a particular aversion to me and supplied her with ever more wounding insults. Even Matti could barely silence her, but there was one other person in whose presence she always minded her manners and that was Jéhu, on whom she depended for the care of her horse. I sometimes fancied that their shared passion for the equine race set them apart from the rest of us mortals and even from Father, whose feeling for horses was utilitarian rather than passionate.

33

Jéhu is important to my story for, although rarely in the foreground, he was yet a black presence of whom I was constantly aware and who could not be overlooked in any company. Not particularly tall, he was nevertheless compact of bodily beauty, strength and agility and his way with horses commanded respect from everyone, but especially from Father, who promised him that he would be a full-time groom just as soon as enough land was cleared and enough sugar sold. When I first read about Centaurs what other picture could form in my mind but that of shining black Jéhu forming part of shining black Hector? I have thought, looking back from another century and indeed from another age, that Jéhu, Negro though he was, could have been the kind of son that Father would have wished for himself. At this time he bore no mark of the lash on his back and at the age of seventeen must have been worth at least £120 and perhaps even more.

Jéhu's face, I have to admit, was scarcely Grecian, and not even handsome by African standards; in fact, it was one of the ugliest I have seen upon a human being. No two of his features were symmetrically placed and his teeth, although splendidly white and strong, were irregular as to size and shape and as to the directions in which they pointed. In the presence of Father and his overseers and of other white people Jéhu never dropped his eyes as Betsy did, but the laconic wit for which he was celebrated emerged from a countenance which was unchangingly guarded in expression; yet when he and Betsy were alone together their faces were mobile and expressive of deep affection, and they talked to each other with great animation and with acute interest in what the other was saying. It was hard for me not to be jealous as I observed them thus from one hiding place or another. I began to think that they were indeed brother and sister, as Tony had said; there was a family resemblance in their movements and their actions if not in their features. When I questioned Betsy about their relationship and the topics of their conversations, she refused to answer. Later, if she was giving me some news, she would preface it with: "They are saying — " but would never attribute it to Jéhu, nor would she acknowledge their relationship.

I learned, as time went on, that Jéhu often visited Matti in her lean-to after dark, and sometimes when she was in the provision-garden. My young mind was unable to appreciate why his visits were discreet and surreptitious, but since Matti was discreetly and surreptitiously encouraging the friendship between Betsy and myself, I had some understanding that Jéhu's visits to her might be just as innocent, but would be frowned upon by my parents, who were prone to strange disapprobations quite unsupported by Reason.

I return reluctantly to my tale, for the next event I have to describe was not a happy one. It was on a Sunday afternoon in the year 1776, when Betsy and I were nine years of age and our joint education had been proceeding for three and a half years, that Father discovered our conspiracy. I was lying upon my bed listening to Henri rocking and snuffling, and I was dreaming no doubt about far places where there was no sugar, secure in the belief that Father had taken Tony away on an all-day visit to a friend's estate near Castara — the occasion was a crop-over party and would involve a sea-bath — when his dreaded voice came from nearby.

"What in the Devil's Name?" he was shouting, "Where did you steal this book? And who was teaching you to read it?"

Terrified, I cowered upon my bed, for I knew instantly what had happened; I wanted to flee, but I could not move, except to reach under my pillow for my little bag of jumbie-beads.

I pieced together later that Father and Tony had returned early from their visit and for some reason walked their horses so quietly that no one heard them; the dogs had accompanied them on the outing and were too exhausted to make a noise. After stabling their mounts they decided, uncharacteristically, not to disturb the afternoon calm and were proceeding quietly past Matti's lean-to toward the back galerie steps. The lean-to door was open and — behold! — there was Betsy seated upon a stool and reading aloud to Matti and Jéhu from a book. For a moment or two, Father related afterwards with an oath, he thought she was "play-acting", but as he watched aghast she turned a page as cool as you please and he could see her eyes moving back and forward across the page as she impudently read aloud the English words. (What the words were and from which book they were being read I know not.)

Immobile upon my bed, I could only listen to the silences which greeted Father's ever more infuriated questions, and wonder how Matti's power would deal with this emergency.

At last, Father lowered his voice but to my horror it became more terrible than his shouts.

"Jéhu," he said, "return at once to your quarters and do not be expecting to look after the horses again — I will be ensuring that you are given the heaviest work. Matti, I will be speaking to Madame about your part in this; and as for this insolent child of yours — "

I heard no more, for at this point Tony tip-toed into my room, closed the door, and put her finger to her lips.

"Was it you who taught Betsy to read?" she asked.

"Yes."

"Oh Dickie, what a silly soft fool you are! Father will flog you to death if he finds out now. You had better hide under the house until he is calmer. Come! be quick! and try not to wake Henri."

She opened the door and when she saw that the way to the front galerie steps was clear she signalled to me urgently that I should run. I moved fast, if in ungainly fashion, and was soon sitting in the hidey-hole shaking like a jelly.

Tony had induced me to move not a moment too soon, for the house was soon trembling as Father mounted the steps and rampaged from room to room, slamming doors and trampling and shouting. Poor Maman, unfit for anything, was angrily interrogated and then abandoned as Father's rage spilled everywhere. Tony seemed to be clattering after him — they were both still in their riding-boots.

"Papa!" I heard Tony say loudly.

"Be quiet, Antonia!" Father answered.

"Papa! Listen! I know something which you ought to hear."

"I am the last to learn everything! What is it you know then?"

"It is not Maman's fault that Betsy learned to read. It was Dickie who was teaching her. He has just told me."

"I believe you! I believe you! Where is he? Where is the miscreant?"

"He is hiding under the house, as he always does."

Father gave vent to a sound so loud and strange that there is no way of conveying it on paper, then found his voice again.

"Fetch him out!"

There was a silence which spread outward from the house, as if even the fowls of the air were listening to hear what my fate was to be.

"Antonia, go and fetch that brother of yours from under the house. Go this minute!"

"No, Papa. You would flog him so hard that you would be sorry afterwards."

There was no reply from Father that I could hear.

"Papa!" came Tony's voice, "you are not raising your whip to your only daughter? Lash me then! I dare you!"

"Oh Jonas — " came Maman's weak moan, followed instantly by a strange prolonged cry from Henri, now awakened from his customary heavy slumber.

"Ah! Bab-bab-bab-bab-bab — " it echoed and seemed to re-echo, diminishing away into nothingness and sounding as though it were uttered by some creature of the forest fleeing swiftly into the distance.

"Mother of God!" cried Father, his profanity followed by creaking sounds which suggested to me that he had flung himself into his armchair, bereft of speech. Someone, Milly most likely, ran up the steps and took Henri away.

No one in the house above me moved and a long silence ensued, a silence broken at last by the soft shuffle of slippered feet and the clink of glass — perhaps it was Maman pouring a brandy for herself? — no, she would be giving Father a tumbler of his *usquebaugh*. Then there was quiet talk, as though Father and Maman, and perchance Tony also, were conferring privily. Suddenly Father erupted into a shout.

"I am telling you that he is my son, and I will be chastising him when he is needing it and by God he is needing it now! As for the others, I am in need of ready cash."

"But Papa — "

"Madame, this daughter of yours is daring to defend a crime, I am telling you, a crime! Just one Negro reading a book today and tomorrow a thousand will be infected!"

Here Tony must have made to speak, for Father shouted: "Not another word! Go to your room, Antonia!"

There followed the clatter of Tony's boots as she made for her chamber; she was, after all, only twelve years of age.

By now the sun was setting and the *cocricos* were making their ugly grating calls from the nearest forest. Straining my ears, I could hear nothing from Father or Maman but I could have sworn that Tony had quietly removed her boots and was leaving her chamber; a board creaked — yes, she was descending the steps; a dog wagged its tail, making a thumping noise against a board — she was under the house and wriggling her way to the hidey-hole. As she entered and rose to her feet a last horizontal ray from the setting sun lit up the sums which Betsy and I had scribbled upon the lumber walls and a tell-tale scrap of paper lying upon the table. Tony picked up the paper and held it to the light.

"Dickie," she whispered, "you have not been teaching Betsy to write as well as read?"

"Yes. Why did you tell on me? You did not have to."

"You are a *mook*, Dickie. It was safer for me to tell Father now, while you were out of his reach. Are these all sums?" She was pointing to the walls.

"Yes. Why did you tell?"

"Can Betsy do sums too?"

"Yes, she is good at sums."

"Oh Dickie, you deserve what you are going to get."

"What-what-what — ?" I stammered.

"You are to get six licks upon your backside with a thin bamboo, which is better than being lashed on your back like a nigger."

I started to sob. In this nineteenth century words have not yet been coined to describe the confusion in my heart. I *knew* that Tony was right about the bamboo being less painful than the whip; I *knew* that she had cunningly deflected the worst of Father's wrath; I *knew* that I ought to be grateful to her, but on the other hand I *knew* that if Father had lashed me already the worst of the pain would have been over by now — the bamboo was still to come and my backside was quivering in anticipation of the blows; I *knew* that I had offended my Father deeply, but had no sense of my own wickedness; in short, I was a nine-year-old boy bewildered by the determination of the world to confuse his mind and injure his body.

Tony had more news for me and, despite my sobs, I could hear what she was saying.

"Papa wanted to sell Matti and Betsy right now; he even wanted to be selling them separately, and said that Matti would fetch £150 and Betsy £25, and that Katy was as good a cook as Matti any day and we could buy another washerwoman for £40 and have £135 left, which would help to build a store on the quay at Scarborough, but Maman and I gave him plenty of *usquebaugh* without too much water and he agreed at last that Maman may keep Matti, but Betsy is to be a present to me for my thirteenth birthday — she is to be my maid, but since I do not have enough clothes to keep her busy she is to be Henri's nurse to keep her out of mischief when I am not needing her. She is to help me to be neat and tidy and lady-like — ha-ha-ha-ha! Papa is going to build three new rooms across the yard — a big one for Henri at the far end where no one will hear him rocking his bed, and a little one for Matti and Betsy, and another little one for Milly and Sara, and all the fowls and hogs and Negro children are to be moved away from the house — "

Tony went rattling on, but I could not comprehend any more of what she was saying, for her words about the selling of Matti and Betsy were burning into my brain. I had known that they were slaves since I had been capable of knowing anything, but had assumed that they were not like field slaves, but in some separate and inalienable category. Now that Matti had had the threat of sale hung over her head, how could she exercise her benign protective power over me? Now that Betsy was Tony's personal property, how could she and I be friends any more? She was to be kept busy all day. I remembered that Betsy owed me no less than two hundred jumbie-beads from our last transaction — would I ever see those beads? I sobbed and wept and snuffled until Tony had to take some notice of me.

"What a cry-baby you are, Dickie!" she said, still in a whisper, "Boo-hoo-hoo! Six licks are nothing!" She slapped my backside, as though I were a pony. "Brace up, Fatty!"

I refused to be comforted, or to have my courage stiffened. Tony tried again.

"You are not the only one to be suffering. Who is going to look after my horse now that Father has sent Jéhu to the cane? Old Cuffy can barely manage the mules, never mind taking on the horses too — Papa says he was no bargain at £40. I will have to be a stable-hand myself."

"But you are not going to have licks."

"If you are afraid of licks, go to Papa now, before he drinks any more of that Glenlivet and becomes dangerous. Go on!"

I knew that Tony was right, for she was the master tactician when it came to dealing with Father, but I wanted to postpone my punishment.

"If Betsy is your maid, you will not stop her from being friends with me?"

"Dickie, when I am out with Papa you may be educating the hogs for all I care. Grunt, grunt! Slurp, slurp! You would be getting more like them than you are already. Shall I tell Papa that you are coming to take your medicine?"

I was still hesitating when I felt a faint draught on my cheek and smelled clean clothes and cocoa-nut oil — such a contrast to the stench of horses and leather and dust from Tony! — and knew that Betsy, daring all, had crept close to the hidey-hole and had been listening to us, although for how long I could not tell.

"All right then," I said to Tony, "you may tell Father that I am coming."

Tony went down on all fours and wriggled away and in a moment Betsy was through the tunnel on her side and was standing close to me in the darkness. She found my hand and pressed a little bag of what I knew to be jumbie-beads into my hand.

"These are what I owe you," she whispered. "There is a note in the bag; it says that you are to be brave."

Soundlessly, she departed, and I was alone again, but somewhat comforted and ready to summon what courage I could from my meagre store of that commodity. My efforts were interrupted by Tony shouting from her chamber: "Betsy, come!"

Betsy did not appear promptly enough, it would seem.

"Where are you, Betsy, you slow-coach? You had better learn to come quickly now that you belong to me, Miss Black Blue-stocking!"

(My memory is at fault here; Tony could not have known about those ladies with pretensions to learning, but I can hear her scornful tone of voice as she shouted for Betsy, and she certainly would have used the insult had she known of it.)

It was some time before I was brave enough to face Father. When at last I stood before him, with my hand upon the jumbie-beads and the precious little note in my pocket, he was indeed crimson of face, but quite mellow. I was afraid that he was going to ask me if I understood that I had done wrong, for I knew that I was not brave enough to answer "no"; however, he wanted the matter over with. He did not trouble to rise from his chair, but called me to him; at which Maman turned her head away and placed her hands over her ears. He bent me over his knee and administered six blows over my trowsers, not using a thin bamboo as Tony had predicted, but his thick gnarled walking-stick — he called it his "cromac". As it descended upon my rump I yelled my agony to all who would hear. When he had done, Father cast me from him.

"Ugh! It is like beating a sack of lard," he complained, whilst I lay writhing upon the floor, trying to stifle my yells for I knew that Tony and Betsy were listening. "There will be no more educating of little Negroes, eh?" added Father heavily.

I was quite unable to speak, but Tony's voice came stridently from her room.

"No more reading, writing and 'rithmetic for you, Miss clever-clever Betsy! Not *that* dress, stupid! I said the *dark* blue one!"

Father ignored this interruption.

"Answer me, sir!"

At this point Maman intervened. "Jonas, he has had enough punishment," she said, taking me in her arms and attempting to comfort me, in which she was only partially successful, for I abhorred the odours of brandy and French perfume almost as much as I abhorred those of raw sugar and rum. How I longed to be in Matti's arms instead! When I quietened, for my agony did abate somewhat, Maman whispered into my ear: "Dickie, what you did was *méchant*, very wicked, and very cruel to Betsy, who will never be happy at all if her head is filled with nonsense — it might even hurt her poor little brain, which is not a big one like yours and your father's. You do understand that now, Dickie my darling, do you not?"

"Someone is whispering," came Tony's voice again, "and they will be whispering about you, Miss Betsy! Ow! You are tugging! You will have to learn to brush my hair properly — it is not a frizz like yours, you know!"

I would have broken away and run to the kitchen to be with Matti had I not been doubtful as to whether her power had been extinguished by the day's happenings. However, she appeared at bedtime, carrying the sleeping Henri; I waited until I judged that she had settled my poor brother and ran to her. She welcomed me silently, as though everything in the world had not changed; undressed me as though I was a tiny boy again; soothed my buttocks with some decoction which she had brought; and put me to my bed with her usual firmness and affection. When she had bid me her silent goodnight and closed the door, I opened Betsy's little bag and emptied out the jumbie-beads with the intention of counting them to ensure that Betsy had given me the correct number, but I was diverted from my purpose when I found the tiny scrap of paper upon which her note was written. It was indeed brief and, as prudence required, unsigned. It read: "I owe you 197 and not 200 but if you will be brave for me I will be faithful."

These words, and especially her demand that I be brave "for her", seem unlikely as coming from a nine-year-old Negress now that I have put them to paper, but they are nevertheless exactly what she wrote in her own elaborate but legible hand. I whispered them aloud to myself several times over before acting the conspirator, as I am sure Betsy intended, and holding the scrap of paper to the candle-flame. The words vanished as the paper was consumed but I can still hear them echoing in my mind and heart, like the dying fall of an old song. The cadence and meaning of them — yes, even those about the debt in jumbie-beads — still have the power to move me to tears, for although my nature may have made it hard for me to be brave, yet it was far harder for Betsy to be faithful to a Young Master whose sister owned her body and was entitled to sell it to strangers at any time. (My readers, do not mistake me; I was never amongst the crazed supporters of Emancipation — Reason was always my Guide.)

I jumped from my bed and kneeled down beside it, not to say my prayers but to lay out my jumbie-beads upon the white sheet in sets of ten; sure enough, there were nineteen sets and seven beads left over. I returned them all to the bag most carefully, blew out the candle, and lay down again, vowing that since I had not been as brave as I might have been I would never be less than faithful to Betsy and to the conspiracy which was our friendship.

CHAPTER III

Father allocates to me Duties unusual for my Age; Betsy and I attend to Henri with happy Results, but she and Tony exhibit disconcerting Behaviour; a new World is opened to us, but it is not altogether a happy one

"You are the son and heir, as I have told you one hundred times and more," said Father, when he could bring himself to speak to me again after beating me, "and you will be doing something to help me."

My heart quaked, expecting as I was to be dragooned into another sun-stricken visit to the fields or to the sugar-houses.

"Stand up straight when I am speaking to you, Richard, and look me in the eyes like a man!"

It is not easy for someone of the shape I was then to assume a military posture, or for someone of my spirit to gaze up into fierce blue eyes, but I did what I could.

"Since you are so clever at the writing, and I am not, because of this," and here he held up his wounded right hand, "you will be copying all my letters; and since Madame your mother tells me that you can figure too, you will be keeping the estate books and checking the totals of all the bills which come in. Merchants and their clerks are rogues, every one of them."

I must have shewn that I was daunted by this prospect, for he gestured toward Maman. "Madame your mother will help you in the beginning."

Maman smiled wanly, intending to encourage me, I think.

"And so," continued Father, raising his voice, "there will be no time for you to be getting into mischief and thinking about educating the Negroes. Do you understand me, sir?"

42

I nodded assent, glad as always that Father could not see what I was thinking, for I was deciding on the one hand that I would go to almost any length to avoid another beating, but on the other hand and contrariwise, that if the chance arose to continue my friendship with Betsy, I would be brave for her and seize it.

Father must have congratulated himself on his perspicacity on many occasions, for I proved to have a talent for copying and improving his letters and indeed, later on, for composing them; and I possessed an even greater talent for keeping his accounts and maintaining what he called his "muster-roll" of Negroes; so that, as the years went by (and by the end of this chapter I will be fourteen) I became a precociously accomplished clerk and accountant. Father would sometimes ask me brusquely whether the estate had the money for this or that purpose — perhaps a new windmill of the latest design, or some Créole or well-seasoned Negro families from other estates (for Father could not bring himself to buy Africans of uncertain health, new landed at Scarborough from slave-ships).

What Father did not understand was that these new duties of mine were not nearly as onerous as he imagined, and left my afternoons almost as free as before, with consequences which I will relate in due course. What I did learn from my duties was that Father's rash and intemperate nature did not fit him for the commercial part of the business upon which he was engaged. He had been brought up to be a soldier, and had learned to be a skilful enough sugar-planter, so that he managed his estate well and was a good Master to his Negroes (however cruel he was to me); but he allowed political and military events, no matter how far from Tobago, to anger and excite him and to warp his judgment; he made hasty decisions and entered into unfortunate agreements and rarely found that the disposal of his sugar and rum were as profitable as he had anticipated. He did not understand tumultuous events for what I have learned them to be — golden opportunities for the alert and calculating man of business.

As a further consequence of the handicaps imposed by his nature, Father's regular outgoings were far too heavy. He had borrowed too much and in Bordeaux of all places, where the bankers are even more rapacious than those of Edinburgh, and his interest and capital repayments were unconscionably high. Moreover, he insisted on retaining no less than six dissolute overseers, of whom one drunken sot acted as distiller. They were all hardy fellows of Father's age, and well-versed in the use of firearms, and while they had been needed as a private militia when Tobago was neutral and "deserta", they were not all required to keep the Negroes in subjection in a British Colony with an official Island Militia and with regular troops available nearby in Barbadoes. I later learned that Father was under obligation to these troublesome creatures and owed them a special loyalty, but he would have been better advised to employ only one or two of them and to have used the salaries thus saved to take on a skilled white carpenter, a white cooper and, most needful of all, a sober Presbyterian distiller. In the years before I learned my business, an honest accounts clerk would have saved him quantities of money.

At about the time of the events in my last chapter Father sold his sugar and rum at an incredibly low price, as his ill-kept account book still shows. He then dissipated what little profit he had made by paying a huge sum for a parcel of contraband American shingles in order to placate Maman, whose complaints on the subject of the thatched roof and the vermin which inhabited it must have wearied him.

The nailing on of the shingles and the building of the new rooms for Henri and the servants brought Negroes around the house in much larger numbers than I had been accustomed to and I spent much of my spare time watching them; seen at close quarters thus, most were much more cheerful and friendly than they were in the fields, perhaps because they were not engaged in back-breaking tasks; some would even wish me good-morning and ask how I was. Others, those bought locally, I suppose, did not seem to understand or speak patois and had only a rudimentary grasp of English — they tended therefore to be morose and silent and to be subject to teasing by the St. Domingue Créoles who made up the bulk of our stock. Whether they spoke patois or not, nothing seemed to please the Negroes more than for one of their number to have a mishap — hit his thumb with a hammer or drop a heavy timber on his foot.

It was watching the Negroes at work under the Scottish overseers that convinced me of the need for a white carpenter, for the Negroes were patently unused to European building fashions and the overseers were no better, although for other reasons — they seemed to regard building work as beneath their dignity. In consequence, the shingles were fixed higgledy-piggedly and the new rooms were as roughly built as the house, with ill-fitting doors and jalousies.

Tony, needless to say, was to be seen everywhere, making herself a nuisance by criticizing everyone and everything, and teasing Father by contemptuously comparing our house and its new additions to the handsome American frame house which her friends at Castara had erected with great ease. I noted that Father would often invent an errand for her and she would gallop away, to the general relief.

Prominent amongst the Negroes, mainly because of the respect accorded him by the others, was Gilbert, an elderly white-haired Créole who had been brought from St. Domingue with the family. (In case my story ever reaches an audience outside the West Indies, which will be when I have been dead for a long time, I should explain that the word "Créole" then meant "born in the West Indies" and does not signify "of mixed blood". Gilbert was as black as Matti.) Although strong for his age, Gilbert did not seem to possess any particular skill, except that of leadership, which he exercised with the greatest discretion. I took particular pains to observe him closely after I saw Betsy with her arms around his neck, whispering into his ear. When she saw me looking, for she knew all my secret observation-posts, she ran quickly away. I shall have occasion to refer to Gilbert again.

When the building work was completed, Henri and Matti and the others were moved into their new quarters and the land surrounding the house (the "policies", as Father called it) was improved by moving away all the livestock, the Negro infants and their day-time minders. The lumber under the house had been used up on the new buildings, so that I no longer had a hidey-hole to which I could escape. With Henri moved across the yard I was free of his endless rocking and had my chamber to myself; I could have read and studied and day-dreamed to my heart's content, had not that heart been filled with unhappiness.

In the weeks after the discovery of our joint crime and whilst the building work was in progress, Betsy and I did not dare to look at each other when our paths crossed. She crept into the house each morning with clean clothes for Tony, helped her to dress, and after she had spent some time tidying and cleaning went off to relieve Milly of the care of Henri. Every time that Tony returned from the fields she would call for Betsy to leave Henri and be subject to her whims. Sometimes, to judge from the noises which emanated from Tony's room, Betsy had to perform every possible duty which could be demanded of a lady's maid, but at other times Tony would dismiss her with curses and blows, shouting that if she could look after her own horse, then by God she could look after her own self. I am sure that Betsy's heart was filled with unhappiness too.

During these weeks I found that my lessons had entirely lost their savour and Maman had a hard time interesting me in what my books contained. As I have explained, Father's letters and accounts could not occupy me for long and I spent much time moping; even my friends the sucriers and the fire-flies could not console me. The papaya tree had been cut down in the interests of neatness, so I was abandoned by the humming-birds.

I need hardly write that it was an intervention by Matti which improved my state. One empty afternoon I was sitting at the table on the back galerie with my head on my arms when she passed close to me.

"Henri lonely for you," she said, without stopping. The four words were such a long speech for her and so quietly spoken that I am, to this day, unsure whether she said them aloud, or whether her proximity wakened my sleeping conscience to the fact that in my misery I had been neglecting my poor brother and I heard those words inside my head. I looked up at Matti's retreating back; she turned and gave me the briefest nod and swivel of her eyes toward Henri's door across the yard.

"Maman!" I shouted, knowing that she would not hear me, but anxious that everyone around the house should know where I was, "I am going to see Henri."

I fetched my hat, lest the sun do me an injury on my expedition, and was soon standing outside Henri's door and in the shade of the narrow galerie which had been built along the side of the room next the yard. My heart beat fast as I reached my hand to the latch for I knew that Betsy was inside, forbidden to leave Henri except when called by Tony. My heart was beating thus, my readers must understand, not because Cupid had sped a precocious dart in my direction, but because I knew that if Father found out that I had exchanged as much as two unnecessary words with Betsy, my backside would have had further acquaintance with his "cromac" and Betsy would have faced sale to strangers or, worse, banishment to the cane; and in either case, an end to any hopes of an education which she might still be nurturing.

I took a deep breath, and then another, but my heart seemed ready to burst out of my breast; I took a third, lifted the latch and stepped into the dimness of Henri's room, which I had entered only once before, whilst it was under construction. It was high and airy and spotlessly clean, the new floorboards not yet dark with polish. In one corner, I knew from the sound of his bubbling snore, Henri was asleep upon his bed; in another, upon a stool where some light reached her, sat Betsy. She had a short plank of wood across her knees and upon it was one of her scraps of paper. Her pencil was in her hand and she was looking up at me, her eyes wide open and her black lips in the shape of an O. I tried to breathe quietly, but succeeded only in making myself more breathless. Betsy dropped her eyes, bowed her head and looked at her paper, composing her face into the mask of stupidity behind which Negroes are wont to hide their thoughts.

As I gazed at her, my one and only true friend, my breath began to come more naturally but I knew not what to say, and when I spoke, I stammered: "B-B-B-Betsy!"

She looked up at me, her eyes suddenly bright again with sagacity, and with tears.

"I cannot do these division sums," she said in a tremulous voice I had not heard her use before, "I do not understand them at all."

"Division is easy," I replied, thinking to comfort her.

"It is easy for you," she said, her tears trickling down her cheeks, "but I have no arithmetic book, and I have to try and overhear what Madame is explaining to you and her voice is not loud at all and Miss Tony's room is too far away from your table."

Thus I learned that Betsy had been spinning out her duties in Tony's room and pressing her ear to the jalousie in the hope of continuing her education; I learned also that she was capable of tears — even when I had bruised her head she had remained dry-eyed — and that her tears had power over me.

"Let me shew you how to do division," I said, all the dangers which I had rehearsed to myself suddenly receding to the back of my mind.

"Oh yes, please!" Betsy answered.

We made a space on Henri's wash-stand and I had cleared up half-a-dozen points of difficulty when we were interrupted by Henri's voice from the bed.

"Ah, beb-beb-beb-Bessy!" he said.

Betsy turned her head.

"Do you want po-cham?" she asked.

Henri made a wordless bubbling noise.

"Say po-po properly, then." Betsy's tone was firm, but the answer did not come immediately.

"Ah, po-po-po-po — " said Henri.

Betsy went straight to him, lifted him from his bed, pulled down his clothes and sat him on the po-cham.

"Ah, pi-pi-pi-pi — " muttered Henri as he passed water.

I was thunderstruck; in all Henri's six years I had not heard him utter a meaningful sound.

"But Henri can say words!" I whispered.

"He can do more than that. Watch this!"

Betsy lifted Henri to his feet, adjusted his clothing and gripped his hands firmly in her own.

"Henri is going to walk to Dickie! Come on, Henri, walk to Dickie! One step! Two steps! Three steps — "

Henri's steps were hesitant and unsteady, like those of a year-old child, but they were indubitably steps. When Betsy had walked him

47

up to me she put his hands in mine and he greeted me in his old way.

"Ah, dab-dab-dab-dab — " he cried.

"But how did he learn all this?" I asked, already knowing half the answer, and with a whole new idea burgeoning in my head.

"I have nothing else to do but teach him. I have no books to read and it is no use doing sums if I do not know whether the answers are right or wrong."

Henri's head wobbled on his neck as he turned his face from me to Betsy and back again. His protruding pale blue eyes, which I had always thought of as empty, showed that he was listening to us and perhaps even understanding a little of what we were saying.

"Does anyone else know about this?" I asked.

"It was my mother's idea. She gives me benay-balls for Henri. He will try very hard for a benay-ball."

(I do not know if "benay-balls" are still made in Tobago as they were in my childhood; they were a primitive sweetmeat concocted from raw sugar and small seeds.)

"Ah, benay-benay-benay — " shouted Henri, very loud.

"No," said Betsy quietly, "not until you whisper it."

"Ah, benay-benay-benay — " whispered Henri.

Betsy produced the marble-sized ball from the pocket in the front of her dress and put it into Henri's mouth.

"That will keep you quiet," she said, then raised her eyes to mine. We looked at each other for a space, sharing our thoughts without speaking, as true friends will.

"I could be Henri's teacher in the afternoon," I said.

If Betsy's brain was smaller than mine, it made up in speed of thought what it lacked in size.

"Out on the galerie," she said, "where everyone can see you, after he has finished his sleep; and I will be behind the door, doing my lessons."

"If someone comes, you could jump out through that back window," I whispered, my excitement mounting.

We shared our thoughts silently again, while Henri sucked his benay-ball messily, but contentedly. At six years of age we had entered into our first conspiracy with only a nebulous conception of the dangers we were risking; at nine, the dangers had been spelled out to us, but we knew ourselves to be more dexterous in deceit and, moreover, we had proved to each other that we were capable of maintaining it over a long period. Nevertheless, the plan was hazardous in the extreme.

"We could start now," urged Betsy, "If you walk Henri out on to the galerie I will finish those division sums which you gave to me."

"You must be sure that the back window is open," I warned, "and if it is too dangerous we will not do it again."

I walked Henri to the door, murmuring encouraging words; once in the doorway, however, the benay-ball fell out of his mouth, he collapsed to the ground and refused to move. I tried to lift him to his feet.

"Ah, bab-bab-bab-bab — " he bawled.

"Do not ask him to do too much at once," whispered Betsy from behind the door. "Do just a little at a time and he keeps quiet. Talk to him now; keep saying 'Dickie' and see if he will learn it."

In twenty minutes or so Henri was beginning to respond to my teaching, helped by the sight of another benay-ball which Betsy passed to me through the slit between door and door-post.

"Ah, did-did-did-did — " said Henri once or twice, and then refused to say more. I gave him the benay-ball, and was at a loss at what to do next.

"Sing him a song," came Betsy's whisper, "I am almost finished."

So I sang, as best I could, a French song which Maman had recently taught me. Henri gazed at me intently with his round eyes half out of his head and a syrup of spittle and benay-ball dribbling down his chin.

We managed to end this strange combined lesson without drawing attention to ourselves. (Betsy's division sums were all correct and much more neatly set out than mine ever were — as I fell asleep that night I was determining that I would emulate and surpass her in that respect.) Over the succeeding weeks and months and indeed years we kept the subterfuge going, varying it according to circumstances. There were long and frustrating gaps, for example, when Father was struck down by fever and about the house for three months, but we always resumed our meetings as soon as we possibly could. I was commended warmly by everyone except Father and Tony for my devotion to Henri and for the progress which he made under my tuition. His rocking was considerably reduced and I even succeeded in training him to attend to some aspects of the cleanliness of his person himself, thus defeating Milly, who could not be dissuaded from treating him as if he were a babe in arms.

As to Betsy's education, my readers will by now have appreciated her quality and I need hardly write that she quickly made up the ground which she had lost. Indeed, she was soon challenging me to move through our books faster than Maman would permit. Our quarrels, on this and other matters, could no longer involve fisticuffs, so we had to fall back on silence as our weapon.

49

"I do not care what Madame says," Betsy would argue, "I think we should be moving on to Chapter Eight — we do not need to revise Chapter Seven at all. Why do you not convince her of that?"

She would then have to sit in Henri's room for hour upon hour each afternoon while I refused to talk to her.

"Is Jéhu really your brother?" I asked once, and sat with Henri for three long afternoons while not a sound came from behind the door.

However, our need of each other's friendship was so great that in the end the silent offended one would relent and answer the other.

Looking back, I think that we were more cautious than we need have been, for Matti was on our side, as always, and did not fail to warn us with her slit bamboo if danger threatened. Martin and Milly and Sara were terrified of Matti and would have died rather than offend her, so there was no risk of exposure from them. Maman took good care not to hear or see anything unpleasant or disturbing, while Tony took less and less interest in myself and Henri as she acted more and more as Father's deputy around the estate. Her statement that she did not care if I made friends with the hogs, with a view to their education, was never put to the test.

Although Tony had lost interest in Henri and myself she was very conscious indeed that she was Betsy's owner. It was no surprise to me that she issued orders to Betsy in the most vulgar and impolite fashion, and if she was dissatisfied with her performance of her duties abused her unmercifully at the top of her voice, for that was the manner in which she treated me when she deemed that I had given her offence.

I would not have my readers think that Tony was nothing but a Jezebel who bullied Betsy unceasingly. Father would sometimes be absent on a Sunday and on a number of these occasions the two girls would play at "dressing-up" together. I would hear much giggling from Tony's room next door as Betsy was arrayed in clothing belonging to Tony.

"Oh, how that blue sash suits you!" Tony would exclaim in her husky contralto voice, "Give me a little kiss then, my beauteous Betsy!"

It was at a point like this that I would leave my chamber and hurry to Henri's room to escape the girlish shrieks which inevitably followed upon the giggles.

Not only did the two girls (who were mistress and slave, remember) indulge in "dressing-up" in Father's absence and with Maman asleep, but Tony would order Betsy to read aloud French novels to her. I would overhear Betsy's voice rising and falling musically and would press my ear to the wall between my chamber and Tony's and hear some such passage as:

" *— de voir dans sa chambre et au milieu de la nuit un homme qu'elle ne connaissait point. Elle frémit en m'apperçevant et fit un grand cri. Je m'efforçai* *de la rassurer; et mettant un genou à terre: Madame, lui dis-je, ne craignez rien. Je ne viens point ici pour vous nuire —* "

On the Monday morning after such girlish employments Tony would be complaining loudly, just as usual: "These boots are not properly clean, Betsy, you slut. You know what will happen if I do not have proper service from you? Well then, go and clean them again."

In the afternoon too everything would be normal: Betsy entirely herself again, my earnest fellow-conspirator, plainly attired in her striped linsey and as anxious as ever to pursue her studies. Only a trace of French perfume, which had attached itself to the cocoa-nut oil and clean clothes of her wonted fragrance, betrayed that my friend had had other interests upon the previous day.

Occasionally Tony would take Betsy away with her for a whole Sunday when she went visiting with Father, averring that no lady travelled without her maid. (For reasons upon which I need not elaborate Maman rarely went visiting with Father. I did not ask to go and was never invited.) Tony would ride off upon her horse — like all her horses, it was a hand or two taller than was proper — while Betsy, neatly dressed, would sit demurely side-saddle upon Flora, the sleepy pony which I had refused to ride. Putting a slave-girl upon a pony was nearly as reprehensible as Tony riding astride but Betsy, from what she told me, was careful not to challenge anyone by attempting to *ride* Flora; she merely sate upon the creature as if it were an ass. In any case no one, not even Father, cared to pick a superfluous quarrel with Tony in those days.

On the Monday afternoon following one of these absences of Betsy's she would have plenty of news for me, garnered in the servants' quarters of whichever estate house or government quarters had been visited and conveyed to me in whispers from behind the door of Henri's room. One such news report stands out amongst my memories.

"Miss Tony borrowed a fresh horse," related Betsy, "and went to gallop it on the beach, so I was helping the butler — they have a butler there, his name is North and he has a pair of shoes, I know because he shewed them to me — well, I was helping him to serve the Madeira wine and the shrub, only he called it 'rum punch', and he said I was a smart girl and not to listen to what the white people were saying, but I could not stop myself from listening — you know that, I never can stop myself from hearing, can I? — so I heard the man they call Governor Campbell talking to your father, to the Master I mean, and they were so angry with each other that they were purple in the face, both of them, and the Governor was shouting, well, not exactly shouting but nearly choking. 'Mr Mason,' he said, 'a Negro uprising is a possibility and war with France virtually

51

certain and you are under an obligation to His Majesty to contribute to the training of the Militia.' The Master was standing up as tall as he could and he was trembling as well as purple in the face. 'MacCallum,' he said — why did he call him that? — 'I have fulfilled my obligations by releasing as many of my overseers as I can spare for service in your draggle-tailed Militia, and each one of them is worth more — ' I had to go away for more glasses so I did not hear any more. I do not know what the Governor means by a Negro uprising, for I am sure there is not going to be one just now, but he would be the first to know if there were going to be a war with France, would he not?"

Governor Campbell was in office for only a short period before his death in 1777, so his quarrel with Father must have taken place when Betsy and I were ten years of age, when we could barely have understood what war with France or a Negro uprising might entail. However, barely understood fears are as poignant, if not more poignant, than fears of that which we know, and Betsy and I would look at each other with terror when we heard news such as that which I have just related. Then, being children, we forgot our fears in the urgency of other more immediate childish concerns.

Father's contretemps with the Governor set me to wondering about him for, in an island of strangers, he was to me perhaps the greatest stranger of all. I had always known, from my infancy, that he had been a soldier, and remembered with respect his coolness and boldness on the night of Captain Paul's sudden appearance; but I did not know in whose army he had served. I knew he was from Scotland, a country he mentioned so rarely that it was burned into my consciousness, but I knew nothing about the family he (and therefore I) came from, except that we were *not* "snivelling Whiggish Presbyterians", as he described his Scottish neighbours. (When one such came on business I used to watch out for him to snivel, but I was never lucky, and had to conclude that this was just one of Father's exaggerations.) He never admitted to being a Roman Catholic like Maman and would make shift to disappear just as quickly when a priest visited to say a Mass and hear confessions as he did when a minister from the Kirk appeared, intent upon proselytism.

Maman seemed to know as little as I about Father's family and was unwilling to tell me much about her own family either. My handsome dashing father had not been wearing uniform when she met and fell in love with him in Paris. Her family barely approved of him and her dowry, instead of being one of their large plantations in St. Domingue, had been a small one. When it had not proved profitable, the sugar crops failing for lack of sustenance in the soil, Father had quarrelled with the *famille*, sold the plantation for much less than it was worth, and taken his family, his overseers and his Negroes to deserted Tobago. Maman thus confirmed my growing doubts about Father's capabilities as a man of business. He had not confided to her the extent of his indebtedness, for she appeared to know nothing of the payments which he was making to Bordeaux, even when she was supposed to be helping me to check the books; truly, there are none so blind as those who will not see.

"And why did we come to Tobago?" I asked.

"Oh Dickie, *you* did not come to Tobago; you were born here, with only Matti to help me; and so was Antoinette; and *le pauvre* Henri too, and — " Here Maman shed tears, for she was remembering her dead children in all their beauty. "The soil was so rich and the climate was to be so healthy because of the cooling winds, and the house was to be on a hill away from the swamps, and so it is, but there is no difference, and I — "

I tried to comfort Maman, but I was soon in tears myself, for I had often dreamed of an older brother who might have defended me from Tony's Amazonian attacks — if only one of the three, Charles or Louis or Ranald, had survived, surely I would have had an ally.

By this time Maman could not help me with my education either, for her convent education in Paris had been narrow — strong on piety and music and drawing and needlework, but weak on worldly subjects suitable for a boy. She sometimes spoke to Father about my going to school in France, thus terrifying me with the prospect of leaving familiar Braemore (and Matti and Betsy and Henri) and setting out across an ocean subject to fearful storms and hostile privateers. However, Father said that he could not afford to invest good money in poor risks like my education (and I am still uncertain whether this was an instance of his poor judgment or no); nor would he allow Maman to write to her *famille* for help. Maman was therefore reduced to consulting her favourite visiting priest and even one of the Presbyterian ministers — both were adamant that I needed to start on my Latin immediately and offered to give me instruction, but Father poured scorn on the proposal, on the grounds that it would have brought "black crows" about the house. Betsy, to my surprise, was also hostile, stating that she did not want to learn a gibberish which no one spoke.

Maman, in despair at my importunings, eventually ordered books from Paris and Edinburgh, but she cannot have been well advised, for the volumes which Betsy and I awaited with such eagerness turned out to be so pious and insubstantial that we could only rarely find in them any matter worthy of debate.

Our formal education thus reached an impasse and Betsy and I tried very hard to invent ways of making progress on our own. We had some success, first by writing each other letters in both English and French and correcting each other's grammar, spelling and punctuation as best we could. We did not sign our letters and passed them to each other by means of a secret post-office — there was no aspect of conspiracy with which we were not familiar! When we had exhausted all the everyday topics appropriate to letters, we took to composing ever more fantastical stories of a childish kind about the Kings and Queens and other inhabitants of a mythic island called "Ogabot" (which is, of course, Tobago spelled backward). None of the exercise-books in which these stories were written has survived, and I can remember nothing of them, except that in one of Betsy's "epics" the Masters (called "Orgens") were black-skinned, and the slaves (called "Retsams") were white of hue. Despite these diversions, our minds were longing for more solid fare, but it was not until the year 1780, shortly before our thirteenth birthdays, that relief came; as always, Matti had a hand in the affair.

Betsy had grown, for the time being, quite as tall as I, although her limbs were more stick-like than ever and the impasse in her education had made her countenance permanently sulky, or so I feared. On the day in question, however, I could hear the old enthusiasm in her voice as she spoke to me from behind the door at the start of Henri's lesson.

"Master Richard! Your Father has a big box of books!"

"Ah, boos-boos-boos — " said Henri, who was now in the habit of attempting to repeat the last word of any sentence which he heard, although he was not to be dissuaded from prefacing his speeches with "Ah".

"It is hidden in the roof," added Betsy, "right here in Henri's room."

"Are you sure?" I inquired with my usual caution.

"Of course I am sure. My mother saw inside the box when the Master was having it moved here at night; she thinks we are old enough now to read the books. I have brought a ladder so that you can climb up."

Curiosity now battled with caution. I had never seen Father reading a book, although he was an avid reader of such newspapers and pamphlets as came our way; what kind of books would he keep hidden away in a box? Would they be worth the dreadful risks involved in climbing up Betsy's ladder and investigating the box? I looked around the yard; all was afternoon calm. If an eye were watching, it would be Matti's.

"Henri and I are coming in to see," I announced.

"Ah, tumming-in-to-see, tumming-in-to-see — " said Henri, rising to his feet unaided and adding: "Ah, walk-please, walk-please — "

I took his hand to support him and we went inside. The "ladder", I saw at once, was no more than a short and slender tree-trunk with cross-pieces nailed to it at irregular intervals. Betsy took charge of Henri and I approached the ladder with some trepidation. I commenced to climb, but was trembling so much that I was afraid that I would cause the ladder to fall. I took a deep breath and steadied myself; then mounted to a point where I could see an iron-bound wooden chest resting on some planks which had been laid across the joists. There was enough light for me to see the black iron plate pierced by the keyhole and the letters "J.M." painted beneath. What thirteen-year-old, even one of my easily dampened spirit, would not want to examine the contents of such a chest? What thirteen-year-old, with a Father such as mine, would not be afraid to raise the lid? I descended the ladder and met Betsy's expectant black eyes.

"We will have to be very careful," I said.

"What is the matter?"

"I will hold Henri," I replied, "while you go up and open the box."

"You know what would happen if I was found up there!" whispered Betsy, spitting out the words, "I would be accused of stealing and sent to the cane, or sold!"

"Ah, sole-sole-sole-sole — " whimpered Henri, echoing Betsy's sibilant undertone.

"I do not wish to open the box today," I said.

"I was brave enough to fetch the ladder in the middle of the night. Are you a coward, as Miss Tony says?"

"Yes," I admitted sadly.

"Ah, yes-yes-yes-yes — " said Henri.

Betsy sucked air noisily through her lips and teeth in the West Indian's most expressive gesture of contempt. She dropped Henri's hand brusquely, went straight to the back window and climbed out, thus commencing the longest and most ferocious silence which I had yet encountered. Her face, on the few occasions on which she permitted me to see it, was identical to her mother's in its heavy-lidded African disgust with a despicable European world.

On my side, I was stubborn in my cowardice and in what can only be described as remnants of my pride. I paid particular attention to Henri's lessons, with the result that he made his first unaided step under my tuition and in Betsy's absence, but my heart was filled with unhappiness.

This unhappiness was scarcely diminished by Betsy's light-hearted behaviour on a subsequent Sunday, when Father was again absent. She and Tony seemed to be playing at "dressing-up" and were giggling away odiously, much as on previous occasions, so I made my escape to Henri's room, dismissed Milly, and engaged myself with my brother as single-mindedly as I could. I lifted him on to a swing which I had

had fixed to the roof of the galerie and pushed him gently to and fro, untunefully singing a song which I had composed especially for such occasions. Henri was bubbling with the pleasure of the swing's motion and might have joined me in the song had I not been silenced by Tony and Betsy appearing on the back galerie of the house.

Betsy was wearing a long white dress (how brilliant is the image of it in my mind as I recall it!) with long white gloves, a white head-dress and veil, and white shoes. She was twirling a white parasol, one of Maman's, as to the manner born. I diverted my gaze from this embarrassing apparition and beheld Tony, dressed in a frock coat and what I later learned to be a pair of Father's tartan trews; round her neck she wore a full cravat and on her head was an old-fashioned gentleman's wig, which looked as though it had been newly floured. Believe me, this outfit of Tony's was more embarrassing to me than Betsy's.

As I watched, Tony put her hand on her heart and bowed low to Betsy.

"Would you care to walk with me a little, Mademoiselle?" she asked.

"With pleasure, Monsieur!" simpered Betsy coquettishly, dropping a full curtsy and laying her hand upon Tony's sleeve.

They then proceeded to walk up and down the galerie, Tony with a manly stride and Betsy in a mincing caricature of Maman's languid gait. I turned my back in dismay and tried to give all my attention to Henri; I gave him a benay-ball, although he had not earned one, and pushed him gently back and forwards; yet I could not help hearing more nonsense.

"*Mademoiselle, ne craignez rien!*" came Tony's voice, "*Je ne viens point ici pour vous nuire.*"

At this, Betsy shrieked and even more nonsense followed, which I cannot bring myself to report although I remember it with crystal clarity. When that was done, I heard Tony declare that the two of them must cross the yard to visit Henri and myself; but upon commencing the descent of the steps they discovered, with more shrieks, that Betsy was so unused to shoes that she could barely stay upright. I turned my head — I could not help myself doing so — and saw poor Betsy stumbling and almost falling at every step as she attempted to walk across the rough and stony yard. Tony became too impatient of this to continue play-acting the gentleman.

"Hold up there, Betsy!" she cried, as though Betsy were a horse, and seizing her around the waist she conveyed her roughly, and with many more horsemanlike adjurations, as far as Henri's swing.

Henri had at last noticed the apparition in white and was gazing at it with wide open eyes. When it came close to him he recognized it as Betsy and fell off the swing in a heap at her feet. She bent down to help him up, but he clasped her around her knees and buried his face in the skirt of the white dress. As Betsy gently disengaged herself it became obvious that Henri had wiped his streaming nose upon the silk; and worse, that he had also wiped his mouth thereon and left a large smear of benay-ball and spittle syrup.

Tony's always fragile temper snapped; she smote Henri sharply upon his head and turned her wrath upon me.

"Dickie, remove this idiot out of my sight!" she cried in Father's tones.

Henri, after a moment's silence, set up such a wordless howling that we all took fright, looking round fearfully lest Matti had seen or heard. Where was she? None of us knew. Silly dressing-up she tolerated, but striking Henri was another matter. Betsy's brain was the first to function, as usual.

"Master Richard, you know how to quiet him," said she, slipping off the white shoes and fleeing back to the house, followed by Tony, whose countenance, almost as fiery as Father's, shewed that Fury and Fear were battling to be uppermost in her breast.

I lifted Henri, carried him into his room and closed the door. "Poor Henri," I told him, "Poor Henri has a sore head. Sore, sore, sore." I caressed him and petted him and rocked him to and fro and, as Betsy had rightly predicted, I quietened him.

I learned later that Matti had not in fact returned from a Sunday afternoon visit, and that although Henri's wails did reach Maman's befuddled senses, I had quietened him before she appeared on the galerie to ask the empty yard what was the matter and, since no one answered, drifted back to bed.

No dire consequences followed upon the afternoon's happenings and within a few days Betsy revealed that the blue-stocking in her was as strong as the coquette, if not stronger. One afternoon, when I went to take over the care of Henri, I was met, not by the fierce silence which I had come to expect, but by an excited whisper.

"I have been reading one of the Master's books!"

I hastened to take Henri outside so that we could converse in our usual cautious manner.

"You will be sold one day!" I said to the door, knowing that Betsy would be just behind it.

"The book is worth the risk," she answered doughtily.

57

"Was not the chest locked?" I asked.

"Yes, but I took Madame's keys when she was asleep and I unlocked it. There must be a hundred books inside, but many of them are in what looks like Latin, and many more are dull books about how to fight battles with infantry and cavalry and muskets and cannon; I took the most interesting one of the others and shut the lid again, but I did not lock it. Then I put Madame's keys back."

I was almost overcome by faintness at Betsy's cool effrontery — the silly girl playing the flirt in a silk dress was made of black iron — yet not so overcome that I was not agog to hear what kind of book had so excited her. She was not slow in telling me.

"The book is called *The Strange and Exciting Adventures of Robinson Crusoe.*" Even when she was roused Betsy's enunciation remained measured and precise. "It is about a young man whose father is telling him not to run away, but to stay at home and enjoy the middle station of life, which is better than being too rich, or being sold into a life of slavery."

"You will have to put it back," I warned.

"But I have read only the first twenty pages. Robinson does disobey his father and he runs away to sea and there are storms and he is captured by the Moors — I do not know who they can be — and they make him a slave and I think he is going to try to escape and I want to know how he does it — "

"My Father would kill us — " I began, for I saw clearly that he would never approve of a Negress reading such a book under any circumstances.

"It is the most enthralling book I have ever read," declared my friend, tempting me, like Eve, with the Forbidden Fruit.

Unlike Adam I resisted, though feebly, recapitulating to Betsy the dangers of the course upon which we were setting out. She answered me not and I could imagine how she was regarding the other side of the door with raised eyebrows and pursed lips, but the word "coward" remained unuttered and so, like Adam, I fell; we were soon arranging that Betsy would read the book all afternoon and then hide it in our "post-office" for me to retrieve and read by candlelight at night. I took to wearing an old cape of Father's when crossing the yard, and a strange cap of his which he called his "bonnet", pretending that I too was playing at "dressing-up" but really because the cape had a deep pocket in which I could conceal the book. I also took to putting the "bonnet" upon Henri's head and he became greatly attached to it, and would demand it loudly as soon as I appeared in it.

From then onward there was little shortage of matter for debate between Betsy and myself. Whilst we were of one mind about the thrilling nature of Robinson's adventures, we argued back and forth through Henri's doorway about the morality of his actions and could hardly avoid the issue of slavery.

"Robinson had no *right* to sell poor faithful Xury to the Portuguese captain," said Betsy one afternoon, "and as for setting off to buy Negroes in Africa, it served him right to be shipwrecked."

I tried hard to counter this argument, but found myself in difficulties when Betsy declared roundly: "It is not right for people to buy and sell other people." The only answer to this is that Negroes are not truly people, which is a commonly held belief, but scarcely one to which I could confess if I wished to retain Betsy's friendship.

"But what about Man Friday?" I challenged. "He *offered* to be Robinson's slave."

"I do not care about him; he was a stupid Charaibe like Martin and Milly."

"It is not in the book that he was a stupid Charaibe."

"But it says that he was 'not quite black, but very tawny' and that his hair was 'long and black, not curled like wool'; and he must have been stupid. Fancy offering to put his head under Robinson's foot, and to call him 'Master', when he was not compelled to."

"But Robinson had guns."

"Ah, gun-gun-gun-gun — " interposed Henri, but we ignored him, so intent were we on our debate.

"If Friday had been a real man instead of a Charaibe, he would have helped himself to the guns."

It is a measure of the degree to which we trusted each other that we talked thus, but I would not have my readers believe that such conversations were at all common in the West Indies. Trust between Negro and white, between slave and slave-owner, was the most fragile of commodities, but somehow Betsy and I managed to preserve it between us.

Betsy, being a woman, or almost a woman, was ready to turn the argument around in female fashion and apply it to herself and her predicament.

"What would you do," asked she, "if Miss Tony became angry with me, or needed money to buy a horse she wanted, and sold me?"

I have to admit that I had often contemplated the horror of this possibility, in the middle of the night, when fears are at their worst.

"I would buy you back," I answered boldly.

"Where would you find the money?"

I was nonplussed.

"I am worth a lot of money to a lady," said Betsy, not without pride. "Madame says that I am very clever with clothes already, and I am quick and clean."

"I would steal the money!" I said, for I knew where Father kept his cash and I thought, not for the first time, that I might even be able to falsify his account book and conceal the theft. His arithmetic was not at all good and he might not notice a bogus entry.

"Everyone knows everyone in Tobago. People would know that you had stolen that much money; and anyway, they would all think that you had bought me for one purpose only."

At thirteen, I did not know the meaning of the last part of Betsy's remark and decided to ignore it lest I reveal my ignorance. As to the rest, what could I say? Despondently, I pushed the now sleeping Henri on his swing and did not answer.

"We are commencing one of our quarrels, are we not?" commented Betsy, after a long silence.

"No," I said.

"When you inherit my mother, will you set her free?"

"Yes, of course."

"And my father, and my brother, if they are still with the estate?"

My silence must have told Betsy that I did not understand her.

"Gilbert is my father, and Jéhu is my brother. We do not tell many people. It is better so."

Speech failed me again. That Gilbert was Betsy's father was a surprise but instantly became part of the natural order — the quick intelligence which I had covertly observed and admired would have been passed on to a daughter. Jéhu being Betsy's brother was a more problematic matter, for it was but a few days since I had seen him and the memory of that occasion was painful. Father had compelled me to walk to a particular cane-piece with an urgent message and I had passed close enough to Jéhu to see that he had a huge raised welt across the full width of his handsome muscular back. It was a welt of the kind which is caused by an overseer's whip being applied to sweating skin in full sunshine early in the day, and the wound then being left untended (and bathed in more sweat and more sunshine) until work is finished at sundown. Although I knew that Father would not have applied the lash himself — he punished only recalcitrant sons — nevertheless the welt had troubled my thoughts to an extent which welts on other Negroes' backs had not. Now that I had learned for certain that Jéhu was Betsy's brother, the welt became even more horrible to me.

I tried to forget the mental image of the pain it must have caused, but Betsy must have read my thoughts in my face — she was ever good at that.

"Will you set them free?" she asked urgently.

"Ah, free-free-free-free— " echoed Henri, only half-awake upon the swing, but becoming more observant every day.

"Yes," I said. (Oh my readers, did I have a choice?)

"That is a promise?"

"Cross my heart — " I began.

"I do not want any of your cross-my-hearts. Say 'I promise'."

"I promise."

"Good! I will take Master Henri now," said Betsy, emerging from behind the door. "No, wait a moment!"

She bent down and lifted her skirt, modestly revealing no more than a bony ankle and its string of jumbie-beads. After some effort she managed to untie the anklet and knot it again without losing any of the beads; she then handed it to me.

"I want you to keep it," said my thirteen-year-old friend, "and give it back to me when I am free."

I was taken aback. "Where shall I keep it?" I asked.

"You are a silly fellow sometimes, Master Dickie. You have more secret places for hiding things than anyone else here. You know where to keep it."

"Ah, keep it—keep it—keep it — " said Henri as Betsy lifted him from the swing to conduct him inside; and to conclude the afternoon's proceedings, which had strayed far from poor Xury and his sale to the Portuguese captain.

Despite Betsy's questing intellect it was I, and not she, who was attracted to the inscription on the fly-leaf of *Robinson Crusoe*; it read, in a florid but uncertain hand: "Ex libris James Macdonald." This aroused in my mind fancies that James was some distant relative, most kindly disposed toward me, who would one day arrive to take me away to happier climes. That he was a man of my own kidney was shewn by a note which he had pencilled (in the same florid hand) on the margin alongside the paragraph where one of Crusoe's men cries out "Land!" just before the ship is wrecked. The note reads, and since the volume is still in my possession, I am copying it word-for-word herewith:

"This Land may be the Island of Tabaco, Latitude 11°15′N, Longitude 60°40′W, a Place where a Man might Settle in Peace, since it hath no Government."

Who James really was, my readers will learn in due course.

When both Betsy and I had finished reading *Robinson* I perceived that I myself would have to exchange it for another book from the chest, or risk one of my friend's silences and most certainly lose more of her respect. This time no tell-tale ladder would be required, for Betsy with her usual foresight and ingenuity had brought along Sandy, the best of the Negro carpenters, and had persuaded him to hammer some very large nails part-way into a main timber in positions which made it possible for either of us to climb up to the chest. Betsy disguised the true purpose of the nails by hanging Henri's clothes and other articles upon them.

On the fateful day, I left Betsy on guard with Henri on the galerie while I, having put *Robinson* inside my shirt, climbed up to the chest. I had lost some of my childhood obesity, but I was scarcely agile; in fact I could best be described as clumsy, so my ascent was nerve-wracking and left me panting. Having caught my breath, I lifted the lid of the chest, only to discover that it was lined with lead and extremely heavy; I therefore had to use my left hand to hold it open while replacing *Robinson* with my right and thereafter lifting the other books to examine their contents in the dim light reflected up from the yard through the eaves. Amongst the Latin works and the military manuals which Betsy had described there were quite a number of others which promised to be more interesting. I had examined and rejected two or three and had picked up another (which had no title upon the spine) when Henri suddenly shouted "Ah, wow-wow-wow-wow!" at the top of his voice, presumably because he had seen one of the dogs. I was so startled and disconcerted that I dropped that monstrous lid and trapped the little finger of my left hand. The pain was excruciating. I had to lay down the book in order to lift the lid and free my finger, which immediately spurted blood. What should I do? It was hard to think clearly when all my mental powers were occupied in preventing myself from crying out; for cry out I must not, lest Betsy and I be discovered *in flagrante delicto*.

After a few moments, which I thought were eternity, I picked up the book, now bloodstained, and put it inside my shirt; I then climbed down by the way I had ascended, blood spattering the wall as I did so. Once on the floor, I tried to stop the flow of blood with my right hand and walked to the door.

"Betsy!" I whispered, "you will have to come in and help me. I have hurt my hand."

Betsy entered, leading Henri. They both gazed wide-eyed at the blood on my hands and clothes.

"Ah, sore-sore-sore-sore — " cried Henri, and I noticed, even through my pain, that this was the first time he had uttered a word spontaneously and out of fellow-feeling, rather than in parrot-fashion, or as a demand for attention.

"Go straight to my mother," said Betsy, ever practical.

"Take the book out of my shirt," I said, and without hesitation she retrieved the bloodstained volume.

I walked to the door of Matti's room, knocked upon it and when she opened it to me, fainted clean away.

When I recovered consciousness I was lying upon my bed and my throbbing little finger had been bandaged. (The bone had been broken and, in the absence of a doctor, mended crookedly, a fact which is becoming more and more apparent nowadays as my flesh shrivels and my skin becomes transparent.)

The next afternoon I ignored my still painful finger and kept my tryst with Betsy, for I was eager to learn what our new book was about. As soon as I had sat Henri upon his swing Betsy spoke from behind the door, without preamble.

"The book is very difficult," she said. "I am not sure that I understand it."

"What is the title?" I asked, somewhat impatiently.

"*The Tragedy of Macbeth by William Shakespeare*. It is a play, and it is all in a kind of poetry, and there are three stupid witches in it. Listen to this!" She read from the witches' speeches in Act IV and despite her mocking tone my hair commenced to stand on end, starting with that at the back of my neck and moving inexorably upward.

> Scale of dragon; tooth of wolf;
> Witches' mummy; maw and gulf
> Of the ravin'd salt-sea shark;
> Root of hemlock digg'd i' the dark —

Knowing Betsy as I did, I was not surprised that she was as scornful of Shakespeare's witches as she was of Obeah women — "they are just old women who have learned something about getting babies born and about making medicines and poisons from plants." I was of a different cast of mind — I knew for a certainty that back in Scotland, and in the dark Old World of Europe, there must be ageless fleshless female creatures dressed in filmy grey and with colourless eyes deep in their sockets, ready to pursue me mercilessly should I cross their path.

> Pour in sow's blood, that hath eaten
> Her nine farrow; grease that's sweaten

From the murderer's gibbet, throw
Into the flame —

"Stop!" I cried. "What is the rest of the play about?"

"I told you. I do not understand it yet. Pray allow me to read you some more."

"No, Betsy! Spare me!"

"Very well, Master Dickie, I will read it to myself," said Betsy. "You are far too tender-hearted."

"Ah, bob-bob-bob-bonnet — " shouted Henri, for although I was swinging him industriously I had forgotten to place Father's bonnet upon his head. I remedied this omission and when he had tired of the swing I commenced his walking lesson, but my heart was not in it, for I was waiting for Betsy to finish *Macbeth* and tell me what it was about, at the same time steeling myself for it to be yet more unpleasant. Perhaps it was the mention of sow's blood which made me remember the stains on the leather binding of the book. I walked Henri back to the door.

"Have you cleaned the blood off the book?" I asked.

"My mother wiped off as much as she could. She says that if she used water it would hurt the book more than if she left it."

"If my father — " I began.

"My mother says that the Master did not touch the books for more than twenty years before he moved them over here, and when he opened the box he did not take out even one; instead, he muttered an oath in that strange language which he sometimes uses, slammed down the lid and locked the box again. We will be grown-up before he finds the blood on *Macbeth*."

The blood on *Macbeth*! Would that I had found *Gulliver's Travels* instead! I will not weary my readers by describing the long struggle we had to understand that most incarnadined play, only that I can remember, as if it were yesterday, Betsy saying to me: "Lady Macbeth had to *make* Macbeth brave, just as I have to *make* you brave; only, she was doing it for wickedness and I am not." Thus spake my little rationalist friend, in the most off-hand manner, but I, being who I was, lost much sleep over the content of the play — the interventions of supernatural beings, the murderous dynastic ambitions of the protagonists, etc.

My nights were not helped by the loss of my friend in fancy James Macdonald, with whom I had often walked hand-in-hand into the land of sweet dreams. He had inscribed his name on the fly-leaf of *Macbeth* just as he had with *Robinson*, but in Act I Scene ii he had taken a pencil and underlined "the merciless Macdonwald" and then noted in the margin:

"Mine Ancestor, whom I Hope to Emulate!" Thus he consigned to oblivion my peace-loving friend and replaced him with a fierce warrior "of kerns and gallowglasses supplied". There was no respite now from the unease of my lonely waking thoughts or from my dreams — nay, nightmares — except in the company of my one and only true friend and trusty fellow-conspirator.

CHAPTER IV

*From the 23rd of May till the 2nd of June 1781 we are in great Peril; I act
in a Manner which does not accord with my Nature, but receive no Reward
or Commendation for my Pains; I observe, but do not understand, my Father's
Actions; I recruit a Bodyguard; and Betsy and I continue our Education*

"*Mon Dieu!*" cried Maman, rising from her chaise longue in great alarm,
"*qu'est-ce* — ?" She and I were sitting on the galerie and I had been reading
aloud to her from a French novel, partly for her entertainment and partly to
eradicate the last traces of patois from my accent, but I stopped instantly, for
I too had heard the sudden unfamiliar sound breaking in upon our morning
calm. It was a distant hammer-blow, faint yet portentous, coming from the
direction of Scarborough.

"It will be the soldiers practising with their cannon," I said, anxious
to reassure Maman, but only too aware that the Artillery Captain always
passed word round the Island when a practice was to be held and that we
had had no such word. It was only two years since we had heard gunfire
and on that occasion American privateers had succeeded in cutting out ships
anchored at Scarborough; and since Britain and France were at war there
was the possibility of an attack by French privateers, or even by the French
Navy, with or without shiploads of troops.

Another detonation followed; and then another; and yet another. The
intervals between them were much shorter than was usual at a practice
firing. I leaned over the balustrade of the galerie, shaded my eyes, and
gazed in the direction of the sounds, but could see nothing. Quickly I ran
to my chamber and fetched the telescope, of which, as befitted my position
as the family observer, I was the custodian. With shaking hands I removed
it from its leather case, opened it and rested it upon the balustrade; as I did

66

so I heard from Maman's chamber the tremulous clink of bottle upon glass which told me that she had retired to pour herself a brandy.

Braemore estate house was, as I have already described, built upon a hill and it commanded vistas in almost every direction, but it was not high enough for the blue Caribbean Sea to be visible to the north and west, or the Atlantic Ocean to the south and east, although both were only two or three miles away. The horizon to the south which I was scanning was a low forested ridge and the first unusual sight upon which I was able to focus the glass was a flock of white birds flying about distractedly. Then, I saw a faint plume of white smoke rise above the distant trees, only to be dispersed instantly by the wind. A few seconds later a detonation followed. I was wondering in my anxious way what rational explanation there could be for the interval between the smoke and the sound when Maman grasped my shoulder.

"Oh Dickie, where is Papa?" she asked.

I was about to answer that I would use the glass to look for Father, as I sometimes did for my own private purposes, but Milly chose that moment to distract my attention by emerging from Henri's room carrying him in a manner he particularly disliked.

"Ah, bam-bam-bam!" he was bawling at the top of his now remarkably powerful eleven-year-old voice.

Before Milly had reached half-way across the yard, Betsy ran out of Tony's chamber, seized Henri from Milly and set him upon his feet. As she conducted him towards us he was quiet, which made the gunfire sound louder. Next, Sara appeared from Maman's chamber and stood quaking beside her mistress. Then Matti appeared from the kitchen and walked across the yard at her usual unhurried pace, followed by Katy the washerwoman with her basket still on her head, and Martin, Father's useless body-servant. We were soon a motley group, standing silent upon the galerie and listening to the gunfire, which was now coming at irregular intervals. For comfort, I sought Betsy's eyes, but she would not raise them to mine, pretending to be entirely occupied with keeping Henri quiet.

"Oh Matti, where is the Master?" asked Maman, still gripping my shoulder fiercely.

As if in answer, two pistol shots came from the direction of the new cane-piece, about a half-mile off, where Father was most likely to be. They were quite clearly the signal from him which meant "Standing Orders" — the daylight version, which were quite different from the night-time orders. Father had been reminding me in an off-hand but insistent manner in the preceding weeks precisely what my duties were when I heard the shots, but now I could not call to mind a single one of them. For reasons which I could not fathom all the women except Betsy were looking at me expectantly. Quite insensible of my actions, I closed the telescope and returned it to its case. My breathing became congested and I could feel all my limbs begin to tremble. Then Betsy spoke, behind my back and *sotto voce*.

"Infirm of purpose!" I heard her say. "Standing Orders!"

This was, needless to say, just the spur I needed.

"Standing Orders!" I shouted in a voice that emerged from my throat as a fourteen-year-old *basso-profondo* and then rose willy-nilly to a thirteen-year-old piping treble as I added, "Into the house, everybody, and lock up everywhere. I will ring the bell."

As I ran to the end of the house to ring the bell Tony arrived at a furious gallop.

"The French are landing! Papa is just behind me!" she yelled, leaping from her horse and failing to tie it to the post, an unheard-of liberty. "Cuffy!" she shrieked, as she ran to her chamber and disappeared without another word.

As I hammered the bell with all my might it occurred to me that I had not heard any more gunfire. I ran back to the galerie, which was now deserted. The noise coming from behind the locked doors and jalousie was diabolical, as Milly was having one of her hysterical attacks and Henri was imitating her. Tony was upbraiding Betsy vehemently and most of the other females were attempting to calm each other and themselves with loud talk.

"Silence!" I roared, and there was a moment's hush, followed by Henri's voice from my room.

"Ah, science-science-science!" he cried, trying to imitate my roar, and failing.

"Be quiet, Henri!" I admonished him, my voice starting as a bass but rising to a treble again. "We must listen for the cannon."

"Ah, quiet Henri — " he muttered, and said no more.

In the silence which followed the beating of my heart was so loud that I could not be sure whether the cannon were still firing. I was saved from this uncertainty by Father cantering into the yard and dismounting calmly. Never before had I been glad to see him, but I was glad now. Old Cuffy, who had already collected Tony's horse, now appeared to take Father's, as if nothing untoward was happening.

"Madeleine!" called Father, and Maman opened her chamber door and ran to him.

"Jonas!" she wept, throwing herself into his arms.

68

He held her close to him and seemed to whisper into her ear.

These words and actions, as my readers will be aware, were uncharacteristic of the Father I had grown accustomed to, but were strangely reassuring to me; the more so, as the gunfire had ceased for the moment. Father continued to hold Maman round the waist while he spoke loudly and in measured tones so that everyone in the house could hear him.

"No one on this estate has anything to fear from the French unless there is a mistake. You must all be staying at your posts and being vigilant. Fergus, Donald and Malcolm will be here to protect you."

At this point there was the thump of a cannon. Father turned his head in its direction as if listening for more, but none came. He seemed to tighten his arm round Maman's slender waist.

"What you have been hearing is the gun at Minister Point. The gunners must have been trying to stop the French from landing, but so far I have not been hearing the French firing their ships' guns. We will be finding out in good time what is happening. Duncan and Alastair will be joining the militia to do their duty. Donal Bain is already drunk, of course, and no one will be risking their lives to help him in any way. I will be where I can best do my duty to you all, as I have sworn to do. Where is Antonia?"

"I am nearly ready, Papa," Tony called from her chamber.

At this moment the overseers' families began to arrive — middle-aged Negresses of different shapes and sizes accompanied by at least a score of Mulatto children of all ages; children I had only seen when they came on rare errands to the house. They all crowded into the yard and Matti, after an inquiring glance at Maman, began to allocate them quarters in the house and in Henri's room.

Amidst this further confusion Father embraced Maman again, shouted to Cuffy to bring a fresh horse, and looked at me for a second; then he looked away as he spoke.

"You did well to ring the bell, Dickie, but if you were a real Rory, you would be coming with me to be my dispatch-rider." He raised his voice. "Antonia!"

Tony, who had been loudly berating the family who were moving into her room, now appeared. She was dressed as a boy-soldier, and a very handsome one at that. She had changed her skirt for breeches and the gay silk kerchief which she had been wearing over her shoulders she had replaced with a drab cotton cravat. Her hair, as always, was tied up and hidden under her hat. Somewhere she had found a leather belt with a holster (which, however, contained no pistol) and she had drawn on a pair of gauntlets in order, I guessed, to conceal the slimness of her hands. The smoothness of her cheeks could not be concealed, of course, but could well have belonged to an eager boy of twelve or thirteen years rather than to a young woman of just turned seventeen. To complete her disguise, Tony's dark brows were knitted together in a fierce military expression.

"Papa!" she declared instanter, "I must have a pistol!"

There followed a short altercation remarkable for the manner in which Father kept his temper. Much to my surprise, he resolved the matter by announcing that Tony would indeed have her pistol, but that I must have one too, whether I wanted it or not. It is a measure of the rapidity and novelty of the events on that day that before I could make any protest at all Father had produced pistols, powder-horns and leather bullet-pouches from the "gun-room" (really a stout press) and handed them to Tony and myself. I held mine awkwardly while Father told me that I must find Fergus as soon as possible and be instructed in its use; Tony, on the other hand, deftly slid her pistol into her holster and adorned herself with the horn and pouch as if she had been used to handling them from her cradle.

As they cantered away I set off on my search, which was not a long one, for the concealed outpost where Fergus was stationed. On my way I passed Quashiba, Donal Bain's tall African mistress, walking towards the house. She was carrying her inebriated master over her shoulder as if he were a bundle of rags. On her head was a large basket of provisions and from her free hand depended two remarkably complaisant fowls, their eyes bright as they looked around. Behind her walked Maria, Donal's short-legged red-haired Irish wife; she was leading a she-goat which was followed by two kids and a ranging questing hog of the leanest possible aspect. I remembered Betsy telling me that Maria, as the only European woman outside the estate house, used to queen it over the Negresses and never lifted a finger if she could help it. My pistol, with its solid metal butt, was becoming heavier and heavier in my unhandy hand and I heartily wished that I had someone like Quashiba to carry it for me.

As I approached the outpost Fergus barked at me in his loudest overseer's voice: "Get your head down, Master Richard! You must really be crawling to me from there."

When I had done as he said and reached his post, somewhat encumbered by my weapon and accoutrements (including the telescope, from which I would not be parted) Fergus became apologetic, raising his hat to me and showing his grizzled head.

"I would not be shouting at you, Master Richard, sir," he explained, "but 'see and do not be seen' is the first rule of this kind of warfare, and although there is no enemy declaring himself as yet, it is as well to start by being careful and to go on being careful."

To a born observer like myself this was advice that accorded with my predilections. My practised eye told me that the outpost, or lookout, had been selected by a person who knew well what he was doing. Seated with his musket to hand behind a slight hummock and concealed by low bushes, Fergus could overlook all the provision-grounds and cane-pieces through which our house could be approached from the Great Courland Bay direction as well as a stretch of public road which, though little used, I had often wished I could see from the galerie. Fergus could also overlook most of the sugar-houses and every one of the Negro-houses and would therefore have early warning of a threat to the former or trouble from the latter. I could understand why he, the senior overseer, was posted here.

When I requested that he teach me how to use the pistol Fergus proved to be a knowledgeable instructor and since I was not altogether inept as a pupil, despite my unhandy hands, I was soon able to load, prime and cock the pistol, though in the circumstances I could not fire it.

"When it is a matter of aiming in earnest," advised Fergus, "I am of the opinion that it is best if you are pointing the pistol as if it was your forefinger."

When I demonstrated to him that in trying to do this I was considerably hampered by the heavy weight of the firearm, he told me not to tire my hand by carrying it all the time, but to thrust it into my belt, and perhaps the Master would find a gentleman's holster for me if I was asking him, choosing one of those suitable moments when he was in a generous frame of mind which were occurring from time to time. It was borne in on me that stopping this man from talking would require some effort and assertion on my part. At the same time I was deciding that the manliness conferred by the pistol need not extend to enduring the persistent beating of the sun upon my shoulders.

"I am returning to the house," I said firmly, and Fergus put his hand to his hat in a kind of military salute.

Not many of my readers will know that the war in 1781, which was no more than a skirmish, and by which the forces of His Most Christian Majesty conquered the Island of Tobago, lasted only ten days. However, that was long enough to convince me that for the non-combatant caught up in it war consists of discomfort, ennui and fearful apprehension in ever-varying proportions.

When I returned to the house I found that my room had been requisitioned for half-a-dozen Mulatto boys aged from nineteen years down to six, and that I had only my bed to myself. Their natures were quarrelsome, their manners rough, their language even rougher (as befitted the sons of their fathers), and their lack of cleanliness a matter over which it is best to draw a veil. Waiting in their company for something unpleasant to happen was a disagreeable prospect, so I appointed myself, *faute de mieux*, as a kind of mobile patrol to our little garrison and spent the rest of the daylight hours roving about restlessly from one patch of shade to another and never venturing far from the yard. I was not hungry and nobody thought to feed me, not even Matti.

Just before sundown Tony trotted into the yard upon a very tired horse. She called to Maman and myself to hear her news, but away from the house so as to be out of earshot of "the rabble", as she called our guests. She took no notice of Maman's anxious inquiries about Father and his whereabouts.

"It was not very exciting," she said. "We saw the French ships — there were five big ones and four small ones. When Papa and I arrived at Scarborough they had left Minister Bay because the gun there had been firing at them and the sea was too rough for the boats with the French soldiers in them, but nobody was killed or drowned or anything like that — *quel malheur!* So they were trying to sail into Rockley Bay instead, but Papa said the wind and the current were too much for them, so they sailed away as if they were going round Columbus Point. Papa detailed me to follow them along the shore as far as I could, but I lost them and did not see them again, even though I went all the way to Sandy Point and then to Pigeon Point. I had to come back because Papa ordered me to be home before sunset."

"Toinette," said Maman, "surely Papa sent a message for me."

"You are to stay where you are and stock up with more food and water. I will go and tell Fergus now."

"But where is Papa?"

"Oh, Maman, do be sensible!" answered Tony. "I do not know where Papa is, and if I did he would have ordered me not to tell you or anyone else. I am to meet him at a secret rendezvous in the morning so that I can receive my orders for the day." She saluted smartly and trotted away, calling for Cuffy, and Maman and I were left to look at each other, wondering about the import of all this news. We did not have time to wonder long for soon Tony returned on foot, bringing Fergus with her and the arrangements for collecting food and water were agreed and put into action. Maman retired to the house, but I resumed my restless patrolling. The darkness fell quickly and there was much confusion as the families returned to the house with their provisions, including more goats and live fowls than I had ever seen in one place at one time.

I carried on patrolling as the confusion and noise in the house gradually subsided. As the lamps and candles were extinguished one by one and only the new moon lit the yard I was assailed by the fear that a night-patrol of fierce Frenchmen, having landed on some lonely unguarded beach, would make a surprise attack and put us all to the sword. Bloody images from *Macbeth* lurked in my imagination ("unseamed him from the nave to the chops") and would not be dispelled by Reason insisting that the French had *not* landed and would hardly choose to attack the only estate on the Island where French was spoken. Despite these fears I began to feel the need for sleep but could not think of any place where I would be comfortable and safe from surprise attack as well.

I was crossing and re-crossing the yard aimlessly when I was interrupted by a creak from the slats of a jalousie.

"Dickie, you fool," came Tony's soldierly voice from Maman's chamber, "what good do you think you are doing out there, wandering about like a jumbie?"

As I approached the jalousie an infant cried out and was instantly hushed.

"There is nowhere for me to sleep," I whispered.

"There is room on the floor in here," answered Tony tartly.

The impropriety of this suggestion appalled me. Nothing would have induced me to sleep in my parents' room, and in company with Tony, so I did not answer. She must have had some inkling of what I was thinking, but decided to scoff at me nevertheless.

"You will never make a soldier," she said, "if you do not lie down and sleep when you have the opportunity. That is what Papa says."

"What if the French —?" I began to ask.

"If you are so scared, why not stand sentinel with Donald, or whoever is on duty? They will give you some backbone."

This was one of Tony's most sensible suggestions and I put it into effect straight away. On the way to the look-out I jumped at shadows, stumbled over a recumbent goat, and took my pistol out of my belt several times, only to be reminded that it was too heavy for my hand. Malcolm was on duty and asked me without rancour if the Master had ordered me to ensure that he did not fall asleep at his post. I assured him that this was not the case and joined him in gazing over the dark countryside and watching the racing clouds as they obscured the moon and stars and then moved on again. After several hours of Malcolm's taciturnity my head began to nod and I composed my self to sleep with my back against a tree-trunk.

When the sun woke me by shining horizontally into my eyes I discovered that it had rained heavily, but perhaps not for long, while I slept, but that I had been protected from the wet and the morning chill by Father's big cloak. I looked around and found that Fergus was on duty.

"Your woman was bringing that cloak," he said.

"My woman?" I asked, blinking wearily and shading my eyes against the sun with my hand.

"Young Betsy is yours, I have been hearing, young sir," said Fergus, "and she is a most useful and reliable female."

"But Betsy is only fourteen," I protested, "and she belongs to Miss Tony."

"Yes, yes, she is a woman, as I was saying, and yourself would be wise to be taking some trouble to keep her, I am of the opinion, for women like that one are not to be found growing upon the trees in the forest, waiting to be plucked."

"Has anything happened while I was asleep?" I asked, too confused by the revelation that Fergus knew something, however garbled, about my friendship with Betsy to answer or rebuke his knowing and obsequious familiarities.

"Well, Master Richard, the Negroes have been sneaking from one of their houses to another, holding confabulations. One day off work, and the prospect of another tomorrow, and maybe even one the day after that, if indeed they can see that far ahead, have gone to their heads altogether; but they have not been bringing their big drums out of the places where they are hiding them from us, which is a good sign. They have only been tapping gently upon their tamboo-bamboos in a peaceful manner, almost as if they were whispering." He turned his head suddenly and shouted: "Get your head down there!" Then his voice softened as he recognized the newcomer. "Ah, Missy Betsy, it is yourself!" he said, with an ironical emphasis upon the "Missy" which my West Indian readers, if there are to be any, will easily imagine.

Betsy was, of course, mistress of the silent approach and I had not heard her. Bending low in obedience to Fergus's command, she was carrying in one hand a platter with bread and large pieces of cold fowl upon it, and in the other a steaming cup. In differing circumstances her progress would have been comical as she endeavoured not to spill the liquid in the cup, but on this morning neither Fergus nor I were inclined to laugh at her. A curtsy being impracticable she bowed her head to me and then, very briefly, to Fergus. She set the platter upon the ground next to me and handed me the cup, which was filled to the brim with coffee, black and fragrant, and sweet too, I could be sure, just as I liked it. She looked me full in the eyes and held my gaze for several moments, but I understood not at all what she was meaning, for my mind was disturbed by what Fergus had said about her, and I was conscious that he was watching us closely with those sidelong eyes of his. Perhaps she meant that I was not to trust the man

74

— her nod to him had been just short of insolent and clearly implied that she did not. Then, without a word, she turned and crawled away on all fours. When she reached the point where it was permissible for her to stand up she dusted down her skirt with familiar dainty gestures and set off for the house, holding her back straight and putting one broad black foot in front of the other in her own precise way, and I recognized my true friend, who resembled the "woman" of Fergus's fancy only in the manner in which she carried her small head upon her long thin neck. This suggested, or suggests to me in retrospect, that her pride was a woman's rather than a mere girl's.

"She is just as I was telling you," said Fergus, who was gazing after her too, "a clean and most valuable woman, and with eyes only for yourself, Master Richard, and of course for your money too. They can be smelling where the money is, the women, just as soon as they are born of their mothers; and as for her colour, if there is no alternative but a Negress then the blacker the more faithful, I am of the opinion, and indeed she is prompter with your rations than my Sally is with mine. Could you be obliging me with a piece of that fowl now?"

For once I was beyond hunger, so I gave Fergus the platter, reserving to myself only a small piece of bread to eat with my coffee, upon which he did not appear to have any designs, perhaps because he had a soldier's canteen, from which he took rum-smelling swigs to wash down the fowl.

As we ate and drank Fergus insisted on favouring me with more of his "opinions", to my dismay.

"I would be fancying Betsy for myself, to be sure — after she had put on some flesh of course — and would have been raising the matter with the Master with a view to buying her, and he might well have obliged me, but my Sally would not be allowing it I am afraid, she has become quite a Tartar since I signed the papers. Then, to keep Betsy in the family, I was thinking of buying her for that upstart son of mine, you must have been meeting him, sir, his name is Charlie and he is nearly twenty years of age and he is needing a woman to polish his buttons as we old soldiers say and Betsy would be a match for the lazy fellow; but since I am now understanding that the charming creature is earmarked for your good self I cannot be pursuing the matter, which is just as well perhaps, for after all a young woman brought up in the big house, even as a servant wench, would find it hard to become accustomed to our simple ways — "

I determined to change the subject, and not to allow Fergus to revert to Betsy.

"What will the French be doing at this moment?" I asked.

"I could only be guessing about that, sir," Fergus replied. "I cannot be reading the minds of their commanders. Your Betsy now, will be. . . ."

"Fergus," I interrupted, "if I ask you a question, will you promise not to tell my Father, or anyone else, that I asked it?"

Fergus gave me a quizzical look out of the corner of his eye; the straight gaze, I was learning, was never for him.

"Very well, then," he said, "I will not be telling Himself."

"And no one else?"

"And not another person, upon my honour."

I hesitated, remembering that Betsy did not trust him. However, he helped me to speak by shifting his red-rimmed eyes to the horizon and giving it his sidelong attention.

"If the French land," I asked, "upon whose side will we be fighting?"

Fergus did not laugh, as I had feared he might; instead, he pondered a while, obviously choosing the right form of words for his answer.

"I am thinking that the Master will be deciding that in the light of all the circumstances."

"You mean . . .?" I said, and began to stutter, almost like Henri, "you mean . . . you mean . . . you mean . . .?"

"I am meaning that I will do whatever the Master tells me, for I am sure that what he decides will be best for Braemore and all of us who are living in it. Were it not for the Master I would be minding a single cow on some barren foreshore in Scotland, or working my heart out to gain a living in the Carolinas, or freezing to death in Canada."

These statements left my mind even more confused than it had been before but I had no opportunity to clarify what Fergus meant for Donald and Malcolm arrived to discuss what their dispositions should be for the day ahead. Their conversation did not help to answer the urgent questions still uppermost in my mind, for they talked obliquely about the French as "our friends in the ships" and about the British as "our friends of the 86th Regiment" or as "our friends in the Militia". I would like to have overheard what they would have said had I not been present — both Donald and Malcolm had glances as oblique as their words, true soul-mates for Fergus.

After the three of them had decided that there was nothing to be done but take up the same day-time outposts as they had occupied the day before, I returned to the house, having discovered yet again that my new-found degree of courage did not extend to exposing my tender self to the fierce attentions of the sun, which was now well above the horizon.

The confusion about the house was indescribable, so I shall not attempt to describe it. I was wandering about from patch of shade to patch of shade, still stupefied from lack of sleep and from the effects of my talk with Fergus, when a strong hand, it could only have been Matti's, grasped me by the elbow, guided me to her room and pushed me inside, closing the door quickly behind me. There, in the narrow space between the two beds, Betsy was washing Henri's face, a rag in one hand and a calabash of water in the other.

"Ah, bam-bam-bam — " shouted Henri when he saw me, but he quietened when I greeted him in my usual manner by ruffling his hair.

"Henri, you bad boy, I thought you had forgotten 'bam-bam-bam'" complained Betsy, picking up another rag to dry his face and then speaking to me. "I told my mother that you have not slept and she wants you to sleep here until the Master returns." She pointed to the narrower of the two beds, plainly her own.

I must have conveyed my doubts by the expression on my face, for Betsy said sharply: "No one will dare to come in here. No one dares to displease my mother."

"Miss Tony — " I muttered.

"Leave Miss Tony to me. Lie down."

When I obeyed and lay down prostrate she left Henri and removed my hat and boots. Her hands, for all their slimness, were as firm as Matti's.

"Now put your pistol under the pillow," she said, "and pull all these things round in front of you." She helped me to arrange the horn, the pouch and the telescope where they would not interfere with my sleep. "Are you comfortable now?" she asked.

"Yes," I answered sleepily, "but if the French — "

"If the French come, no one will be at all interested in where you are hiding," said Betsy calmly.

"Ah, bam-bam-bam — " said Henri from the floor.

"Where did Henri sleep?" I asked.

"I could see that those Mulatto boys in your room were going to tease him cruelly, so I brought him here where he feels safe."

"Ah, safe-safe-safe — " cried Henri.

"Good boy, you *are* forgetting 'bam-bam-bam'" Betsy was saying as I drifted off into the Land of Nod.

Is it not strange, my readers, that I too should have felt safe in that Negro hut? It was spotlessly clean, but primitive and poverty-stricken in the extreme, though our field Negroes would have thought that a bed each for a mother and daughter was rather the extreme of luxury. Betsy's pillow had been neatly stitched together out of part of a grain sack; it smelled of sun-bleached burlap, of some fragrant grass with which it had been stuffed, and of cocoa-nut oil.

I had not slept long when I was awakened by the sound of Tony shouting, her voice penetrating the general hubbub with ease. "Betsy! Where are my boots? I am leaving in five minutes and they had better be ready *now*!"

"Dickie!" whispered Betsy into my ear, "if Milly cannot be spared you will have to mind Henri." She left, closing the door carefully.

As I could see that Henri was comfortably ensconced on Matti's bed, playing with his rosary and humming tunelessly to himself, I permitted myself to close my eyes again. The last thing I heard before unconsciousness stole over me was Tony shouting: "Betsy, you slut, have you no idea of cleanliness at all?"

I had travelled far into the domain of Morpheus when all at once there impinged on my reluctant ear the sounds of many cannon firing at once and of Henri bawling "bam-bam-bam — " at the top of his voice and close to my ear.

I was on my feet in an instant, retrieving my pistol from under Betsy's pillow, putting on my hat and thrusting my feet into my boots. The cannon-fire was very much louder than that of the day before; it was more continuous and plainly derived from many more cannon; and it was coming from the opposite direction, that is, that of Great Courland Bay to the north. It had the effect of silencing everyone at Braemore for a few minutes; everyone except Henri, of course, for he maintained his "bam-bam-bam-bam . . .!" as an idiotic *obbligato* to the majestic thunder coming from beyond our horizon. I made to open the door, intent on discovering whether Father had returned whilst I was sleeping, and if he had not, going to join Fergus, but Henri's voice changed from a shout to a scream.

"Ah, Dickie-dickie-dickie —!" he cried, not wanting me to leave him. Without thinking I kneeled down to the posture which informed him that I would carry him on my back if he put his arms round my neck. He stopped shouting and did as I suggested, nearly dislodging my hat in the process. I then stood up and emerged from Matti's room on my way to war, with my far-too-heavy pistol in my hand, my other accoutrements dangling in front of me, my hat tipped over my eyes, my boots unlaced, and my idiot brother riding me *cocioco*.

The few women who had ventured out of doors had run back into the house, leaving several goats half-milked and many fowls a-flutter, and all the doors and jalousies were shut. Alone in the yard stood Charlie, the Mulatto son whom Fergus so despised, his curly head cocked to listen to the gun-fire and his habitually mournful brown face lit up with excitement, fear, and a desire to be doing something, all in equal proportions. Since it

78

was becoming only too apparent that Henri's flaccid muscles were not up to the task of supporting the weight of his body upon my back and that he was about to slip to the ground, I determined that I must have the help of this strapping nineteen-year-old.

"Here, Charlie!" I called, "take this!"

When he saw me holding out the pistol to him his eyes opened wide and he started back in astonishment.

"Quick!" I bellowed, for I was almost bent double in my attempt to prevent Henri from falling, and my quite indispensable hat seemed about to join the ants in the dust.

Charlie took the pistol from me, grasping it gingerly but with a large firm hand while I stood erect and supported Henri with both my hands under his backside.

Ignoring the continuing gunfire, which was now slightly more intermittent than it had been, I requested Charlie to straighten my hat and when he had complied asked him if the Master had returned. When he replied in the negative, I asked him if he knew how to load and fire a pistol.

"Yes, sir," he answered, making a show of cocking the weapon and then aiming it, "I have watched my father."

"Have you fired a pistol?"

Charlie gave me his father's sidelong look.

"Well, Charlie?" I insisted.

"I have fired my father's pistol when he was drunk," he said with the guilty glee of a disobedient son, which I could recognize only too easily. I began to see a possibility.

"Did you hit the target at which you were aiming?"

"I smashed a bottle, Master Richard, at twenty paces."

"Come and take the horn and pouch then," I commanded, holding my voice in the bass register by the force of my will.

The horn and pouch were duly disentangled from my person, after some little difficulty with the telescope and with Henri's arms. When Charlie had slung them round his own neck, he lifted his chin and squared his shoulders manfully, but whether to defy his father or the rumbling cannon I could not say.

"Now follow me and keep your eyes open!" I ordered and Charlie did so, apparently not noticing that my voice had risen by an octave or two because of a particularly loud burst of detonations.

At the proper distance from Fergus's outpost I put Henri on the ground and we all three crawled towards it, Henri chuckling at what he took to be a new game, and forbearing to shout back at the cannon.

When we arrived, Fergus's sharp soldier's eye immediately saw the pistol in Charlie's hand.

"In the Name of the Devil, where were you getting that?" he asked.

I could now see the rolling smoke from the guns and even feel their explosions in my chest, and was becoming more and more anxious to ask Fergus what was happening, but I perceived that he was deeply concerned about the pistol and that I must clear up that matter promptly.

"Charlie is carrying the pistol for me," I explained.

"You had better be taking it back from him, Master Richard," said Fergus gravely.

"But you know yourself that it is much too heavy for me," I argued, "and why should not Charlie carry it for me, and fire it if it has to be fired?"

"Because he is never obeying me," said Fergus. "He is much too big for his boots altogether."

"Charlie will obey me," I announced with some bravado, attempting to bolster my courage by imitating Father's voice and manner. "He will be my body-guard."

I was rewarded by a look from Charlie which spoke of continuing excitement at the prospect of fighting, resentment towards his father, and a willingness to swear undying loyalty to me — or perhaps to anyone who would let him retain the pistol.

"And whatever will Himself be saying," inquired Fergus, "when he finds Charlie of all the persons here flaunting that fine Doune pistol, and Himself's favourite powder-horn, which he had from his grandfather Clan Ranald, also as well?" The sidelong look was again in evidence. "Perhaps I should be having the Master's pistol, while your bodyguard is having mine." He laid down his musket and produced a plain and worn but well-oiled piece from his holster.

"My bodyguard will carry my Father's pistol," I said, my voice rising to a piping treble again, "and I want to know what is happening over there." I pointed to the smoke still drifting over the trees on the horizon to the north.

"Very well then, indeed, Master Richard, sir," said Fergus, returning his pistol to its holster, settling his musket across his knees again, and remaining silent, contrary to his nature, while his son's shoulders straightened even more as he moved closer to me in a protective manner. I was heartened enough by this to challenge Fergus more vigorously.

"I asked you what is happening," I squeaked, "and I am entitled to an answer." There was a long pause.

"Redcoats have been marching along the road," said Fergus to the horizon.

"Thank you for telling me that, but surely what the ships' cannon are doing is more important?"

"The ships, is it?"

"Yes, the ships, what are they doing?"

"They are firing on the battery at Great Courland and the guns of the battery are firing back."

"French ships?" There was another long pause.

"I do not think that the English navy would be firing on one of their own batteries; although, to be telling you the truth, such things have been known."

I perceived that it was an easy matter to prod the man into being his own garrulous self again.

"Will the French try to land?" I asked, my nightmare visions from the night before rising to haunt me in broad daylight.

"As I was saying, Master Richard, that is a matter for their commanders to decide and to be telling you the truth I am wondering where the English navy is — " Here he cocked a professional ear and held up his hand for silence, but Henri, who had been playing quietly with some pebbles, raised his voice again.

"Ah, science-science-science — !" he bawled, almost as if he had understood Fergus's gesture.

"Whisht!" said Fergus, and Henri desisted, although he could still be heard quietly trying to imitate the sibilance of this unfamiliar interjection, and failing.

"I am thinking," said Fergus, after listening hard, "that the guns at Courland have stopped firing and that there will be gunners not needing hats for they will be lying in the sun with their heads shot off, poor souls." He pondered, his head still cocked. "The French ships are still firing but they will not be trying to land on a lee shore if they do not have reason to believe that the English navy is all sunk, or engaged elswhere, perhaps with the American rebels, so I am of the opinion — "

Here Fergus was interrupted again for Betsy had made her silent approach on all fours and was now squatting with her eyes upon him, as if asking permission to speak. "What can I be doing for you, my dear?" he asked.

"Massieu Fabrice," she answered in patois, using his patois name, "Madame want to speak with you." She had dropped her eyes and her half-witted expression was a triumph of dissimulation. Charlie was taking no notice of her at all, I was glad to see.

81

"Madame knows that I can *not* be leaving my post at a time like this," said Fergus, answering patois with his own kind of English, as all the overseers did.

"She want to know if the Frenchmen coming and what the Negroes doing." Betsy's eyes were still on the ground.

"You may be telling Madame that it is possible that her compatriots will be here before the day is out, and if they are, I am hoping that they will be remembering that they are subjects of His Most Christian Majesty and will be behaving in a Christian manner, although I am taking the liberty of having my doubts upon that score; and as for the Negroes, they are mostly lying upon their beds like rational persons, blessing their good fortune in not having to work today." This was a manifest lie, for there was still an air of alarm and restlessness about the Negro houses, but I supposed that Fergus thought to reassure Maman. "And some of the women are lighting fires to start their cooking and I am praying that none of them has any pork left from those two hogs with which the Master was so free last Sunday, for the smell and aroma of fresh-killed pork roasting would be bringing the Frenchmen round us like flies, since it is likely that they have been eating shipboard rations for a few weeks."

"Ah, pork-pork-pork-pork — " interposed Henri, who had wearied of trying to imitate Fergus's "whisht!" and wanted us to take some notice of him again. Betsy put her hand on his shoulder and hushed him.

"Me go back to the house and tell Madame what you say," she said, "and me take Massieu Henri with me, for he not good at playing *cache-cache*. He make too much noise."

"If you had been mine or Charlie's," said Fergus as he watched the dusty soles of Betsy's retreating feet, "I would have had you speaking the English by now as well as understanding it."

I glanced at Charlie to see what he thought of having my friend Betsy bestowed upon him but his face was already that of an impassive soldier who puts duty before personal considerations. Fergus, of course, had more to say.

"What a soldier's woman she would be making, Master Richard! She knows already that Master Henri would always be breaking the second rule of this kind of warfare, which is 'hear and do not be heard'."

As if in answer to this apophthegm the guns stopped firing and an extraordinary silence fell, the more intimidating as we did not know whether or not it was going to last. Even the dogs were silent and not a bird twittered as Charlie and I looked to Fergus for his opinion as to what was happening or was about to happen. He was in no hurry to enlighten us.

After the guns had been silent for perhaps ten minutes, Fergus deigned to speak. "It is unfortunate that there is no way of knowing what is going on," he said. "The French may have seen the English navy, or had word that it is coming, and decided to sail away before they are caught in the wrong place. On the other hand indeed, they may have stopped firing their guns because they have knocked out the battery and can be making a landing. We must just be waiting and being vigilant until we hear from the Master; Himself is always the first to be finding out and passing on intelligences and Miss Antonia will not be sparing her horse at all at a time like this."

There followed a period of dreadful apprehension, such as I have previously described as a concomitant of war. The hubbub from the house gradually recommenced and a few discreet sounds could be heard from the Negro-houses, but the familiarity of these noises was no comfort to me as I swept the horizon with the telescope, looking for I knew not what.

After a while I discovered that I was obtaining no shade from the bushes round the outpost, as the sun was now overhead. It was burning my shoulders so painfully that I feared I might be forced to abandon the lookout, where I was amongst the first to learn what was happening, and seek the shade of the house, where news would be scarce. To my shame, I was also afraid of losing such respect as I had gained from Fergus and Charlie. However, when Fergus asked me in his most obsequious manner whether he himself could act as my bodyguard for just a few minutes while Charlie fetched us something to eat and drink, I seized the opportunity to have Charlie bring me a carriage-umbrella of Maman's which I had long coveted and which I thought I could now properly requisition, citing "the exigencies of war". It was no dainty aid to coquetry like a lady's parasol, but large, stoutly built and dark green and as suited to my purposes as Robinson Crusoe's was to his. Neither Fergus nor Charlie dared to raise even so much as an eyebrow as I opened it up; Fergus even offered to help me when I decided to conceal the umbrella with a few leafy boughs, as though I were Malcolm in *Macbeth* and Braemore forest were legendary Birnam Wood. When all was arranged to my satisfaction I recommenced my anxious peering through my telescope.

The seemingly endless period of waiting ended, as before, with the sound of a galloping horse.

"Missy Antonia," said Charlie, and I learned that watching through a telescope is not the best way of keeping a whole countryside in view.

Sure enough, Tony was soon galloping up to the post and pulling up her horse dramatically. Fergus stood up and saluted and I noticed that he did not dare to tell Tony to "get her head down". Without dismounting she shouted her news.

"The French have landed at Great Courland, hundreds of them! I saw them! They were leaping out of their boats into the water and running up the beach with their muskets in their hands and the gun at Black Rock was firing at them till it blew up and there was blood in the water and Mr. Collow is going to set fire to his canes to distress the French but people are saying that the canes will not burn because the rain last night was very heavy over there — "

Tony's eyes were dancing wildly and her face was working strangely at the mere thought of the cane being fired. (As to the "blood in the water" I could not but recall with horror that she was no stranger to the sight of blood — even Father did not know that she insisted on being present when a hog was killed and would describe to me afterward, despite my appeals to her to stop, how the blood streamed from the creature's nose into the pail.)

Tony's excitement must have been conveyed to her horse, for it caracoled and reared alarmingly, so that she had to stop her disjointed reporting of events, and thus give Fergus an opportunity to ask a soldierly question.

"Miss Antonia, what are the Master's orders?"

"Oh yes, of course," replied Tony, looking somewhat nettled, "Papa says you are to raise a flagpole and have both flags ready so that when he gives the order you can raise the one and hide the other."

"A flagpole, is it?" said Fergus almost phlegmatically. "Himself might have been thinking of that years ago." He turned to me. "Master Richard, since your bodyguard is so big and bold and well-armed, perhaps he could be going to find Sandy the carpenter in the Negro-houses and telling him that a flag-pole is required in the shortest possible time and that I expect to see him come running with it. Your bodyguard could also, if he is capable of remembering two messages at once, be passing the word around the women that they should not be roasting pork for the reasons I was telling you, and indeed they would do well to be hiding all the food in their possession."

I had only to nod at Charlie for him to salute smartly and march off with his shoulders squared and his hand upon the pistol. (I flatter myself that at fourteen years of age, and purely in pursuit of self-interest, I had transformed a sulky boy of nineteen into a creature who bore a passing resemblance to a man. Would that I could have performed the same transmutation upon myself!)

Tony had by now succeeded in regaining full control of her horse and having caught sight of my umbrella proceeded to roast me about it, much to my relief, as I did not care to contemplate her scorn should she have noticed that I had parted with the pistol.

"Dickie the soldier with the umbrella!" she exclaimed, laughing at me loud and long with the deep-toned laugh which seemed, as she grew older, to become ever more taunting and mirthless.

"You are giving away the position of this outpost," I retorted. "You should take your horse right away from it."

"You and your outpost! The French will be over-running the whole of Tobago in no time. You will see; we will be raising the *fleur-de-lis* on that flagpole by tomorrow, if not today."

"Was the Master saying that?" inquired Fergus with extreme calm.

"No, he was not, Fergus Macdonald," replied Tony, proceeding to mimic his manner of speech, "but myself has been seeing the French soldiers in very very great numbers, and they will be too many for the English altogether, I am of the opinion."

"I am finding myself in agreement with your opinion, Miss Antonia," said Fergus, obviously accustomed to Tony's ways and unperturbed by them.

"Indeed, I am thinking that that is very sensible of you altogether," said Tony, "and since we are being of one mind on these matters, I will go and change this horse." She cantered off to the stables and we could soon hear her making old Cuffy's life a misery.

Minutes later Charlie arrived, escorting Gilbert and Sandy, who were carrying a pole between them. The latter's hair was of a reddish hue, which may have accounted for his name. He had brought with him from Africa an unusual capacity for quickly finding exactly the right piece of timber that was required for any purpose; and since he had no English or patois, and steadfastly refused to acquire them, his capacity for understanding the signs and gestures which people used to describe to him the needed timber was even more remarkable.

After some gesticulation it was decided that the pole should be erected against the end of the house, at the peak of the gable. Sandy went off, apparently confident that he could raise the pole by himself. Gilbert was left behind, looking solemnly from me to Fergus and back again, as if desiring permission to speak, but uncertain to whom to apply. Fergus would have postponed the permission as a matter of principle, but Gilbert's countenance so resembled Betsy's when she had important news to impart that I determined to hear what he had to say immediately.

"You may speak, Gilbert," I said.

"Young Master," he said in patois, bowing his white head gravely, "we hearing the French going to burn down all the estates where the Masters gone to join Militia."

(I saw, in a flash of enlightenment, that the ideas of war which I had gained from *Macbeth* and from my history books were likely to be erroneous; there might be no sword-fights or cavalry charges in Tobago. Instead, the main weapons of war, apart from soldiers' muskets, would be fire and the threat of fire. According to Father, nearly all the estate-owners were as deeply in debt to their bankers in Glasgow and Edinburgh as he was to the carrion-crows of Bordeaux. In a conflagration which need last no more than an hour a planter could lose his cattle-mill or windmill, his boiling and curing houses, and his distillery; without these the cane ripening in the fields would be worthless and his stock of Negroes, nearly half an estate's capital value, would become a liability which had to be fully fed, although not fully occupied, until the *usines* could be rebuilt. If warehouses filled with sugar and rum were put to the torch a year's profit would vanish too. If the estate house went up in flames the owner would have to borrow even more in order to refurnish himself and his family with the necessities of a civilized life, imported by sea at great expense. Farewell then to the dream of returning home with a vast fortune!)

"Who was telling you about all this burning?" asked Fergus of Gilbert with calm disdain.

Gilbert ignored this question, but maintained his respectful stance. When Fergus did not choose to repeat himself Gilbert continued even more solemnly.

"On other estates we hear Negroes being given freedom if they fight French."

Fergus, who was still alertly watching the countryside, shrugged his shoulders; then with a sudden urgent gesture requested me to pass him the telescope.

Gilbert continued: "We want be free and we not want French to rule in Tobago like in St. Domingue, so we fight French if we made free and given muskets and cutlasses by the Master, or the Young Master here."

I saw that I might have to be responsible for great decisions if Father did not return soon, or at the least send orders. Fergus, however, was unperturbed and did not remove his eye from the telescope.

"So that is what all those confabulations were about," he said, "discussing who would be most likely to set you free; and I suppose you have been deciding in your great wisdom to fight for the Master who knows every rascally one of you by name and who was giving you fresh pork last Sunday? But have you been considering that the Master may be on the side of the French and wanting them to win, even and although they were never seeing fit to award him or his faithful followers the pensions which they have been earning over and over again. Moreover and furthermore, if he was to be giving you arms — "

Here Fergus stopped his flow of words and paid close attention to whatever it was that he could see through the telescope. At the same moment I noticed that a group of about twenty of the strongest and most active of our young Negroes were standing regarding us from a distance of about two hundred yards. Easily distinguished amongst them was Jéhu, quite clearly their leader and waiting for a signal from his father. Knowing something of his quality, I could envisage what a formidable soldier he would make, leading his platoon of labour-hardened Negroes, all well-accustomed to the sun and handy with the cutlass, with which they could decapitate a Frenchman as easily as they could cut cane-stalks. Charlie, who was proving to be silent as well as obedient, must have been moved by a similar thought, for he stepped even closer to me in a manner which might have been protective, or fearful — I knew not which.

"Master Richard," said Fergus, and when I turned to him he handed me the telescope, "if you would be so good as to be looking at that large tree with the yellow flowers on the highest point of the hill over there." I pointed the glass as he directed. "You are seeing it?" I nodded. "Now be looking a trifle to the right, where there is a gap between two smaller trees, and you will be seeing some persons moving."

The eyepiece misted over and my hands trembled as I wiped it clear with a corner of my neckerchief. At last I succeeded in focussing upon the moving figures *en silhouette* against the sky; they were, without question, men carrying muskets with long bayonets fixed upon them, and their hats were of an unfamiliar shape with feathers at the back, and they bore an unmistakeable air of cautious, but resolute and murderous, purpose.

"Well now, Young Master," asked Fergus quietly, "and what are you making of these persons?"

"They are French soldiers," I quavered, taking the telescope from my eye, just in time to see Gilbert signal urgently to Jéhu, whereupon all the young Negroes except Jéhu himself vanished amongst the surrounding vegetation.

"Indeed they are," said Fergus, and I could now see that there was unease beneath his calm exterior, "and I am wishing that the Master had issued clear instructions as to who is the enemy into whom I must sink my dirk. If it is to be the French, then I am seeing how, with your permission and consent of course, we could ambush any small party detached to set fire to Braemore. It would involve issuing Jéhu and his friends with cutlasses, and promising them freedom, and losing quite a few of them to French muskets and pistols and bayonets, which are longer than cutlasses — "

Here I looked at Gilbert's face, but it was quite expressionless. I did not have Fergus's faith that he understood little English; my Betsy's father was unlikely to be so stupid.

" — on the other hand," Fergus was continuing, "if it is the English and their Lowland Presbyterian friends who are to be the enemy we need only be sitting here and waiting, because the French, as you have seen, are busying themselves occupying the highest ground and it will be very difficult for the English to dislodge them, if indeed the Militia are having the stomach for watching their houses burning *and* mounting an attack up a hill. As to a party sent to burn Braemore, I am sure that Madame and yourself could be dissuading the French in their own language — "

Here my courage began to ebb away and only the last shreds of my pride prevented me from decamping to Matti's room, where I was sure I would be safe under the protection of her power and where I could discuss with Betsy what I had best do in these truly awful circumstances. My readers will perhaps forgive me if I reiterate that I was fourteen-and-a-half years of age.

Fergus, however, was continuing to range the countryside with his eyes. Now he motioned to me for the telescope and I handed it over. He trained it on the valley through which passed the only public road in our vicinity, which I have already mentioned. It was little used because it was ill-made and subject to flooding. Who was using it now?

When Fergus had examined the road for a few moments he passed the glass back to me.

"You would be doing well to look closely at those persons on the road," he said, "and be learning that war is not all glory."

I think that I had known that truth from my cradle, but I dutifully put the glass to my eye again, focussed it upon the valley road, and saw a procession of redcoats and mules moving with extreme slowness. The redcoats on foot were hobbling and supporting themselves with sticks, whilst the ones on mules were drooping and sagging. Many had bandaged heads, with stains that matched their coats — or so I imagined for I am not sure I could see bloodstains at that distance. As I watched, an open-sided cane cart jolted into view, followed by another; their Negro drivers were leading the mules, and even at that distance I thought I discerned that they were doing so with solemn care. On the carts lay redcoats whose heads rolled from side to side with every jolt — it was impossible to tell whether they were dead or only wounded.

"How many of those poor wounded souls would you be seeing, Master Richard?" asked Fergus.

True to my nature, I had already been counting them without knowing it.

"There are twenty-nine or thirty," I answered promptly.

"I was thinking so myself, and that would be very heavy casualties for the force at Governor Ferguson's disposal, which cannot be mustering more than five hundred — "

Suddenly, and from an unexpected direction, there was the sound of a galloping horse.

"The Master!" exclaimed Charlie, recognizing the hoof-beats before anyone else. "Shall I give you back the pistol, Master Richard?"

"No," I said, holding on to those last shreds of pride and hoping that I would prove to Father that I could act manfully in his absence.

Father rode straight to the stables and must have dismounted quickly for soon he was walking towards the lookout while engaged at the same time in a shouting match with Tony, who was accompanying him. Gilbert made an attempt to move away, but Fergus ordered him to stop, saying that the Master might have need of him. Charlie coughed nervously, very close to my umbrella.

"Fergus!" shouted Father as he approached, "break out the *fleur-de-lis*, just to make sure that Braemore is not set alight by our friends."

Very quickly Fergus turned to Gilbert and said quietly: "Are you hearing that? The French are our friends!"

Gilbert disappeared smartly indeed for a man whose ordinary movements were slow and dignified. Jéhu was not to be seen either.

Fergus shouldered his musket and set off for the house; as he passed Father and Tony he called out loudly: "As a subject of His Most Christian Majesty I am honoured to be raising his flag!"

Father was about to turn away when Tony drew his attention to me, still sitting in the lookout with Charlie behind me. He stopped, stared, and then approached me, his blue eyes growing harder and harder as he took cognisance of the arrangements which I had made for my comfort and protection.

Even now, so many years later, it is too painful for me to describe what followed in any detail. Suffice it to say that Tony looked on with an equivocal smile while Father ordered Charlie to hand over to him the pistol and its accessories — "No Mulatto will be wearing a gentleman's pistol on my estate!" — and when poor Charlie had complied, turned his suffused countenance upon me. I could see that he was about to lash me with his tongue when Tony intervened.

"Dickie has been quite brave," she said. "He patrolled all night with the pistol and then he started his own army by recruiting Charlie, who looks as if he might make a soldier."

"Antonia!" cried Father, "why are you intent on provoking me? I will be dealing with Richard as I see fit, and without any help from you." He once again turned upon me. "Remove yourself, your disgraceful umbrella, and your so-called soldier out of my sight. I am not caring where you go, so long as I cannot be seeing you!"

At this I signalled to Charlie to follow me and made off as quickly as I could, intent on reaching Matti's room, but still protecting myself from the sun with the umbrella — the latter being interpreted by Father as a defiance and causing him to utter one of his incomprehensible Gaelic expletives to my departing back.

Before we reached Matti's door I halted and instructed Charlie to march into the yard flourishing the umbrella, thus creating a diversion which would enable me to reach my hiding place undetected, or so I hoped. Having left the umbrella on the galerie he was to find a hiding place of his own, but within earshot in case I had need of him.

Before we parted I gave him a half-johannes (worth eighteen shillings sterling) which I happened to have about my person. (This coin had been surplus when I had last balanced the estate accounts. I made a habit of secreting such monies against a time when there might be a discrepancy in the accounts in the form of a shortfall — a practice which I commend to any young accounts clerk into whose hands this narrative may fall.)

On Matti's bed I found Henri fast asleep and snoring, with the usual bubbles emerging from his mouth. Dejected, I lay down on Betsy's bed and listened anxiously for any sounds of battle or of a French party being dissuaded from setting fire to us all by the sight of the *fleur-de-lis*, but I could hear only the confused noises coming from the families crowded into Henri's room and into the main house. However, it was not long before my one and only friend arrived. Without surprise, Betsy gazed at me with her dark liquid eyes.

"I have to hide here," I whispered.

"I know," she answered.

Thus we agreed, without further words, that our conspiratorial friendship should continue without a break. For the rest of the war, so-called, I allocated to myself the duty of caring for Henri in Matti's room during the day whilst Betsy was performing the manifold duties demanded of her by Tony, Maman and Matti. At the same time she contrived to gather and to convey to me on her infrequent visits more reliable intelligence about the military conflict than I would have thought possible, so that I was not near as ill-informed as I had feared I might be.

During the night, while Matti and Betsy occupied their room along with Henri, I secretly joined the Mulatto boys in my own room, being guarded in my bed by Charlie who slept on the floor beside me. He had broken into his half-johannes to procure himself a fearsome knife and lorded it over his fellows in a manner which was comical to watch, but which contributed not a little to my comfort and peace of mind. Everyone except Father knew where I was hiding, but since everyone was living hugger-mugger also, no one was moved to make criticism.

As to the war itself, it passed Braemore by as Father had arranged that it should, but I learned from Betsy that rumour and counter-rumour accompanied the marching and counter-marching of the military and the sailing and counter-sailing of the navies. However, the burning of captured estates by the British to flush out the French and the burning of other estates by the French to intimidate the planters into deserting the Militia (in which, of course, the French were successful), these were no rumours, for they were confirmed by the evidence of our eyes and noses.

Even from Matti's windowless room I could see through the chinks in the rough walls that the sky was darkening as neighbouring estates to windward of Braemore went up in flames and smoke, and I could smell the dread aroma of sugar, rum, molasses, *bagasse* and wooden buildings all aflame together.

All these events electrified Tony, so that Father's dispatches were carried to their destinations at breakneck speed; their effect upon Henri was less fortunate. Already showing signs of being disturbed by the many interruptions to the routines by which his simple life was governed, he also discovered a strong aversion to the smoke. On a number of occasions when I was asleep in the day-time upon Betsy's bed (for I found it impossible to sleep at night, even with Charlie to guard me) Henri awakened me by shouting: "Ah, bun-bun-bun-bun — !" and by beating his fists upon my chest and spraying his spittle into my face. (Thus he discovered that his spittle was a far more potent weapon than his fists, and he continued to use it to express displeasure, or to gain his own way, for the rest of his life. Never again was he to be quite the amenable creature he had been in his early childhood.)

Two days before the British forces capitulated to the Marquis de Bouille and the Comte de Grasse, the overseers Duncan and Alastair returned to Braemore (having deserted from the Militia, according to Betsy) and Father decreed, on one of his brief visits, that since the war was as good as over the overseers' families should return to their homes

91

and normal estate activities re-commence — cane-field weeds wait for no man. Gilbert and Jéhu and their followers amongst the Negroes therefore found themselves back in the cane-fields as before, their brief hopes of freedom dashed. This was a matter upon which Betsy did not volunteer one word to me; when I tried to ask her about it she acted as though she were deaf; when I persisted in my questioning she whispered, almost savagely: "Pray interrogate me no more upon that topic, Master Richard!" However, I knew from her speaking of English and not patois that I was not in deep disgrace and that indeed she might have some special news for me, if I cared to wait until she was ready to tell me and did not upset her with further questions.

Sure enough, it emerged upon the following day that my friend, never one to let slip an opportunity, had taken advantage of all the confusion to replace *Macbeth* and to purloin no less than three other volumes, which she had selected with the greatest care and for sound reasons — *Gulliver's Travels* because it seemed to be like *Robinson Crusoe*; *Oroonoko* by Mrs. Aphra Behn, because it was about Africa; and, treasure of treasures, Doctor Samuel Johnson's *Dictionary* (in the one-volume edition) because we need no longer puzzle over the meaning of a word new to us if we kept it by us.

Betsy had already found the time to start reading *Oroonoko*, a book which is now considered lewd and quite unsuitable for a young girl, or indeed for her elders. She giggled so much as she told me about the early chapters that she convinced me that they would not be of interest to me, but I am sure that she was in no way corrupted by them.

That we continued our education most diligently even during the perils and discomforts of war is a measure of the importance which we attached to it. May I commend equal diligence to any of my readers who may be still in their school-days, and assure them that they are indeed fortunate that they have a school or college to attend, and teachers to guide and educate them.

CHAPTER V

The French attempt to impose Conditions for Capitulation which make a Negro Uprising likely; M. Le Comte Dillon makes his Appearance; Tony discovers an unsuspected Talent; My Friend and I overcome some Differences of Opinion

"Oh Master Dickie!" exclaimed Betsy in a voice full of foreboding, "the French are going to hang all the Negroes who fought for the British."

She was speaking from behind the door of Henri's room, for she and I had resumed our afternoon arrangements just as soon as Governor Ferguson and his tiny force had been surrounded by the vastly superior French on the height of Caledonia and negotiations over the terms of capitulation had begun. I was hesitating over how to reply to her when Henri forestalled me.

"Ah, hang-hang-hang-hang — " he said, uncannily selecting for repetition, as was now his wont, the word of greatest moment in the sentence he had just heard.

"Be quiet, Henri!" I said impatiently, at which he threatened to spray me with his spittle, so I threatened him in return: "I will not lift you on to your swing if you do not behave, do you hear me?"

This appeared to be effective and I was able to turn my attention to Betsy. However, I still hesitated, for I was not ready to impart to her some intelligence about the proposed hangings which I had in my possession.

"But none of our Braemore Negroes fought for the British," I temporized. "They are in no danger."

"That is true, but some of them might join an uprising if Negroes from other estates were to be hanged for obeying their Masters and behaving with undaunted courage."

"Are you sure about this?" I asked, appalled to have my fears about a possible uprising confirmed in this way.

"Oh Dickie," replied Betsy, abandoning my title as she did only when her feelings were intense, "you know me well enough — I do not indulge in spreading false alarms. My mother says we do not want hangings and we do not want an uprising and my father agrees. We think you could persuade Madame to speak to the Master, who has friends amongst the French. Would you try to persuade Madame, Dickie? Would you please?"

Betsy begging a favour in this uncharacteristic manner threw me into a state of considerable confusion. To gain time to order my thoughts I lifted Henri on to his swing as a reward for remaining silent and pushed him back and forwards gently.

"Have you been eavesdropping?" I asked.

"No! When have I had the opportunity?" countered Betsy, "But I can tell that you have; I can hear in your voice that you have intelligence which you have not given to me yet. Please tell it to me! *Please!*"

I understood from this that my friendship with Betsy was in jeopardy unless I acceded to her pleas. Despite Fergus and his disagreeable view of Betsy as a slave-woman earmarked for me (and for purposes which, at fourteen years of age, I only half understood, and which I was afraid might undermine the true intimacy which we had shared) I was determined to maintain that friendship come what might; in truth, I could not brook the thought of life without it. I therefore related to my friend all that I had learned early that morning, when I had taken pains to overhear Father talking quietly with Maman just before he and Tony rode off on their mysterious business.

"That's wicked, wicked, wicked of Arthur," were the first words that I had heard from Maman. "He will provoke the Negroes to revolt and we shall all be chopped to pieces, or ravished, or burned to death! I cannot believe it of him — he was always such a gentle boy — and it is not like him to be vindictive — "

"No doubt he is obeying his orders," had answered Father, "as he is bound to do if he has ambitions to be Gouverneur of Martinique or Guadeloupe."

"But Arthur is far too young — "

"Madeleine! Consider! He was old enough to be made a Colonel at seventeen; and I am hearing that he took command at Savannah when d'Estaing was wounded and covered himself with glory, even in that defeat. He will be a Gouverneur before long, never fear!"

"At the price of our lives!" Rarely had I heard Maman so animated.

"I am agreeing with you, my dear, that it would be most impolitic and unwise of Arthur to be punishing those Negroes at this moment. Let us be hoping that he has been given some discretion and can be influenced — "

"Why do you not have Arthur to dinner? Then he would *have* to listen to me!"

"Arthur is not mine to command, my dear — " The more vehement Maman became the milder were Father's answers.

"Then tell him that Madeleine de la Tour du Pin commands him, in the name of our friendship and of the friendship between our families, to appear before her and explain himself — "

There ensued a silence, and I had to deduce that Father had gestured toward the brandy-bottle, for Maman's voice fell to a whisper so low that I could barely hear it.

" — and I will not drink a single glass until you have brought Arthur here and I have spoken to him. I know that our lives may depend upon my abstaining. If you are going to meet Arthur today, go *now*, in the Name of God!"

At this point Tony burst upon the scene — she rarely knocked upon doors.

"Who is this Arthur?" she demanded, "and why have I not heard of him?"

I waited for Father to explode in wrath at this presumption, but it was Maman who answered.

"Arthur is M. le Comte de Dillon, Commandant of the Irish Régiment de Dillon, and I have known him since he was a little boy. When he comes here, I shall introduce you to him."

"But I have met him already," exclaimed Tony, "if he is that young Count who is commanding the *Avant-garde*. I came upon him with his aides and his escort at the ford over the big river, just beside the waterfall, and he asked me for directions and was surprised when I gave them to him in French and even more surprised when I told him that with a seat like his he deserved the best horse in Tobago as spoils of war — he has the firmest seat I have ever seen, except for Jéhu's of course. He looked rather angry, but then he laughed and said that if I was a cadet in his régiment he would ensure that I had good manners as well as a good seat by chastising the said seat. Oh! how embarrassed he will be if he comes here and Maman introduces us and he discovers that he has threatened to chastise a lady's seat! Papa, if we meet him today I absolutely forbid you to introduce me as your daughter!"

"Come, Antonia," said Father briskly, "There will be time enough later to be discussing handsome young officers. We must first see if this

Island can be saved from folly and ruin." He raised Maman's hand to his lips. "Be assured, Madame, that I shall be passing on your command."

When I had conveyed the gist of this conversation to Betsy she announced immediately that she must disappear for half to three-quarters of an hour and would I please be sure to inform any inquirer that I had not seen her and did not know where she was. As I pushed Henri to and fro upon his swing and untunefully sang to him his favourite song, I fell to wondering how Betsy's father and brother would view the news she had hastened to give them, for of course I had no doubt but that it was to them that she had run. Although I was only fourteen years of age, and my mind was a welter of confusion about many things, I yet perceived clearly that Negro leaders such as Gilbert and Jéhu, and I was sure that they were indeed the leaders, were constrained by the passions of their followers and could not be sure of preventing an uprising, although they might direct it and moderate it to some degree.

Whilst I did not doubt Betsy's statement that Gilbert was against an uprising, she had said nothing about Jéhu's view. Would he really want to prevent an uprising? He was a young man of spirit, if ever I saw one, and he would not be likely to forget that lash across his shoulders any more than would other Negroes who had had many lashes. It was only a few days since I had seen Jéhu and his platoon of potential warriors after they had calmly weighed the pros and cons and decided to offer to fight for the British. How different would be their aspect if they were inflamed to red-eyed rage by the wanton and cold-blooded hanging of their fellows? Once they had started on the slaughter of white people, would they make distinctions between friend and foe? If Jéhu encouraged an uprising to settle an old score, for which side would his sister Betsy be carrying messages?

It was this thought more than any other, I think, which made clear to me that the Negroes who had been threatened with hanging must somehow be saved, but what could I do? What could Maman do, if "Arthur" were no longer the gentle boy whom she remembered, but an unfeeling and ambitious soldier? What could anyone do against thousands of French troops?

When Betsy returned she found me staring vacantly into the distance, with Henri asleep upon his stationary swing.

"Master Richard!" she whispered sharply, and when I had awakened from my reverie and turned my eyes upon her, added: "You will speak to Madame?"

"I will do what I can to help her to remain sober."

"And you will urge her to speak to Count Dillon?"

"I am not convinced that my speaking to Maman would do any good."

Betsy sucked air through her lips and teeth and then said, in a most acid manner: "You are never convinced of anything, Master Richard."

She went into Henri's room and refused to speak to me. When it was time for her to resume care of Henri she did so without a word to me or a glance in my direction, so that I knew that I had given great offence to my friend, and that at a conjuncture when it would have been advantageous to keep any friend I possessed.

Thus to my trepidation about an uprising was added the emptiness of heart and mind which was always consequent upon a quarrel with Betsy. It was therefore comfort of a kind to see Charlie signalling to me as I crossed the yard on my way back to the house. He was positioned just within hailing distance, as I had forbidden him to approach any closer to the house. I fetched my umbrella and sallied out to discover what intelligence he had for me, his signals having suggested some urgency. He saluted steadily enough as I approached, but I could see that he was vastly excited.

"Yes, Charlie," I asked, returning his salute.

"Sir, I know of a pistol — " He could not utter more.

"What pistol is this?"

He did not stammer, but his jaw clenched and unclenched strangely until his words spouted out in a rush: "Sir, if you will give me three half-johannes I can buy a good pistol and a horn with powder and a pouch with bullets." This was, I suspect, the longest speech which Charlie ever made.

The pistol, I knew instantly, was either "spoils of war" — that is, stolen by a soldier and therefore legitimately acquired — or the proceeds of a crime, that is, stolen by a Negro. The exceedingly low price suggested the latter.

I hesitated for a few moments, then remembered Tony giving her condescending approval to my "starting my own army". Why should I not? The very thought soothed my trepidation and filled my empty heart and mind.

"If I buy this pistol, Charlie, it will be more than ever necessary that you obey me instantly, without question and to the letter. Moreover, no one must know that you have it." I had no real belief in the efficacy of this speech, but lo! Charlie responded to it as though I were a general.

"Yes sir, I will obey," affirmed the great foolish creature, standing upright in the most exaggerated military posture it is possible to imagine, "no sir, I will tell no one."

"And will the person who is selling it keep his mouth shut?"

"Oh yes, sir. He — "

"Your life may depend upon his silence."

"Sir, his life depends upon my silence. I would — "

"Enough! Salute me, then wait until I bring you the money."

Later that evening Father sent word by a friend who was returning from Caledonia to his estate near Buckoo that he and Tony would be remaining away until the morrow, and that we were to be calm and maintain our usual vigilance. Even after this news Maman remained sober, although she could not but be irritable and querulous. Nevertheless, I risked asking her for the keys of the strong-box in which we kept our petty-cash, on the grounds that I needed to make entries in the account-book and check the cash. She gave them to me with only a sigh or two and there and then, within her line of vision, I abstracted three half-johannes and made a false entry in the book. I heartily wished that I had been deceiving Father in this brazen manner, rather than Maman, whose whole mind was taken up with resisting the allure of her brandy-bottle.

This was the first time I "robbed" Father to make a purchase of which he would not have approved. It was not the last.

Maman proceeded to heap coals of fire upon my head by telling me that since I was so grown-up and acting so responsibly she wanted me to keep the keys myself. Suppressing the promptings of what I suppose I must call my conscience, I secured the keys to my belt, made some excuse to Maman, and ran out into the darkness to find Charlie.

When I had taken only a few steps I ran into Fergus, who was patrolling the policies; he was most anxious to discover if I knew why the Master had not returned and to give me his opinion on the possibility of an uprising. He was thinking, he said, that the Negroes were unnaturally quiet (and indeed not a drum nor a tamboo-bamboo was to be heard) but if the Master had decided to stay away he was of the opinion that the news must be good.

I dismissed Fergus with an approving word about how safe we all felt when he was on patrol and went on to find Charlie and give him the money. He was so overcome that he could not speak but, soldier-like, did not forget to salute before he went off "at the double".

On the following day (which was, to be precise, the second of June 1781) the estate's day-to-day routine continued to mend itself and I could observe through the telescope the overseers and their gangs working in the cane-pieces and the grass-gang fetching fodder for the animals, but around the house we were awaiting Father's return from moment to moment. During the morning I saw Betsy once or twice but she refused to acknowledge my glance, and in the afternoon she showed me the whites of her eyes (as Tony might have said) and silently forbade me to take over Henri's lesson. Betsy thus denying me speech with her emptied my heart and mind again and I wondered if I had unwittingly committed some offence even graver than refusing to pester Maman about speaking to the Count. There was no sign of Charlie and his pistol and I became so melancholic that I would have welcomed a murderous mob of Negroes advancing upon me with their cutlasses raised.

I was jolted out of this unwholesome condition by Father and Tony cantering into the yard in high glee, just half-an-hour before sundown. There was no need for eavesdropping; the four of us gathered on the galerie while the servants listened openly from doorways and Betsy pushed Henri upon his swing.

Father, he revealed, had been acting as an interpreter and go-between despite not being trusted by either side, "and quite rightly!" he laughed. He had persuaded Governor Ferguson to accept some of the more stringent of the French terms whilst at the same time inducing Count Dillon to moderate other demands. The final obstacle to agreement was the matter of the forty Negroes who had fought for the British and here it was Tony and not Father who had carried the day; she was only too willing to describe how she had achieved this end.

"Oh Maman! I did more galloping than I have ever done, but I took care not to wear out the horses I borrowed, and sometimes, you know, because of my fluency in French and English, I was asked to carry messages by word of mouth when there was not time enough to write them down. Well, on several occasions I had to speak to M. le Comte Dillon himself and he gave me such fierce looks, as though he was expecting me to be insolent to him again; and once he took hold of my arm — oh! but his hand was strong! — and told me that he had been a cadet at my age but by God he was not sure that he had looked as smart as I, or ridden a horse so well; then he squeezed my —" here poor Maman blenched, "— one of my nether limbs, Maman, and remember he thought that I was a boy! He squeezed it harder than he had squeezed my arm and I am sure he could hoist me into the saddle as easily as Jéhu used to; I feared for a moment that Papa was going to give the game away but he was a darling for once and continued to address me as Tony, and none of the officers and planters who knew me revealed that I was a girl, but of course deceiving the French would not be against their Presbyterian principles. Anyway, M. le Comte concluded by telling me not to distress myself about being a little thin for my muscles would develop if I continued with an active life and rode every day of the week, and he would have me in his régiment as soon as I was old enough.

"Near the end of all the stupid arguing, when Governor Ferguson sent me to say that he and the planters would *not* hand over the Negroes to be punished, M. le Comte conferred with his officers for a while, then held up his hand for silence. Then — I was so surprised! — he turned to me and said: 'let me hear the cadet's opinion; he seems to have his head screwed on in the right way.'

"So I stood to attention and as tall as I could — I was dismounted, of course — and I said that I knew the Braemore Estate niggers very well indeed, and they were the most contented and peaceable in the whole Island, but even they would be liable to revolt if provoked by the hangings proposed by M. le Comte; and as for the Negroes on the other estates, it was not difficult to conjecture what their feelings would be if the best and bravest of them were sent to the gallows for bearing arms in a manner which M. le Comte, as a soldier and a man of honour himself, could scarce deny was honourable."

"Toinette!" exclaimed Maman, "I had not thought that you could speak so eloquently!"

"Speeches about honour must sound better in French," replied Tony, "for M. le Comte shouted '*Touché!*' and his officers applauded me and they all laughed and agreed to withdraw the demand and the capitulation is to be on the terms given to Dominica."

At this Maman clapped her hands and all the servants joined in, even Matti at the kitchen door, so I clapped my hands also; Betsy was clapping Henri's hands for him, but she was not smiling like the others and she would not look in my direction at all. Tony, however, had not finished, and chattered on while Father listened indulgently.

"Papa sought out M. le Comte and told him that Maman commanded him to appear before her and he said that he would obey just as soon as his duties would permit and I am just longing to see his blushes when Maman introduces us and he perceives that in addition to threatening to chastise a lady's seat he has in fact squeezed her — oh Maman, your face! but why is it only a gentleman who can shew a fine — yes, I know what the Mother Superior would have said, so I will not say it, but how I will laugh at M. le Comte de Dillon! Oh, how I will laugh, and then demand an apology! I will make him kneel down and beg for forgiveness — "

I shall not trouble myself or my readers by recording more of Tony's gloating. Suffice it for me to write that this day of the capitulation was probably the happiest of Tony's life, involving as it did galloping upon horseback, deceiving a person in high authority into thinking she was a boy, and achieving by her own astuteness a diplomatic and political victory which made her something of a heroine in Tobago, and especially amongst the Negroes, who even had a lewd and scandalous song about "Miss Tony and the Count" which they sang when they thought no white person was listening.

The Count early sent word that he proposed to call upon us on the following day, since his stay in Tobago was to be short. The morning and afternoon of the great day were devoted to elaborate preparations which engaged the whole household except for myself and Henri. I, having tried on my best shirt, coat and breeches, and my buckled shoes, found them all grown too small for me, but decided that since I looked awkward in any suit of clothes whether old or new, they would have to suffice. I then resumed my more comfortable clothes and returned to reading *Gulliver's Travels*, intending to change again at the last possible moment. Henri, of course, was to be kept out of sight in his room, with Milly enjoined to keep him silent at any cost.

I could hear over the walls that Maman and Tony were deeply engaged with their toilettes, and that Betsy was running to and fro assisting them. Tony, it seemed, was being remarkably co-operative, probably because she judged that the more feminine she appeared the greater would be the Count's mortification; she was even accepting instruction from Maman in the coquettish use of her fan.

Maman had learned somehow that "*cher* Arthur" was now a widower, his wife, Thérèse-Lucy, having died in unfortunate circumstances, leaving him with a young daughter of unusual accomplishments and effervescent spirit on his hands. From the same source came the news that he was searching for a second wife to help to nurture and educate this *nonpareille*. It had occurred to Maman, in a fit of uncharacteristic sanguinity, that he might be interested in Tony, and this had now become an *idée fixe*. Father, on being apprised of Maman's hope, was less than enthusiastic, perhaps because he was now quite dependent upon Tony's help with the estate, or perhaps for other reasons. I was made strangely uneasy by the prospect of Tony marrying and longed to consult with Betsy, but that creature was still refusing to talk to me. However, in the quiet of the night, and by thinking hard, I brought myself to a knowledge of exactly what my friend would have said. It went thus: "It would be the height of folly for any man to take on Miss Tony as she is now — domineering, bad-tempered and illiterate, and to ask her to become a step-mother to a little girl at seventeen years of age would be grossly unfair to both parties."

Father returned early from the cane and Martin's meagre capabilities were soon being stretched to their limits by his demands for this or that article of clothing and for the polishing of silver ornaments.

The "last possible moment" arrived and I had to put down *Gulliver*, attire myself in my ill-fitting clothes, and emerge from my chamber. I was immediately made ashamed of my hobbledehoy appearance, for the first person I met was Father, looking truly magnificent, if already a little overheated, in a Highland outfit of plaid and trews which I had not seen before; its abundance of silver buttons, buckles, clasps, etc., explained the need for Martin's efforts with the silver polish. (It was not until later in the evening that, ever observant, I noticed that insects had eaten many holes in the tartan stuff of Father's costume and that it would not have passed muster in daylight!)

Matti and her minions had not been inactive. Our dining-table was covered with our whitest and least-darned linen cloth and upon it were set our finest silver, crystal and porcelain, all winking bravely in the light of tall candles (of which I knew the exorbitant cost, since I had myself entered the bill for them into the estate account book).

The Count proved to be a young Irishman of about thirty years, attended by two even younger aides, all three very dashing in their glittering uniforms. His escorts, of rough but soldierly appearance, were promptly committed to the care of Fergus and his fellow-overseers, who greeted them like old friends.

The Count's arrival caused some consternation amongst the ladies, for they were not yet ready to appear. However, Father was unperturbed and straightway introduced me to the three officers as his son and heir. After some general conversation, during which I edged away to a dark corner in an attempt to hide the sorry state of my clothes, the Count sought me out and put me at my ease by inquiring keenly about the prosperity or otherwise of the sugar, cotton and indigo plantations on the Island, a subject which I was able to discuss in a grown-up manner. As we talked he looked around at our still primitive house and noticed, I am sure, that we had no butler to serve us our wine but only a slow-witted footman (Martin) and a servant girl (Betsy, exceptionally attentive and dexterous, but unsmiling, in a neat new dress). Long before the ladies appeared I saw that he had inferred from his own observations, and from the intelligence which he had prised out of me, that no daughter of this house would have a worthwhile dowry.

When Maman and Tony effected their entrance they were resplendent in low-cut gowns of an elegance I had not dreamed that they possessed. Tony's appearance was the more surprising — firstly, in that her sunburned face and neck had been powdered to match the paleness of her shoulders and arms so that she was as pallid as was Maman when she first emerged from her chamber of a morning; secondly, in that the front of her gown had been arranged to suggest that she was the possessor of a bust, an attribute which she had hitherto shewn no signs of desiring, let alone displaying; and lastly, in that her hair, which she usually wore *à la négligence*, was now piled upon the top of her head in a coiffure which matched Maman's in its height and elaborate style.

The Count went down on one knee and kissed Maman's hand, with many flowery compliments; he then turned to Tony, who offered him her (rather too sun-browned) hand, fluttered her fan coyly, and curtsied low, all in the manner which Maman had been inculcating so emphatically all day. The Count went down on one knee to her also although, as I learned later, strict politesse would have required no more than a low bow to the daughter of the house.

Maman and "*cher* Arthur" then commenced a most animated conversation about the affairs of their respective families which was abruptly cut short when Maman was called away by her duties as a hostess. The gallant soldier then turned to Tony, whose eyes had not left his animated face as she listened to him with a patience which I, standing nearby in a dimly-lit corner, found hard to credit. She was plying her fan studiously and looked younger than her years.

"Madamoiselle," the Count said, "I must compliment you, not only upon your appearance tonight, which is delightful, but upon your horsemanship, upon your accomplished command of both English and French, and not least upon your admirable devotion to the welfare or our hard-working friends the Negroes. I must also apologize to you that I did not, when I met you in the field the other day, immediately recognize that you are an unmistakeable de la Tour du Pin, the very image of your so charming and beautiful mother, whom I have worshipped as a Goddess since I was a little boy; had I recognized the fair lineaments of your Maman's *famille* I would have taken notice, very much earlier, of your opinions and of your knowledge of this Island; I would also have taken pains to introduce you to my young gentlemen, who are all of good family — "

Tony, not often at a loss for words, was quite unable to stem the Count's flow of pleasantries and appeared to be mesmerized. She was similarly tongue-tied whilst sitting between the two aides at dinner, ignoring their attempts at small-talk and gazing, apparently spellbound, at the Count across the table. By this time, I must say, I had lost interest in Tony and the rest of the company for Betsy had been brought in to assist Martin to serve the meal and I was covertly watching her from under lowered eyelids and attempting to gauge her state of mind, for she had not spoken to me since I had proved less than zealous over preventing the proposed hangings. However, she gave not the slightest sign, not a flicker of an eyelid, even when she bent over me to change my plate, to indicate

103

that she might relent and be my friend once more. (How I longed to be six or seven again, playing with jumbie-beads under the house!) Several times during that interminable dinner I resolved that, to save my pride, I would ignore the insouciant creature and listen to the conversation around me, which was vivacious if not profound, but when I thought I had succeeded in putting her out of my mind, a slim black hand would appear to remove my plate and, willy-nilly, I was again following that smooth black African mask as its owner moved around the table, and trying to guess what thoughts were filling that small head.

The evening ended with something of a contretemps. When the Count indicated that he and his aides must return to camp — and I am sure that Father was deeply mortified that he could not offer them a bed for the night — it was discovered that their escort had been reduced to near-insensibility by the "clairin" or puncheon rum which had been supplied to them in generous quantities by Fergus and his fellows. Despite the soldiers' condition, the Count insisted that they be heaved on to their mules, after which the officers mounted their horses and the whole party, at my suggestion, were guided back to camp by Charlie, whom I had found squatting under my chamber window, anxious only that I should put him and his precious pistol to good use. He received handsome remuneration for his services and became even more dog-like in his devotion to me.

After the Count had left, and I have omitted to describe all his gallant au revoirs to Maman and Tony, the latter withdrew to her chamber, screamed for Betsy (who, I am sure, had not been off her feet all day) and commenced to abuse her at the top of her voice and in language which she usually confined to the stables, the cane-fields and the sugar-houses, where she had learned it.

Several days later, as I was pushing Henri rather aimlessly upon his swing, Betsy spoke to me at last from behind his door.

"I am not going to speak to you until you have taken *Oroonoko* out of the post office and read it right through." There were none of the giggles which had accompanied her previous references to the book, and she added solemnly, "You must read James Macdonald's inscription too."

"Why is this book of such importance?" I asked.

No answer came and I perceived that the book had upset Betsy and perhaps even widened the breach between us, for she seemed to be making it a condition of our friendship that I should read it and be prepared to debate it with her.

After dark I fetched the volume from the "post office" and took it to my chamber to read. I had some foreboding that I would not enjoy the book, but it turned out to be even more unpleasant than I had feared.

The inscription, written in James Macdonald's own hand, caused me great discomfort and I shall find the transcribing of it distasteful, but I owe it to my readers and here it is:

> Mrs. A.B. desired to be Loyal to our Cause and to the Cause of Kings everywhere but she has Betrayed us by Writing this Book, which Panders to Lustful Desires. If, God being Willing, I beget a Daughter, I Pray that this Book will not Fall into her Hands; if I Beget a Son I Trust that he will not read it until he is of an Age to resist the Temptations which it sets Forth; if I come to Own a Plantation across the Atlantick, which is my Hope and Desire, I will take steps to Ensure that None of my Negroes get Wind of it and its Sentiments.

The matter in *Oroonoko* which so discomposed James Macdonald is not such as can be discussed in writing in this nineteenth century, as my twentieth-century readers may or may not understand. Suffice it for me to write that I did not equate the beautiful African Princess Imoinda — "fair queen of night" — with any young Negress I had seen, and certainly not with Betsy, whom I did not regard as beautiful in any respect. ("Poor little thing," I had heard Maman say with sympathy, "how ugly she is!" Even Fergus did not imply that she was beauteous, however enthusiastic his view of her utility as a slave-woman mistress.) No, Betsy's bodily attributes were of no interest to me; far more important was it that she was, or had been, my friend and fellow-conspirator, and possessed an intellect attuned to mine with the greatest exactitude.

On the other hand, when I read of Prince Oroonoko — "admirably turned from head to foot" and with a countenance of "a perfect ebony, or polished jett" — I could only call to mind the physique and physiognomy of Jéhu. As a consequence, the latter part of Mrs. Behn's book, wherein is described the Negro uprising led by Oroonoko, his killing of the fair Imoinda to prevent her falling prey to his white enemies, and his death by unspeakable dismemberment, all this was so horrible to me that I slept not for many nights. (Indeed, I have not opened the volume from that day upon which I first read it until this morning, when I lifted the front cover to copy out the inscription and then ruffled through the early pages to find the words which I have just quoted. I dare not read further and I am left wondering whether I should not destroy the book to protect the innocence of a certain beloved but inquisitive young person.)

I waited in some trepidation for Betsy to break her silence and ask me what I thought of the book, and it was after several afternoons, several long afternoons of unhappiness, that her fierce whisper came.

"Well?" she asked. "Have you read *Oroonoko*?"

"Yes," I replied.

"What is your opinion of it?"

"It is a disgusting book," I said, almost choking over my words, "I think we should put it back immediately and take out another."

"But what did you think of what the white people did to Prince Oroonoko?"

"I do not wish to speak about it."

Betsy tried hard to inveigle more detailed opinions out of me, but I remained obdurate and she eventually snapped at me.

"You will have to change the book yourself if you are so anxious to be rid of it," adding, as an afterthought, "Master Richard."

Thus the breach between us continued and my attempts to bridge it by mentioning the more exciting parts of *Gulliver* were of no avail. It was at this time, and entirely due to this prolonged silence of Betsy's, that I became a prey to the first of my attacks of true Melancholy; it might have proved fatal had not Henri periodically aroused me from it in his own idiotic manner. He was now eleven years of age and had become dissatisfied with a diet of speech lessons, songs, and the motion of the swing and was demanding longer and longer walks. If I was sunk in Melancholy and refusing to hear his polite "Ah, walk-walk-walk- please-please-please — " he would spray me with his spittle until I had perforce to accede to his importunings. I would then fetch my umbrella and support him round the yard to talk in his own language to the dogs tied up under the house, to Katy as she spread clothes on the hibiscus bushes which she used as bleachers, or best of all to Matti in the kitchen, for she would tempt him with scraps of food and refuse to part with them until he had spoken two or three words of English, or sung a line or two of a song. There were those, including Father, who were of the opinion that Henri should never have been born, but I sometimes wonder if I would have reached manhood without him. Nature's ways are not always fathomable by Reason.

I think that the friendship between Betsy and myself might well have ended at this point in our lives (that is, in our fifteenth year) and that this chronicle of my Life and Times might have been very different, but for her own reasons my friend forgave me — and she had much to forgive, as my readers will agree — and I forgave her, which was easier in that I had only some obstinacy on her part to forgive. (Oh my readers, choose your friend, if choose you can, for his or her forgivingness!) I myself exchanged *Oroonoko* and *Gulliver* for two new books, which I took time to select carefully — they were *Pilgrim's Progress* and *Roderick Random* — and we re-commenced our debates and even exchanged letters (which, of course, we did not sign). However, as I will explain in the next chapter, our friendship was a more troubled one than it had been.

Before I finish this chapter I should inform my readers that I have sometimes been accused, in the base dialect which I swore would never proceed from my pen, of telling "nancy stories", that is, boastful lies such as those told by the wily spider Anansi in the simple-minded tales which Negroes tell to their children and sometimes to each other. In my youth and middle age I would have rebutted this accusation with vigour, but in my old age, with nothing to be gained or lost, I can look back and see that I was in the habit of not treating Truth with the respect she deserves, and that this habit has crept into my narration of my Life and Times.

Even in this chapter I can see, upon re-reading it, that I have deceived my readers in one or two particulars, the most important being my account of the conversation which I had with Count Dillon on his visit to Braemore. The truth is that the Count did not have to *prise* the information about our poverty out of me; I most willingly set forth our financial situation in the clearest of terms, making quite sure that my parents could not hear. I wanted to rule out altogether a marriage between Tony and the Count, not so much out of concern for Tony's happiness as from a conviction that such a marriage would have entailed my losing Betsy for ever. She had become indispensable to Tony as a maid and, to a not inconsiderable extent, as a companion, for Betsy wrote Tony's letters for her and read out the replies, as well as reading romances aloud to her.

Less important, but more like genuine "nancy stories" in that they resound to my credit, are my descriptions over the last few chapters of my dealings with Charlie. Could he rise from his unmarked and unhonoured grave, and be persuaded to be disloyal, he might give a version of events in which I would appear in a less favourable light.

CHAPTER VI

My Friend and I have to contemplate the Possibility of Separation; we take what Steps we can to prevent it; Braemore Estate prospers with Help from myself; we continue our Education; and my Enthusiasm leads me to the Edge of Disaster

"My parents are again talking about sending me to school in Paris," I thought it needful to inform Betsy one afternoon, some months after the capitulation, when Henri was asleep upon his swing. We were continuing with our afternoon arrangements much as before, but were sorely tried by Henri's demands for walks and by his increasingly loud and frequent interruptions to our discourse. I shall not similarly try the patience of my readers by reporting every occasion upon which he hindered us in this manner.

"You would receive a proper education," replied Betsy very quietly, "and be removed from all those things which so displease you in Tobago." Her enunciation was particularly careful and precise, as though she was reading aloud from a letter she had written. "Have they spoken to you about this, or is it that you have been eavesdropping again?"

"They have told me," I said, "but I do not want to go to Paris."

"You do not want to go anywhere, Master Richard. You have not even been to the sea for a bath. You are a stick-in-the-mud, I think."

Despite our recent reconciliation my friend was still short with me: sometimes, as now, speaking her thoughts plainly; sometimes implying criticism by not answering me; and sometimes, if our paths crossed at other times of day, giving me looks so piercing that I had to wonder in what way I had offended. I was beginning to comprehend that our friendship had a price, perhaps because my friend was turning into a mysterious being, that is, a woman. (Dressing-up games with Tony had ceased; clothes were now

108

serious business.) In my innocence I knew not what this price might be, nor in what currency I was expected to make payment.

"Do you think I should agree to go to Paris?" I asked.

"If you want to be an educated gentleman, you *must* go," came the cool and reasoned reply.

"But, Betsy, *you* know why I do not wish to go."

"I know only that you are a stick-in-the-mud."

Suppressing some irritation, I rehearsed in my mind my reasons for not wanting to go to Paris, and for wanting to stay at Braemore, which were two sides of the same coin. Most of the former were of great force. I was afraid of the ocean (which I had not yet seen, remember, let alone ventured upon) and of the battles and sinkings and drownings which took place thereupon. The noise and crowds of Paris, so vividly and nostalgically described by Maman, sounded as though they might be worse than had been the noise and proximity of the overseers' families as they crowded into our house during the "war".

"You must know why I do not want to go," I repeated, but Betsy would not answer, so I had perforce to continue rehearsing more reasons in my troubled mind. I was afraid of loneliness. Would I find a friend on the ship? Would I even find a friend in the school in Paris? Would not all the boys be ordinary boys, rough and ill-mannered and cruel? (I had the notion, from listening to Father, that "ordinary" boys were all like Tony.) If, by a lucky chance, there were quiet boys like me, would they not be so far ahead of me in their studies that they would smile scornfully at my lack of Latin and at my Créole ignorance of the world and refuse to speak to me?

When I turned over the coin and considered my reasons for wanting to stay at Braemore I discovered that a Paris education was something which I must resist with all the resources of cunning at my disposal. How I wanted to keep the sanctuary of my own room (now recovered from its desecration by the Mulatto boys) and the dreams of quiet places which I could dream only there! How I wanted recourse to Matti when I needed her! How I wanted to continue with Henri's education! How I desired, most of all, to keep my one and only true friend, however carping and critical she had become!

At not quite fifteen years of age I did not know how to say that last to her. She, on the other hand, proved to be well able to speak her mind to me, and in the most pertinent and shocking manner.

"If you go away," came a fierce whisper from behind Henri's door, "I shall be ravished the day after your ship leaves!" Her voice, despite the sibilance of her whisper, had a new and unfamiliar resonance.

"What do you mean?" I whispered back in acute alarm.

109

"It is only because I am known to be your friend that I have not been ravished already. Surely you know that?"

How was I to answer her? I had heard the word "ravish" before, and always in hushed or hysterical tones (as from Maman), but its precise meaning was not at all clear to me.

"Who–who–who?" I stammered, unwilling to admit to ignorance.

"Ask Fergus and his cronies. There are others too — some higher and some lower, but all of the same mind — "

"But surely Matti — ?" I said, calling upon the name of the protector of our childhood.

"My mother cannot be everywhere, and when men are determined or drunk, and armed, what can she do? She is just a slave-woman, and she has been ravished too."

For some time I had been doubting whether Matti was truly as omnipotent as I had thought her in my childhood, even though she had regained her apparently predominant position after Father had threatened to sell her, but had never spoken my thoughts aloud. To hear Betsy articulating them, not as doubts but as self-evident truths, was profoundly disturbing and moving. From now on, my friend was telling me, I, Richard Mason, was her protector. I cast around for means of comforting myself and found that I was comforting Betsy also.

"My Father did say that I may not be able to go to France until the Peace is signed," I said.

"Then I hope the Peace is never signed," answered Betsy, and would say no more upon the topic; yet her words stayed in my mind and ruled my actions until that sad time when I was no longer able to be of help to her.

Late that night I consulted Doctor Johnson's *Dictionary* and strained my eyes on a long quest from word to word, from meaning to meaning, and from instance to instance, without ever arriving at true enlightenment. "They cut thy sister's tongue and ravish'd her" and "Tell them ancient stories of the ravishment of chaste maidens" — such statements were of little help to precise understanding. The drift, however, was clear — Betsy was right to be afraid of ravishment, violation, debauchment, or forcible constupration, which all appeared to be some form of dastardly attack upon a woman by a man, or men.

After putting down the *Dictionary* and extinguishing my candle, I lay awake almost until sunrise, wrestling with one of the hardest decisions of my life, that is, that my clandestine friendship must be brought part-way into the open and that it must be made even clearer than it was already to everyone at Braemore that Betsy was under my especial protection — every one, that is, except my parents. (This decision taken, the other decision, that I would do everything in my power to prevent my being sent to school in France, cost me no sleep.) Thus it was that, when Father and Tony were absent, Betsy and I were seen together now and then as we cared for and "educated" Henri. Tony soon got wind of this, of course, and would sometimes tease Betsy by addressing her as "Mrs. Dickie" or "Madame Richard Mason" but, to her credit, she retained some sisterly feeling for me and never let Father hear her. I charged Charlie, now well-practised in the use of his Spanish pistol, with acting as Betsy's bodyguard if she left Braemore on any pretext; this duty he discharged faithfully and there grew up between them an alliance unusual between a Negress and a Mulatto, who was presumably one of her potential ravishers. (I leave my readers to guess who was the dominant member of this alliance.)

Two years elapsed before the signing (in 1783 at Versailles) of the definitive Treaty which confirmed France in her possession of Tobago. During that interval our social life flourished; French officers and officials called regularly at Braemore, some of them with their wives, while Maman managed to accompany Father and Tony on visits to Government House and to the officer's quarters. Although Maman insisted that Tony was elaborately dressed on these occasions, none of the young officers to whom she was introduced was able to silence her in the same manner as the indomitable Count Dillon; they therefore had to endure the incongruous spectacle of a lovely girl talking loudly and enthusiastically about horses, about the bloodier aspects of the war, about her part in it as a dispatch-rider, and about the difficulties involved in driving the niggers back to work again after their experience of idleness during the war. It is not surprising, then, that Maman's efforts to present Tony as a possible bride were discontinued as too humiliating altogether and my sister was allowed to dress as she pleased, with results which my readers can imagine and which caused Maman to have recourse to the brandy-bottle again.

As to estate affairs, we began to prosper. The French kept their Treaty obligation to "protect the inhabitants of the Island in the enjoyment of their estates and of everything in their possession." They allowed us all, Catholic and Protestant alike, access to the French and European markets through the *"exclusif"*, since we were no longer foreigners to be denied these markets. Whilst this appeared somewhat restrictive of trade while France and Britain were still at war, it proved an advantage in the years of peace which followed and we began to dispose of our sugar and rum at prices which put us in the way of repaying our creditors and rapidly becoming what was then judged to be wealthy.

My readers may be wondering if experience had improved Father's capacity as a man of business now that we were exploiting these opportunities;

I can assure them that no such miraculous change had taken place. What had changed was that my influence over him was gradually increasing due to my knowledge of the account books and to my control over the cash which they represented; if I disapproved of a proposed purchase I could prove to Father that we did not have the money for it; if I disapproved of a proposed sale, I could similarly prove that it would bankrupt us, or at least make a loss we could not recoup. I thus imposed my good business sense upon his recklessness and impulsive ways.

I was helped in these manoeuverings by the change to French currency. Father could not retain in his head the exchange rates between French livres and Portuguese half-johannes (then our commonest gold coin), especially as he had never been able to keep track of the varying rates between the pound sterling (or sovereign) and the Spanish currency (doubloons, pistoles and milled silver dollars). By the time the U.S. silver dollar arrived in the West Indies he had altogether given up trying to understand. My mind, on the other hand, could leap from one currency to another, on to a third, and then back again, all with the agility of a goat seeking the most succulent herbage, an agility I had learned early in my life from trading jumbie-beads and other "currencies" with the shrewd and guileful Betsy.

If Father had cause, or thought he had cause, to question my estimate of the amount of money we had available at any time he would call Maman to check the books. Maman, whose brain was customarily too befuddled to perform the required arithmetic, would make a pretence of totting up the columns and would announce in the end that dear Dickie was quite correct. Sometimes, to save her face, I would allow her to find a discrepancy of a few sols, or even a livre or two, but in the main this was not necessary.

Tony would have liked to argue with me about financial matters, and would have made up in noise what she lacked in arithmetical ability, but I took care not to offer more than a token resistance when the purchase of expensive horses was in question and to support her against Father if they disagreed about how much should be paid for a horse. Thus we came to a tacit agreement that if she could have the finest of horses, whether Créole or imported, she would not question my stewardship of the account books.

I write "account books" in the plural because, as time went on, I found it advantageous to keep two, and then several more, each one covering a different aspect of the business, so that I could detect where money was being lost and suggest appropriate remedies. Father found these separate books intolerably confusing and often shouted abuse at me when he failed to understand them. At times I became disheartened when my attempts to control Father's rashness failed, as fail they sometimes did, but regained courage when I recalled that the estimable Count Dillon had been a *sous-lieutenant* before he was sixteen and a *colonel* before he was seventeen. Why then should I not be a skilled man of business at the same age when the Mason family was in so much need of one?

During these years I never forgot the danger to Betsy — if I had, the narrow-eyed look which so many men gave her would have reminded me — and I used these strategems with the account books to prevent my being sent to France and thus abandoning her to the mercies of ravishers. For several years I was able to prove that there was not enough money to pay my fees and support me in Paris, unless I became a dependant of the *famille* de la Tour du Pin, a possibility mooted by Maman but which Father's pride could not stomach. Thus Betsy, Henri and I continued our singular alliance, now much less of a conspiracy, but still not a matter to which we wished to draw too much attention.

We all three grew in stature, of course. I became very tall for my age, and heavily-built rather than obese; Henri added roundness of body to roundness of face, although his arms and legs remained spindly; Betsy had stretched into a tall young woman, thinner than before if that were possible, and I found it hard to look at her pole-like contours for more than a second or two at a time, although if pressed, which I never was, I might have conceded that some of her motions resembled those of a bamboo-tree in a light breeze. Tony, who had neither grown taller nor put on weight since she was seventeen years old, saw Betsy in a different light. "Come here, Miss Mocojumbie!" she would shout across the yard and Betsy's dark orbs would open very wide and then half-close expressively before she obeyed.

The small head on the top of Betsy's elongated body was still in excellent order and she was still anxious to persevere with our joint education. We carried on reading Father's books two by two, rarely selecting new ones from the chest until we had exhausted the matter in every chapter.

Betsy's moods during these years were more fluctuating and unpredictable than at any previous time and she seemed to delight in disagreeing with me purely for disagreement's sake. I recall that the contrary creature took sides with Roderick Random's father and argued that he was quite right to throw his son out of the house, penniless, for marrying without his consent; and quite right too, to send Roderick "an account of the expense he had been at in his education, with a view of being reimbursed." For my part, I thought that this was cruel (although, as a budding accountant, I wished that Mr. Smollett had given details of the "expense" Roderick's father had been at, properly itemized and totalled, to help me in my arguments with Father over going to France). In retaliation, I made sure that I disagreed with Betsy when she complained that Mr. Smollett only once mentioned Negroes, and that only in passing, in all of his six chapters about the West Indies, and that therefore he had not written a true book. I pointed out that the book was a novel and not required to be truthful, since it was a kind of extended nancy-story, which led us to an inconclusive debate about the nature of truth in novels. We were, of course, in dire need of a mentor, for we often lost our way and came to some strange conclusions, some of which the more alert of my readers will have noticed already. I do not remember that we debated Roderick's making money by means of a slaving expedition between Africa and Rio Plata, perhaps because we already knew each other's minds on that terrible topic.

In one respect Betsy did not take her education quite as seriously as I did, for she insisted on diluting her studies by reading all of Maman's library of French romances, now added to by consignments from Paris and by those Tony borrowed from French officer's ladies. She justified this waste of time by arguing that she needed to keep up her French, but I refused to read or discuss these banal outpourings, although I would occasionally eavesdrop upon Betsy reading them aloud to Tony, for I had discovered that there was a kind of pleasure to be had from the mere sound of Betsy's voice, whether uttering romantic inanities or crooning primitive patois songs to Henri.

While Betsy was thus unprofitably engaged I occupied myself by reading the journals and pamphlets which were arriving in ever-increasing numbers from France and which Father freely passed on to me. From these I gained a sense of the unsettled state of people's thoughts and feelings in that great country, even though I had to deduce the republican and libertarian ideas being propagated from the rebuttals printed, for Father's papers were all Royalist. As a very young man, hardly more than a boy, I was naturally attracted to radical ideas, as we now call them, and would have read the writings of the great French and American deistic and revolutionary writers if I could have laid hands on them. To Betsy, of course, rationalist and libertarian ideas came naturally and I could only marvel at her comprehension of them, since I had not seen her reading a single one of the journals etc., which I perused with such painstaking care. (Later on we read and debated *Candide* and other enlightened works in both French and English; these we obtained, not from Father's chest, but through clandestine dealings with junior ship's officers, *sous-officiers* in the army, and other disaffected Frenchmen.)

In the year 1784, when I was approaching seventeen years of age, my enthusiasm for business brought me to the edge of disaster, for I persuaded Father to delay the sale of our estate produce until prices were at their highest; as a consequence we made a profit so substantial that I could no longer keep up the pretence that we did not have enough money to send me to school in France. However, as I shall describe in the next chapter, Fate intervened and, as so often in my life so far, used Betsy as her messenger to bring me news of great import before anyone else had heard it.

CHAPTER VII

My Responsibilities are vastly enlarged; Father makes me an unexpected Gift;
and gives me unsolicited Advice about my Friendship which leaves me at a Loss

"Mr. Grant is dead," said Betsy one afternoon, in her character as Fate's
messenger.

"But he was here only a few days ago," I protested, "trying to borrow
money."

"If it was fever it was slow," she maintained, "if it was poison it was
quick. They are burying him now."

Betsy did not need to elaborate on her meaning — Mr. Grant of
Craigellachie, the adjoining estate, was a brutal Master and had obtained
his just deserts.

"The Negroes at Craigellachie are hungry," added Betsy with some
urgency, and again her meaning was plain — trouble on a neighbouring
estate could easily spread to ours.

The rudiments of a plan were forming in my head, but before I can
describe it I must explain further. Mr. Grant had been trying to borrow
money because he was bankrupt and could not even afford to buy food. He
was one of the many foolhardy planters whose greed exceeded their wisdom
and who did not grow provisions or raise livestock on their estates either
for themselves or for their Negroes, preferring to use all their cleared land
to grow only those crops which could be sold in Europe for huge profits,
and to buy imported foodstuffs; as a result he was liable to disaster should
any untoward occurrence prevent his garnering or selling those crops. The
Negroes on Craigellachie, already poorly fed because of mismanagement,
had been struck by a mysterious sickness; all were weakened and not a few
had died. Since the whole sugar-harvest was threatened, Mr. Grant and his

116

overseers descended to brutalities so vile that even the French officials were constrained by protests from priests and others to invoke the *Code Noir* and threaten Mr. Grant with prosecution.

Father had curtly refused to lend Mr. Grant any money, with my whole-hearted concurrence, but he did agree to lend him enough foodstuffs to feed his household for two or three weeks and his Negroes for a single week. Shortly after this week had passed Mr. Grant was dead, as reported by Betsy.

Within twenty-four hours we heard, this time via Tony, that Mrs. Grant had incontinently embarked herself and her two sickly children (the survivors of the five with whom she had arrived in Tobago) on a ship bound for America which chanced to be sailing that day, with the intention of reaching Greenock as soon as was humanly possible. The following day we learned that she had empowered an agent to sell the property, of which she desired neither part nor parcel, and the day after that her creditors were pressing and that she had told the agent that she was willing, nay anxious, to cut her losses.

Craigellachie Estate, its fine new frame house, its crops, livestock, buildings, and stock of Negroes were therefore to be had for very much less than their true value if the deal could be closed before word of the bargain spread around the other French Islands or reached Bordeaux or Nantes. It had been a condition of the Capitulation that Tobago estates could only in future be sold to French citizens, so we were in a more favourable position to make an offer than our British neighbours. There was also a British law, confirmed by the Capitulation terms, that no Tobago estate might be larger than five hundred acres, but that was not an insuperable obstacle due to our friendship with French officials and to their being accustomed to much larger plantations in other French Islands.

It was I, encouraged by Betsy, who put the suggestion to Father that it would be in our interest to use our substantial profit to buy Craigellachie outright. We would then, I urged upon Father, have an estate of twice the acreage; acquire a much finer house (thus saving the trouble and expense of rebuilding Braemore); and still owe the same amount to the bankers. After several long arguments, from which Maman and Tony were excluded as too easily swayed by their emotions but upon which I encouraged — nay, enjoined — Betsy to eavesdrop, Father slapped me on the knee and cried: "By God! I'll do it!" He then added hopefully: "And you will ride with me to see the agent?"

This put me in a quandary. I knew that it would be prudent for me to be present at the meeting with the agent, but I could not wave a wand and overcome my lifelong aversion to the equine race and I had never attempted to walk farther than the few hundred yards from our house to the sugar-houses. If I walked the four and a half undulating miles to Port Louis (as the French had re-named Scarborough) I might arrive in a state of such exhaustion that I would be more of hindrance to Father than a help and would lose some of the grudging respect which he now accorded me. (The roads in Tobago were not yet suitable for even the strongest carriage; I would sooner have mounted a horse than have sat upon a jolting cane-cart; and I had never heard of, let alone seen, a sedan-chair.)

"No," I told Father, "I do not ride." At this, Father merely frowned and shrugged his shoulders.

To be brief, Father set off immediately and returned the following day, having agreed the exact price which I had suggested. He announced the purchase publicly in triumphant tones and after Maman and Tony had expressed their astonishment and delight he turned to me.

"I would like to be shewing my appreciation for the part you were playing in this," he said. "Is there anything you would like to be having for yourself?"

"The only thing which Dickie really wants," sneered Tony, "he cannot have, for she is mine, and I am not parting with the dear provoking creature to anyone!"

"Toinette!" whispered Maman, glancing in alarm at Father, who chose to ignore Tony and continued to regard me with his eyebrows raised. I had not been prepared for this offer and since Father seemed to be expecting an immediate answer I made a request which mature reflection would surely have persuaded me to be rash in the extreme.

"May I read the books in the chest in Henri's room?" I asked.

"How in the Name of the Devil were you knowing that there were books in that chest?" said Father, shewing the early signs of an angry outburst, his eyes bulging, a pulse beating on his temple, and his hands trembling.

I answered not, but gazed into his hard blue eyes with a courage and steadiness which surprised me. To my further surprise, Father succeeded in calming himself — looking back, I think it might not be irrelevant that he now had to raise those eyes to mine.

"Very well then, Richard, you may be reading my books; indeed, I will make you a present of them if you will promise to remember that most of them were written to be read by gentlemen and not by ladies or the lower orders."

"Betsy *will* be pleased," said Tony, and my glance at her must have appeared murderous, for she made a *moue* at me, in a kind of apology.

"What is that?" demanded Father, "What —?"

"I meant," Tony interrupted him, "that Betsy will be pleased with the servants' rooms at Craigellachie, and with that handsome room on the little hill which will be just right for Henri, being at a distance."

Father glanced at his daughter suspiciously, then huffed and puffed and called for four glasses of brandy (his supply of *usquebaugh* having been exhausted and not replenished in those uncertain times). He gave one to each of us and proposed the toast: "To our happiness at Craigellachie!" As I raised my glass and then put it to my lips without taking even the smallest sip, for I could not stomach brandy, I swear that I heard Henri calling from across the yard: "Ah, hap-hap-hap-hap-ness — " and then Milly hushing him. Betsy would of course have positioned herself where she could hear our conversation.

(The manner in which Father spoke about "his" books revealed to me that James Macdonald and Jonas Mason were, almost certainly, the same person; a discovery which I hid in my heart, not even sharing it with Betsy, until I learned more of the matter by accident, as I shall recount later.)

Having thus successfully persuaded Father to buy Craigellachie, I was able to point out to him that we no longer had enough money to send me to Paris, and that in any case my services were now indispensable to him, and for two reasons: firstly, for checking the Craigellachie inventory; and secondly, for devising and maintaining a proper set of account books to ensure the maximum profit from our new investment. Father agreed, with a reluctance which was now more formal than substantial, that my departure might be delayed until we had sold another crop.

I cannot recall the details of our family's move to the fine house at Craigellachie except that I myself made the journey of three-quarters of a mile on foot, perspiring profusely, and accompanied by Charlie carrying my umbrella to protect me from the sun. The noise of Henri's distress at finding himself in unfamiliar surroundings, the running to and fro of the servants, the loading and unloading of our possessions, and the general confusion, all would have been a burden to me had I not been entirely occupied with trying to understand the Inventory, which had been drawn up in great haste and with scant regard for accuracy. I discovered little esteem for the three gentlemen who had "according to the best of their knowledge and judgement valued and appraised the property of said William Grant, as particularly herein before set forth", and then put their signatures to the document. To do them justice, they must have had some qualms, for they had scratched in, between "judgement" and "valued", the qualifying phrase "as well as circumstances will allow us".

Father gave me twenty-four hours to check the list of three hundred or so Negroes in the Inventory, a period which he proposed to spend handing over the management of Braemore Estate to Tony, with Fergus as her assistant meantime. At sunrise I had a table set up under a large and shady cedar-tree which graced the "policies" of Craigellachie and my umbrella fixed to a stake in the ground for extra protection, while Charlie stood by in case of any trouble. I had arranged that Mr. Grant's Barbadian Red-leg overseers would bring along the Negroes one by one so that I might interview them and check them against the list. Within a very short time my heart was sinking in dismay at what was confronting me. The Red-legs were the most degenerate and disreputable gang of white men that it has been my misfortune to deal with — they pushed, pulled and kicked the Negroes around, and scowled and cursed and muttered their way into instant dismissal just as soon as I apprised Father of their quality. They had not even troubled to learn the Negroes' names and were uncertain as to the categories in which they belonged: for example, carpenter, cooper, field-hand, grass-gang hand, midwife, washerwoman, etc. Since many of the Negroes had not yet learned English and knew not their English names themselves, an accurate check of the Inventory was likely to be impossible.

As to the health of the Negroes, this gave me cause for even greater dismay, all being emaciated and exceedingly dirty and far too many having large sores of the kind that are deemed incurable. The few who were capable of speaking English spoke it in a surly manner; almost every back shewed marks of the lash, some very recent; and the hatred borne to the Red-legs was patent.

As the morning wore on I was confirmed in my conjecture that Mr. Grant had, for the sake of cheapness, bought too many second-rate Negroes, and even the refuse, straight off the slave-ships, and had spent nothing on purchasing that seasoning of healthy and complaisant Créole Negroes which is the steadying influence on any estate (even to this day, ten years after Emancipation). Moreover, the small proportion of Negresses (which I had noted as I studied the Inventory on the previous evening) proved that Mr. Grant had belonged to that group of estate-owners who believed in "buying" rather than "breeding", a policy which led, of course, to much frustration, dissatisfaction, and even despair.

When the Red-legs informed me that I had seen all the Negroes who were fit to walk to my table, and that the rest were either invalids in the sick house, or pregnant women confined to their own houses, I perceived that I would have to make the rounds of all the houses if I was to have an accurate "muster-roll" to present to Father. (The Negroes were, I should perhaps remind my readers, a large part, indeed almost half, of

120

our new investment.) I therefore told Charlie to detach the umbrella from its makeshift stand and to shade and protect me wherever I went. As he lifted the umbrella above my head he took the opportunity to whisper to me in shocked tones that the Red-legs' muskets and pistols were rusty, a fact which I had not noticed and which led me to fear that, if the creatures had not the heart to defend their weapons against the ravages of the climate, they might not have the stomach to defend me, or even themselves, against Negroes deranged by hunger and ill-treatment. I determined to put this fear aside and to carry on with my tour of the houses as if nothing was amiss.

This tour proved to be one of the most disagreeable events of my life; not only were the few pregnant women and small children even more emaciated than the supposedly able-bodied whom I had already counted, but the many sick were untended, the houses were dilapidated and overcrowded and there was indescribable filth everywhere, inside and out. Many of the children were Mulattoes and in as sorry a state as the others, which will indicate to my readers that the Red-legs, and perhaps Mr. Grant himself, had been free with their favours to the few Negresses; had not troubled to ensure that their own offspring were saved from starvation; and had offered the Negroes further cause for jealousy and discontent.

In short, the Estate was of the category which provided much ammunition for the Abolitionists, who were just about to start their agitation in Parliament under the leadership of the shrimp (Mr. Wilberforce) which was to grow into the whale which all but swallowed the prosperity of the sugar-trade in the West Indies. For the first time I truly understood what a good Master Father was, however much he affected to despise Negroes. "I like to be seeing a bloom upon their coats," he was wont to say, as if they were horses. He was amongst the first in Tobago to pay a midwife for each live child she delivered, and to reward with gifts of cloth and extra food such mothers as looked after their children properly.

When I returned to the house after this dreadful tour, I instructed Cumberland, the butler, to line up the house servants in the yard, in order that I might check them against the list. This Cumberland was a plump and smiling Mandingo who smirked and bowed and scraped his way out of my favour almost as quickly as the Red-legs had lost it in their own way. He was valued in the Inventory at £200 sterling, an estimate which suggested that he possessed skills, or performed services, of a particularly valuable kind; I was never to discover what they were. The rest of the servants were well-fed enough, of course, but otherwise unremarkable, except for one young Negress of squat and powerful build who was described as a "children's nurse" although she looked like a field-hand. She was notable for her appearance; for the manner in which she rarely stopped singing to herself; and for having retained her barbarically resonant African name of "Janga". My readers will be hearing more of her.

A description of how we rescued Craigellachie Estate from dereliction and worse, and achieved a bloom upon the Negroes' skins, would be more appropriate for a dissertation upon estate management such as is contained in the indefatigable Mr. Bryan Edwards's *History of the British Colonies in the West Indies* (an encyclopaedic work in three volumes which I have found indispensable). Suffice it for me to write that within six months matters were vastly improved; land had been cleared for provision-grounds; and most of the Negro-houses rebuilt. Within two years Craigellachie had earned a small profit and seemed destined to be as prosperous as Braemore.

Did I continue to venture forth with my umbrella to assist my father with estate business? my readers may ask. My answer is that I went out only when the business was truly urgent and important, for example, when it was necessary to see whether essential building work had been completed, or to check that all the hogsheads and puncheons were properly filled and matched the figures in my books. I did, however, celebrate my seventeenth birthday (in the year 1784) by going to Port Louis, not on horseback but upon my own two legs, or Shanks' pony, Charlie accompanying me to carry my umbrella and my account books. My object was to see our produce loaded on to the ship (the *Amélie* of Nantes) since I had heard rumour that hogsheads sometimes went a-missing betwixt estate and warehouse, betwixt warehouse and quay, and betwixt quay and ship. I was so busy checking the bill of lading against our cargo as it descended into the lighter, and then watching the hogsheads being hoisted from the lighter on to the ship, that I barely had time to look at the ocean on this my first near view of it. I found it unremarkable — flat and blue and covered with small waves monotonously moving from left to right; I could not imagine what pleasure there could be in entering it for a bath.

My business completed, I was in haste to return to Craigellachie before nightfall, as I had not seen or spoken to Betsy before leaving, and none of my days were complete without some interchange of words with her. However, after tackling the steep inclines, and these are many in that part of Tobago although none are markedly high, I would have to sit down and rest. Charlie did not seem to be incommoded by the hills and would sometimes make a few remarks while I caught my breath. On one of these occasions, with the intention of boasting rather than instructing, he nevertheless laconically made clear to me the meaning of the word "ravish" and of one or two other words of great significance to an innocent young man such as I, who had never before held a conversation on such intimate matters with another of similar age.

Upon reaching home, I discovered that I did not wish to seek out Betsy until I had pondered Charlie's information, and was making straight for my chamber when I had the misfortune to be intercepted by Father. He inquired about the success of my outing to Port Louis and congratulated me upon ensuring that we were not robbed, but his mind appeared to be elsewhere and we became silent, as I had nothing more to say to him. We stood thus for several minutes and I began to think that I must ask Father to excuse me, for my mind was in turmoil, when he "hrrrumphed" several times and then spoke to me as though he had rehearsed what he had to say.

"It is understandable, Richard, that at your age you should be wanting to take a mistress. I would request you not to let Madame your Mother know of whatever arrangements you make, as the knowledge would be upsetting her. Furthermore, I would be advising you to confine your affections to a clean and healthy young woman, and to avoid the loose Mulatto women in Port Louis, who are all dirty and infected. I do not propose to say more, for I am sure you are understanding me and will take notice of what I am saying."

Another embarrassed silence followed which I broke by stammering: "Th-th-th-thank you, Father." He excused me with a nod and I stumbled away to my room, where I fell upon my bed, my mind in even greater turmoil and confusion. I lay there for a long time without moving; I could not bring myself to rise and seek out Betsy, or to light a candle and wash off the dust of my journey, or even to console myself by reading a book. When Cumberland, who was still with us unfortunately, knocked upon my door and announced that supper was ready, I called out to him that I was not hungry and would he give my apologies to my parents. I continued to lie there, wide awake, until sunrise, ultimately coming to the conclusion that I should maintain my friendship with Betsy as though Charlie and Father had never spoken.

This decision I carried out with some success; a success which was the more easily achieved in that Betsy also seemed to have determined that our friendship should continue on the same terms as before, that is, that there was a price to be paid but that the bill would not be presented in the near future. Yet I am convinced that even Betsy, who so often knew of the workings of my heart before I knew of them myself, even she was not sensible of the pangs and frets from which I was suffering and which led me to wonder at times whether I was not being attacked by evil spirits, if such could be deemed to exist, or by hot and cold agues which would prove, should the doctor be called, to be unknown to medical science.

CHAPTER VIII

At Craigellachie I meet my Friend less often than I had hoped; on a certain fateful Day I learn about my Name and Tony suffers an Accident; I rebut Accusations of Dishonesty

I had hopes that the family's move to Craigellachie would enable me to meet Betsy more often and with less fear of unwelcome interruptions. These hopes were only partially fulfilled, for reasons which are many and complex and which I shall now attempt to describe.

The room "at a distance" which Tony had referred to as so suitable for Henri was situated upon a knoll some two hundred yards from the main house. It had been built, at Mrs. Grant's insistence, as a *belvédère*, but hurriedly and rather roughly. It was well raised above the ground and its commodious galerie faced the Trade Wind. Mrs. Grant had hoped that, if she and her children spent their days there, its elevated and airy situation would enable them to escape the wasting fevers which were fast making Tobago notorious. It had proved to be ineffectual in this respect and would have remained empty and no more than a monument to Mr. Grant's extravagance, or been offered to an overseer, had not the ever-alert Betsy pointed out to me, as soon as it was known that Craigellachie was for sale, how congenial a room it would be for Henri; how convenient in that it was far enough from the house for Father not to hear and be angered by Henri's cries; and how practical in that it had several servants' rooms attached to it, one of which opened on to the main room, making it signally useful for whoever was nursing Henri.

Matti was inclined to oppose the plan to move her into one of these servants' rooms, averring to Betsy that she preferred to be nearer to her kitchen and to the main house, and that she did not trust the one or two more savoury Red-legs whom we had retained, or the Craigellachie Negroes, who were tricksters and thieves to a man. I won her over by installing Charlie in the largest of the servants' rooms where, when I had no useful employment for him, he spent his time sitting in his doorway, oiling his pistol and ogling any young Negress who chanced, or chose, to walk past. It may have been he who was responsible for a number of brownish-black Sambo children who were born (and, of course, added to our stock) at this time.

When I put these arrangements before Father for his approval he raised his eyebrows and pursed his lips, looking me up and down appraisingly the while.

"I take it this means that you are remembering what I told you about those Mulatto women in Port Louis?" he inquired.

"Yes, of course, Father," I replied, now surer of his drift than I had been a month or two before, and intent on sounding manly.

"Excellent!" he exclaimed, which I took to be his concurrence to the plan, since he said no more on the topic.

This assent set my mind at rest to some degree, and the plan was implemented straightway. Unfortunately, Father discovered that a grassy terrace immediately in front of the *belvédère* was the best place from which to shew visitors the extent of his two estates and would bring them there at any time and without warning, so that Betsy and I, *tête-à-tête* in Henri's room, could never be sure that our debates would not be disturbed by Father's parade-ground voice pointing out the abundance of his crops and the industry of his Negroes. Although he did not ever make a move to enter the *belvédère*, such was his antipathy to Henri, yet the sound of his voice, or even the threat of it, was enough to make my tongue cleave to the roof of my mouth, so that Betsy, who was made of sterner stuff, found it hard to provoke me into speech.

Our meetings were also limited and curtailed by another circumstance: in 1786 M. le Comte de Dillon returned to Tobago, as Gouverneur no less, bringing with him his new wife, Marie de Girardin de Montgirald, a haughty young widow whom he had married in Martinique and who was distantly related to Maman. Tony was delighted to see her hero again and apparently bore him no ill-will for the adroit manner in which he had foiled her design to "roast" him; she was certainly not jealous of Mme. la Comtesse, for they quickly became close friends; so close indeed that Betsy often had to pack *portmanteaux*, mount an ass, and accompany her mistress on long visits to Government House, leaving Henri to suffer in the care of Milly for most of the day while I was occupied with estate affairs. In the afternoons, though, I made sure that I spent an hour or two with him, attempting to salve the loneliness from which we were both suffering.

"Ah, Bessy?" Henri would inquire sadly at intervals, looking around in perplexity.

"Betsy will be back soon," I would reassure him.

"Ah, soon-soon — ?" he would query, and the empty caverns of my heart would echo with his words. He was now sixteen years old.

Despite these separations and the pain they caused me, the frets, pangs, and fevers from which I had been suffering and which I described in the last chapter, subsided somewhat, I know not why, and Betsy and I, at nineteen years of age, were better friends than at any previous time, even that golden time when we were infants together and played and squabbled under the house. I had already decided that Betsy was the best sister any young man could have wished for when Maman, even more maudlin than usual one evening, informed me that Matti had wet-nursed Betsy and myself together (rather than separately, as Maman would have preferred). From this I inferred that we were, in a sense, truly brother and sister, having drawn our primary sustenance from the same ample source. However, it was becoming clearer and clearer that Father and most of the servants believed that she was my mistress and we were therefore accorded convenient privileges, usually with knowing smirks. (Matti knew the truth, as she always did, but for her own purposes helped us to maintain the fiction.) Not being in the relation attributed to us, and confident in our friendship, we ignored the smirks and the *double ententes* and profitted from the privileges. We were so united in our spirit at this time that we rarely quarrelled and with free access to Father's books and to others which we obtained from various sources, our education proceeded steadily; Betsy would even take a book with her to Government House.

It was after one of her visits there in attendance on Tony that I had early intelligence from Betsy that Count Dillon was about to demand of the British planters that they renounce all allegiance to the Crown of England (so-called) and swear fealty to that of France, on penalty of being required to sell their estates (to French citizens) and leave the Island. This demand originated in Paris, I am sure, and had to do with the doubts which His Most Christian Majesty must have been entertaining about the continuing loyalty of his subjects, 1789 being only three years away. Nevertheless, it affected the lives of everyone at Craigellachie and none more than Betsy's and mine, as I shall now attempt to relate as clearly as I can.

There came a fateful day, such as seems to strike every so often in human life, upon which events conspired to occur all at once and to confuse this chronicler (who desires only to construct a plain narrative and to convince his readers that he is telling the truth and not a conglomeration of nancy-stories).

On the afternoon of this day Henri was writing his name with a piece of coal upon the scrubbed boards of the floor of his room. This was the height of his scholastic achievement and he was exceedingly proud of it, often writing HENRI over and over again for an hour or more, oblivious to the world around him. Betsy and I were not slow to take advantage of the peace this offered us and were engrossed, our heads close together, in a quiet but vehement argument about something we had read in a book — I could almost swear that it was *Candide*, for M. Voltaire's irony gives much room for differing views as to his meaning.

Our debate was suddenly halted by the sound of voices from the terrace outside — in a moment we knew that we were overhearing Father and another man engaged in lively disputation. They must have approached on foot, for there was no sound of hooves or jingling bits, nor yet any of the stench of horses which my sensitive nostrils so abhorred and would quickly have detected. The two men approached close to the building and were soon standing at the foot of the high flight of steps which led up to the galerie.

"I am already a French subject," came Father's voice clearly through the wide-open door and jalousies, "and surely need not be swearing yet again to be loyal to His Majesty."

Without thinking, I crouched down and crept to the jalousie, where I could most easily continue to hear without being seen. Meanwhile Betsy was making her way noiselessly to the other side of the door, seizing a *cocier* broom and bending down as if she had been surprised whilst wielding it. Henri appeared to have heard nothing and continued to write his name.

"Nevertheless, it would be politic to do so," answered the other man in a voice which I had heard before, "and to have Roderick, or Richard as you call him, swear also — "

"Richard knows nothing of this," interrupted Father.

"Yet he manages your affairs, and very capably indeed, so you tell me," said the other man, and in the midst of my perturbation at what was being said I recognized the strange contorted Edinburgh accent of the Island's only physician, Doctor David Whyte, a man somewhat older than Father whom, it was now apparent, he trusted as he trusted no other. "It would only be just for you to ensure that there is no mistake about his name and about his right to inherit."

"Ach, David man, he manages my affairs well enough, but he is managing his own even better," answered Father, "for he is borrowing Estate money, my money by God, to finance his own ventures, and then putting the money back when he has made his profit. He does not know

127

that I know this and I will not be challenging him until the time is ripe, but you may be sure that if there is a dispute about inheritance Dickie, who should be called Rory, would be ending up the victor. He is as sharp as a lawyer and as fond of money as a banker."

"Nevertheless, Hamish my friend, he is your son and he deserves to learn that you, and therefore he, could be heir to a Chieftaincy in view of all these unfortunate forfeitures, deaths, disappearances and begettings of daughters of which I have just informed you."

"David," said Father, and his voice was solemn, "I have made up my mind that I do not wish to pursue the matter of the Chieftaincy just now, for I would have to obtain a pardon from the Monarch (whose name I cannot bring myself to pronounce) and that could only be secured by intrigue and bribery, by servile flattery, and by treachery to all that we fought for in Forty-Five." His voice rose, as anger replaced solemnity. "I have had my belly-full of Kings, Courts and Governments and I — "

"If these are your sentiments about Kings," interrupted Doctor Whyte sharply, "you would do well to swear your oath tomorrow, before word gets around that you are a Republican, or worse. You would also be well advised to swear in the name, however commonplace, of Jonas Mason, owner of Braemore and Craigellachie Estates in this Island of Tobago, and to have Richard swear in the name of Mason also; then both of you would be recorded in the Chancery Minutes, which could be used in evidence in case of difficulty."

"That is all very well," said Father, "but every time that I swear to be loyal to His Most Christian Majesty of France" — and he placed a most ironical emphasis upon the adjective "Christian" — "I am remembering that the first oath I swore was to King James and the House of Stewart, and I do not understand how one oath can be cancelled out by another — "

"You are too nice," replied Doctor Whyte. "If I were blessed with children on the right side of the blanket I would swear fealty to Auld Nick — to the Devil Himself I mean — to ensure that their inheritance was in no danger."

"David," said Father, "rest assured that I will be taking into account all that you have been saying. Now, as to the examination which I requested, the creature known as Henri is no doubt within, still requiring a nursemaid at the age of sixteen."

The rickety building trembled as the two men mounted the steps to the galerie. I had been so intent on hearing all that was being said and so shocked by the news that I had a name other than the familiar one of Richard (or Dickie) Mason that I could not move a limb, with the result that when Father passed from the galerie into Henri's room he found me still crouching in my eavesdropper's pose.

"What in the Name of the Devil — ?" he bellowed.

"Ah, name-of-debil!" bellowed Henri in reply from the far end of the room.

Betsy dropped her broom, which she had been plying industriously, and ran towards Henri to hush him while Father advanced upon me with all the bodily indications that he was about to give rein to a bout of evil temper.

"You have been eavesdropping, sir!" he shouted. "I have been suspecting you for years but I have never caught you until this minute! You are too sly altogether for a simple trusting soldier and planter such as your father."

"Ah, Fath-er, Fath-er, Fath-er!" shouted Henri, taking no notice of Betsy's hushing and continuing to repeat the word over and over again in a distinct manner. It was a word which he had never uttered before in his life.

Father half-turned toward Henri and became so red in the face and breathed so heavily that it seemed that he was about to have a seizure of some kind. Fortunately, the good Doctor stepped forward and took his elbow, while Henri submitted to Betsy's efforts and calmly returned to writing on the floor.

"Jonas, I think you should sit down," said the Doctor.

Father slowly raised his hands above his head and began to move them as though he were climbing a ladder. The Doctor signalled to me to fetch one of the two chairs upon which Betsy and I had been sitting; I did so and placed it behind Father's knees. The Doctor then pressed gently upon Father's shoulders until he was sitting upon the chair, breathing stertorously and apparently unconscious, although his bulging eyes were open and staring strangely.

"Richard," said Doctor Whyte, "we must cool his blood as quickly as possible. Fetch me that towel."

He shewed me how to wave the towel to and fro so as to create the maximum current of air directly upon Father's face, then called out to Betsy.

"Lassie, girlie, girl, you bring water and piece of cloth to bathe Massa's face. You understand me?"

Betsy, I need hardly write, already had a calabash of water and a cloth in her hands. The Doctor raised a quizzical eyebrow at her as she instantly set about bathing Father's crimson and purple face.

"There are as many degrees of mental incapacity amongst Negroes as there are amongst idiots; unless, of course, she has been painstakingly trained." Thus he muttered to himself before turning to me. "Richard, I do not like to leave your Father. Could this creature be trusted to fetch my black bag from the house? I left it with your butler."

"Yes," I said, "she is quick and to be trusted," and then, since I knew that the Doctor would not understand my words, I told Betsy in my rankest patois that there were degrees of stupidity amongst doctors as well as amongst idiots; she responded with no more than a lift of her contemptuous eyelids, handed the cloth to the Doctor and went off quickly.

The Doctor eyed her retreating form.

"She is dainty for one so tall," he said with a lubricious sigh; then, as my friend disappeared down the steps, addressed himself pedantically to me: "Young man, Nature made those feet of hers for only one purpose, to support a great weight; it is sad to think how obese she will become."

(I think now that had I decided to shoot dead, or to have Charlie shoot dead, every man in Tobago who looked upon my black sister to lust after her I would have decimated the male population of the Island, white, Mulatto, and black.)

Father's face was gradually becoming less congested under the cooling effects of my towel-waving and of the Doctor's perfunctory wiping of his face. When Betsy returned with the black bag the Doctor fetched out a small green bottle, opened it cautiously and moved it to and fro under Father's nose, causing him to sneeze several times, straighten his back and look about him in a puzzled manner.

"Jonas," said the Doctor, "I must cup you; there is no other treatment for your condition."

There was a pause; then Father said: "Go ahead, David."

"Ah, go head Dabid," echoed Henri without looking up from his writing, "go head, go head — "

I am ashamed to write that as the Doctor inserted his scalpel into a vein in Father's arm I lost consciousness and fell to the floor. When I recovered I was still prone, with Henri's pillow under my head. Betsy was wiping my forehead and Henri was kneeling by me, his face displaying a degree of concern which would have been comical had I not known that it was genuine. Betsy wrung out her cloth in some fresh cool water from the jar on the galerie and handed it to Henri who thereupon wiped my face with commendable gentleness and efficacy.

I could hear the Doctor's voice rising and falling — I knew not whence it came — warning Father against the dangers of overindulging his passions, but I was still too weak to attend closely to what he was saying. When Henri's attentions, and Betsy's, had brought me fully to my senses I sat up. The Doctor noticed this and left Father in order to examine me.

He felt my pulse briefly and touched my forehead with the back of his hand.

"Since you have such an aversion to the sight of blood," he said, "you will be glad to know that you do not require to be cupped." He turned to Henri, who was still kneeling beside me, but now using the damp cloth to wipe his own face. "You seem to have some skill in nursing, young man. What is your name?"

Henri looked up at the Doctor without the slightest gleam of understanding in his expression. It would be tedious to report all the further questions which the Doctor asked, for Henri answered not one, nor did his uncomprehending countenance change its aspect. Upon the Doctor becoming impatient, however, and asking: "Can you not even sing a simple song for me?" Henri turned to Betsy with a glimmer of what I recognized as hope.

"Ah, sing-song, sing-song?" he asked.

Betsy raised her eyes to mine for a second and I shrugged my shoulders, for I must confess that I had not heard Henri sing since I ceased pushing him on his swing and commenced taking him for walks instead, and the manner in which he used to sing then, being an imitation of mine, was unlikely to please the Doctor or indeed anyone with musical feelings. Betsy, however, had more recent knowledge of Henri's capabilities; she knelt in front of him, took his round face between her two slim black hands and began to sing a lullaby in her sweet and true contralto voice. The melody was French and plaintive, but the rhythm had acquired a lilt which resembled the distant beating of a Negro drum. Henri listened to the first stanza, watching Betsy's broad lips and moving his own in time with hers. When Betsy reached the refrain he could just be heard singing along with her and by the time she had reached the end of the second stanza he was singing out clearly; at the refrain of this Betsy stopped singing, but continued moving her lips, so that Henri was singing alone. His voice was neither a boy's voice nor a man's voice, but somewhat like a high tenor of exquisite purity, and he sang the remaining four stanzas and refrains with a pathos which was almost insupportable, never withdrawing his gaze from Betsy's mouth.

When they had finished the last refrain Henri continued to look fixedly into Betsy's face as though expecting something. I must confess that I was waiting for him to demand "Benay!" but instead he whispered "Ah, sing!" and started to sing the last stanza again. Betsy joined him and I will swear to my dying day that they sang that stanza and refrain in harmony. We were not a musical family — Tony's versions of sentimental ballads and Negro topical songs were accurate enough, I believe, but scarcely counted

131

as true music — and I am convinced that this was the very first time upon which my ear had been seduced by the delights of harmony.

"Incredible!" Doctor Whyte muttered, "The blind have led the blind and neither have fallen into the ditch!"

I looked at him and saw that the moistness of his eyes matched the moistness of mine but Father, still seated upon his chair and by now white-faced, was of another temper.

"Well?" he inquired of the Doctor irritably, "is he or is he not an incurable idiot?"

"Ah, incubal idjot, incubal idjot!" said Henri quietly, his attention now switched to a lizard high up on the wall.

Doctor Whyte looked from Father to Henri, from Henri to Betsy, and from Betsy back to Father again; apparently at a loss for words. He then blew his nose noisily upon a large handkerchief, which looked as though it would have benefitted from Katy's most energetic attentions, followed by a long sojourn upon a hibiscus bush.

"Well, David?" insisted Father, "Are you willing to sign an affidavit that he is unfit to succeed to any heritable or moveable property in the event of — " Here he shot a look at me and hastily looked away again. "Antonia deserves — "

"Ah Jonas," said the Doctor, "I have been unmanned, no doubt only temporarily, by seeing and hearing how much humanity your son Henri shares with the rest of us; more humanity, and here I am agreeing with the great Mr. Hume, than is shared by the Negro race, although this female specimen appears to be endowed with some kind of primitive sensibility, akin possibly to that of the Orang-Outan, as instanced by Mr. Edward Long — " Here Father shewed his impatience with this digression by huffing angrily, and the Doctor must needs try to calm him: "Jonas, man, remember what I told you about exciting your passions. Yes, it is my opinion as a physician that Henri is unfit to succeed and, yes, I will sign an affidavit to that effect."

At this Father rose to his feet and announced that we must return to the house for refreshments and requested the Doctor and myself to offer him support on either side, as he was still a trifle shaky on his legs. Ignoring Father's silent disapprobation, I fetched my umbrella and opened it, then offered him my arm, which he took with a shew of reluctance. Our progress was somewhat slow, because of Father's condition and, to a lesser extent, mine, so that I had time to wonder how I might excuse myself from the refreshments in order to retire to my chamber and ponder in solitude the news about my name being Roderick (or Rory) Macdonald, son of James (or Hamish) Macdonald; or better still, return to Henri's room and discuss the news with my friend — that she might be kin to the Orang-Outan troubled me little, since I assumed that the name referred to some African tribe.

This planned escape into solitude, or back into Betsy's company, did not happen, for the fateful day had not done with us yet. (There is now a doubt in my mind as to whether this day was in fact one, and not two, or perhaps even three. My memory, despite its boasted capaciousness, is playing more and more tricks upon me.)

As the three of us approached the house we espied the unmistakeable figure of Jéhu walking towards it from the other direction, that is, from that of Braemore. He was his usual self, dressed in nothing but trowsers and a coarse hat, but he was carrying the limp form of Tony in his mighty black arms as though she were a child. Her eyes were closed, her face under her soldier's forage cap was ashen-grey and her ankles appeared to be tied together with her kerchief. At first I thought that she was dead and I experienced an ignoble wave of relief that my tormentor had gone for ever, a relief mingled with acute sorrow that I had lost the doughty sister who had so often protected me from Father's wrath, but as Jéhu drew nearer we could see that she was smiling a faint derisive smile and that her right arm was not limp but was wound tightly around the great column of Jéhu's perspiring neck in a manner which was plainly intended to shock and dismay the right-thinking onlooker. Her favourite and most spirited horse Metaphor (that, believe it or not, was the creature's name) was following behind, limping badly.

Jéhu was walking with a dignity which would have done credit to his father Gilbert, or even to His Worship the Mayor of Port-of-Spain on a ceremonial occasion, but his eyes were as wary as ever. Doctor Whyte took charge instantly, directing me with a glance to continue supporting Father, whose arm was trembling in my grasp, then examining Tony's limbs briefly and silencing her when she tried to explain what had happened. He decreed that Jéhu must not lay Miss Tony down, but must carry her all the way to her chamber and lower her onto her bed with the minimum of disturbance to the left nether limb, which was certainly broken.

By the time Jéhu was inside the house with his burden, word had spread around the house and yard about Miss Tony's injury and servants were converging from all directions. Father shook off my arm and made as if to follow his favourite child into her chamber, but the Doctor barred him from entry, declaring that he would have no one in the room save Madame and one female servant. As he spoke, Maman could be heard at the back of the house screaming across the yard for Matti. Whilst awaiting their arrival Father and I and the curious

133

throng watched through the open door as Jéhu essayed to lay Tony upon her bed.

"Whoa, you clumsy nigger, whoa! whoa! whoa!" she cried as her injured limb first touched the bed, "Steady there Jéhu, steady boy, steady, WHOA!" Jéhu had perforce to straighten his back as she clutched him round the neck even more tightly and with both arms; then, as the Doctor took a hand and helped Jéhu to lower her to the prone position he was able to disengage himself, as Tony slowly unwound her arms, screwed up her eyes and bit her lip. Jéhu then tried to back away, but she grasped his great black forearm with both of her small brown hands and spoke to him in a shaky whisper, but loud enough for us all to hear.

"You go see to Metaphor, Jéhu. You no let old Cuffy touch him, oui!" Then, in English, she went on: "No, Doctor, I *will* speak; I am giving my instructions to my *groom* about my *horse*. I will listen to you when I am *quite* finished." The Doctor was duly quelled and she reverted to patois: "Cuffy go ruin Metaphor, even if injury not serious. Only you to touch him, Jéhu. Then come tell me how bad. You understand me?"

Jéhu hesitated before looking through the open door to where Father was standing. Their eyes must have met, for Father nodded.

"Oui, Mamzelle Toinette," said Jéhu, and Tony lay back upon her bed, shutting her eyes and clenching her hands.

At this point Matti arrived, escorting Maman, who was as ashen-faced as Tony but ready to be of use in the sick-room. The Doctor firmly closed the door.

Father, now in command of himself, cleared the salon of idle onlookers by frowning and staring around him, then took Jéhu out on to the galerie to question him and I followed. I am afraid that I cannot do justice to the rustic yet poetic simplicity of Jéhu's patois account of the affair: transliterated into English it sounds merely commonplace.

"Massieu," he began, "me planting with Massieu Malcolm's gang when me see Metaphor walking loose with bad limp and he legs wet higher than he fetlocks, so me reckon Mamzelle Toinette been thrown off near river. Me leave gang quick-quick and me no have time to ask permission — " here Jéhu gave Father a questioning look which Father did not deign to answer, "— so Massieu Malcolm go be looking for me, oui! Anyhow, me track hoofprints back to ravine near windmill and there Mamzelle lying at bottom. She not let me fetch anyone; she say 'Is only broken leg, Jéhu. You carry me home — that quickest and safest.' So me ask she for she kerchief and me tear it in two and me tie she broken leg to she good one to keep it firm and me carry Mamzelle home like she tell me. Metaphor follow me."

134

I have reported this speech as though it was uninterrupted; in fact, it was interrupted several times. Firstly, when Doctor Whyte emerged to announce that Tony had a simple fracture of the femur, which he could set immediately if someone could find splints. This caused a great shouting for Sandy, who arrived out of breath with his adze in one hand and two pieces of wood of the right length in the other. When Sandy had shaped the pieces of wood to the Doctor's requirements with a few deft blows, the Doctor returned to Tony. The other interruptions were occasioned by groans and shrieks from Tony as the Doctor addressed the task of setting her limb. At particularly poignant shrieks we all three grimaced and looked away from each other, knowing that broken bone was grating upon broken bone as the Doctor attempted to match them together. Sometimes Jéhu stopped speaking so that we could listen to Matti uttering comforting words — we knew that she must be holding Tony firmly on the bed, such a task not being for Maman.

When Jéhu had done, Father spoke to him loudly, no doubt to drown the continuing groans from Tony.

"You done act sensible, Jéhu," he said, "and you go be groom from now. No, you go be *head* groom from now. Metaphor need tending. Jump!"

(Thus Jéhu returned to favour. His promotion to head groom pleased old Cuffy as he was no longer required to perform duties which were beyond his failing powers, and displeased Fortune, the Craigellachie stockman, who had harboured hopes of being head groom when Cuffy was superannuated.)

When the Doctor had finished and emerged from Tony's chamber he was remarkably sanguine.

"Jonas," he said, "your daughter's limb will mend in quick time, in view of her youth and her exceptional hardiness. She has promised me that she will lie as still as a corp and that she will allow herself to be nursed in every particular by her maid, that willowy but well-trained creature whom I saw earlier and who must stay within your daughter's call at all times."

The Doctor was right in one respect: Tony's limb did mend quickly. However, it was not because she lay still. After tormenting poor Betsy, and indeed the whole household, from her bed for a little under a week, she managed to rise and hop about her chamber, supporting herself upon the furniture. When this proved insufficient for her restless energy she called me into her presence and badgered me into sending for Sandy. She explained to him in dumb-shew what she required and he sped off into the forest, returning in a jiffy with a pair of barbarically-fashioned but perfectly adequate crutches. Tony rapidly learned the knack of using these and commenced to hop about the house, making life even more of a misery for everyone with her taunts and jeers, which were given their keen edge, I surmise, by the pain she was suffering.

Tony took particular delight in invading the room which I had designated as my office (or "compting-house" as I sometimes described it to myself). There she would sit for an unconscionably long hour, questioning me importunately about the exact extent of our wealth and making cuttingly derogatory remarks about my devotion to the ledger, the account books and the correspondence-book. Often I made shift to escape from her unwelcome attentions to Henri's room; once there, however, I had to content myself with Henri's company, for Tony insisted that Betsy obey the Doctor's orders to the letter and remain at her beck and call night and day. Thus I was unable to debate with my friend the news which we had overheard about my name, for it was that name, or rather those two names, which concerned me far more than the news of the clan chieftaincy. For a week or two I pondered them so much that I became a stranger to myself and would wake up in the dark watches of the night wondering which one was truly mine — Richard Mason, budding young estate accountant and trader of Tobago in the West Indies, or Roderick Macdonald, descendant of "the merciless Macdonwald" and of I knew not how many other bloodthirsty warriors. If my unpredictable Father, James Macdonald, decided that in future we must answer to our real name, would I be required to live up to it in some way and perhaps even be turned into another person?

This confusion is with me even now, and is still capable of disturbing me of a wakeful night, although I have never publicly used any other name but Richard (or Dickie or Dick) Mason.

To conclude this chapter on a lighter note I had better reassure my readers about Father's statement to Dr. Whyte that I had been financing my own ventures out of estate money. It was true that I had been occasionally trading on my own account, but it was not true that I had been using Father's money. On my very first venture I used instead an accumulation of small sums which were left surplus after the estate accounts had been balanced. This accumulation was, I believe, and still do believe, neither estate money nor Father's money, but money in a kind of limbo, money of which I, as the accountant, was the trustee. Now Charlie had brought me word of a damaged hogshead of sugar which had been left on the quay at Port Louis because there was no room for it on the ship in which it was to be cargo. I knew that if I could have it covered with a tarpaulin before the next rain-shower and then repaired before the arrival of the next ship due from France, the supercargo on that ship would dispose of it for me in exchange for a percentage of the profit. The price being asked, though laughably low, was a few livres more than the money-in-limbo which I held and I was resigning myself to losing the bargain when I mentioned the matter to Betsy. She immediately revealed that she possessed a hoard of small coins in five or six different currencies; she ran to fetch it and when counted it proved to be a few sols more than was needed to make up my deficit. She offered to lend it to me, although not without trying to negotiate a share of the profit in excess of the proportion she was due, on the grounds that I would have had to abandon the venture without her contribution; on this occasion at least I succeeded in agreeing an equitable division of the profit. In brief, this first venture was a success and we used the profit from it to invest in our next, and so on, although the amounts at this time were never large and poor Betsy's freedom fund (as she called her hoard) could not keep pace with her growing value as a lady's maid of many talents.

Yes, my readers, after the success of that first venture I *did* return the money-in-limbo to the Estate strong-box where I was able to use it later to cover an inexplicable deficit.

CHAPTER IX

I accompany Father on a Visit to Port Louis; we discuss important Matters on the Journey; habitual Eavesdroppers are eavesdropped upon and there is an unfortunate Outcome

"Dick," said Father curtly one morning, a day or two after I had learned of my true name, "you must come with me to Port Louis today to take the Oath of Allegiance to His Most Christian Majesty of France, King Louis the Sixteenth."

"I am at your service, Father," I replied.

"I need not explain further?"

"I do not think so, sir."

"Will you ride?"

"I would prefer to walk, Father, if I may."

"I had thought to relieve the tedium of the journey by explaining to you one or two matters of import in circumstances where we cannot be overheard." He shot me a keen but not entirely hostile glance.

"Father, if you will tell me at what hour you wish me to be at Government House, I will take pains to be there punctually; and as to not being overheard, we could walk upon the beach at Rockley Bay."

Father was remarkably calm, but a vein was beating ominously on his temple as he replied: "Richard, as your father I could order you to ride, but I will not do so. Instead, I am challenging you to decide the matter by the toss of a coin." He produced a gold louis. "Heads we both ride, tails we both walk — or vice versa if you wish."

I might have refused Father's challenge had not Betsy chosen that moment to emerge from Tony's room with a bundle of linen over her arm and a volley of abuse from Tony about her head. She could not possibly have been eavesdropping, so that she cannot have known of the dilemma which I was facing, but the proud carriage of that head reminded me of the many occasions upon which she had reproached me with cowardice. As she disappeared across the yard I could feel my neck stiffen in emulation of hers, but Father was becoming impatient, as always.

"Richard, I abhor walking as much as you abhor riding but you have my word that I will walk, if that is the way the coin falls."

"Very well, Father," I said, adding, out of filial contrariness, "but I would prefer: 'Heads we walk, tails we ride.'"

"Ha! Excellent!" exclaimed Father and flipped the coin with his thumb; it rose flashing into the air, dropped to the floor and went rolling away while my heart turned over. It then fell flat with the head of King Louis uppermost.

Thus it was that for the first and last time Father and I walked side by side to Port Louis and back, with Martin and Charlie following at a discreet distance. Since the day was overcast Charlie was carrying my umbrella, which probably made it easier for Father to be friendly, which he was trying to be.

"Dickie," he said as we walked along at a gentle pace, "what you were overhearing the other day about the Chieftaincy is something which you would have been entitled to learn when you were twenty-one. I think it would be best if you were keeping it all to yourself and not even telling Antonia about it. I need not elaborate upon that?" He turned his head to look me in the face and I nodded.

We had a hill to climb, so we were silent for a while. At the top, when we had caught our breath, Father spoke again.

"There are Macdonalds and Macdonalds," he said, "and our clan is but a minor one, but we have an honourable history and we chose to be loyal to King James and for that we have been proscribed and banished and our lands have been forfeited and — " His voice was rising in anger, but he stopped speaking and made an effort to calm himself. "I am not to give way to my choleric humour, Doctor Whyte tells me." He was again silent for a while, then asked with some emphasis: "Young Betsy, now, she was overhearing too?"

"Yes, Father," I said, for I could scarcely deny that she had overheard.

"And she would understand what she heard?"

"Yes, Father." I said, though I would dearly have liked to persuade Father that she was a half-wit.

"Not stupid, eh?"

"No, Father."

"Lively, is she?" asked Father in a tone of voice which I had not heard before and which I did not like at all.

"She has a lively understanding," I said, attempting to conceal my feelings and having some success, for Father turned to the topic of Negro intellectual powers and forbore to quiz me further about Betsy's temperament.

"You do not agree with my friend David Whyte about the mental incapacity of our ebony fellow-creatures?"

"No, Father."

"Neither do I, my boy. We who have to be living and working close to them know them better than those philosophers in Edinburgh and Aberdeen, who sit upon their fine mahogany chairs and sharpen their fine quill pens in order to be writing nonsense about creatures which they have never seen. Negroes may not be quite as clever as we are, but they are twice as cunning." He paused. "Can you be trusting your light o' love to keep her mouth shut?"

This was indeed a terrible question. Could I trust Betsy? I do not think I had ever asked it of myself, for our whole lives had been one long conspiracy, and the foundation of that conspiracy was that we trusted each other without question even when we had quarrelled and were "not speaking". We both knew that we had secrets from each other, but we did not allow even that knowledge to undermine our trust. I had not been surprised or disconcerted that Betsy had concealed her "freedom fund" from me, and I knew for a certainty that it was no indiscretion of hers which had discovered our private ventures to Father. (I was, in fact, intending to use this visit to Port Louis to make inquiries as to who might have talked too much; the finger of my suspicion was pointing at Charlie, who was becoming too fond of rum to be quite the reliable messenger he had once been.)

I was able to ponder thus and to delay answering Father's question because we were negotiating a particularly ill-made and ill-maintained part of the road, where it was necessary for the foot-passenger to consider every step with some care, a necessity which caused Father to lose some of the equanimity which he was trying so hard to preserve. As soon as we had reached a smooth and level portion of road he spoke to me sharply.

"Surely you can be telling me whether that young Negress of yours is to be trusted?"

"Why is it so important that our true name should be concealed?" I dared to ask.

"Believe me," said Father earnestly, "I would not be concealing it if it were not important. I have made powerful enemies in my time, in high

140

places and in secret places, and I do not wish to have their attention drawn to me and my family."

I hesitated, for it occurred to me that Betsy withheld few secrets from Matti and yet I dared not say so to Father. To cover my hesitation, I spoke confidently.

"I will ensure that Betsy tells no one," I said.

"If there is any doubt at all about her obeying you," replied Father, "a good thrashing would be in order, for nothing less than silence will suffice, if you value your skin, do you understand me?"

"Yes, Father."

"In that case, Dickie, we need speak no more upon this matter."

The rest of our walk was silent, for neither of us seemed to have anything to say to the other. In Port Louis we presented ourselves to M. le Comte; he inquired solicitously after Maman's health, and after Tony's, and promised that he and Madame la Comtesse would visit Craigellachie just as soon as his duties allowed. Father and I duly swore our oaths, and while Father went off to visit friends, I inquired after, and was directed to, the garrison recruiting sergeant. I spoke to him privily about Charlie's manly bearing and proficiency with weapons; he expressed some interest and when the potential recruit was introduced to him made a most eloquent speech about the manifold advantages of life in the French Army. Charlie was quickly induced to enlist, the smart uniform being perhaps more persuasive than the sergeant, but he wept, although I did not, as I relieved him of his pistol, assured him of my continuing patronage, gave him a generous gratuity and bade him farewell.

On the walk home Father, ever hopeful, tried to interest me in the state of the crops in the fields by which we were passing, and in the unkempt and ill-fed condition of the Negroes as compared to ours. I tried my best to reply but could hardly explain that sugar and rum only became of interest to me when they were ready for trade; or confess to him that my mind was taken up with speculating when I would be able to speak with Betsy — surely she could be released from Tony's clutches for half-an-hour when I was in such need of her wise counsel!

This half-an-hour did not arrive until a few days later when Mme. la Comtesse arrived unannounced with her escort and retinue to visit her dear friend Toinette de Mason. I, having kissed the lady's hand and made the required polite remarks, excused myself and hastened to Henri's room, for out of the corner of my eye I had seen Betsy scampering off there. Together — what a pleasure it was to be in congenial company again! — together we induced Henri to settle to writing his name upon the floorboards; as soon as he was fully engrossed I did not beat about the bush.

141

"Betsy," I asked, "have you told your mother about what my father and Doctor Whyte were saying when we overheard them?"

"No," replied she, "but she probably knows about all that already."

"And would she have told anyone else?"

"My mother stores information of that kind in her heart and only imparts it when it will benefit her family or herself."

Somewhat reassured, I turned to the other matter which was troubling me so much.

"What do you think of my name being — " here I whispered lest Henri pick up the name and repeat it, "— Roderick Macdonald?"

"I knew your head would be full of that nonsense," teased Betsy, "What does it matter what I think?"

"I value your opinion more than any other person's," I said, already aware that females need a modicum of praise to maintain them in a happy frame of mind.

"You are flattering me," she laughed, shewing her fine teeth which, unlike her brother's, were set straight and evenly spaced. How their whiteness was set off by her black lips!

"I am not flattering you," I answered, "for it is a most important matter and I want you to tell me what you think."

She hesitated, then smiled at me roguishly as though she would tease me further, but I did not return her smile and the sight of my long face must have re-awakened the sympathy due to a brother whose mind was troubled.

"Master Richard," she said, "there is nothing untoward about having a secret name. I have one also."

I stared at her in disbelief, then stammered: "But-but-but-but — " and was instantly echoed by Henri crying: "But-but-but — " However, he did not look up from his writing.

"It is more of a secret than yours," continued Betsy, "and no white person will hear it until we Negroes are free."

"Is it an African name?"

"It is a secret name, so please do not ask me about it again."

"But do you not sometimes wonder which name truly belongs to you?"

"I am Betsy and you are Master Richard Mason, but inside our heads we can be other persons with other names if that is what we wish."

"Betsy, I do not want to be — " here I had to whisper again, "— Roderick Macdonald, whether inside my head or outside of it. If I were, I would have to be a clan Chief and fierce and warlike and you know well that — "

"— I know well that you are not like that, Master Dickie, but it is no bad thing to be a Chief. Think of the way in which the overseers love, fear and respect the Master, who is their Chief, and how he is more loyal to them than other Masters are to their overseers. It is the same with us; we love, fear and respect our Chiefs — " She broke off as though afraid that she had said too much.

"But you have no Chiefs," I said.

Betsy did not reply; nor did she change her expression. I perceived that I was venturing on ticklish matters, for a Prince Oroonoko who had been captured and enslaved might not want his identity made known to his owner, lest that owner be afraid of his influence over his fellow-slaves and sell him, or worse. I reverted to what I saw as the heart of the matter.

"So you agree to keep the secret of my name and lineage?"

"Yes," came the swift reply, "just as you have agreed to keep the secret that you are going to free me and my family when you succeed to Craigellachie and Braemore."

"But Tony may not — " I hesitated.

"When you are the Master, and perhaps Chief of the clan, Miss Tony will be subject to you, just as she is subject to your father now."

At this point we were interrupted by a series of loud thumps and bangs, as though someone outside the *belvédère* were striking its planks with a heavy stick. When the noise ceased there came Tony's voice in a furious shout.

"What in the Devil's Name is this about Dickie being a great Chief and my being subject to him? And who said that he could free Betsy, who is my very own property?"

Henri was alarmed by all this noise and ran toward us crying: "Ah, bam-bam-bam — !" as though he were a little boy again. He flung his arms around Betsy. His cry was answered by another rain of blows upon the building.

"Betsy," came Tony's voice again, "if you do not shut that idiot's mouth I will — " She fell to cursing in a voice which commenced as loud and strong but which diminished in force until it was almost feeble.

I ran out on to the galerie and looked round the corner of the building. Tony was seated upon the ground with both legs stretched in front of her and holding the injured one as though it were hurting her; her face was as ashen-grey as when Jéhu had carried her home. One crutch lay beside her, but in her temper she must have flung the other away, for it was lying on the ground at least ten feet from her. I ran down the steps with the intention of going to her aid, but she would have none of me.

"Keep off!" she warned, speaking through clenched teeth and raising her crutch as if to strike me, "you lying, spying, conniving *macommère*-man! You are nothing but a filthy hog, sniffing around for anything you can gobble up, and your black *mocojumbie* of a Mistress Betsy is no better! Fetch Jéhu!"

When I did not comply immediately, her voice rose to a scream. "Fetch Jéhu!"

As I ran to the stables the sun beat mercilessly upon my head and shoulders for I had neither hat nor umbrella. I found Jéhu at work with a curry-comb upon Tony's mare Méduse and upon my giving him the news of Tony's plight he leapt upon the creature's back and trotted her away to the *belvédère*, leaving me to escape from the stench of the stable-yard by myself. When I reached the house Jéhu was already carrying Tony up the steps and there were female shrieks coming from every direction. I hastened to my room to fetch a hat and set off for the *belvédère*, where I found Betsy still comforting Henri. We looked at each other with fear in our eyes, for we knew that Tony was capable of almost any spiteful and unpredictable action and her anger had been more terrible than my poor pen can convey. I quickly took over the comforting of my brother, while Betsy made for the house as fast as she could, lest Tony call for her.

It would be tedious to relate at length how, in the next few days, Father and I received many lacerations from the rasping edge of Tony's tongue as she complained that, being the eldest, she should have been told the family history first; that she was managing Braemore almost entirely on her own and was damned if she would go on doing so after her leg was mended if all her work was simply going to make Designing Dickie richer; and that if I was going to inherit both Estates I had better mount a horse and learn to drive the overseers and the niggers myself instead of hiding at home plotting, etc., etc.

Mealtimes became Purgatory for both Father and myself since neither of us relished the prospect of escaping like Maman into brandy-induced insensibility. Tony simply would not allow the discussion of any other topic but that of the injustice under which she saw herself as suffering, and when Father ordered her to her room, she continued her verbal harassment of us by shouting over the partition wall. I had only one consolation, which was that she seemed satisfied with concentrating her fire upon Father and myself and forbore to berate Betsy in her normal caustic manner. Nevertheless she continued to keep Betsy by her side all of the time, so that I had no opportunity of meeting my sister and friend.

I never discovered why Mme. la Comtesse cut short her visit in that disastrous manner, nor what induced Tony to attempt to hobble on her crutches all the way to the *belvédère*.

CHAPTER X

Tony accepts a standing Invitation to stay with her Friend Madame La Comtesse De Dillon; Henri and I bid Farewell to Betsy, who is to accompany her Mistress

What a relief it was to all the other members of the household when Tony declared, not three weeks after her accident, that she was now well enough to accept a standing invitation from Mme. la Comtesse to stay for as long as she liked at Government House, and proposed to leave the following morning! No one else thought that Tony was sufficiently recovered to ride that far, but other people's opinions were never an obstacle to Tony's plans and it was patent that Father was forbearing to invoke Doctor Whyte's authority lest he forbid the journey.

Preparations were therefore set in train for an absence of several weeks. In great haste Katy had to wash, dry and press sufficient clothing; Betsy had to pack boxes and portmanteaux; Jéhu had to prepare Méduse who, despite her name, was a suitably quiet mare for Tony in her present condition; and Fortune had to see to mules for all the baggage and to an ass for Betsy, and to prepare himself, for he was going along too.

Early in the morning I escaped from the noise and confusion caused by the preparations for departure and went to be with Henri in the *belvédère*. His welcome was especially warm as he was not used to seeing me at that hour, and since Milly had already fed him his breakfast of cornmeal pap I was able to distract myself by giving him a writing "lesson", one of those which Betsy and I had been devising in our anxiety to help him to progress beyond scribbling "HENRI" upon the floor. I had to use all the power of my will to bend my mind to this task for, as my readers will understand, the thought of several weeks without Betsy's presence in the house, even although I would have found it hard to find the opportunity to speak with her had she remained, was throwing a dark shadow over my spirit.

Henri was beginning to show some interest in the lesson and I was helping him to use his pencil when the doorway darkened; Betsy had approached without a sound and was standing there ready for her journey. She was wearing her familiar "best" grey dress; it was modest, high-necked, long-sleeved and full-skirted and suited her person to perfection. On her head was her grey kerchief, so well-ironed, as always, that not a wrinkle was to be seen. The look on her face, on the other hand, was anything but familiar; indeed, I had not seen its like before. Henri, of course, had been seeing far less of her than he would have liked; he threw down his pencil, jumped from his chair and ran to her, crying: "Bess-Bess-Bessy —" He flung his arms around her and she caressed and cossetted him as she always did, but instead of looking down at him she continued to gaze at me. I rose from my chair and fumbled for words to say.

"Have you packed those two books which you were intending to read?" I eventually managed to ask.

She answered with a single nod of her head and did not remove her eyes from my countenance. Henri, who must have had some foreboding, buried his face in her shoulder and whimpered into it, making a noise like a lost puppy.

Betsy allowed him to whimper for a while, stroking the back of his neck to comfort him, then disengaged herself from his embrace, grasped his hand firmly and walked him over to me.

"Miss Tony will be departing in a few minutes," she said.

"Thank-thank you for informing me-me," I stammered.

"You will be coming to the house to kiss her farewell?" she asked, with just enough emphasis upon the word "kiss" to provoke Henri.

"Ah, kiss-kiss-kiss-kiss —" he exclaimed, while I took a deep breath and said: "Yes."

At this, Betsy lifted her face to mine; I knew instantly what she was asking me to do, but could not move.

"Oh Dickie!" she said, with a catch in her voice, "shut your eyes and pretend that I am your white sister and not your black sister, and I will shut mine and pretend that you are my black brother and not my white brother."

Perceiving, despite all the confusion in my head, that I must be brave for her, and that even closing my eyes was the coward's way, I bent down and, yes, I kissed my black sister upon her full and tender lips; since she too had kept her eyes open I was able to look into their unfathomable depths and see that they were brimful with tears which shimmered on the brink of falling, but did not fall.

146

In a few seconds our lips were apart again and Betsy was thrusting Henri's hand into mine. She walked to the doorway, put a slim hand upon the doorpost and turned herself from her waist to look back at us over her shoulder. (What grace does a bamboo have, a mere shrub, compared to my virginal nineteen-year-old Betsy at that moment, outlined as she was against the azure sky and the flower-bedecked Tobago hills?)

"You have my beads?" she asked, using the words she might have used when she was eight years old, but which now conveyed some much sadder meaning. Her beads? It took a few moments for me to remember her anklet of jumbie beads and the promises it represented.

"Yes," I answered, holding Henri's hand more tightly as I began to share his foreboding.

"You are keeping them safe?"

"Yes," I repeated, great Dread filling my heart, although Reason was arguing that Betsy was to return in a few weeks.

Betsy turned away, moved lightly and silently across the galerie on her broad bare feet, ran swiftly down the steps and vanished from our sight.

"Ah, Bessy-*not*-go, Bessy-*not*-go, Bessy-*not*-go — " howled Henri, his first true sentence wrenched from his vocal chords by the force of his feelings. He struggled to free himself from my grip so that he could follow Betsy; I needed almost all of my strength to keep him in the room.

My readers, and I hope that by now I may call you my friends, you must excuse an old man if he ends this chapter prematurely here, wipes his eyes, removes the tears from the ledger in front of him with blotting-paper, and postpones the writing of the next chapter until he is in command of his feelings again.

CHAPTER XI

I receive News which distresses me and most Others at Craigellachie; the Tide of Revolution washes toward Tobago; Charlie informs me of impending Trouble

When Tony sent word one morning three weeks later that she would be returning from Government House that afternoon I made shift to be present on the galerie to welcome her (and, more important, of course, Betsy). Time dragged slowly but at last Tony appeared, riding the quiet mare Méduse upon which she had left us, but also leading a stallion of intimidating size and spirit. As she shouted for Jéhu my mind was speculating unhappily about where she might have obtained the money to pay for such an outstanding equine, since she had not come to me for it; at the same time my heart was jumping ahead to the conclusion which I most feared.

"Where is Betsy?" I asked sharply as Fortune led into view the ass upon which my friend had ridden away; the beast was now carrying no more than a portmanteau on either side.

Tony did not answer me but dismounted in leisurely fashion, demonstrating that her limb was still stiff. She blew a kiss to Maman, who had appeared in her usual afternoon stupor, then turned her head in the direction of the stables.

"Jéhu!" she shouted, "are you asleep? I have a real horse for you! I will have your hide if you do not appear this minute!"

"Where is Betsy?" I repeated, running down the steps.

"Should you not greet me, your sister, before you ask 'Where is Betsy?'"

I kissed her most briefly, wishing that she did not smell of horses.

"Where is she?" I asked in a whisper.

"Who is this Betsy, that you should be so anxious about her?" She raised her voice. "Jéhu!"

"Henri has been fractious and a nuisance to everyone all the time you have been away," I said. "Betsy is the only one who can keep him happy."

"You mean, Dickie," scoffed Tony, "that Betsy was the only one who could keep *you* happy!" An evil gleam came into her eye. "I have sold the treacherous minx to M. le Captaine d'Aumont, who needed a lady's-maid-cum-nursemaid for his wife, or so he said, but I hear that he is partial to lithesome young — "

At this point Jéhu appeared, breathless, and Tony stopped speaking, as though she was uncertain how much he had overheard, but he went straight to the stallion's head and led him away without a word, leaving Méduse to Fortune.

Tony limped up the galerie steps, then looked back at me with evil still gleaming in her eye.

"M. le Captaine d'Aumont," she said, "*and* Mme. d'Aumont, *and* their children, *and* all their baggage *and* their pretty black nursemaid embarked this morning and the ship sailed for Martinique this afternoon; so do not think that you can hasten off and buy back your precious Betsy!"

I knew that Tony was telling me the truth and not merely teasing me and I vowed at that moment never to speak to her again unless compelled by necessity. I walked away to the *belvédère* where I dismissed Milly and stood gazing at poor Henri, who was sound asleep and bubbling and snoring gently, until sorrow overwhelmed me. I recalled Milly, stumbled back to my compting-house, dropped into my chair, laid my head upon my table and wept salt tears on to my blotting-pad.

There was no one to whom I could speak freely of my anguish. Only Father had some glimmering of my state for when I hinted, in order to explain the hang-dog looks which he had noticed, that I had had a disappointment, he told me bluntly that a wench could know too much and if she did she was better out of the way; and whatever the case to be remembering his advice about loose Mulatto women.

Yet my anguish was shared, as was shewn by the sad consequences of Betsy's sale all around Craigellachie; the light went out of Matti's eyes and she became even more taciturn than ever; the same could be said of Gilbert, for he performed his duties as watchman in a lackadaisical manner, his mind and spirit dulled by recourse to the rum-bottle; while Jéhu's eyes reflected a deep-seated rage which, although he held it under a tight rein, was clearly liable to break free one day. Jéhu obeyed Tony with exaggerated correctness and never mistreated or neglected a horse in the smallest particular, yet his whole being was changed, his witticisms ceased, and I for one was aware that his heart was now set upon far horizons. The little hut against the *belvédère*, where the Gilbert family had dwelt in some unity, was no longer redolent of even that modicum of happiness which is sometimes the lot of slaves, but seemed empty and sad.

Maman could not but perceive Matti's even greater disinclination to speak and became like an infant again in her attempts to gain the housekeeper's attention; between times she relapsed into the Melancholy which had been her usual condition before the stimulus of the French occupation.

I am sure that Tony, although she would never have admitted to it, missed Betsy as much as the rest of us. She had taken on Milly as her maid in Betsy's place and never ceased singing her praises as a biddable creature who did exactly as she was told and had no ideas above her station, but she had only Maman at hand to read aloud romances to her or to read and write her letters, and Maman was only occasionally both fit and willing to oblige her. I resolutely refused to help her in any way, even in arguments with Father over the price of horses.

After Betsy's departure Henri would have reverted to total idiocy, had I not taken over much of his nursing and education myself. He would demand "Bessy-Bessy-Bessy" and when she failed to appear would have a tantrum resembling those in which I have seen very small boys indulge and which involved kicking, scratching, biting and yelling; if I acceded to his request for a "walk-walk-walk" and then crossed him in some way he would slump to the ground and refuse to move; if I attempted to lift him to his feet he would somehow make himself so heavy, such a dead-weight, that no heaving on my part could move him; and if I attempted to reprove him he would spray me with his spittle, but whether to provoke me further, or to express his frustration and anger at a world which had deprived him of his Bess-Bess-Bessy, I could not say. After many months of effort on my part he seemed to have overcome the worst of his misery and we began to make some progress together. In this we were helped by Milly's replacement, Janga, the squat young "children's nurse" who had been trained as such by Mrs. Grant. Unfortunately, Mrs. Grant had also taught her to sing Presbyterian metrical psalms — morning, noon, and night her high treble voice, issuing strangely from her powerful person, could be heard warbling such lines as: "Than honey, honey from the comb, that droppeth, sweeter far." Although Janga lacked the subtle stratagems by which Betsy had made Henri happy, and was somewhat light-fingered, she was good-hearted and he and I became fond of her.

Father, dimly aware that his home was less welcoming than it had been, and no longer able to depend on Tony to the same extent, spent more and

more time in the cane and though our sugar harvests benefitted, Father
was rarely cheerful.

Thus it transpired that Betsy had been the light and life of our whole
Craigellachie household. Without her it was a dreary place indeed; so
much so that I transferred myself, along with my books (both literary
and commercial) to Henri's room and everyone, whether from the estate
or outwith it, who had business with me had to make the journey to the
belvédère. I became expert, after a while, at keeping Henri occupied so
that he did not interrupt me. If I had important business callers, he was
quite happy to go for a "walk-walk-walk" with Janga.

As my anguish about Betsy's cruel fate diminished I began to suffer my
second attack of Melancholy. I felt it creeping over me, ready to engulph me
if I were not vigilant, especially in the hours of darkness. During the day I
kept it at bay by working so hard and purposefully at estate affairs that we
were, within three years, amongst the wealthiest families in Tobago. My
own private hoard increased annually, through my judicious participation
in various ventures, and it was a matter of some regret to me that Betsy had
not left even part of her "freedom fund" with me, for I could have increased
it to the point where it would have bought her several times over, if only I
had known where to find her. (I would sometimes despairingly ask Matti if
she had had news and she would reply with a shake of her head. All I could
ascertain was that after a short stay in Martinique, le Capitaine d'Aumont and
his family had set sail in a ship the destination of which was a naval secret.)

In the dark of the night I kept Melancholy at bay by losing myself in
books, none of which I remember, as I read them for oblivion and not for
the pleasure of debating their contents with a dear sharp-witted friend. On
the other hand, I do remember clearly the pamphlets and newspapers which
arrived from France in an ever-swelling and ever more agitated stream,
for they had a direct bearing on our affairs and I needed to keep abreast of
political developments if I was to profit from them. I read of the activities of
"Les Amis des Noirs" with apprehension, and yet with some understanding;
I was, after all, "un ami d'une noire".

Despite my gloomy aspect I became quite popular amongst the British
estate-owners for I had no aversion to sharing the news from France, which
most of them could only discover from me, as their French was rudimentary
and their contacts in France confined to tight-lipped merchants and bankers
in Bordeaux and Nantes. Father could not bring himself to be polite to
Whigs, so they learned to visit me in the belvédère after having assured
themselves that he was engaged elsewhere. I had no qualms about deceiving
Father in this manner for I negotiated many profitable deals, both for the
estate and for myself, while Henri sat on the floor and wrote his name or

gazed at a Jack Spania wasp building its nest on the ceiling. Some of the visiting planters and merchants were good enough, or clever enough, to bring little presents for Henri.

In 1789, three years after Betsy's departure, the news of the meeting of the States General at Versailles reached us, having crossed the Atlantic in a fast vessel. Not long afterwards we heard of the storming of the Bastille in the same manner. Then, a week or two later still, newspapers with more detailed accounts arrived and I was reading one of them in Henri's room one peaceful afternoon when I heard slow heavy feet mounting the steps; I glanced at Henri, but he had not been wakened by them; I looked round at the door and Matti came into view, panting slightly from the effort of climbing the steep steps.

"Betsy à Paris," she managed to say; then, without waiting to regain her breath, she turned and left me. I knew it would be fruitless to follow her and try to question her, so I sat where I was. It did not occur to me to doubt the truth of the news; if Matti took the trouble to say it, true it must be.

Betsy amongst the mobs in Paris! How my heart ached for my friend! How I wished that I had gone to Paris and been there to greet her and perhaps protect her! (Yet, argued Reason, had I gone to Paris she would not have been sold, and she would have been in Tobago wondering what was happening to me while the mobs raged.)

It made my heart ache even more that, as a rare visitor even to Port Louis, I could not picture what a city such as Paris must look like. The few engravings which I had seen in books were unenlightening. Maman's descriptions, although they had been exciting to me as a small boy, were little better; the most vivid mental images she had conveyed to me were those of carriages which had difficulty in passing each other, hub-to-hub, in the narrow streets where the houses were four and five storeys high; and those of ladies dressed for balls in clothes even more fashionable and elaborate than those worn at Government House or even in Port-au-Prince. How could I visualize my friend in such scenes — would she be pressing herself against the wall to let a carriage past, or would she be riding in one, attending her mistress to a glittering occasion, only to be attacked by a ravening mob? Would she be ravished, if she had not already been ravished by le Capitaine d'Aumont, who was said to be partial to lithesome young —

The news that sparked off these fears was the only news of Betsy's whereabouts to reach Craigellachie during the years she was away, years which could best be represented by a hundred or more blank pages in this leather-bound ledger upon which I have been writing these memoirs, with here a single sentence and there a short paragraph amongst the vast desert of empty lines and columns.

One paragraph would have to concern a visit paid to me, most privily, by Charlie. He came to the *belvédère* at night wearing, not the smart *caporal*'s uniform in which I had seen him once or twice, but ragged clothes. It was not until I had plied him with some of Father's *usquebaugh*, a bottle of which I kept for Scotch visitors, that he was able to speak and explain the purpose of his visit. He told me that since the departure of Count Dillon, who was both loved and feared by all ranks, Republican agitators had been gaining more and more of a hearing amongst the French soldiers, many of whom were Mulattoes like himself and felt themselves to be wronged, though he, loyal fellow, did not. He begged me to be on my guard and to institute measures for the defence of my person. As the *usquebaugh* took hold he even asked me to buy him out of the army so that he might become my bodyguard once again. It is a measure of the alarm raised in my mind by events in Paris that I considered this request seriously. However, the cautious and calculating part of my nature re-asserted itself and I decided that Charlie would be of more use as a source of information within the French garrison and therefore dismissed him with a gratuity of an amount nicely calculated to retain his loyalty but not to buy his discharge.

Father was so busy with an exceptionally fine sugar-harvest that he had either not heard, or not attended to, rumours of Republican disaffection amongst the soldiers. After I had pondered Charlie's news for a day or two I decided that Father must be informed.

"What is that?" he snapped back at me. "Where were you hearing that?"

I was then subjected to an expert inquisition during which the only secret I managed to save for myself was that of Charlie's identity as my informant. Once convinced, Father immediately became the soldier again. He induced Tony to take charge of the harvest by a mixture of cajolery, threats of being confined to the house, and appeals to her loyalty. He and Fergus then looked to the defences of Craigellachie. It had not been sited by a military man for easy defence like Braemore but the roof was made of tiles instead of shingles and there was much readier access to water for extinguishing fires. Father declared that, with some clearing of forest when the harvest was over, the place would be defensible against a rabble of mutineers, sure to be more interested in rum than in Republicanism, although not against a disciplined army; and that we should stay where we were and not return to Braemore, now a semi-ruin occupied by two overseers' families and their hangers-on. The *belvédère*, though an excellent lookout, was too isolated for proper defence, and I was instructed to remove myself and my books to the main house at the very first alarm, there to station myself at a window and act as a last line of defence with my pistol.

153

Tony, much to her chagrin, was to defend the other side of the house with her pistol; she would much have preferred to gallop about on her stallion, whose name I have taken pains to forget, in view of the price paid for him. (Father could not bring himself to mention Henri, but I understood him to mean that if I was concerned enough about my brother I should convey him to the house with me.)

Behind the uncertainty about the loyalty of the French troops lay a much greater uncertainty — the mood and allegiance of the Negroes. To which side would they incline if the army turned Republican? The slogan *"Liberté! Egalité! Fraternité!"* was to be heard everywhere, as though carried on the breeze, and its appeal to the Negroes would be irresistible if they truly understood its meaning.

Father refused to discuss these matters with me at any length, maintaining sturdily that *his* Negroes would remain loyal, even the Craigellachie ones, for they regarded him as a father and knew on which side their bread was buttered. I was not so confident, for I knew how unpopular amongst the Negroes some of the overseers were, Donal Bain in particular; and I knew too how well Jéhu was concealing his true feelings from Father and Tony — he was not forgetting that he had been wantonly lashed or that his sister had been sold for a whim. Since Gilbert had taken to the bottle, Jéhu had shewn his quality by remaining popular with both the house-Negroes and their compatriots in the fields, and his influence was now paramount. Alongside Jéhu's power, but not I think directly connected to it, was the power of Obeah. There had been an upsurge in Obeah practices, the signs were everywhere, and one night as I lay awake imagining all the worst possible consequences of a mutiny amongst the troops I heard from the forest a single note from what was clearly a very large Negro drum. I listened until dawn for a repeat of the note but it did not come. Since the making and beating of drums were flogging matters I should have reported what I heard to Father, but he had been particularly dismissive of some of my apprehensions and I kept the news to myself.

How I missed Betsy! How I needed the cool application of Reason with which she would have soothed the hot fevers of Imagination! What would I not have given for one of her roguish teasing smiles?

I know not how many blank pages to allocate to the unhappy year which followed, for it was not until 1790 that the actual mutiny took place. Prior to the outbreak Charlie came to see me in the middle of the night and told me all he knew, though not without the assistance of *usquebaugh*. He begged me to employ him in any capacity whatsoever — he swore he would be my body-servant and work for no wages — but I persuaded him to return to his duty and have to report to my readers that he was never heard of again.

It was rumoured that he was executed by his fellows for disloyalty to the conspiracy, and I cannot but remember that this disloyalty was really loyalty to myself. Many months later I heard from an old Negro that the body of a Mulatto soldier had been found in the forest and had been hastily buried by the local Negroes with perfunctory Obeah rites, lest his spirit haunt the district. This body may have been Charlie's but it may not have been. The few Sambo children, whom I suspected of being Charlie's offspring, may not have been, for he was not the only Mulatto buck in the area. The only certainty is that his loyal spirit sometimes haunts me in the dark hours before dawn. He would have made an excellent body-servant.

Charlie's news was that there were several factions amongst the mutineers. Some, the true Republicans, were for forming a disciplined Republican army, replacing the officers from amongst the more popular soldiers and taking over the Island. There was a division within this faction between those who wanted to free the Negroes forthwith and others who thought the Negroes should be kept at work and freed after a suitable interval. Another faction were in favour of indiscriminate pillage, rapine and ravishment, while a third had indicated that at the first sign of trouble they would leave for the nearest British Islands, or even for the Spanish Island of la Trinidad (or la Trinité, as we French-speakers called it) which was plain to the eye on the horizon to the south-west; with the Trade Wind so favourable it was less than a day's sail away. All were agreed, however, upon two points, the first being that they should take their revenge upon their officers by beating them unmercifully; the second, that the mutiny should take place at a given hour upon a given day. This last intelligence Charlie would impart only after a fifth generous "dram" of *usquebaugh*. The appointed day was only a week off.

I told Father all this without delay and he forbade me to alarm the household by making the news public; instead we made our dispositions with the utmost discretion, pretending to the overseers and even to Tony that we were merely rehearsing the manner in which we would defend the house and our lives. Two days before the mutiny was due I "rehearsed" my evacuation of the *belvédère* and took Henri into my room in the house. Declaring that he and I found it convenient and comfortable, I did not make the return journey.

My nature being what it was, and still remains, it was almost a pleasure when the mutiny broke out, relieving me of the weight of apprehension which had been oppressing me, enhancing my sensibilities in strange ways, and stirring me to actions of which I would not have judged myself capable.

155

CHAPTER XII

The French Soldiers mutiny; we are constrained to give Shelter to a large Party of Women, Children and Servants; I am perturbed by the appearance of one of the Latter, and volunteer to set out upon a dangerous Mission

The mutiny took place in the year 1790 and the appointed day (according to Charlie's information) was only a few weeks before my twenty-third birthday. I write this that my readers may remember that I was no longer a boy. I was, in fact, a clumsy young man, six feet in height and over fourteen stone in weight; never a day passed but I wished that I was smaller and more agile.

Father, along with Tony, the overseers and myself, had gone to great lengths to make our preparations for the defence of Craigellachie as inconspicuous as possible and to the unobservant onlooker the day, when it broke, would have seemed the same as any other day. Father and the overseers were out in the cane, but were posted at various points near the roads, so that they could intercept dispatch-riders or have early warning of parties of mutineers on the move; the servants were at their daily tasks; and I was pretending to busy myself with my books while listening hard for the sounds of musket-fire — Father had forbidden me to use the telescope. Tony had disobeyed orders and taken herself off no one knew where: this, in a sense, made the day even more like any other day.

The morning passed peacefully and the afternoon seemed likely to pass in the same manner. At about three o'clock, however, Tony galloped in to announce that she had met a loyal dispatch-rider who had been sent to spread the news around our part of the Island that almost all the officers had been surprised by the soldiers, beaten severely and locked up in the guard-room on Fort de Castrie. Parties of soldiers had been seen setting out in all directions but it was not known what their intentions were. The dispatch-rider had overtaken a straggling group of officers' wives and children who, along with their servants, had managed to escape and were now heading in our direction, escorted by some young officers who had been away from barracks on venereal business when the mutiny started and who were unfortunately unmounted. The officers' wives had elected to mount their children upon the few mules and asses which were available and were shewing a fair turn of speed upon their feet, considering the roughness of the road, the delicacy of their constitutions, the unsuitability of their silken shoes and the heat of the late afternoon. The dispatch-rider knew not if any party of mutineers was in pursuit.

Having passed this intelligence to me, Tony announced that she must go and find Father, but at that moment he galloped in, his usually crimson face pallid.

"To your post, sir!" he bawled at me; then, turning to Tony: "Antonia, where have you been all day? You are as bad as a deserter!"

"Father, I was the first with the news because I posted myself miles along the road — "

"Silence! I have ordered the field Negroes to their houses — go now and make sure that none of them are running off to the forest. Go now!"

As Tony wheeled her horse and galloped away, Father raised his voice to a full stentorian bellow. "Jéhu! Fortune! I will be having your hides! I need a fresh horse!"

When only Fortune appeared, Father seemed ready to lash him with his whip.

"Where is Jéhu?"

By this time I was at my post which, as I have said, was at the window of my chamber and could not hear what Fortune answered or what Father said further on the matter of Jéhu's whereabouts. That he was absent without leave on such a day was almost as unsettling to me as Father's abandonment of the calm authority upon which we all so depended in times of crisis, and I looked forward with increasing dread to the imminent dangers.

(Later, I concluded that while Father was notably calm in the face of an external enemy he yet found disloyalty and mutiny extremely disturbing, whether from soldiers or his Negroes; perhaps, too, his long-standing anger with me arose from my very nature being a form of disloyalty to his notion of what a Macdonald son should be.)

When Henri awoke I had fetched out my pistol and was checking my powder and shot; he was not aware of the general excitement and watched me as I went on to adjust the slats of the jalousies so that I had what Father

157

called "a field of fire" through the narrow gaps while not being visible from the outside.

The house was full of the chattering of women, but this was suddenly stilled when, from the direction where the forest was thickest, came the sound of drums — not the disciplined rat-a-tat-tat of military kettledrums, nor yet the hollow wooden resonance of tolerated tamboo-bamboos, but the deep throbbing of forbidden Negro big drums, now being brought out of their hiding places and used, I fancied, for Negroes on one estate to talk to and warn Negroes on the next, and so on along the whole length of Tobago. Tony must have failed in her mission, and the drummers escaped to the forest.

Henri had some glimmering of my fancy that the drums were talking to each other and decided to answer them himself, in a manner which so closely resembled them that it was uncanny.

"Bam-a-da-bam-bam!" he went, "bam-bam-a-da-bam-bam-bam!" and so on and on and on.

"Silence that idiot!" came Father's furious command, as though there were another mutinous soldier or Negro in the camp.

Poor Janga, her eyes rolling with fright, came running in to quiet Henri but he would not stop the delightful game and I had to send her across the yard to Matti for benay-balls. The drums continued — how I wished that Betsy was with me to tell me what they meant! — and answering drums came from many directions. Henri, with a benay-ball in his mouth, could only spray syrup instead of imitating them.

My readers must imagine the drum-beats continuing during what I describe next, even when I do not mention them. They were intermittent, but insistent, and though the white members of the household and our soon-to-arrive guests pretended not to hear them, black servants would occasionally turn a head, or purse lips and open eyes wide, as if considering a message they had heard.

As the sun set in considerable glory the party of officers' wives about whom we had been forewarned straggled into the yard, followed by the young officers who had been acting as rearguard. From my post I could hear Father ordering the latter, in peremptory military French, to take up positions round the house, but before they went he berated them for the condition of their pistols and warned them to be alert, if they valued their paltry lives. One young fellow was posted outside my window and since he appeared to be heeding Father's warning I relaxed my vigilance and crossed my chamber to the doorway, whence I could at once keep an eye on Henri and watch the new arrivals as they entered our spacious hall (which was also our dining-room and our salon); it was already overcrowded and more women and children and servants were climbing the steps to the galerie outside, intent on adding to the crush. I saw that it might be difficult to make certain that no disagreeable people were billetted upon Henri and myself.

Most notable amongst the officers' wives who had already entered the hall was a tall, beautiful and vivacious young woman, whom I had not seen before. Her dress, considerably torn, disordered and splashed with mud after her journey, was cut low in what I took to be the latest fashion from Port-au-Prince or Paris and revealed the marble magnificence of her neck, shoulders, arms and bosom. She was leading two very unhappy little girls by the hand in a manner which shewed plainly that she was unused to the office of nursemaid. The little girls' dresses were most fetchingly designed to match their mother's but were also in pitiful disarray. I was dazzled, nay entranced, by the effulgence of the young mother's beauty and stood gawking at her from my shadowy doorway, forgetting mutineers, Negro-drums and my duty to be at the window and alert. For her part, she did not appear to be at all conscious of my regard.

I suspect that my female readers, if there are to be any, will now be wondering whether I have not at last reached the point in my story which they have doubtless been awaiting with impatience, when Cupid will successfully lodge an arrow in my breast and I will become subject to Beauty's dominion. Rest assured, dear ladies, (and the dearer for having persevered thus far with my commonplace chronicle) rest assured that Cupid was taking aim at that very moment and that I am about to describe the pain and joy of the wound which he inflicted upon me; pain and joy which seemed to be intensified and not weakened by the sound of the savage drums and the fear of death which accompanied them.

As I watched the delightful Frenchwoman, her two little ringletted moppets took further fright at the ever denser crush around them and started to weep noisily and to pull at her skirts. She shook them roughly, her face contorted with fear and anger, and admonished them in a voice so harsh that it made even her elegant French sound unmusical. A moment later there entered from the galerie an apparition which could only be likened to her shadow — a black nursemaid as tall and nobly formed as her mistress. She was carrying two pallid babes, one on either arm, while a further two infants grasped her skirts. The last rays of the sun were shining into the house and I saw that the maid was dressed in the same fashion as her mistress, but while the mistress favoured bright lustrous silks and sparkling jewels, the maid's simply cut but elegant dress was of a plain linen stuff and her neck and arms were unadorned; while the mistress's hair was piled high in a triumph of the *friseur's* art, the maid's was concealed by

159

a plain kerchief tied in a neat but unfamiliar fashion which combined modesty with coquetry; and, of course, while the mistress's skin shone marble-white, the maid's anticipated the approaching night with its ebony. It seemed as though the mistress had consciously planned these contrasts to emphasize the brilliance of her own attractions. However, perspiration had run in rivulets down those "marble" shoulders, streaking the powder which accounted for their whiteness and revealing many mosquito bites and other blemishes, while the maid's skin shewed neither powder nor blemish, only "polished jett"; and there was yet another contrast which was hardly in the mistress's favour — the maid was evincing no impatience at all with her four distressed little charges; instead, she was gently fondling them and reassuring them with soft endearments which, though I could not hear them, I knew to be in patois.

Almost against my will, and with fright and confusion filling the house, I continued to observe the maid rather than the mistress. When at last she looked around and saw me in my doorway her eyes, full of fear and yet tender from her comforting of the children, found mine and remained tender. She did not drop them as most Negresses would have done; nor did she attempt to ogle me, as most Frenchwomen seemed inclined to do, even in that dreadful situation; nay, she held my gaze with her own in a manner which was so frank in its admission of fear, and yet so bold in its conviction that fear could be overcome, that willy-nilly my heart began to beat faster and faster and louder and louder in my ears, as though it wished to drown the sound of the threatening drums; my breath came with difficulty; and the world seemed to stop turning on its axis. At the same time my vitals were gripped with a pain so exquisite that I cannot begin to describe it, despite my promise to my lady readers that I would do so. I can only write that a cutlass blow, savage enough to end my agony, would have been a blessing to me at that moment.

I became apprehensive that I would be observed in this abject state by other people. I turned my head away from the nursemaid's gaze to look around and lo! not one person in the throng had noticed my condition; nor had any of them noticed — how blind were they! — that they had a goddess in their midst. Instead, they were all jabbering like terrified monkeys. Deranged by their indifference, I began to doubt whether I Richard Mason, properly Roderick Macdonald, had truly exchanged significant glances with a Negress whom I had never seen before, and in circumstances of extreme danger. I glanced back at the creature who had disturbed me to the point where Pain and Joy had overcome Fear. She had found a quiet corner and was lowering herself gracefully to the floor, spreading out her muddy skirts the more easily to wrap her arms —

how fine and round and smooth they were! — around her four charges. They responded by competing to hold her and nestle into her and caress her, as if they were sure that they were safe in her embrace, despite all the discomforts and dangers of the day.

The goddess, the Sable Venus, must have become aware that my covert glance had lengthened into a discourteous stare for she looked up at me and in the fading light our eyes met again. Our communion lasted for only a few moments for we were interrupted by Father appearing from the yard and addressing the jabbering throng.

"Be silent!" he commanded in a fierce whisper, "and do not attempt to light lights!"

Instantly, and as though in defiance of Father, there were confused shouts and irregular musket-fire not too far from the house. Terror gripped the women; hands flew to mouths; many sank to the floor half-conscious; the few mothers of young children held them more tightly; while Henri, shouting "Bam-bam-bam!" pushed his way under my arm, saw the black nursemaid in the very last of the light from the western sky, and stumbled toward her crying "Bessy-Bessy-Bessy!" He flung himself on the floor and tried to worm his way into her embrace between the two sickly babes. She held Henri at bay as best she could until I moved forward to take hold of him, followed by Janga, who had appeared out of nowhere. As we hustled the spitting and spluttering Henri back to my chamber I could just see that Maman had also appeared and was kneeling on her *prie-Dieu* in front of the image of the Virgin, and that most of the other women were joining her, their faces ghostly pale in the light of the tiny lamp in front of the holy image. The beautiful mother essayed to kneel too, but was incommoded by her two little daughters.

"Betsee!" she screamed, "take these children away from me now!"

Father, who had been moving quietly down the galerie steps, turned back and his figure again filled the doorway, while the intermittent musket-fire continued.

"Antonia!" he whispered even more fiercely, "You are at your post?"

"Yes, Papa!" came the reply from the other side of the house.

"Richard!" he called, still in a whisper, "You have your pistol?"

"Yes, Father." I had quickly moved back to my post at the window.

"I am ordering you both to shoot the next woman who is making a noise, and that idiot, too, if necessary!" Father waited to ensure that this threat had had the desired effect, then tip-toed away. A moment later I was aware that a woman's figure had entered my chamber, accompanied by small children. There was a movement in the air which carried toward me the scent of cocoa-nut oil, freshly pressed linen and a trace

161

of French perfume. I knew then that Henri had not been mistaken, that the apparition, the black nursemaid, was no goddess; she was my flesh-and-blood sister Betsy and, as her first words testified, she had most down-to-earth concerns.

"Master Richard," whispered she in patois, "me need you po-cham for these children."

I do not think that I need describe the attendings to nature which followed. They would have proceeded smoothly and quietly had it not been for Henri, who had to be restrained from participating as if he were one of the infants, and from imitating the now infrequent musket-fire. Janga's great strength was a boon to us that night.

With the po-cham restored to its rightful place, Betsy gathered the children, all six of them, and took them to the corner of the room farthest from the window, where she somehow managed to hold them all in her embrace, and soothe them into readiness for sleep. She even found space for Henri and his rotund twenty-year-old person.

The musket-fire stopped altogether, and the moon rose, shining through the jalousies in narrow stripes which illumined Betsy's form and confirmed that she belonged to the harsh world of mutinies and musket-fire and po-chams, and not to any Olympia or Arcadia. Yet confusion reigned in my heart. I longed to pay homage and swear fealty to the goddess who did not exist, and perhaps even bend down and kiss her feet, yet I was wrathful that I had failed to recognize my fierce little rationalist friend and that she had betrayed me by "putting on flesh" (in Fergus's rude phrase); by learning to display her charms with discreet elegance à la mode de Paris; and by using the perfume I so disliked. I turned my attention back to my guard-duties.

The musket-fire did not re-commence and nothing else was to be heard around the house; even the crickets seemed to be holding their breath. Then the Negro drums started again, very quietly and slowly; even to my white ear their sound was somewhat reassuring.

"Soldiers now so drunk they lying down," came Betsy's patois whisper behind me. "Only one or two still standing and they ready to fall any time. We safe till morning, when they wake up with sore heads and bad tempers."

Father must have obtained the same intelligence from his own sources, for shortly afterwards he entered the house to announce loudly that the mutineers were insensible, that lamps might be lit and that all those with weapons should join him on the galerie instantly for a Council of War. This armed party, once gathered, consisted of Father, three grey-bearded overseers (including Fergus), the three young French officers, Tony, and myself.

"I am needing someone," said Father, "to volunteer to be taking a message to the Governor — on foot, I am afraid. The despatch will have to be verbal to save time and it will be to the effect: one, that I have all these people safe here for the moment; two, that I may need reinforcements in the morning if any of the Negroes join the mutineers; three, that I am in need of all the intelligence he can be sparing me; and four, that I am awaiting his orders." He turned to the young officers. "I take it that none of you are knowing Grant's Trace?" They shook their heads and shrugged their shoulders in true Gallic fashion. "Ha! When I was a lieutenant I was making it my business to know every nook and cranny of the country I might be fighting across." He turned away with another snort of disgust and spoke to the overseers, regarding their ageing and corpulent bodies with pursed lips. "I am needing you here," he said briefly, "for you are still good shots."

"I know Grant's Trace," I interposed before he could say more. "I will go to the Governor."

My offer was met with astonished and unbelieving silence for, as my readers will recognize, volunteering to carry a message through a dark forest, with mutinous and drunken soldiers at large and Negro drums beating, was hardly in keeping with my character. None of those present knew that I was not myself that night — I would have walked to the gates of Hell itself and back again, to prove I knew not what. The confusion in the house and in my mind and heart made even the darkness of the forest seem an inviting prospect, especially as there was a bright moon to light me on my way and no sun to cast its burden of heat upon my shoulders. I put my hand upon the butt of the Doune pistol.

"I will go," I said, "since it is a matter of walking."

Before Father could reply Tony's mocking laugh rang out.

"I will go," she mimicked me, putting her hand upon the butt of the pistol and laughing again more cruelly than before.

"Indeed and indeed, Richard will go," said Father quickly, as though afraid I might change my mind.

"But Father," expostulated Tony, "he is a coward and he does not know — "

"Be silent, Antonia! I know you are wishing to go, but I will not be sending a woman on this assignment. Be silent, I said!"

Father then proceeded to instruct me about the trace which Mr. Grant had cut with the intention of clearing more land, but which had reverted to a hunter's track. Neither muskets nor drums had been heard from its direction and I only had to follow it for two miles or so when I would come to a main road. If I approached this with caution, keeping my eyes open for guard posts, I could cross it and find my way by another trace to Port Louis and Government House.

Thus briefed, I went off to the kitchen to see Matti and be fortified with a cold fricassee of mutton and some fresh bread which Matti had baked before she had been forbidden to continue cooking.

"You have seen Betsy?" I asked.

Matti shook her head.

"She is much changed," I ventured.

In the darkness Matti turned away and did not answer by the slightest gesture. I remembered the missing Negroes.

"Where are Gilbert and Jéhu?" I asked, and realized that Matti would not answer this question even if she could.

Father accompanied me to the edge of the forest and I set off along the trace, regretting, despite my unreasoning wrath, that I had not received Betsy's approbation for my boldness. Perhaps, I consoled myself, that might be bestowed upon me later, if I survived.

CHAPTER XIII

I set off upon my Mission and am joined by Another; we are unable to reach our Destination because of a Disaster; on the return Journey we meet with various Adventures; Tony indulges in a Fit of Rage

For ten or fifteen minutes I walked along Grant's Trace boldly enough, my footfalls silenced by the mould of the forest floor. (I knew, of course, that there were no dangerous wild animals in Tobago.) Then I reached a steep uphill part, lost my breath, and stopped for a moment. Behind me I heard, not a footfall, but a faint chink of metal upon metal. I was sure I was being pursued. I laid my hand upon my pistol, which at Father's insistence was already loaded, and would have withdrawn it from its holster and cocked it, had not a voice spoken to me from a short distance.

"Dickie!" it said, and I knew it for Tony's, "I am coming with you!"

When she drew near I could just make out by the light of the moon that she was back in her soldier's gear and that the chink I had heard must have been made by the pistol she was holding in her hand, knocking upon the buckle of her belt.

"Why have you come?" I asked.

"I am sure you will make a botch of it, Dickie, and if you do not, I do not want you to have all the glory."

I knew Tony too well to raise any objections so I turned and started to climb the hill again. I could hear her behind me, but she made no attempt to overtake me as I had expected her to do. I reflected that people skilled on horseback are often poor walkers, slower even than those of sluggish temperament such as myself. Ah! but tonight I was anything but sluggish; I was being goaded by unfamiliar and relentless Furies!

We journeyed on, uphill and downhill in Tobago fashion, until we

were not far short of a crest where, in daylight, the ocean would be visible and
Port Louis concealed only by a small hill. I could hear Tony behind me, her
breath coming in gasps as she laboured to keep up with me; I too was walking
with my head down and breathing hard. Suddenly I became aware, out of the
corner of my eye, of a faint rosy glow in the sky, as though a premature dawn
was breaking. Without saying anything to Tony I quickened my pace and
when I reached the crest there was no doubt about the source of the glow —
there was a great fire in Port Louis. Ruddy tints were reaching the clouds in
the sky and even from our viewpoint, three-quarters of a mile off, flaming
particles could be seen flying along, tumbling in the strong breeze. Tony
came up behind me and seized my arm in a fierce grip.

"Port Louis on fire!" she exclaimed. "How lucky that I followed you.
We must hurry!" Her words emerged between gasps much louder than those
caused by her loss of breath on the hill. "Come on, Dickie!"

I would have liked to ponder the implications of the conflagration for
a while, but Tony was of another mind and set off down the hill at a great
pace, forcing me to follow her, for though I would have much preferred
to have been alone, I knew that it would be folly for us to become separated
now. Two pistols were better than one, as Fergus had told me once.

I had difficulty in keeping up with Tony and had to reflect that persons
accustomed to horse-riding can perhaps move as fast upon their own legs as
anyone else if their spirit moves them to do so. Running downhill thus, we
quickly gained the main road, which followed the bottom of the shallow
valley. I would have liked to approach it with caution, lest there be mutineers
or hostile Negroes upon it, but Tony crossed it without stopping and started
up the steep trace, known as Willow Trace, on the other side. Here,
half-hidden amongst the dark trees, were huts belonging to free Negroes
who gained their livelihood from cultivating small provision-gardens and
working in the town and on the quayside. Their dogs, knowing that we were
strangers, barked at us but no one spoke to us, let alone offered to question our
passage. When we reached the top of the hill we found a group of the Negro
men from the huts; they were gazing at a sight I hope never to see again —
fire engulfing a town and blazing out of human control as the wind blew
sparks and huge pieces of flaming palm-thatch in front of it, and sent long
tongues of flame licking hungrily across the gaps between houses and stores
and huts. None of the Negroes spoke and neither did I; Tony, whom I had
expected to dance with joy as she did every *camboulay*, stood rigid and still,
breathing deeply and watching the flames as though bewitched.

Shortly after our arrival the flames reached a store on the quay and
puncheons of rum must have burst open with the heat, for rivers of blue flame
appeared, flowing across the ground towards the sea. "Goad a'michty!" said

one of the Negroes with awe in his voice, releasing the tongues of the others, who began to name to each other in quiet undertones the buildings which were being destroyed and their owners, and to speculate as to the prospects of work and wages for them on the morrow.

The population of the town were not to be descried, and I had to assume that they had seen the hopelessness of any attempt to extinguish the flames and had withdrawn into the darkness. (We learned later that the mutineers were firing at anyone who tried to protect his house or rescue his moveable property.)

For my part I was concerned whether our sugar and rum were amongst those being consumed by the raging flames, for we had a store in Port Louis and I knew that, although some were safely at sea, some were awaiting shipment, including a few hogsheads which were private ventures of my own. I also had some hardware, nails, bolts, hinges and the like, which I had imported from the United States via a devious route and which I was about to sell around the Island through an agent. Father despised iron-mongers and would not invest in such goods, but I had already discovered what a profitable trade they were, and even at that moment I saw that, if my stock had not been damaged by the fire, I could look forward to charging high prices when Port Louis was being rebuilt.

I am ashamed to admit that I had been to Port Louis so rarely that I knew not whether our warehouse was amongst those being reduced so rapidly to ashes; it was certainly not amongst those being named by the Negroes. I was cursing myself heartily for this failure to attend to such an important part of our business, and vowing that I would visit our quayside property more often, when we heard a large party of men climbing the steep part of the trace behind us. The free Negroes vanished without a sound. I drew my pistol, but the precaution proved unnecessary for the party consisted of Mr. George Glover of Hampden Estate, a gentleman known to us, three of his overseers and thirty or forty of his Negroes. Mr. Glover, speaking in his strange English accent (that is, as though he had secreted an extraneous object, say a child's marble, in his mouth) told me that he had seen the glow of the fire from his house and had been approaching Port Louis along the main road with the intention of saving his produce on the quay and giving what assistance he could to the townspeople, but had been stopped by well-armed and disciplined mutineers.

He had turned back and was now attempting to approach the town via Willow Trace. When I told him that we too had property at risk he invited me to join him and his party: he had not noticed Tony, still standing entranced and motionless. When I commented politely, but in an inquiring manner, on his trust in the loyalty of his Negroes, he told me in his pedantic

English way that "he and his Negroes had a reciprocal regard and a mutual determination to resist this licentious garrison, misled as they were by the mad democracy of French tricksters."

When I called to Tony that we were about to move on, her return to full consciousness was instantaneous and complete.

"Oh yes!" she cried, "let us approach closer to the fire! I cannot wait to feel its heat upon me, but I am tired of walking. Mr. Glover, sir, pray let me have one of your Niggers to ride — a strong one with good legs!"

Mr. Glover was taken aback, but had time neither to accede nor to protest, for Tony was already running along the line of Negroes illumined by the fire and picking out the tallest and most sturdy, a simple fellow who shewed his teeth in a broad grin when she stood in front of him, looked him up and down, and felt the condition of his arm. I half expected her to lift his foot to see if he were properly shod.

"You will do," she said, punching him lightly in the midriff. "What is your name?"

"Duke, Massa," he answered.

"Bend down, Duke, and let me mount on to your shoulders."

Duke did as he was told and the party set off, with embarrassment on every man's face, an embarrassment which was not diminished by Tony's next speech. I wished heartily that she was not my sister and even more heartily that she, or I, or both of us, were elsewhere.

"Mr. Glover," she shouted, "you should ensure that your Niggers wash themselves more often. A sea-bath would do wonders for this Duke fellow."

Our attempt to reach Port Louis was unsuccessful for we had not proceeded far when we were stopped by a party of carousing soldiers, drunkenly shouting "*Liberté!*" at frequent intervals. They had lit their own fire in the middle of the trace and were barbecuing the carcase of some animal upon it; they would not let us approach, firing muskets into the air when we made the attempt. Tony started to remonstrate with them in French from her perch on Duke's shoulders, but I persuaded her to desist, pointing out in English that the French we spoke was the same as that spoken by the officers whom the mutineers so hated. Unfortunately she took my point as licence to abuse them loudly and at length in her lowest and vilest pat3ois, which caused consternation amongst them; they drew together around the fire and had Mr. Glover not given the order for our party to withdraw up the trace, they might well have decided to fire upon us. Back at the junction of the trace with the main road we met another estate-owner, Dr. Thomas Currie, of Lowlands, a Scotsman known to me; he had with him several overseers and fifty Negroes. He had made three unsuccessful attempts to reach the town by other routes and was now returning to his estate. He advised me that it would be extremely risky to try to reach the Governor, who might well be surrounded, and Mr. Glover agreed. Both gentlemen offered to detach one or two overseers to escort Tony and myself back to Craigellachie, but I persuaded them that it would be safer for us to return in the same silent and privy manner as we had come. Convincing Tony that this course was the only prudent one was no easy matter — she was for riding Duke as near to Port Louis as possible and making a grand circle round the town to see the fire from as many points of vantage as she could; in so doing, she was sure, she would find a way to pass our message to the Governor. It was not until Dr. Currie pointed out that the glow in the sky had almost disappeared and that the sunrise was only an hour away that Tony agreed to an immediate return home, and to dismount from the tolerant Duke.

" 'Tis a pity I did not try you at a canter," she said, punching him lightly again. "I will send you some soap, Duke. See that you use it!"

Our return along Grant's Trace seemed much quicker than our outward journey (as seems to be true of so many return journeys). By the time we were approaching Craigellachie the moon was low in the sky and it was darker than at any previous time of the night. I was in the lead and moving as fast as was consistent with caution because I yearned to see the Sable Venus again, lest she had changed herself back into my sister and friend, and I could be assured that I had not lost my senses. My attention must have been fixed on this prospect rather than on negotiating the dark trace for suddenly, all at once, I smelled "clairin" and stumbled over something lying on the ground. I put out my hand to stop myself from falling and encountered the warmth of a human body which made no effort to rise, merely grunting and wheezing. Tony tried to help me to my feet.

"It is a French soldier!" she whispered.

"Dead drunk!" I answered.

"Where is his musket?" asked Tony.

We fumbled and searched and eventually found the weapon lying on the ground a few feet away. Tony picked it up boldly.

"Be careful! It may be loaded," I whispered.

We tried to discover whether it was loaded or not, but it was hard to be certain one way or the other, what with the darkness and our unfamiliarity with the French mechanism. Tony soon grew impatient.

"I will carry it as it is," she announced, "if you will bring his powder and shot. It will be one less to fire at us in the morning."

Distrusting Tony's temperament as I did, I could not be happy with this arrangement but decided against arguing with her, lest she raise her voice and inform the soldier's comrades, who might not be as insensible as he, of our whereabouts. We knew nothing of where the Negroes might be, nor of their intentions. Unhandily, I contrived to relieve the soldier of his satchel and slung it over my shoulder.

"If that fellow was supposed to be guarding this trace," said Tony, "we should reach the house without trouble." She set off, marching in careless fashion but at least with the musket pointing to the sky. I was following, not enjoying the weight of the soldier's satchel on my shoulder, but keeping close to her, when we both heard a drum being tapped in a perfunctory manner somewhere nearby. We stopped instantly and Tony brought her musket down in front of her. After listening for a while and not hearing the drum again we were creeping forward step by step when I saw a flicker of light ahead of us and just to one side of the line of the trace. I grasped Tony's arm to warn her and a movement of her head told me she had seen the light too. Without making a sound, we crept forward again until we could see a small fire burning in the midst of a clearing where a forest path crossed the trace. Round the fire, talking quietly, were a number of Negroes, all with familiar faces.

On a tree-stump, as if he were the leader, sate Gilbert, on his right hand was Jéhu, seated on the ground, and on his left Adam, one of the Craigellachie coopers, crouched upon a low stump with a large drum between his knees. As Tony and I watched, uncertain of the purpose of this meeting, Adam touched the surface of the drum with his fingers, producing a low uncheerful noise, which sounded for all the world as if the drum were making a pessimistic contribution to the confabulation. The black faces all wore serious, even gloomy, expressions. There were no signs that Obeah was being practised and I began to realize that this was a meeting of the Negro leaders, a council of state rather than a religious ceremony, and that the drum was to be used for passing messages rather than for accompanying the sacrifice of a goat or chicken to the old African gods.

I was marvelling that the Negroes had posted no sentries and were therefore unaware of our presence when Tony stepped forward into the firelight, still holding the musket in front of her. The Negroes looked up at her and retained their sad expressions. Adam lifted the middle finger of his right hand, which was resting on the rough skin of the drum, brought it down three times and the drum whispered "Miss Tony!" so clearly that I trembled and put my hand upon the butt of my pistol. Tony was cast in a different mould.

"Gilbert!" she said in patois, "Master Richard and me want know if any soldiers between here and the house."

There was a delay while the Negroes conferred in mutters, a process made harder by the fact that while our Braemore Negroes had a little

170

English, our Craigellachie Negroes understood virtually none of the patois which Tony had spoken so naturally. When they had done, Adam struck the drum again as quietly as before, but with measured intervals. I could not read its message this time. Was it calling up fifty Negroes, all armed as Tony was with French muskets taken from drunken soldiers? Or with cutlasses? Even with no arms at all fifty of them could overwhelm the two of us. I half drew out my pistol.

"Me tell Massa Mason about that drum if you no answer me," threatened Tony.

The delay continued, and it occurred to me that Tony was no longer any kind of heroine to the Negroes since she had disposed of Betsy in such capricious fashion. On the other hand, the looks upon the faces around the fire were those of acute disappointment and defeat and I saw that the Negroes were about to sink into lethargic indifference, a condition familiar to everyone in the West Indies who has had dealings with their race.

"Bestir yourselves!" cried Tony impatiently. "Answer me!"

Gilbert nodded sadly at Jéhu, as though giving him permission to be the spokesman and he raised his eyebrows in return. The looks on both their countenances so resembled looks which I had seen on Betsy's that I was all but unmanned. Resolutely, I shut Betsy's face out of my mind and waited for Jéhu to speak while maintaining a proper alertness.

"Mamzelle," said he at last, "the Republican soldiers promise us freedom, but when they come here shouting '*Liberté!*' they only wanting rum and when they drunk it they steal everything they find, and they break everything that no use to them, even our cooking-pots, and they trample our gardens and pull the roofs off our houses; and just now we hearing that the Negroes on the other estates not wanting a Republic — "

"And where the Republican soldiers now?" interrupted Tony. "Is any on the trace ahead?"

Jéhu took his time in answering. He was thinking out every implication of his answer before he made it; he was Betsy's brother, even if his thoughts were somewhat slower.

"They all lying where they fall down," he said, "except for one or two sergeants."

"And they weapons?" demanded Tony, "where they muskets and pistols?"

There was no need to translate those last two words to the Craigellachie Negroes. Jéhu needed only one glance to consult his father.

"Safe," he said.

At this point I would have taken time to ponder what to say or do next, for the hidden weapons were the Negroes' only card, and a strong one at that, but Tony was her father's daughter.

"Sun up soon," she said. "Bring muskets and pistols, all of them, to the house at sunrise and me say nothing to Master about you dealings with Republicans or about that drum; nor will Master Richard."

There were murmurings and translations into English and back again before Jéhu spoke.

"What happen about our houses and gardens and cooking-pots?"

Again Tony spoke like Father and this time on Father's behalf also: "The Master give you extra time off so you can mend houses and he buy you new cooking-pots."

(Indeed he will, I thought to myself, and from my very own consignment of hardware if it has survived the fire.)

Gilbert looked around the circle and as I was following his gaze from face to face I saw a movement out of the corner of my eye; I could have sworn that Adam had lifted his hands but when I looked at him he was sitting perfectly still. His drum, however, had vanished. Gilbert must have received unanimous agreement, for he nodded to Jéhu, who voiced the decision.

"We bring muskets," he said.

"And pistols," asked Tony, "and bayonets and powder and shot?"

"Everything, Mamzelle Tony," answered Jéhu, reluctance in every syllable.

"Good!" said Tony, and turned to me. "Do you promise not to tell the Master about this?"

"Yes," I said, knowing that I would keep my promise but wondering if Tony could truly bring herself to be silent on the matter. In pondering thus I forgot to mention to Tony the disappearance of the drum. She was impatient to be gone and might not have listened to me. "Let us be off!" she said, and set off down the trace at a trot.

The first indication of dawn was lightening the sky as we made great speed into the last little valley just below Craigellachie House. At the bottom of the dell there was a muddy stream which had to be crossed on stepping-stones. Tony was about to put her foot on the first stone when an unsteady voice came from the darkest patch of semi-darkness on the other side of the stream.

"*Qui va là?*" it demanded.

Events followed so quickly that it is hard for me to describe them in proper order. Tony stopped, lifted her musket off her shoulder and pointed it at a soldier who appeared to be trying to jump forward and threaten her, or perhaps me, with a pistol. The musket exploded and the soldier's whole body was knocked to the ground, but not before I had seen his face turn to blackness in the dim light. In the same instant Tony was thrown backward by the musket's recoil; her foot caught on something and she spun round and fell face forward into the mud of the stream's edge. Meanwhile I had drawn my pistol and when Tony fell I quickly crossed the stream by the stepping stones and presented the weapon at the recumbent soldier. He did not move and it was soon apparent to me in the rapidly improving light that he was dead, with part of his head blown off. He wore a sergeant's stripes, I noticed.

When I turned back, Tony was struggling to free herself from the mud and I had to help her to regain her feet and climb on to the bank; she was muddied from head to foot, her eyes and nose were blocked; and she was spitting mud out of her mouth between gasps for breath. With the aid of a handkerchief I helped her to clear her nostrils and her eyes and she immediately started to curse me (in terms which I shall spare my readers) as though I were responsible for her condition.

"Tony!" I begged her. "Pray listen!"

The silence in the forest which had followed the discharge of Tony's musket had been broken by one or two cries, or so I thought. I wanted to know who or what was making them. When Tony stopped her vituperation we both listened and it soon became apparent that the musket-shot had awakened at least two Frenchmen who were not far off and who were blundering about and drunkenly cursing because they could not lay their hands upon their weapons.

"We must hurry," I said. "Bring that musket." I crossed the stream again and took the dead sergeant's pistol. I averted my eyes from his head, round which flies were buzzing in ever-increasing numbers.

"I cannot lift this musket," complained Tony, after she had bent down and tried to retrieve it from the stream. "My shoulder hurts too much. Oh yes, I can. My left arm is not injured."

She skipped across the stones and we commenced to run uphill toward the house. Halfway up the slope Tony stopped.

"I am out of breath," she said. "There is something wrong with me and I cannot carry this musket."

I took it from her and we started the climb again. As soon as we reached the edge of the forest I called out breathlessly to one of the young officers acting as sentinel. He heard me and conducted us to the house. Our entrance into the hall converted the confusion there into chaos. Most of the women, children and servants were lying asleep in higgledy-piggledy fashion all over the floor, on the table and even under the table. The one or two women who were awake shrieked when they saw Tony's condition for not only was she muddy from head to foot, her right arm was hanging awkwardly from a shoulder that could only be dislocated. (No wonder she had not been able to pick up the musket or climb the hill without losing her breath!) The shrieks wakened the other sleepers and further shrieks followed. Some were directed at me, for I still had the muddy musket in one hand and the sergeant's pistol in the other.

To give Maman her due, she did not shriek when she saw Tony but simply took her round the waist and conducted her to the kitchen, where Matti would be able to put the shoulder to rights. As soon as they had left, the officers' wives, in all stages of *déshabillé* and disarray, crowded around me and plied me with questions about their husbands' whereabouts. I was answering as best I could when Father arrived and ordered the women to be quiet and to silence their children so that he could hear my story.

There were exclamations of horror at my news about the fire, which had only been visible from Craigellachie as a glow in the sky; sighs of disappointment when I revealed that we had not been able to reach Government House or the barracks; and deeper sighs of relief when I explained that the mutineers around the house had been disarmed. This last intelligence was confirmed when one of the sous-lieutenants entered, approached Father, saluted, and on being given permission to speak informed him that a party of Negroes was bringing in many French weapons and much powder and shot. Father left to supervize the storing of the weaponry while I remained to accept the florid French compliments of the women upon my bravery, still holding the musket. I was not insensible to the pleasure of receiving these unaccustomed plaudits, but I was not to enjoy them for long, for Betsy now appeared at the door of my chamber carrying the two listless babes. Her eyes found mine and their expression, which the night before had seemed to be compounded of tenderness and fear, now proved to be one of profound sadness mingled with reproach.

"These two not last this day," she said to me quietly and, strange to say, I could hear her voice clearly above the jabber of the other women. "They wasting and too weak to eat." Her eyes left mine and swept the crowd until they found Mme. d'Aumont; then she walked forward to her mistress.

"Me taking these to me mother," I heard her say. "She maybe know wet-nurse or remedy. She only hope. Janga looking after the others."

Mme. d'Aumont sank to her knees and covered her face with her hands as Betsy walked majestically through the mob of chattering women, whimpering children and sullen servants as though they did not exist; and they, seeing the grey faces of the twin babes, made way for her with something approaching awe, as though they could actually see the dread Angel hovering over the twins, his purpose all too plain. I watched Betsy's

174

kerchief disappear as she descended the galerie steps and then, by craning
my neck, I caught a glimpse of her crossing the yard.

Neither my distracted air nor the sad state of the twins discouraged the
wives from resuming their questioning of me about the whereabouts of their
husbands, hoping to elicit some crumb of news; nor did the older female
children desist from regarding me with the adulatory, nay worshipping,
stares due to the hero of the hour. I was not trying to extricate myself
from these irritations with any energy, for I had not energy left, when I
saw Tony regarding me from the doorway. Her person had been cleaned
of mud and she was wearing a *peignoir* and there was rankest hatred in her
eyes. Her shoulder had been "put back", for she was standing straight, but
she was obviously still in pain. Her daemon must have prompted her at that
moment for she suddenly strode towards me and stopped before me; then
she relieved me of the musket with her left hand.

"This brother of mine is no hero!" she shouted, while the wives and
daughters started back and left the two of us in the centre of a circle. "It was
I who persuaded the Niggers to give up the weapons and it was I who saved
Dickie's life by firing this musket at the sergeant who was about to shoot him
with a pistol!" She shook the musket in my face and with her right hand she
tore the *peignoir* off her shoulder and bosom and displayed the horrid bruise
made by the weapon's recoil. "Look, all of you, at the real hero's wounds!"
Her voice grew even louder. "If I had had my way we would have found your
husbands instead of coming back here with our tails between our legs!"

Tony dropped the musket and proceeded to beat me with her fists and
to scream obscenities in a voice so penetrating that it must have reached
the Negro-houses and the French soldiers awakening from their sodden
slumbers; it certainly reached Henri, who was not easily awakened of a
morning, for he began to whine and whimper and then to shout "Ah,
quiet-quiet-quiet-quiet — " As I defended myself from Tony's assault as
best I could I was hoping that my poor brother would not emerge from my
chamber and be hurt in the fray; he did not, so Janga must have been doing
her duty and restraining him. Her other charges, Mme. d'Aumont's four
little daughters, appeared crying for Betsy and had to be satisfied with their
mother.

One or two of the bolder Frenchwomen attempted to tackle Tony and
protect me and were successful in so far as she abandoned the attack, stood
with her head raised and commenced a deep rhythmical baying that froze my
blood and made everyone present take a step back and gaze at her as though
wondering if she had lost her senses altogether. It was Matti — who else? —
who calmed her; she arrived unhurriedly and in no time had restored Tony's
clothing to decency and was kneading her neck gently while propelling her

toward her own chamber, where she quietened in a few seconds. I think it probable that Tony fell asleep almost instantly, for that was her wont after an outburst of temper.

At this point Father returned and took charge again. He looked at me and decreed that I must stand down and sleep, for I was no use to him in the condition in which he saw me. I begged him to allow me to withdraw to the *belvédère*, where there would be peace. Father concurred, as I would be guarded by one of the overseers who was still posted there as a lookout. On my way to that haven of peace I called at the kitchen, ostensibly to find out what breakfast was available, but in truth because I was hoping that Betsy would be there. However, one of the other servants told me that she had gone to look for a wet-nurse in the Negro-houses as the twins were still refusing food of any kind. That my black sister should set out on such an errand of mercy when no one was sure what was happening was a measure of her quality. For all I knew, the Negro women had left their houses and were hiding in the bush. My heart told me that I should follow Betsy, with my pistol at the ready, but my head knew that she was safer without my white face in the uncertain state of everyone's emotions.

As I left the kitchen carrying a breakfast of bread and avocado-pear, which Matti had insisted that I take with me, along with a pitcher of hot chocolate, I glanced into a makeshift cradle in which Betsy had left the dark-eyed twins. Their skulls were already showing through the parchment of their skins; their tiny skeletal hands were in motion, but so weakly there could be no doubt about their approaching end. There was nothing I could do to help them, so I went to the *belvédère* and slept undisturbed until well after sundown.

When I awoke and returned to the house I found that our little world had returned to its normal state in an extraordinary number of ways. The disarmed mutineers had been rounded up by Father with the help of the young officers, who had been put on their mettle by his searing tongue; the Negroes had been put to work on repairing their houses and gardens; and a party of French officers, having escaped from their confinement in Fort de Castrie, had rallied a few loyal soldiers, found some horses and ridden to the rescue of their wives and children. Thus our guests had been taken back to Fort de Castrie, as they would be more easily defended there than at Craigellachie, and more easily evacuated by ship. Small parties of staunchly Republican troops who had held on to their weapons and who had no intention of surrendering were at large in the forests in the north of the Island, but no one knew their intentions. It was surmised that they would be forced to leave the forests in search of food but that might not be for some time. There had been hopes of reinforcements from Martinique or Guadeloupe, but it was feared that there might have been mutinies in those Islands also. I learned most of this intelligence from Father; rarely had I seen him so disturbed.

It was not until I encountered Tony, who had slept off her tantrum but not her ill-will, that I heard the particulars of Betsy's departure. Would I had learned them from someone else!

"Your precious Mistress Betsy has no sooner come than gone, Master Dickie," she said malevolently, "and I must tell you that M. le Capitaine d'Aumont was much more concerned about her safety than he was about that of his lady-wife and his children, even those twins, the elder of which is his son and heir. Oh, he pretended very well, very well indeed. It was: 'Madame, I am thankful to le Bon Dieu that you are safe and well,' and 'Have no fear, I pray you, Madame, you and the children will be safe in Fort de Castrie,' but I could see that everything he said was addressed to Betsy; he could not keep his eyes off her. She plays up to him too, of course, with those big round eyes of hers and that figure she has now; and she makes a fuss of those twins as if they were her own. Mind you, his Madame is one of the stupidest of women and I would sooner have Betsy myself, the little tease!" — Tony brushed a tear from her eye — "Oh, he is her slave, just as you are! Oh, how her stratagems used to make me laugh!" Tony laughed immoderately at my lengthening face, the tears still wet on her cheeks.

What happened after this speech of Tony's I cannot recall, no matter how much time I spend searching through the dusty account-books of my memory, but I shall not fill the hiatus in my narrative by inventing a nancy-story; no, I shall instead bring this chapter to a close as quickly as I can.

The confusion which followed the mutiny continued for many weeks; all Tobago was at sixes and sevens, as the officers attempted to regain control over the mutineers and to make the roads safe from marauders, and life at Craigellachie and Braemore was overshadowed, especially at night, by the fear of attack at any time and from any direction. I had to take my turn at standing guard and during the long dark hours I had time to wonder that any man could be so disturbed in his emotions. I was in turn melancholy enough to think of shooting myself with my own pistol, angry enough to hope that M. le Capitaine d'Aumont would be posted away from Tobago for good and would take the deceitful Betsy with him, and lonely enough to determine that I must contrive a meeting with her, come what may. However, I could not even find a way of conveying a note to her, so unsafe and uncertain was the state of the Island. The only news I had, and that through the unreliable Tony, was that the d'Aumont twins had died in her arms. I found it in my heart to envy them.

These many weeks of man-made confusion in Tobago (and inside my head) were as naught to the far greater confusion which Dame Nature, in one of her fits of heartless rage, inflicted upon us in a few hours, and which I shall describe in my next chapter.

CHAPTER XIV

Dame Nature does her worst and Father makes a momentous Decision; I meet a Friend again but in frustrating Circumstances

Lo! I dreamed that I was fast asleep and that I was dreaming, not of some far and secret place as I would have wished, but of Henri howling: "Ah, hoo-hoo-hoo-hoo-hoo," and picking at my eyelids with clumsy fingers. "Dickie-Dickie-Dickie!" he went on, "hoo-hoo-hoo-hoo!" and would not stop. The dogs under the house seemed to be answering him howl for howl.

I knew that I was asleep and dreaming because the strangeness of all that was happening was dreamlike. Here was Henri, never easily aroused from his slumbers, wide awake in the middle of the night and making the strangest noise I had ever heard him make; the two of us were occupying my chamber in the house and were not where we should have been, in separate chambers in the *bélvèdere*; the dogs were howling in a weird manner, like dogs in a nightmare — not as if they had heard an intruder, but as though they were in mortal dread of some canine incubus; there was not a ray of moonlight, although it was the time of the full moon; and the very air was the air of choking dreams, heavy and hard to inhale and suffocating. In this my dream I too was in mortal dread, dread of the onset of true nightmare — could I forestall it by an act of my Will? Ah, but in dreams we have no Will, we are driven by some relentless Force which we cannot control.

"Ah, hoo-hoo-hoo-hoo-hoo!" Henry continued to howl, still picking at my eyelids and now spraying spittle into my face. The incontrovertible wetness of this convinced me at last that I was awake and that Henri and I were not in the *belvédère* but abed in my chamber in the house because of the danger from the marauding mutineers who were still at large. I was not on guard-duty as it was the turn of Malcolm's son, Alexander, a trustworthy

Mulatto overseer. The dogs were certainly howling eerily, but they might well have been doing so in reply to Henri's strange cries. Perhaps Henri had been awakened by the stiff breeze which was making an uncommonly loud rustling in the cocoa-nut palms; it was even disturbing the tiles on the roof to the point where they were making a rattling noise and, though gusty, it had no element of freshness in it — rather it seemed as though it were composed of the vapours from a cauldron of boiling sea-water.

"Hoo-hoo-hoo-hoo-hoo!" went on Henri and the dogs continued to answer him even more mournfully, if that were possible, bringing sighs and groans and muttered complaints from the other sleepers in the house. Father's voice came clearly and testily.

"Alec! Are you awake?"

"Yes, Master!" came the alert reply.

"Anyone about?"

"No, Master!"

"In that case, Richard," shouted Father, "can you not be keeping that fellow quiet? He is disturbing the dogs."

Obediently, I attempted to persuade Henri to be quiet and to return to his bed, but he was most obdurate in his resistance, continuing to trumpet "hoo-hoo-hoo-hoo-hoo!" as though trying to tell me something of great import, pointing at the roof where the tiles could be heard beating an irregular tattoo, and to the floor, under which the dogs were refusing to be quieted by Alexander.

A few distant flashes of lightning filtered through the chinks in the house and Henri clung to me, wailing "Bessy-Bessy-Bessy!" as the more devout might wail "Mother of God!" When the rumble of distant thunder followed he was silenced, overcome with awe, or so I surmised, at a noise which he could not attempt to imitate. I persuaded him to sit on the floor with his arms around me for comfort while we hearkened to the sound of the wind in the palms and the thunder approaching nearer and nearer.

Suddenly there was a shouting in the yard and a beating upon the door. Then came the voice of Gilbert in great alarm.

"Massieu! Massieu!" he cried and when Father did not answer immediately, added at the top of his not inconsiderable voice "Houragan! Houragan!"

All at once there was a flash of lightning far surpassing in brilliance all that had gone before, followed by a clap of thunder so close-by that it seemed to shake the house.

"Secure the jalousies!" shouted Father. "Dress yourselves, everyone! There is no time to be lost if this is truly a hurricano."

"A hurricano! How exciting! Hurrah!" cried Tony, awakening from

180

deep sleep to full consciousness in a second or two, as she always did. "How glorious! This is the best thing to happen since the fire!"

The thunder was followed by rain of a kind which I had never experienced before — it was not the vertical downpour of the beneficent showers which kept our crops growing and the forest green, but a horizontal lashing of drops so huge and being driven so fast before the wind that they beat into the house through every chink which had been revealed by the lightning and reached everywhere, even wetting Henri and myself in our night attire.

As I hustled Henri into his clothes and tried to ignore the fact that he was calling upon Betsy's name in the most fervent manner, I could not help recalling all the stories I had heard about West Indian hurricanoes; of ships dismasted and driven upon the strand; of crops and forests laid waste; and of buildings and their contents reduced to matchwood. We in Tobago had convinced ourselves that we were too far to the south to be afflicted by these disastrous storms, hence our failure to recognize the approach of one. Only Henri and the dogs, untrammelled by the deceptions of Reason, had apprehended the approach of danger.

The Craigellachie house had been framed in America; it was set upon pillars of imported brick and was probably the soundest estate house in the Island, yet as the wind roared, and increased in strength, and strengthened yet again, the floor began to heave under our feet and I began to doubt whether the wooden frame was fixed to those pillars in a truly robust manner.

"This is what the deck of a ship must be like!" shouted Tony, "Ship ahoy! I can scarce keep my feet! Ahoy there!"

"Antonia!" shouted Father, "we must be leaving the house. Come to my chamber now! Richard, come too!"

Our answers, if indeed we made any, were drowned by a strange and terrible noise from the roof as hundreds of tiles were torn away. I induced Henri to follow me on all fours and together we crossed the salon to Father's door. The rain was now pouring unhindered through the roof and our fine French and Scottish furniture was receiving the same soaking as we were. Once inside Father's chamber we crawled toward the others, who were crouched by the window. There was not a servant or watchman to be seen.

"This is the lee side of the house," shouted Father against the din, "and when I open the jalousie I want you to climb on to the sill, drop to the ground and take shelter under the house. You will be blown away if you do not stay under the house."

He stood up and opened the jalousie, but before he could give a signal Tony leapt on to the sill. She barely hesitated.

"Shelter or no shelter," she cried, "I am off to the stables. The horses may be needing me."

"Antonia!" protested Father, but he was too late, for with a wild shriek of "Man overboard!" she dropped to the ground and vanished into the dark. A flash of lightning shewed us some object being tumbled over and over down the slope toward the stables — it might have been Tony, but it might not have been. (We did not see Tony again while the hurricano lasted and I never learned, because I did not inquire, how she spent the time. No doubt she had a hand in saving the horses, which always meant more to her than did humankind.)

With some difficulty Father and I helped Maman and Henri to the ground; in the process the rain as thoroughly penetrated our clothes as if we had fallen into the sea. We clung together under the house but it was soon evident that this was no safe place, for the wind was lifting the house up and down upon its pillars, which seemed about to crumble. I set my mind to thinking of a place which would offer shelter and safety — the thought and the word came at the same instant.

"The tackle-store!" I shouted into Father's ear, and he took my suggestion without a quibble. The tackle-store was half-way between the house and the stables and was set into a steep slope; its door and roof were made of heavy timbers firmly carpentered.

Father eventually bullied Maman into understanding that we must all hold each other tightly and crawl upon our hands and knees down the slippery muddy slope which led to the store. Our way was lit by incessant lightning-flashes; our lives were constantly in danger from flying tiles and large pieces of timber; and the rain seemed intent upon drowning us.

We were not the only ones to have thought of the store as a refuge, for when Father opened the door a lightning-flash revealed all the house-servants and several hangers-on standing huddled together in the darkness. There was not room for any of them to sit. We pushed our way inside and Father managed to close the door.

There was no possibility of talk in the roaring of the inexorably increasing wind; and no escape from the rain beating on our heads through the gap betwixt wall and roof, or from the water flooding down the hillside and forming a river of liquid mud ankle-deep across the floor. Even Father could not find a seat for Maman and had to be content with supporting her against the door. Along with Janga, whom I discovered to be my immediate neighbour, I had to support Henri, a task which became more and more onerous as first one hour and then a second and a third passed in ever-louder noise and ever more exquisite misery. "Necessity is the Mother of Invention" and rather than have him slump to the floor and sit in the muddy stream I made a kind of swing from a saddle and some harness and suspended it from one of the roof timbers. With Janga's help I hoisted Henri's limp form into the contraption. It proved so successful that Father insisted upon fitting Maman into it also. Thus mother and son spent more hours in a close embrace than they had ever done.

Relieved of Henri's weight, and with nothing to do but keep myself upright, count the lightning flashes, and wait for the storm to end, my mind could not but turn to my friend and sister Betsy. Where was she? Was she perhaps pinned under some fallen beam in the officers' quarters, perhaps even dead? If she survived, and I did too, would we ever meet again? Was she truly Captain d'Aumont's mistress and as devoted to him as she was to his twins? What if she had transferred all her capacity for faithfulness to him? My anger with her grew and grew as the storm reached its climax and began to abate; I convinced myself that the gallant Captain was more deserving of her than I was.

Thus did the night of the hurricano pass in deafening noise and acute discomfort and melancholy thoughts; we heard not the catastrophic events which happened near by and which must have made huge rending and tearing and crashing noises; we became colder and colder and colder and had no means of warming ourselves except to huddle closer to each other; our legs grew more and more tired and ached abominably; only Janga, singing her doleful Psalms and Paraphrases, seemed to maintain a contrarious cheerfulness. By the end of the night, as the howling of the wind subsided, most of the Negroes and even Father were joining in her heretical chanting. I think she took the opportunity to steal my watch, for I am certain that I had it with me, yet I saw it not again after that night.

A little after sunrise the wind and rain stopped as suddenly as they had started and Father risked opening the door. The sights which met our eyes were so dismal that I can bring myself to give only a summary of them. Every piece of vegetation in sight, including huge trees, precious cane, and essential provision-gardens, appeared to have been torn to shreds; Negro-houses and sugar-works and stables had been flattened; not an animal was to be seen; and Craigellachie House had been lifted bodily off its pillars and was lying at a crazy angle at least twenty feet away from them, roofless and uninhabitable.

When we had all left the store and had withdrawn our eyes from the destruction around us, we had perforce to look at each other and the sights we saw then were no less dismal, for we white people were muddy, dishevelled and ghastly pale; the servants were in worse shape, if that be possible, for their faces were of that indescribable shade of greeny-grey which so contrasts with the shining black of the Negro's complexion when in health; and our only Mulatto, Alexander, was of a hue which can only be described as corpse-like.

"Madame, we will all be needing breakfast," said Father, as brusquely as though Maman were an aide-de-camp, "could you be seeing that we get it? Gilbert, go and find Miss Tony or news of her at the least. Alexander, check on every single one of the Negroes and report to me at the *belvédère*; Richard, come with me — we shall be able to assess the damage from there."

The sun was now shining out of a clear blue sky and I knew that it would shortly be high enough to afflict me. Since our route to the *belvédère* passed close to the ruins of the house I represented to Father that prudence dictated that I should find our strong-box with our store of cash, and also my ledgers. He agreed somewhat impatiently and stood gazing around at the catastrophically altered surroundings while I clambered into the sloping ruin which had been my office and searched amongst the wreckage which had slid to the lower end of the room. The strong-box and the press in which I kept the ledgers were intact, but so jammed in that I could not move the one or open the other. Before shouting out this news to Father I made my way to my chamber and amongst the ruins of my clothes-press and other furniture I found my umbrella miraculously undamaged. As I emerged from the house and opened it I saw Maman, Matti and the servants moving around the kitchen and stores, what was left of them, in a dazed manner.

The first half of the path to the *belvédère* was so obstructed by tree-branches and other debris that it took Father and myself at least ten minutes to negotiate it. The top of the knoll, on the other hand, was completely bald; it looked as though there never had been a building there, so thoroughly had the wind and the rain gone about their business. I could not even discern where the foundations had been, and all the timbers had vanished amongst the uprooted trees and tangled branches of the nearby forest. Birds of all sizes, their nests destroyed, were flying about distractedly. I was filled with a strange empty longing when I remembered the many happy hours which Betsy, Henri and I had spent in the vanished building and my fears about my friend revived. Why could I not find Jéhu and instruct him to seek out Betsy and bring me word, just as Father had sent Gilbert to find Tony?

These thoughts of Betsy were interrupted by the urgent necessities of the moment, as they had been so often during the raging of the hurricano, for Father was speaking to me and propounding a scheme so impulsive and indeed so madcap that I was constrained to attend to him as closely as I could.

"I have been thinking for some time," he was saying, "that I have had enough of French Government and of French lack of government. I have not yet, after all these years, been receiving the pension due to me as a former officer in His Majesty's service; it will be impossible to grow sugar, or indeed any other crop, in a French colony if the troops are to mutiny whenever they are dissatisfied with this or that; and now there is this hurricano!" Father spoke as though the storm were due entirely to French indiscipline. "How long will it take to restore all this to proper order?" He swept his hand around his ruined estates. "In a year's time we might have cleared enough of the pieces to produce perhaps a quarter of what we produced last year, but we will have to buy in all our provisions; in two years we might be able to feed everyone and produce half of what we do now; in three years — "

I am not so stupid that I did not discern the direction of Father's thoughts. We looked at each other in silence, and for the life of me I thought that we were like two duellists eyeing each other before setting to. Father, as was his due, made the first thrust.

"Richard," he said, "this devastation need not be cleared up at all, and I will give you the reasons why: firstly, there is free land to be had for the asking in la Trinité; secondly, it is better land than this; thirdly, the Spanish Government will not allow revolutionary and Republican intrigues and conspiracies and mutinies; fourthly, all the French who are being given land there, and I am hearing that there are to be four hundred families, are of the same kidney as I; fifthly, Governor Chacon has promised that newcomers will not be taxed for ten years; and lastly, Richard, I shall eat my hat if this hurricano reached la Trinité — no, *never* has a hurricano been known there!"

This was to be no duel with *epées* — Father had struck me with a bludgeon. He waited for my reply, but I could think of nothing to say.

"Well then, Richard," he declared, "I have decided! Just as soon as everyone has some sort of shelter I shall take Fergus to la Trinité and we shall discover what land is available and upon what terms and conditions."

"Father! Sir!" I commenced, but the bludgeon descended again.

"Make no objections on the ground of cost!" interrupted Father. "I am telling you now that it is your responsibility to be finding the money for the move — we shall be needing to charter a ship or a brace of schooners, and to feed the Negroes while we clear the land, and so on — I leave the particular details to you."

I saw with a sinking heart that this was not a scheme about which Father would be willing to change his mind. I marvelled at the resilience of his temperament — whilst the rest of us at Craigellachie had been numbly enduring the hurricano and were now scarcely in a condition to contemplate its aftermath, he had already reviewed his prospects and made up his mind what he was going to do. Even the extraordinary rashness of his character had an admirable quality and I could not oppose his will. Nevertheless I would dearly have liked to do just that for, as my readers know only too well, I was a stick-in-the-mud by nature and the very thought of being uprooted, conveyed across the unpredictable sea, and set down willy-nilly upon a strange Island, was abhorrent to me. Moreover, my heart, or rather a hidden, confused and conspiratorial portion of it, was telling me that if I wanted to renew my friendship with the provoking Betsy, I would have to remain in Tobago.

Oh that heart of mine and its inconvenient promptings! The memory of my friendship with Betsy was now almost a sickness, of the kind which has to be concealed from the world like a sore on the body, for how could I, Richard Mason, heir to a fortune and perhaps to a Chieftaincy, and an up-and-coming man of affairs in his own right, be a friend to a barefoot black nursemaid? Surely I was telling myself a nancy-story when I dwelt upon those memories of her extraordinary attributes as a child and as a young woman? I might as well have been infatuated with squat Janga and her *crapaud*-like eyes, great jutting teeth and lumpy figure.

Yes, after I had found a pretext to send Jéhu to discover whether Betsy had survived the hurricano I tried hard to put her out of my mind and to attend only to the tasks which had been set me by Father (and to my own ventures, of course — after the two disasters Tobagonians were willing to pay almost any price for my American nails and other ironmongery). My readers must be wondering if my heart had not taken on the likeness of my merchandise, and it may be that it had, for when Jéhu reported that Betsy had indeed survived the storm, but had been sold to a Captain Laurent, a fellow-officer of Captain d'Aumont, I experienced only a brief pang for the four little moppets who had thus lost a favourite nurse. Betsy, added Jéhu with his customary guarded expression of countenance, was now lady's maid to her new owner's childless wife, the lady having insisted that he pay an inflated price for the creature's veritably Parisian skill in millinery. I did not trouble to inquire of Jéhu whether his sister was happy with her new owners and in her new employment.

I shall not burden my readers with the details of how we extricated ourselves from the ruins of Craigellachie and Braemore. It will surely be enough for me to write that we spent many uncomfortable days and nights in makeshift shelters and that for once our Negroes were no worse off than we were. Father duly visited la Trinidad — I shall use its Spanish name from now on in order not to confuse my readers, but when speaking French or patois we naturally continued to refer to it as la Trinité. He returned in a very short time to announce that the Governor, Don José

Maria Chacon, had received him with great kindness and had granted him thirty-two acres for himself and for each member of his family and half of that for every working Negro he could bring with him. (We thus learned how anxious were the Spanish Government to populate empty la Trinidad with Catholic planters; captured by Protestants, whether British or Dutch, the Island would have become an heretical and commercial pistol pointed at the heart of the Spanish American empire.) According to Father, the land he had been granted was of the most fertile he had ever seen and he had met like-minded friends from his days in Paris and St. Domingue who had also been granted land, so that there would be no lack of company.

Both Maman and Tony were delighted at the prospect of the move, Maman in the hope of meeting old friends amongst the French Créoles and Tony because she had heard that horse-races and other outdoor events were more frequent, better attended and better ordered than in Tobago.

A few days before we were due to leave, as I was standing under my umbrella attempting to bring some order to the confusion of carts and mules and Negroes and baggage being got ready for the journey to the quay at Port Louis, I was astonished to see Betsy walking calmly towards the erection of palm-leaves which was serving us as a kitchen. The neatness of her person was a rebuke to the disorder through which she was picking her way. I raised my umbrella high and signalled to her by waving my hand but she chose not to see me and disappeared under the thatch, evidently to visit her mother.

I became agitated at her insolence in not answering my signals and found it hard to attend to the task on which I was engaged — for the life of me I cannot remember what it was. When after an hour or more Betsy left the kitchen and walked away as if intending to return to Port Louis forthwith I furled my umbrella and followed her with the intention of reproving her angrily, but contrariwise I made sure that she would not see me. After walking a few hundred yards along the newly cleared road through the devastated cane she turned aside, climbed down into a little gully and disappeared behind a tangled mass of vegetation. Approaching cautiously, I could hear her speaking to someone. Concealing my height and girth with my usual care, I managed to view her and her companions, who were Gilbert and Jéhu. Their three heads were close together and they were talking so conspiratorially that I could not make out one word. I must have waited for half an hour before I saw that they were about to end their confabulation; I therefore prepared to withdraw silently. Before I did so the three of them indulged in displays of familial affection, Betsy tearfully and the two men solemnly. Then Jéhu audibly uttered the words "St. Domingue!" as though they were a war-cry, or at least a pass-word, and I had to withdraw and find a new hiding-place.

Betsy passed close to me and I thought to follow her, but she set off down the road to Port Louis at a pace which was much too smart for me, and in any case I discovered that her tears had dissipated my anger and that I had no words to speak to her. I therefore unfurled my umbrella and returned to my so-easily-forgotten task and put her out of my mind.

By a strange coincidence I have now reached the last page of this ledger in which I write, and will have to purchase a new one if I am to continue to recount my Life and Times after our removal to the Island of la Trinidad, where I still reside. I wish that I could draw a line across the bottom of this page, reckon up the income and expenditure represented by my life before I left Tobago, strike a balance and be certain whether I had made a profit or no, but Life does not seem to be susceptible to such an accounting and I can only write that as I helped Henri to climb from the lighter on to the deck of the chartered schooner and silently dared the sailors to laugh at him, I carried with me a purse full of gold louis, a waterproof oilskin wallet containing a fair wad of bills of exchange, and a heart which knew not whether it was empty or no.

CHAPTER XV

The Family's Move to la Trinidad is accomplished, although not without Loss of Property; We find ourselves again amongst Strangers, who are divided amongst themselves; I am befriended by a high Official

From Braemore estate house, although not from Craigellachie, the jagged outline of the mountains of la Trinidad were often visible to the south-west and, as I now recall, Betsy and I used to refer to them in our fanciful childish manner as "the Edge of the World". Unlike the mythical land of "Ogabot", which was a friendly place, the mountains of la Trinidad were hostile territory. We terrified each other with tales of the void which lay beyond them, the vast abyss from which no traveller returned. We imagined also that there were strange animals and fabulous beings unknown to science roaming the summits and the deep secret valleys. Betsy was of course the first to disclaim her terror and to insist that all these creatures were our friends, even the monstrous Papa Bois and the sinister Mama Glo, and I would agree with her for our friendship's sake, but afterwards, alone in my chamber, my heart told me that I would be afraid to go anywhere near the mountains except in company with armed and courageous friends lest Betsy's friendly creatures were truly otherwise and anxious only to seize me and carry me to the very tip-top of the mountains and throw me over into the nothingness beyond.

Later we learned from some informant, probably Maman, that la Trinidad was a decayed outpost of the Spanish American empire, empty of human habitation except for a few degenerate Spaniards and some even more degenerate Arawaks. Since our informant did not elaborate, the Island became as intimidating to me as when I had peopled it with monsters, for Betsy had not yet purloined Doctor Johnson's *Dictionary* and we knew not

189

the meaning of "degenerate"; Betsy inclined to the view that it meant that the Spaniards and Arawaks were very poor and had not much to eat, but I was convinced that it meant that their hair had grown down to their ankles and that their nails had become sharp claws.

Later still, my fear of the strange Island was intensified when I learned that a ship, aiming to reach the kindly and habitable lowland parts of la Trinidad had to pass through either "The Serpent's Mouth" (la Boca del Sierpe) or through one of the four "Mouths of the Dragon" (las Bocas del Dragon). What ghastly visions these names evoked, especially when they were spoken in the strange manner which passed for Spanish pronunciation in our family! I have recounted these fears of mine because, although I had grown to manhood and put them behind me, they yet seemed to colour my thoughts as I contemplated the voyage to the Island on which we planned to settle.

Moving ourselves, our overseers and their families, our horses, and all our Negroes was achieved by chartering two Dutch schooners at a price which, because of Father's impatience, was exorbitant. As Father had gone ahead himself with two overseers to make the necessary preparations I was in charge of the whole expedition, although Tony, who was sailing in the larger vessel with the horses, announced that once at sea she would have an independent command and would give her own instructions to her captain.

On the morning of our departure from Port Louis the skies were overcast and the mountains of la Trinidad were invisible behind a dull haze. The two ruddy-cheeked captains assured me that the wind was favourable and that we would be through one of the Dragon's Mouths and safe in Puerto d'Espana before nightfall. I understood from the exaggerated nature of their bluff and hearty manner that sailing through the chosen Boca was an undertaking fraught with danger, and that their assurances were to be regarded as formal rather than sincere.

As the Negroes were herded by the overseers from the lighters on to the schooners I checked every man, woman and child against my "muster-roll". Many of the Africans shewed signs of acute apprehension, as though their memories of the Middle Passage had been revived and they feared that they were to be chained together below decks for a long voyage. However, those of the Braemore Créoles who were old enough to remember the voyage from St. Domingue to Tobago managed to calm these fears, and since every family had been given food for the day and some were carrying their own supplies in addition, it was not long before the decks and open holds of the schooners were crowded with merry picnics. I wondered how long the merriment would last after we had weighed anchor and reached the open sea.

As I sate upon the after part of the deck holding Henri with my left arm and Maman with my right, and with Matti, Janga, Milly and Sara in attendance, I was able to survey the ruins of Port Louis from an unfamiliar viewpoint. The various attempts to rebuild the town after the fire had been swept away by the hurricano; on the surrounding estates not a windmill retained its sails; and only in sheltered ravines was any vegetation still standing. Yet hopes of wresting a fortune from the soil of Tobago were still alive, for I could see gangs of Negroes, men and women, and even small boys and girls, wielding their cutlasses amongst the tangled greenery, and I knew from the alacrity of their distant ant-like movements that their armed overseers were not far away. For a moment or two I wondered where the inconstant creature Betsy was — perhaps she was looking down upon our departure from her Master's makeshift quarters amongst the roofless buildings up there on Fort de Castrie; perhaps that solitary figure of a Negress standing on the rocks by the quay and waving a white kerchief was Betsy herself signalling farewell to her family. My thoughts on this topic were quickly diverted by the bustle and confusion occasioned by the raising of the anchor.

No sooner had we cleared the shelter of Bacolet Point than our schooner gave a prodigious heave and a sheet of salt spray splashed upon the deck, causing consternation amongst the less-experienced Negroes—they shouted and wailed and screamed, while those in the hold had to be dissuaded by the sailors from clambering on deck. Henri clasped me round the waist with both arms and cried "Bessy-Bessy-Bessy!" as was his wont when distressed, and Maman sank to her knees and commenced an "ave Maria", or rather a whole rosary of them. From the other schooner came faint shouts of "hooray!" for it too had set sail and was dipping its prow into the waves. Standing on its rail, holding on to the rigging with one hand and waving madly with the other, was Tony in a state of high excitement; even as I watched she leapt from the rail on to the deck and dropped into the hold — she must have heard her precious horses neighing their discomfort.

The heaving of the ship continued and since it did not instantly founder, and the sailors were laughing unconcernedly, the Negroes stopped their noise, except for some of the young females upon the open deck who continued to scream, but with delight now, as they lined the rail to ensure that the spray would most thoroughly drench their bosoms, which were, of course, unshrouded from the gaze of man. When the two ships had cleared the dangerous rocks which extend far out into the sea off Port Louis they were able to turn downwind and head toward la Trinidad, which was still invisible in the haze. The motion of the ship thereupon became much steadier and the Negroes set up a cheerful singing, accompanied by much clapping of hands and beating upon the deck with whatever implement was to hand. Henri was greatly taken with the music and demanded "walk-walk-walk!", so I paraded him round the deck while he joined in the singing. He did not seem to suffer the slightest qualm of the *mal-de-mer* which was afflicting Maman and one or two of the Negroes; in fact Henri, against all my expectations, found this part of the voyage most enjoyable.

The schooners were sailing along thus peacefully, and I was congratulating myself on my success in leading the expedition and in controlling my own perturbation, when there appeared ahead of us through the haze the mountains of la Trinidad; seen close-to they were enormously high to one reared amongst Tobago's windmill-dotted hills. Their tops vanished among the clouds and they were even more forbidding than they had been in my youthful fancy. They were fringed at their foot by something which I had not imagined, an unbroken line of horrid rocks against which white waves were dashing themselves savagely and unceasingly. The Mulatto mate of the schooner further disturbed my already uneasy mind by strolling up to me and coolly offering the news that there was no safe anchorage on this whole north coast and that we would be entirely dependent upon an old Mandingo Negro pilot to guide us through whichever of the Bocas he judged to be the safest, but even he had not been successful in preventing several ships from running on the rocks and being broken to pieces. It was little comfort when the Mulatto added that once through the Boca and into the Golfo de Paria we would be anchoring in the safest harbour in the whole of the Caribbean Sea.

At midday Janga brought cold viands but Maman and I had no stomach for them, although Henri ate heartily enough and we all three drank down cups of tepid coffee. With the mountains approaching nearer and nearer I conceived the notion that using the telescope might calm my fears, so I removed it from its case, opened it and put it to my eye but succeeded only in making myself more apprehensive, for the instrument magnified the dreadful nature of the scenes upon which I trained it—the mountains seemed higher, steeper and more desolate, the rocks at their foot more fanged, and the waves of the sea more ravenous; but worst of all, I saw amongst the heaving waters two men in a tiny pirogue disappearing beneath each wave and then re-appearing on the crest of the next as though their lives were charmed — what could induce men in their right minds to sail upon such a sea in such a craft? I shut the telescope and returned it to its case, abandoning myself to paroxysms of terror so intense that I could neither hear nor see anything. It was fortunate that everyone else on board was so taken up with their own affairs that not one of them noticed my condition.

When I awakened from this surrender to Unreason I found that the schooner was still sailing westward along the frightful coast but that the mountains were now no higher than the hills of Tobago. The captain appeared to be edging the ship closer and closer to the rocks and to the savagely spouting breakers; the other schooner was nearby and on the same course. After a while, however, it became clear that we were about to enter a deep bay. The waves became irregular and the ship's motion correspondingly abrupt and uncertain. Across the surface of the sea I saw a long snaking line of foam, the water on one side a different hue of green to that on the other, as though two seas were boiling together yet could not mix. White sea-birds flew about distractedly while the sailors scanned the sea intently, as though afraid to miss seeing something vital to their safety.

It was then that I saw, at the bottom of the cliffs which formed the coast, the black mouths of vast caverns into which the sea seemed to be disappearing wave by wave. Were these the phenomena known as the Dragon's Mouths? For a moment my disordered fancy saw our two ships sailing into them under the guidance of a grinning Mandingo, as insolent as Cumberland but far more evil. These thoughts were interrupted by a cry from one of the sailors. "Pilot!" he shouted and straightway we were hustled by the boatswain from the deck and into the captain's foetid cabin, although not before I had noticed that the "deep bay" which we had entered was in fact a long narrow channel between two steep wooded banks. I wondered if anyone on the other schooner had had the temerity to hustle Tony below decks and in what manner she had responded.

It was in close confinement, then, that Maman, Henri and I were conveyed through the most easterly of the Bocas del Dragon which is known as the Boca de Monos, or Monkey's Mouth. It was as well that I had not eaten of Janga's cold viands for I had to spend the whole passage of the Boca in holding Henri's head and trying to comfort Maman, for both suffered acutely from *mal-de-mer* in that stifling cabin. I tried to draw the attention of the captain to our plight, for I was sure that my poor brother would have been perfectly well and happy upon the open deck, but that seaman was intent on keeping his deck clear of passengers. The Negroes, now all below decks, were making a mournful noise, part wail, part musical lament; only Matti, seated upon the deck as though built thereon by the shipwright, had been left unmolested. It was a relief of great proportions when the schooner at last reached the sheltered island-adorned waters off Chaguaramas and we were allowed back on deck to marvel at the huge sweep of low-lying land which stretched to the eastwards as far as the eye could see. I noticed, but quickly averted my eyes from, the southern aspect of the drear mountains which had so disturbed me when I had viewed them from the north. The air of the Golfo de Paria, although fresher than that in the cabin, had none of the lively quality of the air of Tobago; it was stagnant and stale, as if the mountains had imprisoned it and refused to let it escape. The water was of a muddy complexion and gave off stale odours, in contrast to the jewel-like brilliance and invigorating scents of the ocean around Tobago.

The afternoon was by now well-advanced and the sun appeared for the first time that day; it was low and hazy in the western sky. I was chagrined in no small degree when the captain informed me that the other schooner would not be able to work through the Boca until the next morning; he was sorry, he said heartily, but the horses and Negroes would have only one night's pitching and rolling and would be delivered in fine fettle by mid-morning. I would have protested, and perhaps exacted a financial penalty for the delay, but I was anxious to disembark ourselves and our Negroes before sundown and feared to antagonize the fellow.

Our introduction to Puerto Espana, the Port-of-Spain of which we are now so proud, was hardly propitious. To our eyes, from the deck of the schooner, it presented a muddy foreshore crowded with small boats and a line of undistinguished buildings; and the ground being flat there was no indication as to how far back the town extended, unlike Port Louis where the buildings are all displayed upon a hill. To our ears, the town offered a continuous humming noise, punctuated with loud cries and with the incessant barking of dogs. To our noses it wafted the mingled odours of open drains, decaying fish, burning coalpots and much cookery (most of which, unhappily, was being done with rancid oil, unless my nose deceived me).

When we stepped out of the lighter, Father came forward to greet us with the news that our lodging was to be in an unfinished house on the far side of the town and that the Negroes must be marched for a mile or two to a kind of temporary barracks which he had rented. Maman and Henri, both fortunately stupefied into silence by the novelty of their situation, were quickly taken off in a crude carriage drawn by two mules with the servants following on foot, whilst I remained behind with Father to check the Negroes against the muster-roll as they came ashore. Once this was done, and the overseers had marshalled and set in motion the sorry procession, Father and I were free to make our way through the town to our lodging.

As I strode along, half a pace behind Father, through the noisy and foul-smelling streets, I might well have passed for a tall young man who was sure of himself, armed as I was with my pistols — yes, I now wore two — and in the company of a fierce older man with the mien of true command. As I glanced from side to side, however, I knew that my confidence was but a facade and that if Father had not been there I might well have broken into a humiliating run and stumbled over the filth which was lying everywhere. The sky was now dark and the streets were lit only by the lanterns of the better-off foot-passengers and by faint flickers from lamps and candles in the open shops and on the stalls of hucksters. Every person we saw seemed to be a Mulatto — I knew not, confined as I had been to Tobago, that there were so many Mulattoes in the world — and every face which looked into mine seemed to be degraded or degenerate or both; I would not have been at all surprised to learn that they were thieves and murderers to a man.

In addition to the fears aroused by the darkness and the strange faces, I was overwhelmed by the noise — the humming and occasional cries which we had heard from off-shore were now revealed as a cacophony so loud and discordant that I was afraid that some uprising or civil commotion was in train and that soon the dark streets would be filled with raging mobs such as had roamed the streets of Paris. However, as Father moved briskly and in unconcerned fashion from street to street it became clear to me that loud noise was the population's natural element and no portent of impending revolution and bloodshed (and so, I may say, it remains to this day). Hucksters shouted their wares at the tops of their voices in Spanish, French and patois; dogs, curs rather, were barking from behind every fence and gate and door; Mulatto neighbours were conducting loud multilingual quarrels from house to house, and from street to balcony; Negro servants were being urged to their duties by the lash of their mistresses' tongues rather than by cajolery or the quiet threat of the whip; and, with the houses crowded together as they were, music being played in one clashed with music being played in others. (The front galeries of the houses emitting the music were brightly lit and occupied by gaudily dressed Mulatto ladies who called out alluringly to Father and myself, often with favourable comment upon my height; when we took no notice their jocular solicitations turned into noisy abuse, which provoked passers-by into ribald and even noisier jocundities.) No one seemed to be alarmed at, or even to notice, the thumping of Negro drums, which was audible everywhere yet seemed to be coming from nowhere, so faint it was.

I need hardly distress my lady readers by describing the odours which arose from the drains in the middle of the street; let me write only that they detracted somewhat from the savouriness of the aromas wafting from the foodstalls at every corner (for not all of the stallholders had been using rancid oil) but were not sufficient to conceal from me that my abstention from lunch aboard the schooner had made me faint with hunger. Ignoring Father's impatient disdain I allowed my nose to select a stall where the Venezuelan owner sold me a substantial meat and cornmeal *pastel* wrapped in a banana leaf. I ate it with my fingers as I walked and with great pleasure.

I had hoped that our lodging was to be in a quieter part of the town but the half-finished house of Senora Villafana was in the Calle de la Princesa de

Asturias (now Duke street) which was a thoroughfare inhabited by enough people to fill Port Louis several times over, all as determined to make themselves heard above the barking of their dogs as were the inhabitants of the meaner streets nearer the quay.

I passed an unhappy night, the greater part of it spent holding Henri by the hand to quiet him, as even Janga's placid nature had succumbed to the novelty of her experiences and she had become useless; in the morning, however, she had recovered just enough sense to perform her duties and I was able to set off for the quay to meet the other schooner. After some pacing up and down in the mud and much peering through the telescope I at last saw the second schooner approaching and then dropping anchor. Tony, I need hardly write, insisted that the horses were unloaded first. When they were at last ashore, after much whinnying, and the lighters were returning for the first batch of Negroes, she strode up to me leading her favourite horse. I was standing with my muster-roll in one hand and my umbrella in the other, waiting to hand the latter to the first young Negro to come ashore.

"I need no muster-roll to tell me that we are two niggers short," Tony announced abruptly, while her horse slobbered her shoulder.

I looked at her in a questioning manner, but did not speak, in accordance with my vow.

"Gilbert and Jéhu have taken their leave," she said in a tone so strange that I was at a loss to know whether she was rejoicing or mourning or ashamed of negligence — she was plainly deeply moved in her feelings, but anxious to pretend that she was not. "The sharks," she added huskily, "will have dined well on two hundred guineas worth of prime Negro and twenty guineas worth of old gristle and bone."

My emotions on hearing of this loss were as mixed as Tony's but I had little time to examine them for Father arrived and, as my readers will not be surprised to learn, instituted immediate and rigorous inquiries into the disappearance of the two, as well as more perfunctory inquiries into the similar mystery of the disappearance of Donal Bain, which Tony had not thought of sufficient importance to mention to me, although Quashiba could be heard pouring out her grief at the top of her powerful voice to the other overseers' mistresses, who heard her without sympathy. It was assumed that Donal had fallen overboard from the schooner while hopelessly drunk and if he had been assisted in his fall that was a matter of indifference to all except Quashiba, for her staunch ally Maria, Donal's wife, had died some years before. (Without any protector or friend, the tall Negress was returned to a field gang, as she had not been trained in any useful skill and was strong for her age.)

Father's inquiries, rigorous but ill-tempered, met with no result — no one, whether ship's captain, sailor, overseer or Negro, had seen or heard anything suspicious and everyone seemed genuinely surprised. Only I, who alone could recall Jéhu's exclamation of "St. Domingue!" as he ended that confabulation in the ravine, and who alone had seen that unexplained pirogue tossing upon the sea, only I had an inkling whither father and son might have decided to flee and what arrangements might have been made to facilitate their escape; but I, for reasons which I still do not altogether understand, withheld my suspicions from Father. (These suspicions were partially confirmed later in the day when I gave the news to Matti and saw a momentary gleam of complicity in her eye.) In the end Father had to accept that the runaways were lost for good and that he had no redress for, by the terms of the Cedula of Population under which he had been granted land, he was obliged to control his own Negroes and could expect no assistance from the Spanish authorities.

(At that time the world knew nothing of the Negro rebellion which was about to break out in St. Domingue and to send shudders of fear throughout the civilized world.)

The loss of those two familiar faces was felt by us all and made settling into our new life in la Trinidad even more of a trial than it would otherwise have been. Matti, in the absence of her family, became a white-haired old woman almost overnight; her power was scarce diminished but she shrank from the effort of using it. In consequence our household at Senora Villafana's descended into chaos — Sara, Milly and Janga all discovered themselves to be *enceinte* at about the same time, doubtless because of the attentions of the hired Negroes who were finishing the house in somewhat desultory fashion. Despairing of order, I bought for myself, out of estate funds, a well-trained body-servant, Jacques.

Father went off to clear our estate near Arouca, which was known, for reasons which escape me, as *"Sans Peur"*.

(How strange it seems that I can write so glibly that "Father went off to clear our land"! It was, of course, as I am not allowed to forget, the Negroes who cleared the land, many of them dying as they did so from disease, *mal d'estomac*, snakebites and exhaustion, if not by self-administered or other poison.)

Tony spent some of her time with Father, a little with us in Puerto Espana, and some, perhaps most, with a set of rakish young French Créoles who occupied themselves with horseback outings, horse-races, sailing trips and card parties. Maman attempted to enlist Matti and her authority in an effort to persuade Tony to dress in a feminine manner for these fêtes, but Matti was half-hearted and Tony obdurate; as a result, Tony's outfits and manners remained boyish and her teasing devoid of coquetry, so that the young Créole blades regarded her as one of themselves rather than as a likely soul-mate or as the source of a dowry.

Maman, besides attempting to civilize Tony, also made an effort to abstain from brandy as she had done after the French "*prise de Tabago*", and to visit several more or less distant relatives. However, she found these persons haughty, quarrelsome and inclined to despise her for her marriage to a barbarian *Écossais* and for the unsatisfactory nature of her three children, so she quickly relapsed into melancholia and began to shew the first signs of the deterioration in her mental faculties which so distressed us later on. Her condition was not improved by having Henri within earshot for twenty-four hours in the day, for he was finding the strangeness of his new life not at all to his liking. For many months he failed to accustom himself to the incessant clamour of the town and became pettish and so noisy that our neighbours, whose houses were very close indeed to Senora Villafana's, began to complain. Perhaps the manner in which Henri echoed and re-echoed their shouted words made them conscious of the totally unreasonable nature of what they were saying. Mind you, Henri was also capable of deliberately provoking their dogs — their baying, whining, growling, yelping curs — into ever noisier displays of canine fury. It was not until Janga had given birth to her coal-black infant and had taken charge of the equally coal-black offspring of the other two Graces that Henri began to quieten somewhat. He became an affectionate, although unreliable, nurse, capable of tending to the pickneys for half-an-hour at a time but also capable of leaving them unattended without warning, or of surreptitiously pinching them to make them cry and thus bring Janga running. Poor Maman! What a relief it was to her when Father took her to Sans Peur even before the house there was finished, Matti and Sara going with her.

As for myself, I kept Melancholy at bay by setting up a new business, renting a small but sufficient room in the Calle de Santa Ana (now Charlotte Street) and by a most fortunate coincidence finding a reliable clerk on my first day. This red-haired young gentleman, by the name of O'Brien, had disembarked only that morning and had straightway started to knock on doors, looking for employment. He had all the necessary skills for the post I had to offer, and a soft-spoken Irish manner; he told me that he had read in a broadsheet back home in County Armagh about the outstanding beauty and kindness of Spanish Mulatto women and could not rest easy in his bed until he had seen the lovely creatures with his own eyes. He spoke with the sadness of one who is driven by Forces which he cannot control, and would happily die if this one wish could be fulfilled. He had spent all his savings on his passage and was now penniless. He instantly

accepted my offer of bed and board during a month's trial and a weekly
wage thereafter if his work was to my satisfaction. I have had no reason
to regret taking on Mr. O'Brien. I set about buying and selling with my
usual success — indeed with more success than I had achieved in Tobago,
for here I met other traders every day and I could personally supervize the
loading and unloading of my merchandise. In passing I may mention that
my trading-house was, from this time onward, more profitable than Sans
Peur or any other estate known to me.

All my busy activity could not conceal from my mind that I was as
much a stranger in a strange land as I had been in Tobago; more so, for I had
no childhood memories of the new Island to console me when in reflective
mood. My French Créole fellow-merchants and planters, whether white or
Mulatto (and I made no distinction when it came to doing business) appeared
to be more concerned with their politics than with making newcomers like
myself welcome. The first question asked of me by a new acquaintance
was invariably whether I was English, and when I answered "no" there
would follow a puzzled silence and then the further question as to whether
I held pro-English views. It seemed that when I spoke French my accent,
despite all Maman's efforts and despite my intercourse with French officers
and officials in Tobago, was neither *métropolitain* nor Créole, but faintly
anglicized (or Scotticized) and therefore suspect, the speech of a stranger.

These French Créole acquaintances were bitterly divided between two
allegiances — the Royalist, which included most of the French aristos, and
the Republican, which included most of the Mulattoes (and for all I know
they may still be so divided). Both camps were confused in their views
about Britain, or "*l'Angleterre*" as they called it, as indeed I was myself, for
Father had always averred that England was the enemy of all true Highland
Scotsmen who were loyal to the Stewarts and yet here I was, referring in
conversation to the United Kingdom as *l'Angleterre* and even wondering if
it would not be better for trade and for the general welfare of la Trinidad if
it were conquered by that country. Father was in favour of the Island staying
in the Spanish empire, and indeed Spain and her Gobernador had been good
to us, but as a merchant I was coming round to the view that British ways
might be more appropriate for the nineteenth century, now close upon us.

El Gobernador, Don José Maria Chacon (Sanchez of Sotomayor;
Knight of the Order of Calatrava; Brigadier of the Royal Navy;
Governor, Commander-in-Chief and Intendant of this Island of Trinidad
to Windward, and its Dependencies; Deputy Inspector General of the
Troops of its Garrison; Judge Protector of the Royal Revenue of the Post
Office for His Majesty, etc. etc.) thus overloaded with titles in the Spanish
manner, was nevertheless in a weak position, caught as he was between

the two factions amongst the French incomers, now far outnumbering the Spaniards, and representing as he did a Madrid Government who could offer him little support. He was an "enlightened" Spaniard and as such leaned toward England and her institutions rather than to France and hers, as I discovered when I had to meet him over some business matter. Our rapport was immediate and cordial and shortly afterward I was invited to dine with him *en famille*. Speaking English (in which he was fluent) because of the presence of his singularly handsome black mistress, he condescended to share with me his sorrow that he was now a stranger in an Island where he should have been at home, being, as he had successfully concealed from Madrid, a Spanish Créole born in Cuba. I did not presume upon this condescension and we maintained an intermittent but warm and productive friendship — he gave me considerable assistance when I decided to learn to speak Spanish in the Castilian manner, finding a tutor for me and graciously correcting my mistakes and mispronunciations when I addressed him. In return, I was able to provide him with intelligence about the rival French factions, and sometimes to act as his emissary to one or the other of them. I was also in a position, of course, to supply him and his Government with goods at advantageous prices.

To return to the history of my family and to bring this chapter to a close, I will record that within two years Father had completed his estate house at Sans Peur, while I had built a house on a spacious lot on the Calle de San Carlos (now Frederick Street) only three blocks away from my office. The front of my house overlooked the marshy ground whence Don José had had the river diverted and where now stands the pleasant Brunswick Square; to the rear there were separate and commodious rooms for Henri, for Janga and her nursery, and for the rest of the servants. Tony, of course, had chambers both at Sans Peur and in my house and moved between them as her fancy, or her daemon, drove her. With the help of Jacques, who proved to be excellent value for money, I was able to live a life as comfortable as the accursed climate of Puerto Espana would allow, but my heart continued empty and only my evening conversations with Henri, limited in range though they were, kept my sensibilities alive. Melancholy "of darkest midnight born" ever threatened to emerge from her lair and defeat my efforts to keep her confined.

CHAPTER XVI

I return to Tobago in Haste in Order to make a Purchase there; Life becomes more comfortable for Henri and myself; Father broaches an astounding Project which makes me exceedingly uneasy

"Buy me, sell me. Massa bull, Massa cow."

Thus muttered Betsy at last, after a long and stubborn silence. Her words were patois and uttered in a most surly manner. I had been inquiring earnestly whether she would be happy for me to purchase her and take her back with me to Puerto Espana so that she could resume the care of Henri. She had refused to answer me either by voice or gesture and I had had to repeat my question several times. We were standing in full public view just outside the officers' quarters on the highest point of Fort de Castrie in Port Louis and I dared not reveal the agitation which possessed me. The Tobago breeze was ruffling Betsy's full and elegant grey skirts with a force which did not seem to disturb her, although I was having difficulty in retaining my hat and my composure.

"I have many new books, both in English and in French," I said, thinking to tempt her into some animation.

"Me no read," said the perverse creature, without a scintilla of sensibility in her voice.

"Henri is not at all happy, as Janga is too busy with three infants to care for, while I have to be out all day."

She elected to behave as though I had not spoken; her attitude and facial expression changed not at all.

"I will give you permission to visit your mother at Sans Peur as often as you wish."

Betsy lifted her face to mine at last. She blinked her shapely eyelids three times.

"Buy me then. You no have to ask me." She dropped her eyes and turned her face away.

This last remark was no more than the truth, as my readers know already, but for reasons which I did not care to examine at the time, I desired — nay, I needed — Betsy's concurrence before I purchased her. The price being asked for the creature by the white-haired M. le Capitaine Laurent was truly excessive — he was being repatriated to troubled France and presumably needed all the money he could realize. Upon hearing that Betsy was on the market I had sailed from Puerto Espana on the first available vessel, accompanied by Jacques. I was confident that I could reduce the inflated asking-price by business-like bargaining, but M. le Capitaine, under the watchful eye of his young-seeming wife, was adamant. Although Madame did not appear to have any knowledge of the intellectual and linguistic prowess which Babet, as she called her, could boast, yet she had more than a suspicion that I was not interested in Betsy's accomplishments as a lady's maid. Her resolve to wring the asking-price out of me was probably strengthened when I requested that the negotiations be broken off for a few minutes so that I could interview the property in question, assess her value, and possibly review my latest offer in the light of what I might discover.

Thus Betsy and I found ourselves out in the breezy air, with the *fleur-de-lis* flapping furiously on its tall pole, French gunners tending their cannon upon the batteries nearby, and lookouts scanning the ocean in all directions. Here, at least, the damage done by the mutiny and the hurricano appeared to have been repaired, and discipline restored.

"Why do you not answer me in English?" I asked in exasperation.

"Bush have ears," replied Betsy, giving her first acknowledgment that she and I might share some intelligence which was best kept between ourselves.

"Why you so dear, then, if you no speak English?" I asked, reverting to patois myself.

Betsy gave me a sidelong glance without raising her face, then giggled quietly, but with an unmistakeable note of impudence.

"My Madame, how old she, think you?"

"Thirty-five?" I ventured.

Betsy giggled again: "She tell me she forty-five, but me think she fifty!" I must have shewn my astonishment, for Betsy continued: "Me colour and me *frise* she hair; and me massage she *béké* face and neck; and me treat she *béké* skin with herbs and oil; and me dab a little rouge here and there, but clever-clever; and me dress she young and dainty! Is me make she look thirty-five! Other old Madames pay anything for me!"

"So me have to pay three hundred louis for you! Is more than for a good-good carpenter or Governor butler!"

Betsy shrugged her shoulders, while I began to be conscious of a rising tide of irritation within me. "*Béké*" was not a word which a Negress should have used when speaking of one white person to another. Moreover, somewhere at the back of my mind lurked a doubt as to whether Betsy was not acting in concert with her Madame to inflate her price; perhaps — ignoble thought! — she was to have a percentage of the proceeds of her own sale. A nobler thought also rose unbidden, that Betsy had encouraged her Madame to hold out for that price, to ensure that only I would buy her, since no one else in the West Indies would be both willing and able to pay it. How confused I was! Yet at the same time I perceived that Melancholy was in retreat — not yet defeated, but no longer threatening to exercise uncontested dominion over my soul. I decided to revert to English.

"You would not mind tending Henri again," I asked, "after being such a pearl of great price as a lady's maid?"

"You buy me, me must do like you say. How else?"

"You know that you could make Henri's life miserable if you thought caring for him was beneath you."

"Me never *never* make Massieu Henri's life miserable," said she, emphasizing "Massieu Henri" in the most insolent manner, as though to warn me: "Let others beware!"

This was the Betsy of old and I made my decision.

"Me buy you!" I announced loudly and in patois, for the ears of a passing sergeant.

Besty raised her head and laughed, a falsely vivacious, penetratingly loud and unnecessarily prolonged cachinnation intended, I hoped, for the retreating sergeant's benefit. When she had done, she asked in a low voice: "For you-self, or for estate?"

This was a question as penetrating as her laugh, for it happened that all my own assets were at that moment tied up in various ventures and I had come to Tobago intending to buy her, as I had bought Jacques, with estate, that is, Father's money. I had been the happier about this course as it postponed the question of Betsy's manumission until after Father's death. Had I bought her myself she might have argued that I had promised to free her when I owned her, and freeing a Negress was not to be done lightly at that time, what with the Trinidad planters being so terrified by the Negro uprising in St. Domingue, by the Republicans in their midst, and even by insolent individuals with black skins walking about with their heads held high — free Negresses, they averred, were more trouble to the *alguazils* who patrolled the streets of Puerto Espana than were free Negroes. I was also, I have to admit, still afraid of Father's rage — he would never have agreed to free even Betsy.

"I am buying you for the estate," I replied, "for I have no desire to own you." This was an excuse which had the advantage of being the truth, or part of it. The breezy air of Tobago and Betsy's infuriating yet intimate presumption had recalled our childhood battles in the most vivid fashion and I could not contemplate owning her with any equanimity.

"But three hundred *louis d'or!*" whispered Betsy in English. "That is far too much for one Negress — you know what the Master will say!" Her lips hinted at a smile for the first time and I knew from of old that another instance of her penetration was on the way. "You will be making a false entry in the estate account book, will you not?"

"Fetch your things!" said I, barely controlling a desire to strike her and stamping off to M. le Capitaine Laurent's quarters where Jacques was waiting with my bag. I paid out the truly exorbitant price in mint gold louis, for the Capitaine would not hear of bills of exchange, "the times, Monsieur Mason, being troubled and war with the English perhaps imminent." I parted from him and his wife with many compliments and expressions of respect; Madame being somewhat tearful, although not incapable of irony, as she told me that "parting with *chère* Babet was not so insupportable since the darling creature was going to a Master who had demonstrated in the most practical way how much he valued her".

(For the satisfaction of such of my readers as may be interested, I learned many years later that Betsy had indeed informed Madame Laurent that there was one gentleman living in la Trinidad who could be persuaded to pay a huge price for her and that she had been rewarded, not with a percentage of her sale price, but with a handsome gold bracelet.)

Betsy was ready to leave as soon as that price had been paid, her worldly goods in a large bundle upon her head. Jacques, who was discreetly but incurably amorous, offered to help her with the bundle in a familiar manner, but she rebuffed and rebuked him with one glance — "I am not for such as you!" it conveyed in rapier fashion — and followed me down the steep road to the quayside, drawing the eyes of all the men we passed, so that I knew with what grace she was walking. On the sloop, seasoned traveller as she was, she quickly found a sheltered spot upon the deck and set about completing the subjugation of Jacques — watching this distracted my mind from the discomforts and perils of the voyage back to Puerto Espana.

On our arrival at the house in Calle de San Carlos there was amazement and great delight at my re-purchase of Betsy, for I had told no one of my purpose in going to Tobago. Her reunion with Henri was most affecting — they did not rush into each others' arms as I had expected, but stood regarding one another, their smiles broadening and broadening, for several minutes, then ran to embrace each other with all their old fervour. For days, nay weeks, Henri would not willingly let Betsy out of his sight during his waking hours; for something like the same period, or longer in truth, my attention to business, which was usually so strict, weakened somewhat and I would oft-times make an excuse to walk home under my umbrella just for a sight of Henri's happiness in the presence of his goddess.

My life, it seemed on the surface, became much more ordered and cheerful. Matti, by an arrangement in which I had no part, but which bore all the marks of having been instigated by Betsy, was superannuated from Sans Peur as too old and sick for major responsibilities and took nominal charge of my household, with Betsy as her second-in-command. Meals were punctual, varied, well-seasoned in Créole style, and truly delicious; if there was fish, it was king-fish fresh from the quay; if I called for a cooling drink, it appeared as quickly as was humanly possible; when I wanted to read of an evening the lamps were trimmed and ready and, since Henri had regained his regular sleeping habits for the first time since our move to la Trinidad, there was peace and quiet. Father, and even Tony, would comment favourably and with a touch of envy upon the discreet comfort and exceptional cleanliness of my *ménage*; Father continued to assume, as I could discern from his consciously indulgent expression, that I had other even more discreet and private satisfactions of which I did not speak to him.

However, under the surface of my apparent Content there lay not Melancholy, but Frustration and Disappointment, all the more poignant for not being spoken of. Betsy resisted all my attempts to engage her in conversation and I was not again favoured with the vivifying shafts of insolence which I had so enjoyed on that blowy day on Fort de Castrie. When we discussed necessary household affairs she would speak only patois which, although expressive and even poetical in its own way, especially when uttered in a voice such as hers, is no vehicle for intelligent discourse on literature or philosophy, or on world affairs such as the then current war between Britain and Republican France, or on such topics as Thomas Paine's newly published *The Rights of Man*. There seemed to be no way in which I could revive our youthful companionship; if I sat myself down upon a chair in Henri's room and offered to converse, Betsy would laugh in nervous fashion, excuse herself and leave; if I brought a book and purposely left it lying for her to pick up and read, I would find it back in the salon before the end of the day.

There was only one book, thus laid out as bait by me, which Betsy kept and returned after an interval. This was *Poems on Various Subjects* by the young Boston Negress Phillis Wheatley. I had had it from a friend who was a supercargo on a ship trading out of London (where the book was published) and had perused it myself with some interest. When I asked Betsy outright whether she had enjoyed the poems she shook her head, paused, and then nodded, as if to say that she had doubts about the quality of the poems while applauding that they had been written at all.

(The book is still in my possession, though sadly foxed with the mildew that attacks all paper in this climate. As I leaf through it after writing the above, I find that the following lines have been underlined in pencil:

> Some view our sable race with scornful eye,
> "Their colour is a diabolic die."
> Remember, *Christians*, *Negros*, black as *Cain*,
> May be refin'd and join th' angelic train.

Against the first couplet, in Betsy's neat hand, are the words: "In Truth!" and against the second: "Fond Hope!")

The hopes raised in my breast by Betsy's response to this book were not fulfilled in any immediate manner, but I was saved from repining by other and much more fateful events to which I was constrained to turn my attention, and which I must now describe.

One day Father sent word from Sans Peur that he was coming to stay in Calle de San Carlos for a short visit and that I should make myself available on the morrow as he had urgent and important business to discuss with me. My heart sank, for I had had too much experience of Father's "urgent" business to be hopeful about this latest instance, but I judged it both a filial duty and a politic course to comply with his request and stayed at home to await him. When Father arrived he immediately made sure that no servant was within earshot, then broached without preamble an astounding scheme, of which, I may add, I had had no inkling. He informed me that he had an old friend in England, an Englishman of good family to whom he was beholden for a favour which he did not propose to discuss. (I did not know that this Englishman existed, nor indeed that Father could regard an Englishman as a friend.) This Mr. Rochester had a younger son, Edward, who was not entitled to any of the family wealth, which was entailed; he had just left college and and was prepared to consider marriage to Tony, provided her dowry was not less than thirty thousand pounds, of which at least £3,000 must be *in specie*.

I cannot tell my readers which part of this plan astonished me the more — the proposal that Tony should marry, or the singular size of the dowry. Tony was now thirty years of age; no gentleman had made her an offer and if there had been inquiries about her dowry they had not reached my ears. Moreover, she was loudly derisive when any of her friends, whether male or female, formed a sentimental attachment and had given unforgiveable offence to la Trinidad's French Créole manhood by averring on many occasions that her erstwhile Negro groom, Jéhu, was her yardstick of manliness and horsemanship — she barely distinguished the two — and that she had yet to see a *béké* who matched him. As to the amount of the dowry, I could not bring myself to speak of it, so my first words to Father were concerned with my hateful sister's welfare (although, in the recesses of my mind I had already weighed one or two methods of putting thirty thousand pounds together).

"I trust that you have informed Tony of her good fortune," I said, "since she is the one to be married."

"Richard, I am not a fool, whatever you may be thinking of me. You and I have to be seeing about the money first."

"I do not think that Tony will want to marry any man whom she has not chosen herself."

"Rochester tells me in his letter that his Edward is a bold young fellow and the finest of horsemen. He has ridden the length of England for a wager and would be living over the stables if he could. Furthermore, he is a gentleman pugilist and has fought the reigning champion of England to a standstill — the seconds had to stop the fight because both contestants were not far short of insensible. He sounds just the man for Antonia."

"I cannot believe," I said stubbornly, "that Tony wants to marry anyone."

"All women should marry," said Father with some impatience, "and besides, the girl is becoming an embarrassment to me — I am not being invited to certain houses because my friends are afraid that I will be bringing her along. I am also thinking that Madame your mother's state of mind might improve if she saw Antonia married and had some white grandchildren to be proud of." Here he looked at me sidelong as if to inquire whether I proposed to father any white sons. "Finally, Richard, as I have been telling you and will be repeating only this once — are you understanding me? — I am beholden to Mr. Rochester in no small degree."

"But, Father — " I began.

"But me no buts, Richard," Father interrupted. "As soon as you can be assuring me that the money and so forth is ready, I will write to Mr. Rochester and inform Antonia."

I could easily have arranged the books to shew that £30,000 was beyond our resources, but decided to be magnanimous and allow Tony to have at least the chance of marriage. (There was an element of self-interest in my magnanimity, of course, which my readers will easily discern.) By various stratagems, including the purchase of a small sugar-estate in el Valle Diego Martin which I immediately had valued (honestly, as it happened) at twice what I had paid for it, and having Father sign several papers of which he knew not the import, I was able to assure him that land, buildings, Negroes, negotiable paper and gold coin to the agreed amount would be available for the bold and impecunious Mr. Edward Rochester as soon as he had induced Tony to marry him.

After this, events moved swiftly. First of all, one evening Betsy came to me of her own volition and addressed me in English without waiting for permission.

"Master Richard, Miss Tony wants me for her maid again! She asked the Master and he has given his consent. She is coming tomorrow to take me to Sans Peur straight away."

"But why-why?" I stammered, not doubting for a moment that this intelligence was true, "why-why?"

"She is wanting to marry this young Master Rochester from England and she needs to look younger than she is, for he is only twenty-five years old, and she has heard what I can do."

"But you are indispensable to this household!" I burst out. "I need you to see that Henri is properly cared for and you are the housekeeper in all but name, with your mother so old."

Betsy dropped me a full and most graceful curtsy, looking straight into my eyes as she had not done since we returned from Tobago.

"How can we prevent this?" I continued, my voice a tremble. "It is unwarrantable that you should have to submit to — "

Betsy had her answer. When had she not?

"If I were your personal property," she said in her most precise tones, "and you had appointed me as your house-keeper you could insist that I remain here and that I only attend Miss Tony with your permission when she comes to stay." She placed a faint emphasis upon the word "housekeeper" as though to remind me that it would be to our advantage to have our family and friends think that I had promoted my mistress.

We were conspirators again! There is nothing like a deep-laid plot to cement friendship and rouse the torpid soul! I doubted not at all that we trusted each other and my spirits rose. My intellect had been sharpened by my experience of trading in Puerto Espana and I was able to make my decisions promptly.

"You have been my housekeeper since — when was Miss Tony last here? — since two weeks ago. Will you be good enough to inform your mother, Janga and the others of this change and when it took place? Meanwhile, I will go to work on the books — I will own you before sunrise."

Betsy smiled — ah! that conspiratorial smile! — curtsied again and swept away. Doctor Whyte, I noticed, not for the first time, had been wrong about her becoming obese. I called Jacques and had him light a lamp in my study where I kept most of the relevant papers. I then locked the door and commenced a long series of forgeries which removed Betsy's name from the account-books and the muster-roll. Betsy knocked on the door once to offer me refreshment and when I admitted her I noticed that she wore Matti's housekeeper's keys in a prominent position at her waist instead of the less conspicuous position which they had occupied before. Discovering that I needed to alter even more papers, I had Jacques accompany me through the sleepless town to my office where we managed to gain access without wakening Mr. O'Brien, who occupied a ground-floor room with the first of his Mulatto bedmates (a little fifteen-year-old who was so plain that he had been able to purchase her for a derisible sum).

By sunrise, as I had promised, I had a set of documents which would have convinced any investigator that I was the lawful owner of two Negroes, entered thus in my "muster-roll":

Betsy (Créole):	Nurse:	100.00
Jacques:	House:	70.00

I added Jacques to give some verisimilitude; his gratitude when I told him he was now mine was quite touching, and helped him to keep his mouth shut about my back-dating of Betsy's elevation.

Our defences thus prepared, Betsy and I were ready to meet Tony on the morrow. I think that my readers must be wearied of my accounts of my sister's tantrums and vile language, so I will merely state that upon this occasion they were prolonged, loud and quite ineffectual, for in the end she had to agree that she must come to Calle de San Carlos if she needed special help with her toilette or her wardrobe, and that Milly would be given instruction in the treatments her skin would require.

In my experience of victory it is rarely complete, and there is always a price to be paid. This victory over Tony was a case in point, for she decided, so determined was she to make an impression on young Mr. Edward Rochester, to bring Milly, her groom and her horses, and lodge in Calle de San Carlos for an indefinite period, even though the stabling was hardly sufficient. She would have badgered Betsy unmercifully had not that artful Negress been able to claim other duties to do with the running of the household such as going to market for provisions, etc. Nevertheless, even without Betsy at her elbow all the time, Tony's appearance, manners and deportment underwent remarkable improvement so that by the time a letter had been dispatched to Mr. Edward's father and the young gentleman had crossed the ocean she was the very simulacrum of a youthful Créole heiress. Her face, once so browned and roughened by sun and rain, had been transformed by almond-oil and broad-brimmed hats into a delightful shade of pale olive with just a touch of pink in her cheeks when her fancy required it; her black hair, previously so lack-lustre and pinned so tightly on top of her head in order to fit under her hat, now shone like a boat-tail's wing and was tied loosely with a single ribbon in the becoming fashion affected by young girls at that time; her voice, when she remembered her singing-master's instruction, lost its cane-field and stable-yard hoarseness and became almost dove-like; her gait, always light but somewhat boyish, now came under the influence of a Parisian dancing-master and improved to the point that, when she thought hard about it, she could seem to float languidly above the ground.

Watching this metamorphosis, I wondered if Edward Rochester would ever learn that this young lady was capable of singing, or rather shouting, the lewdest of Negro songs in the most debased language, and of accompanying herself upon the tamboo-bamboo or the *chac-chac* in order to place beyond doubt the barbarous perversity of the song's rhythm. I recalled Tony's glee when she cozened M. le Comte de Dillon into thinking that she was a young boy — would she be just as gleeful after she had deceived this horseman and pugilist from England into believing that she was a young girl?

CHAPTER XVII

The arrival in la Trinidad of Edward Rochester; Betsy and I have Cause to mourn; Ill-Omens and Machinations attend a Wedding-Day

I had imagined that Edward Rochester would be a tall fair Englishman, but he was short, thickset and dark — very dark. His luxuriant black hair fell over his forehead and almost met his heavy eyebrows; his face was sallow and was made even darker by facial hair of the kind which needs the attentions of the razor twice a day; more black hair grew in thickets on the backs of his hands; his deep-set eyes were black, glittering and somewhat fierce.

In spite of Edward's appearance we were all of us — Tony, Father and myself — soon in thrall to him: in thrall to his charm; to his lively and informed conversation; to his ability to bend those eyes upon, and attend closely to, any companion of the moment as though he or she were the most elevated person in the world; and, lastly, to his irresistible animal force. His skills as a horseman had not been exaggerated and endeared him to Tony (and to Father) as none of his other attributes did. He took her on longer and ever longer rides over steeper and steeper hill-traces and she pretended that she had difficulty in finding the way and in keeping up with him, so that he thought he was teaching her to ride boldly. At horse-races, Tony reported, he was pre-eminent; she began to speak of him in the warmest of terms and made no attempt to compare him with Jéhu — even I could see that upon a horse Edward Rochester was another Centaur, and perhaps Jéhu's equal.

It was not long before Father was saying: "A frank and manly fellow, and a true son of my old friend Rochester. It will be a privilege to be having him in the family — make altogether sure, Richard, that he knows

211

that Antonia's dowry can be doubled in five years if the price of sugar holds up and he is prepared to work hard."

And I? I was probably the most in thrall to the young man straight from college. He would call of an early morning to take Tony out riding and while I ate my breakfast he and I would have a conversation so lively that I would leave for the office as invigorated as though I had had a second *douche-en-pluie*. I even left my umbrella at home on several occasions, for fear that he would see me with it and think the less of me. He was an acute observer of European affairs, had travelled widely on that Continent and gave me much information from which I was able to profit. He was willing to learn from me about the West Indies and freely expressed his gratitude for the instruction which I gave him. Best of all, he invariably had a ready opinion on any book I mentioned and would correct my untutored judgments in the most jocular and friendly manner; he would also direct my attention to books which I would do well to read. I had never had a friend of the male sex before, let alone an educated one, and my devotion to him was almost unquestioning. I began to ape his English way of speaking and took his advice that I needed a new coat in the same style as his.

As time went on I began to have doubts about one of Edward's qualities and about its possible consequences for Tony's happiness — did the easiness of his manners imply easiness in his morals? He commented one day upon Betsy's attractions — "such a figure, my dear Dick, and such spirit in her eye!" — and when I did not answer rallied me: "You are a sly fellow, I can see, with a taste like my own for ladies who are not too submissive. Is she yours?"

"She is my housekeeper, yes."

"And your property?"

"Yes."

"Property which you would not care to part with temporarily to a friend?"

He must have seen me blench, and understood that he had gone too far, for he bowed as if in apology and dropped the topic.

Nevertheless, such was my attachment to Edward that I contemplated revealing to him the deception which was being practised upon him, for not only was Tony pretending to be ladylike, literate and in her early twenties, but the very existence of Maman and Henri was being concealed. I had agreed to enter this conspiracy, proposed to me by Father and Tony, without any of the elation which was aroused in me when I plotted with Betsy. Maman was placed in the care of a group of nuns who were intent upon setting up a convent in Puerto Espana despite, or perhaps because of, the lawlessness of the town, while Henri was kept concealed in his quarters in the yard and never spoken of.

In the months after Edward's arrival I was so taken up with him that I hardly saw Betsy at all and I was very remiss in my duty to Henri. However, as my unhappiness about the deception increased I became aware that Betsy was unhappy too. After several days of ignoring the urgent messages conveyed by her eyes I made an opportunity to converse with her in private.

"You have something to say to me, I think," I said.

Betsy was silent for a while, then spoke in patois, using the words which Matti (or my conscience) had used on a previous occasion: "Henri lonely for you!"

"Thank you, Betsy," I replied, "I shall make a point of visiting him. But surely that is not all?"

Betsy did not answer straightway and I did not attempt to prompt her. When she spoke, it was in English and very quietly and precisely.

"I am desirous of saying something which I am sure you will not like." She looked at me as if asking my permission to proceed.

"Say it, if you please."

"You must know that I find it hard to forgive Miss Tony for her behaviour to me, and for her cruelty in selling me."

I nodded. This bordered on insolence but was no secret.

"It was my hope that she would marry Mr. Rochester and that he would take her away so that I need never see her again — that is why I was very happy to help her with her toilette and so on — "

What next? I wondered. True insolence?

"— but however much resentment I may bear Miss Tony I have now come to the conclusion that she should not be sacrificed to Mr. Rochester." She looked into my startled face and continued: "I am sure that you are deceived. He is a very wicked man."

"Betsy! Edward Rochester is my good friend!" I glared at the creature but she did not drop her eyes. "He is the finest gentleman I have known!" A silence followed. "Have you anything further to say?" I asked.

Betsy raised her chin.

"Your friend complimented you upon the bodily attractions of your housekeeper, did he not?"

"You were eavesdropping. I might have known!"

"No, Master Richard, I was not eavesdropping. He told me himself that he had done so when he was enticing me to yield to his embraces. He also stated that you had given him your permission to molest me."

I was struck dumb. For the first time in my life I had to doubt Betsy's word — she had been capable of concealment, yes, I knew that, but of an untruth to me, no, or so I would have sworn.

"I think," Betsy went on, intent on sparing me nothing, "that he is not above any wrongdoing. He is a monster of cruelty, lust and greed. He is also a liar."

"What grounds have you for such statements?"

"I have had much experience of men and their wickedness," replied Betsy calmly.

At this I dismissed her curtly and as soon as she had moved away, still holding her head high, I sincerely wished that I had not, for I heard Edward and Tony ride into the yard and I knew what difficulty I would have in speaking to them whilst I was still wrestling with the doubts which Betsy had sown in my mind. I should have asked for more instances of Edward's wickedness, and been ready for him.

As it turned out, I had little chance to speak to the couple, so full were they of excited talk. It seemed that Edward had proposed marriage to Tony — whilst they were both on horseback, of course — and that they had gone straight to Sans Peur and obtained Father's permission and blessing. I managed to utter my congratulations in my usual voice, to kiss Tony and to accept her kiss in return with some semblance of fraternal feeling, but could not help gazing at Edward in horror. Either my first male friend was as Betsy had described him — and how that thought racked me! — or the female friend of my childhood, now my trusted housekeeper, was a liar and a calumniator of the worst order, a doubt which struck at the roots of my being.

Edward, quite unconscious of my gaze upon him, announced that there was no point in wasting time; he would go to find a priest and make a start on the arrangements for the ceremony.

"It is an uncommon piece of luck," said he lightly, "that my father had me baptized into the Church of Rome, for family reasons of great antiquity and little modern relevancy. I prefer to fudge the issue and at home I pass for a loyal member of the Church of England, otherwise I would not have been able to attend college at Oxford. There will be no delay in paying Antonia's dowry, will there, Richard?"

"No, of course not," I said. "Everything will be ready on the appointed day."

Even as I spoke I was reviewing Edward's speech in the light of what Betsy had said — its import was now far more sinister than it would have been before. I decided that I must now dispense with my vow of silence and when Edward had ridden off to find a priest I spoke directly to Tony for the first time in all those years.

"You are truly happy to be marrying Edward?" I asked.

"Oh yes, dearest Dickie!" she replied in her well-rehearsed young lady's voice. "I am devoted to him. Surely you know that!"

"You do not think that he is — " I hesitated, "— somewhat hard?"

"I fail to understand you. I do not know what you mean," protested Tony, still lady-like. Then, with her eyes widening, she took a deep breath and spoke in her own resounding tones. "Every man worth his salt is hard. He is a man, not a long-faced double-dealing stingy old Jew like you!"

My silence in answer to this only served to provoke her further.

"Of course I shall be happy with Edward. He is a man, I am telling you, and not a lily-livered namby-pamby such as you, who would rather keep silence for years than give someone's hide a good tanning when they have deserved it!"

I would have liked time to ponder the implications of this remark, but Tony had more to say.

"We are to have the best stable in Trinidad and when I have shewn him how to run the estate and we have made enough money to go to England we are to have a fine stable there, not the biggest, but the best, and you know what English horses are — "

"He has promised you all this?" I interrupted.

"Yes, of course."

"And he says he loves you?"

"Oh, Dickie, you ask the stupidest questions."

"He seems a little short with you sometimes."

"That is because I enjoy roasting him more than anything — except winning a race, of course."

"He does not become angry?"

"Oh yes, he can be a trifle crusty at times, but that is the way I like a man — ready to do battle, ready to break a horse, ready — "

"Ready to keep a woman in subjection, and to punish her when he discovers that he has been deceived about her age and her lack of accomplishments?"

At this Tony broke into a tirade of such vehemence that I made an excuse and departed, leaving unfinished my inquiry into Edward's true character.

(I wondered then, and I still wonder, why it is that Nature permits two people to persuade themselves that they are in love with each other, when it is clear to any observer guided by Reason that Love is but a small ingredient in the attachment of the one to the other.)

Edward pushed on the arrangements for the wedding so fast and so furiously that I had no further opportunity of talking privately with either party or with Father, or indeed of influencing the matter in any way except by refusing to be Edward's groomsman. Betsy, no doubt resenting my curt dismissal of her, would have none of me, pleading, in patois of course, that she was extremely busy, what with the wedding and with Matti needing much nursing.

Here I must postpone my description of the wedding, for one morning a few days beforehand Janga came to me with tears in her eyes to say that Matti had announced that she was dying and wanted to speak with Master Richard. Although I was about to make my way to the office and was already late because of a visit I had been paying to Henri, I knew that the message was a command which I had to obey. I sent off Jacques to tell Mr. O'Brien that I might be delayed until the afternoon and made my way to Matti's room, which I had not entered before. It was extremely small, although airy enough, and to my surprise was almost filled by a large and handsome mahogany four-poster bed, the curtains of which were of the purest white cambric, delicately embroidered and crisply pressed. Suppressing the question in my mind as to whence such luxury might have come, I bent over Matti, who was half-reclining against the whitest of pillows, her jetty countenance shrunk to the likeness of a dry prune, but the eyes therein still alive and expressive. I could see that she knew of my presence and was trying to speak to me, so I bent even closer.

"Massieu Richard," she said, with a faint query in her voice, "you father father a chief, no?" Her patois still had an African ring to it.

"Yes," I whispered.

Matti lifted one wasted hand and placed it upon mine.

"Betsy father father a chief too, for me a chief daughter. You know this?"

"Me wonder," I said, "but no one tell me so."

"It true true," Matti's voice was growing fainter, "and is why Betsy must make baby for you and that baby be chief."

I knew not how to answer these words, which had pierced to my heart but to the implications of which I was refusing to listen. However, Matti started to speak again, her voice a little stronger.

"Gilbert drown in Boca. Jéhu fighting so hard in St. Domingue he no time for babies. Only Betsy left. She no make baby for nobody but you."

Again I could not answer. Matti closed her eyes and I thought that she had fallen asleep. Then she opened her eyes and smiled at me without speaking, and I knew I was being given a rare and precious reward; I lifted her hand to my lips and kissed it. She smiled again but shewed no desire to speak. We shared a long and strangely happy silence.

"You want priest?" I asked at last.

Matti laughed, a ghostly distant laugh, the first I had ever heard her utter and an even more precious gift than her two smiles.

"Me no need no priest. Me no need no Obeah man. Oil in bottle, spirit in bottle — all same. Chief daughter no afraid of dark."

She closed her eyes and said no more, nor would she answer me by any sign, so I left her. She died not long afterward in Betsy's arms and we buried her quietly at the far end of the lot so as not to detract from the wedding preparations, which were by now well-advanced. I would have wept like a child, I think, if I could have been a child again and had Matti's arms in which to weep. Betsy was also dry-eyed. After the burial I paid a visit to Maman in the rudimental convent and tried to tell her about Matti's death but she appeared not to know me or to hear me when I spoke to her. The nuns seemed unnaturally happy that Maman had succeeded in saying a whole rosary that morning. (I learned later that after saying her rosary Maman had laid hold of a full bottle of altar wine and had drunk it to the dregs.)

The wedding, the shortest permissible ceremony at Edward's insistence, was to take place in the cool of the early morning in the small plain shingle-roofed Church of the Immaculate Conception in the Plaza de la Marina (now superseded by the well-known Cathedral of the same name). The wedding-feast was to be held, not in my house in Calle de San Carlos, but out at Sans Peur, where all the Negroes had been promised the day off work and joy was expected to be unconfined. The newly-weds and Father were to make their way there on horseback as soon as possible after the ceremony, whilst I was to follow in a carriage, with such friends from Puerto Espana as I could muster, and with the baggage.

The weather was propitious; on the day before there were sufficient downpours of rain to flush clean the streets of the town so that on the day itself Puerto Espana stank rather less than it usually did; the morning was delightfully cool, there was no sign of thunder-clouds and there were no unlucky *corbeaux* circling in the limpid air; and yet it was a day which I would rather forget, so full of ill-omens was it.

Just before sunrise I breakfasted as best I could in a household where all the females appeared to have taken leave of their senses. After Jacques had attired me in the suit of English broadcloth cut in imitation of Edward's, I was summoned to view the bride in the dress which had been brought from Terror-stricken Paris at the risk of sailors' lives. It was cut from pale lilac *gorge-de-pigeon* silk which was set off by much cream-coloured lace, in the "dairy-maid" style first affected by Marie Antoinette and, I was assured on the best possible authority, that is, Betsy's, still *à la mode* in Paris. (I took leave to doubt this, thinking that the Revolution had surely put dairy-maids upon a different footing, and that the couturier might well have disposed of an out-of-fashion gown to a customer who could hardly return it — but who was I to express such opinions?)

Since the preparation of the bride was complete, Betsy and Milly withdrew and left me alone with my sister. I was trying to compose a suitable, but very brief, compliment, for Tony did indeed look charming, when she left off preening herself in front of the looking-glass, bent down and grasped the hems of her full skirt and petticoat.

"Would you like to see my stockings, dear brother?" she asked, and without waiting for an answer turned toward me and lifted her skirts; for the fragment of a second before I could turn my eyes away I saw that under their fullness Tony was wearing her drab riding-breeches. They made a strange contrast to her white silk stockings and dainty silken shoes. Shocked into silence I hurried from the room, followed by mocking laughter from Tony. This was the first of the ill-omens which oppressed my spirits.

Father arrived soon afterwards from Sans Peur and quickly changed into his blue coat and nankeen trowsers — I could rest assured that he would not be shewn Tony's breeches.

We did not then own a carriage of our own and I had perforce to hire two of the primitive mule-drawn vehicles available — an open one for Tony and Father at her request, and a closed one for me. When they arrived in front of the house a small crowd collected, composed of servants and Negro children from the neighbouring houses, as well as passing *marchands* and the idlers of all colours who were, and are, conjured so quickly out of nowhere in Puerto Espana. Our French Créole neighbours did not think it beneath them to watch from their front galeries and make loud comments.

When, after some delay of the inevitable female kind, I saw Father leading Tony toward the open carriage, I hurried to the closed one which was, of course, to set off before the bride's. The driver was holding the door open for me and when I stepped inside who should I find sitting there but Henri and Betsy.

"Ah, Henri-go-to-church, go-to-church!" cried my brother; he was at his most animated and seemed ready to shout his pleasure even louder to the skies. His clothing was of the most respectable and his hat a new one. As I hesitated in dismay Betsy opened the far door of the carriage, stepped out, and closed it again, all so quietly that Henri did not notice. Thus my housekeeper had arranged matters so that I had to take Henri with me, or create an unthinkably undignified disturbance in front of Father, Tony, the servants, the neighbours and the crowd. I leaned out of the carriage window to remonstrate with the sly creature, but she had almost reached the corner of the house, her back expressively straight and her barefoot tread decisive — Matti's daughter in every inch of her frame. She had trapped me; I could only signal to Jacques to jump up in front and instruct the driver to set his mules in motion and draw as far ahead of the other carriage as possible.

Henri was excited by the rare treat of a journey by carriage but not so uncontrollably that I could not keep him calm by holding his hand and pointing out the sights. Unlike me, he had no foreboding about what would happen when we reached the church, and he thoroughly enjoyed himself, while I cast anxious looks behind and occasionally urged the driver to greater speed.

We arrived at the church with a few minutes to spare and I was tempted to alight and instruct the driver to take Henri home, but I knew not if the man was to be trusted, even with Jacques to watch him; moreover, I was again constrained by a crowd, for even at that early hour the Plaza was full of passers-by and idlers, all of whom would no doubt have thoroughly enjoyed my discomfiture if Henri had leaned out of the carriage window and complained at the top of his idiot voice about being abandoned. I decided that I must take him into the church and conceal him somehow. I was just helping him to alight when I saw, to one side of the church door and supported by two stalwart nuns, the frail figure of Maman. (At the time I took it that the nuns thought that no invitation was required for the mother of the bride. I learned later that Maman's presence was the result of further machinations by Betsy.)

Before I could recover from the shock of seeing Maman, there arose, from the Plaza along which we had just driven, a tumult of shouting and whip-cracking. I took a firm grip of Henri's hand and turned to look, as did all the onlookers. A sorry sight met our eyes — a procession of new-landed Negroes, perhaps one hundred men, women and children. They were all in a state of bodily emaciation and filthy beyond belief; their acute mental confusion was attested by the way in which they barely raised their heads whilst looking sideways at the strange passers-by and at the building which must have been just as unfamiliar. They were being herded slowly along toward the San José road by some of the most ruffianly English sailors I had ever seen. I wondered which foolish estate-owner had bought the poor creatures or, if they were not already sold, how the Liverpool contractors could make a profit on them — the ship's captain should at least have offered them a dowsing in the sea before exposing then to the gaze of possible purchasers in this state. Contrary to commonly held belief, Negroes are always willing to wash themselves.

My concern for the Negroes was only momentary for it was soon apparent that the noise of whips being cracked came, not from the sailors, who were armed only with staves, but from the drivers of two carriages who were trying to frighten the Negroes into giving way, something which they could hardly do since they were shackled together. Most of the shouting was coming from Spanish soldiers who appeared to be guarding the first carriage, a closed one — good heavens! — it was the carriage of el Gobernador himself! He must have decided to attend the wedding! In the open carriage behind, now stationary because of the fracas, I could just discern Tony standing up in her lilac gown, whilst Father appeared to be begging her to sit. Would either of them see Henri, or Maman, or both?

Henri was oblivious to all this commotion; he was pulling at my hand and crying: "Ah, piggy-piggy-piggy — " thereby attempting to draw my attention to a fine young porker trotting along the street, clearly intent upon escaping from the human clamour but not at the expense of his dignity. One part of my mind was thinking that his well-scrubbed plumpness would fetch his owner a better price than most of the Negroes would fetch theirs, but another was noticing that the two nuns were conducting Maman into the dark interior of the church. Without pausing to reflect whether another course of action would have been more appropriate, I dragged Henri away from his rapt contemplation of the retreating hog and followed the nuns. As my eyes became accustomed to the dim light I saw Edward and his groomsman sitting near the altar in pious attitudes and seemingly as oblivious as Henri to the disturbance outside. The nuns were standing as though undecided as to where they should properly sit.

"Follow me!" I whispered fiercely, and turned directly to the left, where I had spotted a dark corner. The nuns were not slow to grasp my purpose although they were somewhat puzzled by my vehemence, and we were soon seated on a bench where our presence would be almost entirely concealed by the darkness and by a group of those pious women who are to be found in church upon every occasion — their heads were adorned with high Spanish combs and mantillas, or with elaborate bonnets, all of which provided an excellent screen.

I was barely sensible of the arrival of el Gobernador or of his solemn progress to his seat, and I caught a mere glimpse of Tony upon Father's arm, for my attention was fixed upon keeping Henri quiet. In this I succeeded, helped by the briefness of the ceremony and by one of the nuns permitting Henri to play with a crucifix on a long chain. There was no music; if there had been I doubt if I could have dissuaded Henri from raising his voice. Maman, I noticed with some sorrow, was quite unaware of all that was happening around her; her eyes were empty and moist, although the moistness was not tears, and her hands were barely able to hold her rosary. I wondered if Father knew that his Madeleine's days were numbered.

At the end of the ceremony Maman, Henri and I were still hid from view as the pious ladies stood and craned to see Tony walk toward the door upon her brand-new husband's arm. I remained seated while Henri carried on playing with the crucifix, but in the interstices between the ladies' persons I could see that el Gobernador was following the couple up the aisle, condescendingly walking alongside Father, whose countenance was suffused with pride and pleasure — unlike me, he knew not of the strangeness of Tony's undergarments. When Edward and Tony had reached the church door, the pious ladies decided with one accord to curtsy to el Gobernador, so that he saw me for a moment and acknowledged my bow with the kind of smile which implies resignation at the need to undergo such fatiguing ceremonial nonsense. Unfortunately, Father also saw me and my companions; his face paled frightfully, but he continued to walk alongside Don José and to chat to him as though he had seen nothing.

The church did not take long to empty and I knew not which way to turn, for I was in terror as to what Father might say or do. However, almost straight away Jacques appeared from his post outside the door and told me that the Master had had a seizure and that my presence was required.

Outside, I found that the bride and groom and el Gobernador had left and that only the covered carriage remained; it was surrounded by a crowd composed of the wedding guests and onlookers. Taking a firm hold of Henri I thrust my way through the throng and found Father prostrate inside the carriage; his face was apoplectic and a merchant friend of mine was loosening his collar. Thanking this gentleman for his kindness, I helped Henri into the carriage, ordered Jacques to get up and the driver to set off and make good speed. At the last moment I saw Maman and her stout escorts and waved them goodbye. In the general hubbub I am sure I heard Henri crying "Ah, Fath-er! Fath-er! Fath-er!" in some distress.

Father did not regain consciousness, and his head jerked about horridly as the carriage jolted over the vile surface of Puerto Espana's streets, but he did continue to breathe, although stertorously. When we reached home I was able to have Jacques smuggle Henri to his room while I called loudly for help from the house. Edward appeared *en déshabillé* — he was already changing for the ride to Sans Peur — and carried Father to his chamber as though he were a child. (In passing, I noticed that the thickets of hair upon the backs of Edward's hands were joined to a veritable forest upon his forearms.)

In brief, the only trustworthy medico in the town was sent for; he revived Father, cupped him, and warned me gravely in his perfect Castilian that any excessive exertion or agitation could prove mortiferous for my esteemed father and that he must prohibit any journey on that day. Edward and Tony had therefore to mount and ride off to the celebrations by themselves, the latter wearing an elegant new habit with skirts, and riding side-saddle — I wondered how long it would be before that lady's-saddle galled the horse's back. Neither guessed what had caused Father's seizure, nor did I enlighten them.

I was not at all averse to missing both the jolting journey to Sans Peur and the noisy celebrations there, so I decided that I must stay in town and look after Father. In consequence, I cannot give my readers a first-hand account of the eating and drinking, or of the music and dancing, or indeed of anything else which took place out there upon that day. I did hear, at second hand, that while the white guests (there were no Mulattoes) enjoyed themselves at their part of the fête, the Negroes were sullen; having eaten or secreted away all the quantities of food and drink laid out for them, they stubbornly refused to make music, sing or dance. This behaviour was the penultimate ill-omen of the day and was caused, firstly, by our Negroes having witnessed the arrival at a nearby estate of the sorry batch of Africans which we had seen in the Plaza; most being Créoles, they did not express much sympathy for the unseasoned newcomers, but the very sight of the miserable creatures served to damp their spirits. The second cause of the Negroes' sullen-ness was that Edward had tried to bully them into a shew of hilarity, despite warnings from Tony that he was only making matters worse.

The final ill-omen of the day I did not learn of for many weeks — Tony refused Edward admission to her chamber, screaming abuse the while.

CHAPTER XVIII

I am pressed to consider Matrimony, but am discouraged by various Means; we lay Maman to rest; after an Incident at a Horse-Race I become concerned about Tony's Welfare and pay her a Visit

"We are men of the world, Monsieur Mason," said Monsieur Victor de G—, slapping me on the shoulder heartily, "and I know that you will not take offence if I say that you are renowned for the fidelity of your attachments — or when it comes to the ladies perhaps I should say attachment in the singular? — and Madame de G— and I perfectly understand that you might wish to maintain your present arrangements after you — " Here he hesitated, for he was not as great a man of the world as he pretended to be and he did not know how to finish his sentence. He had no less than five marriageable daughters (for the fever had been kinder to him than to many) and was most anxious that I should marry one of them — I might take my pick, it was all one to him, he implied, but Cécile the second eldest was particularly even-tempered and complaisant, and so used to leaving everything to the servants that he deemed her a most suitable match for me.

M. de G— was a French Créole from a family so well-known in the public affairs of la Trinidad over the past fifty years that I am withholding his surname to avoid embarrassment even to his descendants when I reveal that all his daughters' dowries put together would not have added up to the one I had had to arrange for Tony.

How did I answer M. de G—? I raised my eyebrows, pursed my lips and bowed ironically in the hope that I would discourage him without giving him cause for offence, for I had had profitable dealings with him and hoped to have more. Cécile was well enough — I had nothing against the pallid creature except that she shewed no signs of any intellect or spirit whatsoever and, what was more, that she had no lips, only a slit in her face for a mouth. (My readers, if you are amongst white people, look around you and you will understand what I mean.)

M. and Mme. de G— were not the only parents to be approaching me about their daughters, for shortly after Tony's marriage rumours about the generous size of her dowry, some of them accurate and some of them not, swept through la Trinidad's planter society like a bush fire and members of the Mason family were suddenly less than outcasts and strangers amongst the proud French Créoles. Father, though a Scottish barbarian, appeared to be a Catholic and a Royalist and had certainly served with distinction in the French army; Maman's antecedents as a de la Tour du Pin were impeccable; Tony had married a scion of a good English family who appeared to be a Catholic; I was known to be able to rub two pennies together to good effect; and last, but not least, the whiteness of our skins was beyond doubt.

The daughters presented for my inspection varied, of course, from the enchantingly beautiful (in the languid Créole fashion) to the lamentably plain; from dew-fresh sixteen-year-olds to purported twenty-five-year-olds (who demonstrated that they were able to perform at least one arithmetical calculation, that of subtracting ten from thirty-five); and from the speechlessly shy to those whose tinkling French flowed so incessantly and with such disregard for my sensibilities that I am astonished that their mothers had not warned them to hold their tongues. All these aspirants, even those who had been educated in France, had one quality in common — empty-headedness. One, of whom I had momentary hopes, had met a friend of M. Voltaire's in Paris but could not articulate a single one of the great man's ideas, nor had she understood a single word of *Candide* although she boasted that she had read a contraband copy in her convent school.

The tittle-tattle about "the singular fidelity of my attachment" to my housekeeper was largely erroneous, for Betsy and I did not speak to each other, except out of household necessity, for several months after her attempt to prevent Tony's marriage by alerting Edward Rochester to the various deceptions being practised upon him. I was angry, more angry than I had been for years, and she was ashamed, or so I hoped. However, as the procession of candidates for my bed and my fortune continued unabated, and it seemed that my resistance must eventually be weakened by the attractions of some charmer, I began to have messages conveyed to me in privy ways, for example, when I called for a coffee and Jacques was not available to serve it to me, it would be brought by one of Betsy's newly purchased young female acolytes, who would be unaware that betwixt cup and saucer there was concealed a small piece of folded paper. These notes were written in capital letters, were unaddressed and unsigned, and consisted of a summary of the qualities of the young lady currently on offer, along with a note of her dowry. Thus:

SWEET-TEMPERED: MUSICAL: NO LOVERS: STUPID: EX-TRAVAGANT: NOT ALTOGETHER CLEAN IN HER HABITS: MOTHER A TERMAGANT

It was notable that the authoress of these notes tried valiantly to be fair, and that her estimate of the dowry was accurate to within twenty doubloons or so.

These notes certainly served to discourage me from precipitate action, as did the unhappy example of Tony's marriage. After the wedding ceremony and the contretemps of the first night, Edward had taken her straight to the estate which I had bought for them in el Valle Diego Martin — Edward immediately named it l'Orangerie because of its large orange-garden. There, I learned, Edward set about clearing the uncleared part of the land and planting more sugar, although he was reported to be unwilling to take advice from Tony, preferring to consult his neighbour, a Martiniquan by the name of St. Hilaire Begorrat. When they came to visit me in town, or to stay over-night on their way to visit friends elsewhere, they rarely spoke to each other and when they did it was in a sharp and unpleasant manner. On one occasion Tony spoke to a servant in patois and Edward exploded.

"Antoinette," he shouted, "I thought that I had made it clear that you were not to speak in that corrupt and base lingo. Metropolitan French was your mother's tongue and, however mad she may be now, she taught you to speak it in a lady-like manner. There is no need for you to mumble like a nigger."

"Edward," replied Tony in her meek little-girlish voice, "you know well that I do not like to be addressed as Antoinette."

"I will not have my wife known by a name fit only for a small boy," said Edward curtly, "especially as she is considerably older than I."

"As you will, Edward," said Tony, still meek, "but the servants will not understand me if I speak to them in French."

"After all these years of working for you! Of course they understand French!" He then gave instructions in his heavily Anglicized French, which the terrified servant tried to understand, and failed to implement.

As to Betsy, if Edward had occasion to speak to her in French or

English she made it plain that she understood him, but answered him in patois only, speaking the words slowly, as though to a child. This fell just short of insolence, but made Edward very angry and he would clench and unclench his fists as though ready to strike her. Betsy was quite capable of staring him down on these occasions, much as her mother had stared down Father; she had even taken to crossing her hands in front of her.

Maman, although never as truly mad as Edward seemed to think, was nevertheless now in the final stages of her decline. Father grew impatient of not being recognized by her and only rarely rode in from Sans Peur to see her in the "nunnery", so that I was the only member of the family to visit her regularly and to watch her fade quietly toward Oblivion. When her end was only hours away and we were all assembled round her bed, the nuns, ever hopeful, were convinced that she knew that she was taking the last rites, but I could see no signs of consciousness at all. As soon as the priest had gone Father knelt down, weeping freely, and held Maman's hand until she breathed no more.

I need hardly inform my readers that I was not moved to tears and that my grief was far less poignant than at Matti's death; nevertheless, I had been concerned for some time that Maman should not be dishonoured by a poor funeral and had fortunately completed the purchase of a carriage just a week before her death. The very advantageous price included the shiny imported vehicle, its fine pair of horses (named Castor and Pollux) complete with their harness, and a smart Negro driver (who answered to the name of Sam) complete with his uniform.

Although it was only a short journey from the nuns' house to Calle de San Carlos we drove in proper style behind the hearse bearing Maman's remains. We buried her at the end of the lot in the same grave as Matti, a fact with which I did not deem it necessary to burden Father or Tony.

After the interment and the breakfast, when all the mourners had left and Edward and Tony were changing into their riding clothes, Father spoke to me tearfully. He was sipping a glass of the contraband *usque baugh* which I had obtained for him.

"Dickie," he said, "it is a privilege to have the love of a good woman — Madame your Mother was faithful to me until she died and I could wish that I had been as faithful to her. You should be finding yourself a wife and treating her with more consideration than I was shewing to your mother."

I could think of no answer to this.

Father dried his eyes and went on: "You have been meeting some suitable young ladies, I hear, and I could be arranging for even more, if you are fastidious."

"Father," I said, "I am not at all sure that I want to marry."

He eyed me quizzically over his glass.

"Satisfied with your present arrangements, are you?"

"Yes," I answered, as it seemed to be the least dangerous reply.

"But the family is needing a legitimate white heir and it is your duty to be fathering one. In the Name, pick yourself a young and submissive female — of good family, of course — and let Betsy be coaching her in the necessary arts."

"I shall consider your suggestion, Father," I said, somewhat stiffly, marvelling that he could so misunderstand what was occurring within his own family, while recognizing that I had always taken great pains to conceal my feelings and intentions from him. My heart, after my anger at Betsy's machinations at Tony's wedding had cooled, was set not so much upon having her as a mistress but more upon her again becoming the trusted, far-seeing and argumentative sister, friend and confidante with whom I could discuss family and business affairs. (What was more, for business reasons I needed every scrap of intelligence about the political and military situation in St. Domingue; Betsy, I was sure, was in touch with Jéhu and would have as much information as anyone in la Trinidad.) I flattered myself that I was making some progress in this respect, and for two reasons: one, she had been conveying those enlightening notes to me; and two, single books had been disappearing from my shelves, only to re-appear a week or so later, sometimes with annotations in Betsy's hand in the margins. If I asked the stubborn creature whether she had read a particular book she would nod in the affirmative but refuse to discuss the matter in the volume.

I must return to the day of Maman's funeral. Tony had been dry-eyed, although sombre, throughout the interment while Edward had been indifferent and impatient to return to his estate. Afterwards, at the house, Father seemed intent on continuing to impress upon me the benefits of matrimony, even in front of Tony and Edward, who were waiting to say their *adieux*. Thinking to change that dull and distasteful subject by introducing something more dramatic, I asked Tony whether she had heard that Arthur Dillon had been guillotined in Paris.

"No!" cried Tony, "it cannot be!"

"I assure you that it is so," I said, and read out the announcement in a Royalist news-sheet which had found its way into my possession: "*M. le Comte de Dillon est mort — il monta à l'échafaud en criant 'Vive le Roi!'*"

Tony's eyes filled with tears and her breast heaved, whilst Father's countenance turned pale as he dropped into a chair, so that I was afraid that I had broken the news too suddenly for his health. However, he stayed upright, muttering curses upon Danton, Robespierre and the rest, while

Tony's grief grew in violence and she shouted to the heavens to punish Arthur's murderers. Edward regarded his wife with some surprise and then with growing impatience.

"Who is this Arthur Dillon?" he demanded peremptorily.

Tony answered him not and continued to shout. I was about to explain who Arthur was, but Tony's cries became insupportable to him.

"Be quiet, Madam!" he shouted. "Your grief is not commensurate with its cause!"

At this Tony flung herself at him, uttering curses which my readers will not expect me to report, and beating upon his broad chest with her fists.

"Arthur was a gentleman," she screamed, "a true and loyal gentleman! Not a turncoat and monster like you!"

Edward did not tolerate the blows for long; he lifted his wife in his arms and carried her kicking and screaming through the house and across the yard to the stables. There Tony's yells became muffled and then stopped.

"Antonia has met her match at last," said Father.

We looked at each other and I saw in Father's pallid face that he too was assailed by doubt.

"It would seem so," I answered, listening to the sound of hooves as Edward and Tony rode away without the courtesy of *adieux*. I saw them not for many months.

Father soon regained his colour and declared that he was well able to ride back to Sans Peur, and must do so before darkness fell. Despite this apparent enthusiasm to return to his cane-fields, I learned later from Sam, who drove our baggage and provision cart to and from the estate when I did not require the carriage, that the Master seemed to have lost heart since Madame had died and spent a good deal of his time moping and drinking his *usquebaugh* and telling such friends as called that he had nothing to live for. I imagine that the world was of the opinion that I was adding to his sorrows by my dilatoriness about marrying and fathering an heir.

Sam, I may say, was beginning to prove that he was worth more than the carriage, horses and harness put together. He knew everyone from the highest to the lowest in the world of horses; he heard every piece of news that was worth hearing and could not rest until he had passed it around. He could not discriminate between the truly important and the merely interesting, so that one had to listen to much chit-chat in order to come at the real intelligence. He was not, of course, a person to whom one would confine a secret, unless one desired that secret to be broadcast throughout Puerto Espana and ultimately all of la Trinidad. Sam had a fine singing voice (in the raucous Negro style) and one could learn all one needed to know about the current sentiments of the Negro population by attending to the topical songs, some of his own composition, which he sang around the yard and whilst driving the carriage. Of course, one needed some imagination to penetrate the double entente which these songs invariably contained; and then more imagination (of a lascivious kind) to penetrate the second double entente behind the first.

It was Sam, then, who brought me tidings of an untoward event at a horse-race meeting on a large open pasture at el Socorro. This meeting was regarded as the most important of the equine year and crowds of people of all conditions, all degrees of respectability, and all colours of skin had ridden or walked thence from all over the Island; I had judged it in my own interest to give Sam the day off to attend. He reported upon his return that Master Edward was there, with several horses and all his grooms, but that he was not accompanied by his Madame; Sam had assumed that she was indisposed and had had to remain at home. Edward won two races and was fancied to win the longest and most important race of the day upon a large and powerful stallion which he had recently imported and which only he was skilled enough to ride. There was no formality about the ordering of these races and at the last possible moment there appeared a new entry, a lively and medium-sized horse which no one present recognized. It was ridden by a slightly-built jockey, his face invisible behind the kerchief which was needed to protect a rider's nose and mouth from the dust and flying stones thrown up by the galloping hooves. The race being a long one, Sam explained in the rapid patois which I have not attempted to translate, the horses disappeared behind some bush; when they reappeared Master Rochester and the unknown jockey were well ahead of the field and neck-and-neck. They stayed that way until the last fifty yards. (Here Sam's speech became incoherent with excitement and I had to make him repeat himself several times.) As the two horses rushed toward the winning-post the smaller horse edged ahead and Master Rochester, for all that he used the whip like a madman, lost the race by a head.

"Then jockey took off he mask, and he Madame Rochester," related Sam, full of simple pleasure in other people's trouble which could not possibly harm him. "Master Rochester's face like thundercloud. He grab she off she horse, jump on fresh horse and carry she home one time!"

This story had the ring of truth and I did not care to contemplate what the sequel might have been, but I was not to escape hearing that sequel for the following morning Betsy served my breakfast herself, a sure sign and signal that she had important news for me. She stood waiting patiently for my permission to speak, permission which I was in no hurry to give, for her face told me that her news was unpleasant as well as important. In the end I had to nod in answer to the urgency of her stare.

"Master Rochester has whipped Miss Tony and locked her up," she announced baldly in English.

I did not waste time with fruitless ejaculations or by asking for corroboration. "Is she injured?" I inquired.

"Her skin will be scarred for life," answered Betsy, "unless, of course, a white skin heals better than a black one."

"Where is she locked up? Not in one of the slaves' cells?"

"No, she is in an outside room, where Master Rochester cannot hear her shouting from the house."

The words "I told you so!" seemed to hang suspended in the air between us, but remained unsaid. My charming educated English friend had been revealed for what he was.

"What can I do?" I asked, but not aloud, or so I thought. I had forgotten that Betsy could hear my unspoken words, often before I had formed the thought behind them. She lifted her chin in her familiar manner, hesitated, and visibly made up her mind to give an answer to my question, regardless of whether I liked it or no.

"Master Richard," she said, "you were always a stick-in-the-mud. I think you should bestir yourself, order your carriage and go to see your unfortunate sister without delay."

"How dare you speak to me in such a manner?" I demanded in a fierce whisper, very much afraid that the other servants might have heard Betsy and gained a wrong impression.

Betsy's countenance did not change; she continued to stare at me out of scornful eyes and with the ends of her mouth turned down, while the vivifying shaft which she had sped in my direction took effect. I rose to my feet, although I had not finished my breakfast, and knocked over my chair while doing so. Standing, I looked down upon my housekeeper instead of up at her — but then I had looked down upon Father since I was fourteen years of age, and what advantage had that given me?

"Please tell Sam to harness the horses," I said furiously, "and that I will be going to — "

"There is no need to tell the world where you are going," interrupted Betsy, and proceeded to clear my breakfast things on to a tray and take them away.

Although I had arranged the purchase of l'Orangerie I had never been there; nor had I been to Sans Peur. In fact, loath though I am to admit it, I was indeed a stick-in-the-mud and had not left the muddy environs of Puerto Espana except upon the one occasion of my visit to

Tobago. Unsavoury and noisy and hot though the town was, I preferred it at all times to the sugar-estates which I had learned to hate and despise in my childhood; moreover, I found it prudent to visit my warehouse at least once every day, including Sundays. On this morning the prospect of sitting behind two horses for several hours was almost more than I could bear and I considered walking to l'Orangerie accompanied by Jacques carrying my umbrella, but decided that I would not be fit to meet Edward whilst fatigued and perspiring from the exertion.

The road to el Valle Diego Martin passed closer to the lowering mountains than was pleasant, but the journey was not overlong, and I found Edward at his breakfast, he having already spent several hours in the cane. He greeted me civilly enough, ordered fresh coffee for me and forbore to ask me my business until after he had finished the beefsteak and potatoes which he was eating.

"Well, Dick," he said, "so you have finally managed to drag yourself away from your compting-house to honour me with a visit?"

"Yes," I said, not knowing how to proceed, despite having rehearsed several gambits in the carriage.

"If you have come for the pleasure of my company I am afraid that I must disappoint you — I have incompetent overseers, dishonest book-keepers, and the laziest collection of Negroes that was ever over-valued for the purpose of inflating a dowry, so you must excuse me if I return to the cane immediately." He buckled on his belt and pistols, and picked up his hat and whip. "If you have anything to say to me, please be brief."

"Where is Tony?" I asked.

"Madame your sister is confined to her room."

"May I see her there?"

"No."

"I trust that she is well?"

"She is well enough and will be allowed visitors when she has come to her senses."

"Edward, I do not understand what you mean — there has never been any doubt about Tony's senses," I said, stilling any qualms about the truth of that assertion, "and perhaps if I talked to her — "

"As her husband," interrupted Edward, "I may say that I have talked and talked to Madame and I have declared an end of talking. She must learn to obey me and to act in a lady-like manner; to concern herself with the proper conduct of my household and with my comfort; and to give instructions to the house-servants only — I will have you know, Mr. Mason, that your sister has on numerous occasions countermanded my orders to my overseers and to my grooms, and that she has even attempted to intercede with me on behalf of a Negro whom I was punishing for the crime of attempted suicide. I will not have a woman interfering with what does not concern her."

"But," I protested, "Tony has known how to manage a plantation since she was twelve years of age; she knows more — "

"Mr. Mason, sir," interrupted Edward, "do not mention the years of her age to me for that is a matter on which you were party to a gross deception; and I would be obliged if you would refer to Madame your sister as Antoinette."

"Perhaps if I spoke to her — "

"I must warn you not to influence my wife against me."

"Edward, you are being most unreasonable. I beg you — "

"Mr. Mason, I would be obliged if you would leave my house and my land, thus abandoning the company of one whom you find unreasonable."

I made no move. Surely this was a bad dream?

"I am your very humble servant, sir, but I will shoot you if you do not comply immediately." He put his hand upon one of his pistols.

I attempted to make my departure a dignified one, but Edward did not scruple to let Sam and Jacques see that I was being hustled off the premises against my will. On the journey back to Puerto Espana Sam needed no prompting to tell me that he had never known Negroes more unhappy than those at l'Orangerie. Since la Trinidad was at that time dishonoured by brutal and oppressive planters (such as Begorrat) who provided much ammunition for the Abolitionists, Sam's statement was not one to be overlooked. Jacques, although more discreet as befitted a body-servant, nodded his head in agreement with Sam and let fall enough observations of his own for me to understand that Edward's lust for money was driving him to inhuman excesses.

On my return home I was so distressed in my mind that I straightway called Betsy into my presence and asked her to sit, but she said that she would prefer to remain standing. I then informed her of all that had happened at l'Orangerie, and we had a lengthy consultation, during which we began to regain a degree of that intimacy of like minds for which I had so long been yearning. (Truly, "'tis an ill wind that blows no man to profit".) We debated how best we could help Tony and had to agree that there was little to be done, since a wife had to obey her husband and Spanish law and custom were clear upon that point. As to the Negroes at l'Orangerie, Betsy asked me to defer spreading word of their plight until she had questioned Sam and Jacques and had made further inquiries. Upon our convening again, Betsy confirmed that all I had heard was true and pressed me to inform el Gobernador himself, using all the discretion for which I was now becoming well known. This I did, only to discover that my enlightened friend was entirely subordinate to the power of the French Créole planters, who were insistent that French practices with regard to the Negroes should prevail over Spanish law, which was more liberal, at least in intent.

As I fretted about my inability to help Tony, and Betsy fumed about her inability to help her fellow-Negroes, we both had to come to terms with our inability to help Henri, for he had become subject to intermittent bouts of a fever which made it difficult for him to breathe and he had to spend much of his life in bed, keeping as quiet as his nature would allow. When these attacks were at their worst, Betsy and I would sit with him of an evening, holding his two hands until he fell asleep. It is, I repeat, an ill wind etc., for after many months of thus sitting with Henri, sometimes even when he was not ill, we became so accustomed to each other's company that we would continue to sit and talk long after he had fallen asleep. We even took to playing cards together and sharpening our wits against each other as we had done in childhood. As time went on the sums for which we played became less and less paltry, for Betsy rarely seemed to be short of the necessary currency. I suspected, and still suspect, although I have not questioned her upon the subject, that she had been financing ventures of her own (almost certainly concerned with silk, satin, cambric, millinery goods and the like) from incidental surpluses in the household monies, much as I had had to do with the estate cash. Legally, as we both knew well, all her money was mine, as she was my property, but as we also knew well, any attempt on my part to lay hands on her money would have been doomed to failure, so well would it have been tied up in loans, joint ventures, etc. etc. Somehow this knowledge added to our sense of intimacy as we increased our stakes, and then increased them further. Lest any of my readers might think that I deliberately lost to Betsy in order to buy the friendship of which I represent myself as so desirous, I must state unequivocally that I would not have so insulted her intellect — she was perfectly capable of emptying my purse without my help.

CHAPTER XIX

My Sister's Troubles do not abate; Father grows old; after an Argument, Betsy and I come to an Agreement

As a house-servant and a Negress Betsy had sources of information which were denied to me. Had it not been for her I would have known little of Tony's sufferings at the hands of Edward Rochester during the years that followed the incident at the horse-race: how she would be quiet for a week or more in her prison-house and would then be allowed out for a few days to ride with Edward about the estate in daylight and to mope about the house in the evenings; how a quarrel would follow, sometimes out of doors but more commonly in Tony's chamber at night, and she would be incarcerated again, shouting foul abuse at Edward and begging and cajoling the servants to release her. The source of the outdoor quarrels, it seemed, was usually to do with Edward's treatment, or maltreatment, of his Negroes, for he had not failed to emulate the practices of his infamous neighbour St. Hilaire Begorrat. The causes of the night-time quarrels were clear enough, though Betsy delicately confined herself to generalities accompanied by significant looks — I understood that Edward's assertion of his rights did not always meet with immediate submission from Tony.

On one occasion Tony escaped by a stratagem, mounted Edward's big stallion Mesrour and rode him bareback to Sans Peur, a feat which is the subject of a Negro song still commonly sung. (The later stanzas of the song assert that Tony was *enceinte* and lost the child as a consequence of the ride — to this day I know not if there was any truth in this story, though Betsy and I agreed that she was capable of deceiving Edward into thinking she was expecting a child, for she had become as cunning as Anansi — all informants were agreed upon that.)

Edward, naturally, went to look for his wife and his favourite horse. He called first at our house in Calle San Carlos and finding that she was not there proceeded to my office. When he had convinced himself that I had no knowledge of her "escape" or her whereabouts, he announced his intention of riding to Sans Peur and addressed me thus:

"It is time, Mr Mason sir, that the Governor set up a proper asylum in which people like Madame your sister could be locked up for their own good and for the safety of others. Perhaps you could use your influence with the benighted *hidalgo* to that end."

I learned later that Father had surrendered Tony to Edward and that my poor sister returned to l'Orangerie riding upon an ass and with her legs tied together by a rope which passed under the beast's belly. This also became part of the song and I cannot imagine a greater humiliation for the intrepid horsewoman than to be shackled in this manner and then held up to ridicule by illiterate songsters.

That Father had thus yielded to Edward was a measure of his loss of heart. He had delegated most of his business affairs to me, (unaware, of course, that he had little choice in the matter as the papers he had signed when I was amassing Tony's dowry had transferred virtually all his assets to me — a fact which, as a true conspirator, I did not reveal to him in his life-time.) He had also appointed a manager at Sans Peur — it is another measure of his condition that he promoted Alexander to this post; in his prime he would not have considered a Mulatto for any employment.

After a seizure, almost certainly brought on by hearing of the freeing of the Negroes by the French Assembly in 1794, Father began to spend more and more time in Calle de San Carlos. There I tried to calm his immoderate responses to political and military events in Europe and the Caribbean; of an evening I would encourage him to speak rather of his youth which, it appeared, bore some resemblance to Tony's youth in Tobago, involving as it did much horse-riding over hills. However, it seemed that he had been more interested in books than Tony ever was. He and his brothers had had a tutor at home and he had attended the University of Louvain for a year or two before deciding that he preferred the life of a soldier to that of a pedant (if that is the word). Even in the French Army he had continued to read his books, but after marrying Maman he had discovered that she had no interest in any books but romances and pious works of the more insipid kind. When he arrived in the West Indies he had quickly learned that plantation society was entirely inimical to the reading of books, so he had locked his chest and hidden it away. Now, after telling me about his education, he asked me to look out *Robinson Crusoe* for him and he read it, very slowly but with evident enjoyment, at least three times over.

At other times Father would describe to me, unprompted, all the ramifications of the Macdonald clan and speculate where various clansmen were and what they were doing now. They had spread, he explained, from Scotland to France, the Carolinas, Canada, Italy and even Russia. He insisted that I write down the name and address of Mr. Andrew Tulloch, his Edinburgh lawyer, whom I might consult if I wished to find out if I had a claim to the title of Chief or to any of the clan's land.

I listened to Father's rambling discourses with some interest, but often with some impatience, for they deprived me of many a game of whist with Betsy. Upon occasion he would notice my impatience.

"Go to your lady, then," he would say, "though why you cannot be having children I do not understand at all. Brown Macdonalds on the wrong side of the blanket would be better than no Macdonalds whatever."

As if to demonstrate that he was capable of enjoying children's company he took up with one of Janga's three charges, Milly's half-Charaibe half-Negro son Merry, who despite his mother's lack of intellect was growing to be a bright straight-nosed little charmer of the kind who were often selected for export in small batches to Europe, to be sold for high prices to aristocratic ladies as page-boys. Father would call the little fellow from the yard to the back gallery and there indulge him shamelessly, and would sometimes even include Merry's two jet-black age-mates Prince and Earl in the spoiling. When I attempted to reprove him, he was brusque.

"A man without heirs is entitled to be enjoying his small pleasures," he would say pointedly. However, if Betsy remonstrated with him by giving him the same black stare as Matti used to, he would huff and puff, end whatever noisy game he was playing with the little boys, and send them to her to be returned to the yard and proper discipline.

Of an evening, in Henri's room, Betsy and I would often lay down our cards and exchange intelligence about world affairs and discuss them with great animation. Thus was I kept up-to-date about the progress of the Negro rebellion in St. Domingue and about Jéhu's part in it. He had joined the Negro army led by Christophe (and later by Toussaint l'Ouverture) and had been promoted quickly because of his soldierly qualities; His knowledge of English had also been of great use to the Negroes when the British took a hand and sent their doomed army to St. Domingue. Betsy now referred to her brother, with affectionate sisterly mockery, as "M. le Capitaine".

How Betsy obtained all this news I did not inquire; I inferred that she had letters and messages from Jéhu brought by Negro crew on inter-island schooners. We thought it best for Father's fragile health not to share too much of our intelligence with him.

One evening, ask me not to date it, we became very heated in argument over some news from unhappy St. Domingue of a massacre perpetrated by people of one colour against people of another colour. It did not help us to reach accord that the intelligence which Betsy had received differed so markedly in substance from that which I had received from my sources.

"Would you not prefer," I exclaimed testily, "to leave la Trinidad and go to St. Domingue if that is the way in which you view the slaughter of innocent people? I hear that even the Negresses are being given weapons and take great delight in cutting off the members of any whites or Mulattoes they capture."

Betsy drew away from me by sitting back in her chair. She gazed at me steadily out of her black eyes until both our tempers had had time to cool.

"Master Richard," she then said, "I would not make a soldier, for however much I may desire Freedom for myself and my people, I am not at all sure that killing and maiming and burning are the means to achieve what we must have. The hatred they fan into flames will live on in people's hearts, and Liberty gained by bloodshed will be old Slavery and Oppression in a new guise."

I answered this prophetic speech by dealing out the cards and indicating that we should restart our game. Betsy did not object and picked up her hand. In the subsequent play I found I was so flustered that I could not attend properly to the cards and I lost heavily, and went on losing. At the end of our session I did not have enough cash to pay Betsy her very substantial winnings and had to promise to pay her on the morrow.

"You need not pay me in cash at all," said Betsy, and though her voice was matter-of-fact, her eyes were dancing with glee. "I will accept the freedom which you promised me so long ago in settlement of this debt of honour."

Betsy knew well that I had not arranged for her manumission because it was a legal process which could not easily be concealed; because Father would have been enraged, or so I believed, at a Negress being freed at such a young age — manumission to him was a reward for a lifetime of service and unquestioning loyalty; and because any action which appeared to favour Negro emancipation would have caused such a scandal amongst the French Créole planters that I would have lost much business amongst them, and they were, after all, my principal customers. Betsy understood business and the necessities of business, but she also knew almost as well as Mr. O'Brien just how wealthy I now was and was challenging me to use that wealth, and the position I had established for myself in Puerto Espana (for there was even talk of my being appointed to the Illustrious Cabildo, now known more prosaically as the Town Council), and the influence I had with el Gobernador.

"The Master — " I began, but Betsy interrupted me.

"The Master," she said, "has offered me my freedom in return for certain favours, to be bestowed in private."

"But you are my property," I said, stammering over the two p's.

"He seems to have forgotten about that; if, indeed, he ever knew. He is an old man."

"You refused him the favours, of course?"

Betsy seemed to be relishing my discomfiture. Her eyes were dancing again. She delayed her answer until I was ready to shake it out of her.

"Of course," she said, "but I fancy he will return to the subject. He is lonely."

"Would you accept my word —?"

"Master Richard, you know that I would need a paper. Otherwise I might as well wait for the French Republicans or Mr. Clarkson to invade la Trinidad and free me."

I absently shuffled and re-shuffled the cards while I attempted to bring order to the confusion of my thoughts. I did not want to use any of my influence to free Betsy, yet I wanted to please her and to enjoy the new kind of friendship which I was certain would follow when I no longer owned her. Yet if I no longer owned her, she might use her freedom to depart and leave me friendless.

As was usual, Betsy brought order to the confusion.

"If we had a *coartación* agreement," she said, "it need not be flaunted in the public eye."

Coartación, I should explain to my readers, was an old Spanish custom which was unknown to the French Créole planters and which is now totally forgotten in la Trinidad. By it, master and slave fixed a price for the slave's freedom which could not thereafter be changed and which the slave paid over an agreed period out of wages paid by the master. The custom was not enshrined in any law and was more of the nature of a business contract. It could be kept private, unless the slave's status was questioned and one of the parties applied to the *Alcalde*.

I shall not weary my readers with a description of the negotiations with Betsy which took place in Henri's room over the next few evenings. We ended with a *coartación* agreement (witnessed by Don José himself in a typical act of condescension) by which Betsy was to be free in three years. When all was done, I began to fret again and to wonder how Betsy would use her freedom when it came. I therefore questioned her obliquely on the matter several times without receiving a satisfactory answer. Then, one evening as Henri laying wheezing in his sleep, I summoned courage and asked her directly.

"Will you stay as my housekeeper after you are free?"

Betsy looked up at me, then turned her head to look at Henri.

"I shall stay as long as Master Henri needs me," she said, and would vouchsafe no more, no matter how hard I pressed her.

CHAPTER XX

Edward Rochester comes to see me bearing not unexpected News, but makes a surprising Request; I visit l'Orangerie and am distressed at what I find

"Mr. Rochester to see you, sir," said Mr. O'Brien, now my trusted head-clerk, hurriedly putting his head round the door of my office before being pushed ignominiously out of the way by Edward.

"Good morning, Dickie!" said the latter. "So this is where the money is coined!" He looked around my bare little room as if expecting to see bags of gold in evidence.

"Good morning, Mr. Rochester," I said curtly without rising, and inspecting my brother-in-law minutely, for I had not seem him for some eighteen months. He had not changed, except in that his complexion had been burned even darker by the sun, and in that his features seemed set in an indelible sneer, which was at variance with the hearty and jocular manner which he was affecting.

"Antoinette sends you her kind regards," he said, adding carelessly, "— and her love, of course."

"She is well, I trust?"

"Well enough, Dickie, well enough. And how is your esteemed father?"

I knew already that Edward had news to impart, but now began to harbour a suspicion that he had some favour to ask as well. He was so hail-fellow-well-met that I would not have been surprised had he acknowledged Henri's existence for once, and inquired after his health.

This visit was taking place at the beginning of the year 1797, a twelvemonth so full of important events that it may take me more than one chapter to describe them. At the time of Edward's visit they were not, of course, to be foreseen, though some were casting their dark shadows ahead of them.

When I had assured Edward that Father was as well as could be expected, he hemmed and hawed a while and then asked me how the war was affecting my ventures and the safety of the ships in which they were carried. I raised my eyebrows, for I had no intention of discussing my affairs with Edward.

"I did not think to find myself in enemy territory," he said, again referring to Spain joining France in hostilities against Britain, news of which had reached us a few weeks before, "and it is deuced inconvenient to me in my changed circumstances."

Ah, thought I to myself, he is about to divulge his good news; news of which I, with my network of informants, had already been apprised.

"I have just learned that both my father and my elder brother Rowland are dead," said Edward, with a gleam of cupidity in his deep-set eyes. He then paused, giving me the opportunity to offer the formal condolences which I had carefully rehearsed.

"Mr. Rochester, sir," I said. "To lose an esteemed father is sad enough, but to lose a beloved elder brother at the same time must be truly heart-rending. Please accept my deepest sympathy and condolences. I am sure that my father will hear of your unexpected double loss, and his, with dismay and unalloyed sorrow."

The gleam in Edward's eyes remained undimmed.

"Dickie," he said, "you have learned flowery language from your Hispanic friends. I prefer English bluntness. I did not have much time for either my father or my brother nor did they for me. A younger son with extravagant tastes is always an embarrassment, and they disposed of me by the deception to which you and your father were parties." Here he glowered at me for a moment. "But that is now past history, for my father's estates in England are extensive and I inherit every single acre, as well as the family mansion of Thornfield, where I was brought up."

"I must congratulate you," I said, conveying only too clearly the coolness I felt.

"Thank-you, Dickie. I shall not further beat about the bush. Firstly, I propose to take Antoinette back to England as soon as I can obtain a passage. There I will be better able to make arrangements which will be in keeping with her station in life and her condition. I have promised her access to one of the finest stables in England and that has calmed her somewhat, for the time being at least. Secondly, I would like to ask you, as my brother-in-law, whether you would be good enough to manage l'Orangerie for me in my absence. Needless to say, I would make it worth your while."

I was astounded at his effrontery in asking this favour, considering that he had forbidden me to enter his estate even for the purpose of visiting my only sister. Moreover, to agree to manage his stock of discontented and demoralized Negroes would have been folly as great as taking on those of M. Begorrat, whose harshness he had aped with such eagerness. I therefore looked at Edward with a countenance as severe as I could make it.

"I think," I said, "that I should take you to tell your news to my father before I give you my answer to that request."

"Come now, I have much business in town. Surely you can give me your agreement now?"

I was obdurate, for I needed time to work out how best to refuse Edward, and in the end he agreed to call for his horse and his groom and to accompany me while I walked back to Calle de San Carlos.

Father was now almost permanently resident with us in view of his poor health and because he found the Sans Peur estate house a lonely place. When Edward and I arrived we found him sitting on the front galerie at the exact spot where the breeze was most cooling; he greeted Edward with some reserve but shewed none of the hostility towards him which I was experiencing — but, after all, he had not been ordered off Edward's land.

I left them together exchanging barbed pleasantries and hastened to the back of the house to find Betsy, for that morning she had elected to serve my breakfast and had told me the news that Edward had inherited great wealth and was taking Tony to England; I wanted to hear her views on the latest developments. However, she was not in the house, so I instructed Jacques to look for her down the yard and was waiting impatiently on the back galeries when I heard raised voices from the front of the house. Neither Father nor Edward subjected himself to the discipline of Reason, and in consequence both were liable to give free rein to their passions, so I immediately returned through the house with the intention of attempting to calm them, for the medico had forbidden Father excess of any kind, but when I was about to emerge on to the galerie I discovered that my strong preference was to remain where I was, in concealment, and hear as much as I could.

"— Edward," Father was saying, "you are a disgrace to your line — I had not thought that any Rochester could be so disloyal — "

"Mr. Mason, sir, the cause of the House of Stewart has been nothing but romantic folly for the whole of this century — " here Father swore an oath in Gaelic, but Edward continued, "— as you will discover when the British conquer this Island as they have already conquered Tobago; it will be essential if we are to defeat France and Spain together and gain a toe-hold upon South America. Then you may advocate the cause of the House of Stewart at the top of your voice and you will be laughed at for your pains — that is, if anyone takes the trouble to listen to you. Jacobitism is now nothing but a subject for sentimental songs written by Scotch ladies so that their daughters may sing languishingly about Prince Charlie of an evening — "

"Enough!" Father was now beside himself. "Your father was saving my life at the risk of his own, but I have repaid that debt, in so far as it can ever be repaid, and were I not an old man and were you not my son-in-law, I would be throwing you down these steps — "

At this point I became aware that Betsy was behind me, also eavesdropping on the altercation. I turned my head and she curtsied to me. Then, as Father's rage mounted to the point where it was plainly a threat to his well-being, Betsy motioned me to go out to him. This was against my inclination for I had never overcome my aversion to Father when he was in a fury, but my housekeeper's influence over me was strong enough to propel me through the door.

I found that Father's face was crimson as he confronted Edward; his chest was heaving and he was clasping and unclasping his hands in front of him. In contrast, Edward's sallow face had gone sallower and behind his back he was bending and unbending the stock of his whip between his Herculean hands.

"Mr. Rochester," I said, "Pray come to the stable with me. Your groom tells me he is deeply concerned about your horse."

Edward turned to me. "What is the matter with Mesrour?" he asked.

"Your groom did not say, but he was most agitated. Pray come!"

It never fails to astonish me that those infatuated with the equine race can be deflected from almost any course of action by the news that one of their animals is out of sorts. Edward left Father without a by-your-leave or a backward glance and followed me through the salon whence, as was to be expected, Betsy had disappeared.

"Mr. Rochester, sir," I said, when we had reached the steps down to the yard, from which Janga's charges were vanishing at speed, "I have to confess that I have deceived you. There is nothing wrong with your horse, but my father must not be over-excited and I thought it proper to end your quarrel by a stratagem."

"Ha!" exclaimed Edward, "so Antoinette has been truthful in one particular at least. She told me, when she was still capable of rational speech, that stratagems were your *métier* and to be careful whether I believed anything you said."

Seeing that Edward had calmed himself with remarkable speed, perhaps thinking that a man as rich as he now was need never lose his temper, I risked an ironical bow, as between acknowledged liars. Edward did not notice and continued:

"So you desire to keep your father alive as long as possible?"

"He is my father," I said.

"But would you not benefit, as I have, by losing a father?"

"Mr. Rochester, I am a wealthier man than my father and I do not desire him to die."

"A true Christian, I perceive. Now then, I have no time to waste — will you, or will you not, manage l'Orangerie for me?"

"I am no Christian, Mr. Rochester, but an adherent of Reason, and Reason tells me that it would not be in my interest, nor in that of my family, for me to manage an estate for you; unless, indeed, you would care to make l'Orangerie over to me in trust for my sister."

"This is some stratagem, Dickie. Reveal your true purpose or — " I could see that his temper was rising again.

"This is no stratagem, I give you my word."

"You must be mad!" cried Edward. "This is your final word?"

"Yes," I answered quietly.

"In that case — " he shouted, and raised his whip, but thought better of it, and shouted for his horse. His groom, who must have anticipated a sudden departure, immediately led the horse into the yard. When Edward had mounted, he cursed me roundly for wasting so much of his time that he would not be able to return to his estate before dark.

After he and his groom had galloped away I stood motionless until the sun began to press heavily upon my shoulders and forced me to act upon my thoughts. For once, I had no need to consult Betsy, only to inform her. I called for Sam and my carriage and for Jacques, checked over my pistols and ammunition, and set off for l'Orangerie, directing Sam to make the best speed of which the horses were capable.

When I arrived in el Valle Diego Martin I was in some trepidation lest Edward had changed his mind and returned home, or had led me to l'Orangerie by a trick for nefarious purposes. I took the precaution of concealing the carriage on a little-used trace amongst high cane, instructing Sam to look out for Master Rochester; if he appeared, Sam was to signal by a whistle to Jacques, whom I posted half-way between carriage and house.

I approached the house on foot and was met by Edward's butler, who began to shake with fear when I asked to be announced to Madame Rochester. He knew who I was, for Milly was standing just behind him, but was clearly torn between fear of Edward, who had decreed that Madame Rochester was to receive no visitors, and fear of me, another Master who, I was surprised to learn from Sam later in the day, was credited with vast power, being rich as the King of Ashanti and able to buy and sell everyone on the Island, right up to el Gobernador himself. (I suspect that Sam was more likely to foment than to deny rumours of my power and wealth; it redounded to his credit that he was owned by such a one.)

Perceiving this fear, although not yet fully cognisant of its cause, I bullied the poor trembling butler into directing me towards the outside room where Tony was incarcerated, assuring him that I would tell everyone that I had made my way there myself without calling at the house, and that he was blameless. I made him promise to send Milly if any of Edward's overseers should return from the cane and shew an interest in my presence. I also tipped him handsomely for a promise of silence from himself and the other house-Negroes. His last words to me were: "Massieu, don't give she no flint and steel or she burn the place down and Massieu Rochester kill me!"

Tony's room was set amongst other buildings and distinguishable by stout bars over the windows, which were set high above the ground. The massive door was secured by a hasp, staple and padlock, all of which I recognized as having been purchased from a batch of the strongest I had ever imported — they were manufactured by the same firm in the United States as made manacles for slaves and were a fast-selling line of goods, a measure of the unsettled conditions then obtaining in Trinidad.

I can no longer postpone describing my conversation with Tony, much as I would like to. As I approached the door her ever-keen ear must have heard my footsteps for she called out: "Who is there?"

I found myself so moved at the sound of her voice that I could not answer and coughed in an embarrassed manner.

"Whoever you are, you cough like my brother Dickie."

"You are right, Tony," I said, "it is I."

"Oh Dickie! You have come at last!" she cried. "But does Rochester know you are here?"

"No, I have come alone."

"He will kill you if he finds you talking to me. Are you armed?"

"Yes, I have my pistols and I have posted sentries and in any case he told me that he will not return until after dark."

"So you have come to release me from this prison?"

"Tony, I do not have the key to the padlock."

"Fetch a crow, then, and prise off the lock, for God's sake. There are crows in the tool-store."

"Where are the keys for the padlock?"

"Rochester carries one on his person and he has left the other in the charge of that vile man Begorrat."

Begorrat! If he was in league with Edward over the confinement of Tony, and discovered me here, there was no knowing to what violence he might resort. He was notoriously free with his pistols as well as his whip. Tony became impatient.

"Dickie, stop being so dilatory! Fetch a crow and let me out!"

"Does not Edward release you at all?"

"Only when I promise to behave and he can keep an eye on me. Fetch a crow and some strong Negroes, in the Name of God!"

There was no way in which I could avoid infuriating Tony, for I needed time to inspect the woodwork and the iron fastenings of the door and the windows. All were strong enough to withstand any but the most energetic and determined assault by several men armed with sledges as well as crows, a proceeding so noisy that it would alert the countryside and perhaps Begorrat to the fact that something untoward was happening. I could think of no stratagem to obtain the key.

"Has Edward told you that he proposes to take you to England?" I asked, "and to make better arrangements for you there?"

"England!" screamed Tony, "How can I tell if he will treat me better there? He has made all sorts of promises, but he is a bigger liar than you are — how can I believe him? There are madhouses in England and if he locked me up in one no one would ever know and that would be the end of me! And it would be your fault!" Here Tony paused and I thought she was taking breath to continue with her raging, but she quietened as suddenly as she had become enraged and shortly I heard her sobbing — a most strange and unfamiliar sound.

"It is my own fault," she said between sobs, "that he is going to rush me away on the first ship that is available. I told him that the Negroes would start planning to poison him as well as each other if he did not mend his ways but he is so mistrustful that he thought I was threatening to poison him. Dickie, I have married a madman; he is quite without humanity. I have no one to help me if you do not." Here she broke into heart-rending wails, which lasted for a long while.

I was thinking that Betsy and Father and I could surely find a way of releasing Tony if we put our heads together, but before I could tell her so she spoke again, in a pleading voice, like a little girl's, so that I was reminded that she was now reputed to be as cunning as Anansi.

"Dickie, if you cannot release me, and I know it is almost impossible, will you please do me one favour before Edward takes me to England?"

"If it is within my power," I said cautiously, "and I think it is a reasonable request."

"Give Betsy back to me!"

I was bereft of speech.

"Dickie, you are my brother and you know how often I saved you from whippings by Father. Betsy is the only person who could save me from whippings by my husband — she is clever like you and can think of clever ways of getting out of trouble, and she is strong like Matti and can face up to people without losing her temper in the way I do, and she is not your mistress, is she? No, you have not the mettle for that, so you will not mind parting with her."

I stared at that unyielding door in disbelief.

"Dickie, are you listening? I know that she knows that she would be free as soon as she sets foot in England but I would pay her a good wage and we were such happy playmates when we were girls — "

"Tony — " I answered, and could not utter another word.

"Come close to the door. Can you hear me when I whisper thus?"

"Yes," I whispered back.

"I would not mind if Betsy became Edward's mistress, for then she would have a hold over him and he would not plague me so much. He often compares me unfavourably with her — "

"Tony," I interrupted, having found my voice, "Betsy is free already. She made the last payment on her *coartación* just a few months ago — "

"You have freed her by *coartación*? You cannot have been such a *mook*! You are telling me one of your nancy-stories!"

"— and I do not think that she would agree to serve you as your maid whatever the wages you offered her. On the one hand, she does not easily forget or forgive injury, and on the other, she has promised me that she will stay with me as long as Henri needs her — "

"Injury? What injury is it that you are speaking of?"

"You sold her."

"But, Dickie, being sold to the d'Aumont's was the making of her! She came back from Paris with such style and so many accomplishments that she had quadrupled in value. You know what you had to pay to buy her from that other captain. I did her no injury."

"She might have a different opinion."

"And you would encourage her in that opinion! You are — " Here Tony gave vent to a torrent of abuse so violent that I was glad of the stout door between us. As usual, I do not propose to set it out upon paper except to write that it was mainly directed against my lack of manliness in not producing a male heir — as long as I was childless Edward could hope to inherit my wealth through Tony, and his lust for money was boundless. So long as that hope existed, he would never part with her.

I did not tarry to hear Tony out. Instead, I withdrew rapidly toward my carriage and was driven away, a sad and frightened man, convinced that all my wealth and influence would not enable me to release Tony and conceal her thereafter, for Edward had the law on his side. I was not yet ready to father a legitimate heir merely to protect Tony from her husband.

That evening, after Betsy had sung poor wheezing gasping Henri to sleep with his favourite Créole song, I apprised her of what had happened at l'Orangerie. We discussed it late into the night but came to no conclusion except that there was little or nothing that either of us could do to help my poor sister, much as we might pity her when out of the reach of her tongue. As Betsy pointed out tartly, she had married Edward Rochester of her own free will after she had been warned as to his true and dreadful nature.

CHAPTER XXI

A hostile Fleet appears off Puerto Espana; Father's unconcerned Behaviour;
I take Precautions and we are not molested; I suffer a grievous double
Loss

I can assure my readers that there are few experiences so disagreeable or so daunting as to look out from a hole which one has just made in one's own roof and to see from an unfamiliar angle a familiar town where the streets are empty except for occasional gangs of revolutionary ruffians, and where the cattle and goats have disappeared from every patch of waste ground, and then to raise a telescope to one's eye and look straight into the open gun-ports of a dozen or more ships of the line. What were the British ships' intentions? What could be the import of all the strings of signal-flags being run up and down the ships' rigging with such speed and frequency? Were they giving the command which would cause the open ports to belch flames and smoke and send hundreds of cannon-balls or — dreadful thought! — fire-bombs hurtling through the air toward us?

After watching the ships until I became faint with terror I descended into the darkness and airlessness of the shuttered house below and spoke to Father, urging him to leave for Sans Peur whilst there was still time.

"No, Dickie," said Father, looking up from the pistols which he had been inspecting and testing with especial care, "I do not care how many English ships have their ports open and their guns trained upon us, I will not be slinking away in that damned slow jolting carriage of yours." His voice was strong, despite his frail trembling body, and he would not allow me to interrupt him. "Little though I am liking the sight of red-coats, and indeed I was hoping that I had seen the last of them when Arthur chased them out of Tobago, yet I would sooner stay in town where they will

249

be new-landed and sober, and where I will have due warning of them marching up the street and can be ascertaining their strength and their temper and taking measures to defend myself — " Here he held up his pistols in a meaningful gesture, but still would not let me speak. "— No, I will not retreat with my tail between my legs, for at Sans Peur they could march up in a drunken mob, fire the cane half-a-mile to windward of the house and finish me off as they have finished so many Macdonalds since the infamous treacheries of Glencoe and Forty-Six. I thought I was safe on a Spanish Island, but I have instructed Alexander to swear that the owner of the estate is a loyal subject of the King of Spain and would sooner be swearing fealty to King George or the Devil Himself than to a rabble of cut-throat Republicans — "

"Father, sir," I begged, "pray do not speak so loudly! You know that the streets are full of — " I did not need to specify the bands of free Mulattoes and Negroes, all wearing red-white-and-blue *cocardes*, and all armed, if only with cutlasses and *bois*.

"The Mulattoes and the Negroes are not joining together in the same bands?"

"No, of course not, Father, not after the massacres in St. Domingue."

"Well then, indeed, they will be at each others' throats before sundown and we will have nothing to fear from them." Father stood up, drew his sword and made a few thrusts and parries in the air, and then sat down again, somewhat short of breath.

"But, Father," I protested, my ears awaiting the first thump of cannon-fire, "the British ships may commence a bombardment at any moment, and when they land troops there will be fighting in the streets — "

"And are you expecting myself, Hamish Macdonald, to be afraid of cannon-balls and of fighting?" demanded Father, seemingly forgetting that he had ever called himself Jonas Mason, and challenging me to say that I was not afraid of fighting. When I did not respond, for reasons which are well known to my readers, he continued: "If the English land — "

"*When* the British land — " I dared to interrupt.

"Very well then, indeed, you are right, when the British land they will settle the Republican's hash very expeditiously altogether. You have the British flag ready to hang out if needful?"

"Yes, Father," I said somewhat impatiently, for I was anxious to climb up to the roof again, in case the British were making their intentions clearer. I was still the same being who, all those years ago in Tobago, had been impelled to patrol restlessly, checking on all the preparations and precautions over and over again. I had had warning from several of my sources that the British fleet was due to arrive and had looked out our ancient flag, which had been severely attacked by insects and mould since we last flew it in Tobago; its dilapidated state conveniently suggested that we were long-time adherents of the British Crown. I had been provident in other ways too, for I had made sure that we had water sufficient for both drinking and fire-fighting, while Betsy, unbidden, had purchased plentiful supplies of food and coals, and had moved Henri and the servants into the house.

At this point the confabulation between Father and myself was interrupted by six-year-old Merry marching into the salon, followed by his two playmates. Merry was wearing the flag in question like a cloak, while the other two warriors, Prince and Earl, wore hats with the red-white-and-blue *cocarde* of the Republicans. All three carried sticks over their shoulders like muskets. I expected Father to explode at the sight of the *cocardes*, but not at all; he proceeded to raise himself to his feet and to review the parade of barefoot little soldiers with great attention and solemnity, telling them to stand up straight, throw back their shoulders, etc., and then marching them round and round the salon with many commands of "*halte!*" and "*marche!*" and "*tourne!*" He even demanded that they sing as they marched and did not object when they broke into a ragged treble rendering of the revolutionary song now known, I believe, as the '*Marseillaise*'. How the tables had been turned! I thought. Now it was I who held that Silence was a Negro child's best friend, while Father was actually encouraging these black imps to screech a Republican song under the guns of what looked like half the ships of the British navy.

However, Father had not changed altogether, for when he had tired of the drill, he lined up his platoon of three, demanded that they stand up even more ramrod-like than before, and announced loudly in a stern if rather cracked voice that a soldier's first duty was to obey — "*d'obéir, comprenez-vous?*" He then hobbled along the line, bent down his face to each one in turn, fixed them with his fierce blue eyes, and asked in a whisper which seemed to awe them more than his shouts: "What is a soldier's first duty?" If their "*obéir, Massieu!*" was not instant enough or loud enough, he made them repeat it until he was satisfied. This inquisition over, Father hobbled his way along the parade again and asked each one: "If I command 'silence!', what do I hear?" When each of the soldiers had answered with a trembling finger to his lips, Father dismissed the platoon and lowered himself into his chair.

"Those wee niggers might even be making soldiers," he said. "They were flinching and wanting to weep when I was shouting at them, but they were holding their ground like little men."

I forbore to comment aloud at the time, listening as I was for cannon-fire, that Merry would have died rather than lose Father's good opinion, for he loved Father in a fashion so idolatrous that it was beyond my comprehension, while the other two followed their leader without question, as little boys seem inclined to do.

These events which I am describing took place on the 16th of February in the year 1797, not long after Edward and Tony had embarked for New York, bound thence for England. Edward had been so determined to leave the Island which he now heartily loathed, and to enjoy his new-found and unexpected wealth, that he had decided to risk the voyage, which would be extremely hazardous, even in a neutral American ship. (He had departed without learning that the anonymous party who had bought l'Orangerie through an intermediary was myself. The price was so low that the mood and condition of Edward's Negroes was immaterial.)

Father's view that la Trinidad would quickly fall to the British was shared by everyone from el Gobernador down — the Spanish troops were inadequate as to numbers and as to armament and many of them were sick; the forts and the shore batteries were a laughing-stock; and the crews of Admiral Apodaca's five ships anchored at Chaguaramas were known to be hopelessly dejected and unwilling to fight. The white and Mulatto planters were, of course, only interested in preserving their estates and would make no precipitate move. I was somewhat confused as to which outcome of the imminent engagement would serve my interests best. I was sure that there would be greater opportunities of profit for my trading-house under the British flag, but since I was a French subject, I could not anticipate that my relations with British Governors would be as agreeable as those I had enjoyed with Don José.

On that 16th of February I was giving little thought to these greater considerations, concerned as I was for the safety of my own person, of my house and its inhabitants, of my cash-in-hand (which was concealed I shall not reveal where), of my warehouse and its contents, of my office and all my ledgers, account-books, etc., etc. The inhabitants of the house included Betsy who, without advancing any cogent reason except that Henri was unfit to travel, had elected to remain with me; Jacques, who was proving a most alert sentry at the hole in the roof; Father's body-servant Martin, who was even more decrepit than his Master; Sara, now our cook; Janga, still warbling her strange Psalms and Paraphrases; and the three little *soldats*, who were being trained as servants, although Prince's limited capacities suggested that he would grow up to be no more than a yard boy.

I had mounted a twenty-four-hour guard upon my warehouse,

composed of stout free-Negroes armed with *bois* and plenty of water-buckets; I had promised them handsome rewards if my goods survived the Republican rioters and the British invasion intact, but had no faith at all in their stomach to defend the building against an attack with firearms. As to my office, the lugubrious and prolific Mr. O'Brien had installed himself therein, along with his Mulatto family (or families — I inquired not how many he had), judging it to be safer than the ramshackled hut in the yard where he usually dwelt. He had had many opportunities of learning how to dowse fires, he said, the Scotch militia having been in the habit of setting alight the thatch over his head back in County Armagh, but I had little confidence that he could repel even a small party of unarmed thieves, for he belied his nation's reputation by being pacific and cowardly in the extreme.

As I have written above, all these anxieties caused me to move about restlessly. Even whilst Father was drilling his imps I had paid a visit to Jacques on the roof and had seen for myself that the British ships were still stationary and were making no attempt to land troops. It was most strange to descend yet again from the heat and glare of the sun upon the roof to the house below, where Father was emphasizing his unconcern by instilling military discipline into the six-year-olds, but where the true discipline of the household depended upon Betsy. Her power and influence were now at least as great as Matti's had been and Father's drilling of the little boys would not have occurred without her tacit consent. Her equanimity was at least as reassuring to me as was Father's unconcern.

"See anything from up there, Massieu Richard?" she asked in patois, after having appeared from nowhere to resume control of the little boys from Father.

"Nothing new," I replied. "You hear anything?"

"Drums silent, but there go be riots tonight and British go land soldiers at Carenage tomorrow."

"What is that?" demanded Father at the same moment that I ejaculated: "Where did you hear that?"

Betsy did not answer us — instead, she rolled her eyes upward and turned the corners of her mouth down in a grimace which conveyed: "If you would only trouble yourselves to apply Reason to what I have said you would see that it is composed of self-evident truths." Had Father not been present I am sure that she would have accompanied her grimace with a deep sigh, as of one whose patience is near exhausted. I fear I was permitting my housekeeper to treat me with some disrespect since she had become a free Negress and assumed the courtesy title of Madame Gilbert.

As it happened, Betsy's reasoning was right: rioting mobs did roam the streets unchecked all night, so that no one in the house slept, except Henri and the three weary little soldiers. For some reason the rioters did not succeed in setting fire to the town, as had the mutineers on that unforgettable night in Port Louis. It may have been that they attempted arson and were frustrated by the alacrity of the law-abiding to defend their property, and by the lack of a wind (which was also hindering the naval manoeuvres in the Golfo). We were lucky in that they left our house alone; we certainly did nothing to provoke the rival gangs as they fought noisy stick-and-cutlass battles by the light of *flambeaux*. That they had no fire-arms was truly fortunate; Don José had taken the precaution of distributing all the muskets and ammunition in the Government armoury to the Royalist French Créole planters, who had immediately decamped with them to their estates.

When the night was at its blackest there came from the west — the direction of the Spanish naval harbour at Chaguaramas — the noise of huge explosions. Father listened to them with his head cocked and announced that they were not gunfire, but the results of some magazines having been set alight, either on shore or on board ships. The latter proved to be the case, as the explosions were followed by a ruddy glow in the sky, so large and bright that it could only have been caused by the tarry timbers of several ships burning at once. Father and I discussed for some time which ships might have been disposed of thus, but could come to no conclusion. Betsy had been listening to us as she served us a welcome cup of coffee by the light of a carefully shaded candle; she had no doubts on the matter.

"Paniol burn own ship," she said, using patois to emphasize her dismissive tone. (In this instance she was again correct — Admiral Apodaca and his captains had indeed set fire to their own ships.)

My experience of war gained in Tobago had led me to a conclusion which was now being confirmed: to the non-combatant it consists, if I may repeat myself, of discomfort, ennui, uncertainty, and fearful apprehension in ever-varying proportions. For the rest of that night and for the whole of the ensuing day and night we remained cabined in the house, the loudest sounds being Henri's laboured breathing and his pitifully weak calls for Betsy. Despite Father's warning that I was not acting like a soldier and was doing no good at all, I rarely sat still for long, except when I relieved Jacques at the look-out, and spent all my time rehearsing to myself all the worst possible outcomes of the impending invasion.

At midday it fell to me, during one of my spells at the hole in the roof, to see the first puff of smoke from the British ships, after they had been sailing slowly closer and closer for some time. I was immediately convinced that they intended to flatten the whole town, or at the very least intimidate its inhabitants by indiscriminate bombardment, before landing soldiers on the waterfront. However, it soon became apparent that only one or two of the ships were firing, and then no more than one gun at a time, and that they were aiming at the much ridiculed little battery at Fuerto San Andres. (The citizens of Puerto Espana had, even then, a notable talent for ridicule, especially of those in authority or claiming authority.) This tiny fort was, and I have since measured the distance for myself, no more and no less than one thousand paces down the street from our house, situated against a mole which protruded into the sea and which formed a continuation of the street. At the time the distance seemed more like one hundred paces for, in addition to the noise of the battery returning fire as best it could, I could hear a strange whooping sound which could only be that of cannon-balls rushing through the air, and a horrid splintering, which must have been the iron projectiles crashing into the walls of houses.

I had been stunned into an enervate sloth by these events, but when a ball passed so close to me that I felt the wind of it, or fancied that I did, I decided that I should descend from the roof and inform Father and Betsy of what I had seen. I had barely started my descent when there was a particularly loud report from the direction of the battery, several more shots from the ships, and then silence. Into my mind there came the words of Fergus in Tobago: "There will be gunners not needing hats, poor souls, for they will be lying in the sun with their heads shot off."

I reversed my decision to leave my post and looked around. The whole town had been shocked into silence — it seemed as though every yard-dog had run for cover under every house and stood trembling with terror, and that most of the human inhabitants were in like condition. Not a soul moved in the streets. When I lifted the telescope to my eye the British fleet appeared to hang as though painted upon a waveless sea which blent, without a line at the horizon, into a cloudless sky. The barely moving puffs of smoke from the cannon could have been added by the artist for dramatic effect.

The silence was broken by women and children screaming, immediately followed by a great howling from the canine hordes and by men shouting to each other from house to house, sharing whatever news and rumour was to be had. The Republicans had thought better of their rioting and the streets were even more empty than they had been before. There was silence within our house, due to the discipline imposed by Father and Betsy, but it served merely to intensify my fearful apprehension. I tried to apply Reason to our predicament, but the only favourable aspect which

I could discern was that the British had not used fire-bombs, perhaps deeming it in their interest to preserve the town for their own use and advantage.

The general apprehension was not ameliorated in any way by the rumours which were shouted to us by neighbours and by Spanish dispatch-riders and other foolhardy passers-by. It might be thought that the dispatch-riders, on their way to and from Don José's head-quarters on the Plaza de la Marina, would have passed on news on which we could rely but no, their reports were as unlikely as those of the others — the British had lost half their ships whilst attacking the Spanish ships at Chaguaramas and were returning to Barbados — el Gobernador had taken himself off in a cutter and joined the British — the Mulattoes had set up a Republican government — the Negroes had elected a king — the British had taken ten thousand men up the Caroni river in boats and were now marching upon Puerto Espana from the east, having already reached Barataria — the Spanish and French navies had closed off all the Bocas del Dragon and the Boca del Sierpe and the British force was trapped in the Golfo and a major naval battle was imminent as they attempted to fight their way out — there seemed to be no end to the fanciful inventions of the rumour-mongers. It was strange to see Father and Betsy shaking their heads almost in unison with each other as they dismissed one rumour after another as false.

When a particularly dejected dispatch-rider went slowly past upon a very tired horse, I inquired of him for news in my most aristocratic Castilian. He replied without enthusiasm that the British had attempted to land several thousand troops near Carenage but were now most thoroughly mired in the shallows and might never reach the shore; however there were no Spanish troops deployed to exploit the British misfortunes. When Betsy heard this she shrugged her shoulders as though to say "What are the tribulations of the British to me?" but Father became alert and soldierly.

"That will be proving the quality of their officers," he declared. "Good officers will be leading their men through any mud. I am wondering who their General is."

There followed more uncertainty and apprehension until we heard that the British were ashore in their thousands, accompanied by battalions of German Jaegers, also in thousands, and that both were pillaging rum from every estate they had reached.

"If that is the truth," said Father, "and it has the smell of truth, I am not liking it at all. Pillaging is the reward which officers are holding out to their troops to encourage them, but in a disciplined army it is only permitted after the victory is won and not while the victory is still in the balance."

"Master," interposed Betsy, who spoke more freely to Father than she did to me, "if the British and their mercenaries are ashore in thousands, they have won the victory, have they not? The troops will therefore be entitled to their rewards of pillage and ravishment? It is fortunate that I have my pistols."

"Pistols?" asked Father, with surprising politeness.

"Yes, Master," said Betsy, "I have two ladies' pistols and I have concealed them where no gentleman worthy of the name will find them." She gave Father her black stare.

"Do you know how to fire them?" I asked.

"Master Richard, I found no difficulty in understanding the mechanism, or in loading and priming them."

"Capital, my dear," said Father, "but I am not understanding where you are obtaining your knowledge of military affairs. It cannot be from pillow talk with Dickie, who is more likely to fly like a bird than to be fighting like a man. Pray tell me why it is that the British have won already?"

"Who is to oppose them?" asked Betsy. "It is surely plain to the meanest intellect that even if the Republicans were armed they would soon be bottled up in the town between the British navy, the British and German troops, and the Royalist planters, who are not going to fight the British and chance losing their estates."

I could see no answer to the logic of these arguments, but Father had a question.

"And what will the Negroes be doing?" he asked. "We have heard that they have already elected a King."

"I know nothing of Negro intentions," said Betsy, her face assuming its mask of Negro stupidity. "Me go tend Henri," she added in patois, and left us to our perplexity.

Henri seemed to be suffering more than the rest of us from the airlessness of the house, as we dared not yet risk opening the jalousies. Indeed, it was at about this time that Betsy whispered to me that she feared that Henri might succumb to the malady in his chest; he certainly had not the strength to make his usual comments upon events around him.

Towards sundown, after another long period of uncertainty, and when the house was at its hottest and most stifling, Betsy announced that since there was no news of fighting, nor any sign of the approach of the British or German troops across the empty pasture which stretched away to the west, nor yet any disturbances in the streets, she proposed to move Henri to a pallet bed on the back galerie where the fresh air might help him to breathe. Father agreed and, not to be outdone, decided to open the front door and sit on his favourite morning chair on the front galerie with his pistols in his lap and with poor old Martin to hand, ready to help him indoors again should the necessity arise.

Made even more restless by this apparent relaxation of our guard, I moved around the house, from front to rear, up to the roof and back down again, wondering if I should send Jacques to ascertain whether my office and warehouse were safe. It chanced that I was standing beside Father when we had our first sight of the British. They were a small patrol and they appeared from a narrow track through the cane on the far side of the pasture opposite our house. They moved toward us with extreme caution, obviously alert and ready for any eventuality. As they came closer we could see that there were half-a-dozen of them led by a young officer.

"Show that infamous flag!" called Father quietly and Jacques quickly hung it from the eaves. The movement attracted the attention of the patrol, who stopped and assumed a defensive posture. If these men had been drinking rum, they had recovered with remarkable speed.

"Who is showing the flag? Declare yourselves!" shouted the officer in a strangely familiar accent.

"Jonas Mason, estate-owner, at your service!" replied Father.

"You are British, Mr Mason?"

"I was born in the northern part of the United Kingdom, yes. You are a reconnaissance patrol?"

"Yes, sir. My orders are — "

"Who is your General?" Father interrupted.

The young officer, and he was very young indeed, hesitated.

"Surely that is no military secret?" barked Father.

"Sir Ralph Abercrombie is our General."

"He bears a fine old Scotch Whig name," said Father with an irony of which perhaps only I was aware. "I am hoping that he is worthy of it."

"His officers and his men are devoted to him already, Mr. Mason, because of his genuine concern for our welfare. He is also most anxious that loyal subjects of King George and anyone else who is favourably disposed to His Majesty should not be hurt or inconvenienced during the imminent attack upon Port-of-Spain."

"Pray inform Sir Ralph that there is no one in Port-of-Spain, as you are calling it, with the arms or the stomach to be opposing him, although indeed the Republican *canaille* and the Negroes will need to be overawed by a shew of force — three or four companies of men as disciplined as yours should be sufficient."

"Thank you, sir. Now I must be continuing with my patrol, as I have strict orders."

258

"You are a smart fellow. May I be having your name, that I may commend you to your General?"

"Lieutenant Simon Fraser, at your service, sir," said the young man, and I was watching the cautious and alert manner in which he led away his patrol towards the waterfront when I heard a strange sound from Father. When I turned to him I found him lying collapsed upon the floor, his face set in an angry grimace but entirely drained of its usual choleric hue; his pistols had dropped out of his hands and lay beside him. Old Martin had appeared from wherever he had been hiding and was gazing down at his Master, his rheumy eyes as expressionless as ever.

"Call Madame Gilbert!" I told him, and he shuffled away.

When Betsy arrived, I had only had time to kneel down and listen for Father's heartbeat, which I could not detect. She wasted no words.

"He is dead, Master Richard," she said, calmly, and without even a catch in her voice. "He should be taken into the house."

I looked around and called for Martin, but he had vanished. (He never reappeared, although he knew I would have felt an obligation to feed, clothe and house him for the rest of his life. He was reported to frequent *cantinas*, now known as rum-shops, in the hope of free drinks.)

Not wishing to call Jacques from his post on the roof, Betsy and I lifted Father's frame — I had not reckoned on it being so slight — and carried him to his bed. As I closed his eyes, Betsy having indicated that it was a son's duty, there arose a great wailing from the back of the house. I recognized Janga's voice, those of her three little charges, and Sara's, and inferred that news of Father's passing had reached them. However, when Betsy went to investigate she did not seem able to calm them at all. She returned to Father's bedside with tears trembling in her eyes.

"Master Henri is dead!" she said, allowing her tears to roll down her face. "I should have taken him to Sans Peur. Come, Master!"

I followed Betsy to the rear of the house, where Henri lay motionless upon the pallet-bed, a peaceful smile upon his round beardless twenty-seven-year-old countenance.

"Me jus' turn me head and he pass," were Janga's only words before starting to wail again.

I shall not weary my readers, or distress myself, by describing the days that followed in detail. Don José promptly and politically surrendered to General Abercrombie early the following morning and in the hushed hiatus which followed I, or rather my freely disbursed wealth, found coffins, grave-diggers, and a priest, so that well before sundown on the next day we were able to bury Father and Henri beside Maman and Matti at the far end of our well-fenced lot, just beyond our small provision-patch. In the circumstances I did not attempt to invite any of Father's French Créole cronies, who would no doubt have been fully engaged in the defence of their estates and the control of their Negroes. I was therefore the only family mourner. Betsy marshalled the servants at a respectful distance and prevented all unseemly display, except that as Father's coffin was lowered into the ground Merry ran forward to watch its descent from close by; but even he acted thus with great solemnity. When the priest was done with his incantations and the grave-diggers were setting about their work, Merry picked up a flat piece of wood and made as if to help them. After looking to Betsy for her nod of approval I encouraged him to do so. Then, thinking that I too owed my father and my beloved brother a final gesture of respect, I abandoned my umbrella, seized a spade from one of the grave-diggers and followed Merry's example. Every so often I had to look up from my shovelling of earth to see whether Jacques on the roof was signalling the approach of danger.

It was many months later, long after the estimable Lieutenant Fraser had departed with the British force for engagements elsewhere, that I learned why the mere sound of his name had caused Father to suffer a fatal apoplexy. It appears that another Simon Fraser, a Highland Chief with the title of Lord Lovat, had played a double part in the Rebellion of 1745; he was in consequence despised and detested as a Judas by those whom he had deceived, both Jacobite and Hanoverian. In fact, said my informant, even Lord Lovat's execution in London had not posthumously reconciled him to the Jacobites.

CHAPTER XXII

*My Housekeeper and I reach an Agreement which has unforeseen Consequences;
I come into Conflict with the new British Governor, but the Danger to my Liberty
is averted by Assistance from an unexpected Quarter*

For some time after the first British Governor, Colonel Thomas Picton, had taken control of the town (which I must now call Port-of-Spain) and of the whole Island, my life was so filled with activity that I grieved not for Henri, nor for Father. I had discovered my warehouse cleared of all its contents, while the free Negroes whom I had hired to guard it had vanished — presumably into Caracas, where most Republicans and criminals had taken refuge from the merciless Picton and his minions. My ledgers, on the other hand, had survived the disturbances (due to the devotion of Mister O'Brien) and it was not long before I made up my losses and began to profit handsomely from supplying the needs of the British forces and of the flood of British incomers intent on making their fortunes.

I made no attempt to obtrude upon the British officials except in the way of business; instead, I went daily to my office and harried poor faithful Mister O'Brien and my lazy clerks. Daily, too, I visited my warehouse to ensure that every consignment unloaded at the quay was checked item by item against the bill-of-lading, and that every order was dispatched promptly. I returned home late in the evening to eat the excellent suppers personally prepared by Betsy — even now I find it hard to refer to her as Madame Gilbert — now employed as my housekeeper on terms of a week's notice on either side. I would have preferred the usual month's notice, but she would have none of it, no matter how hard I tried to make her see Reason. So obstinate was she that I feared she might be considering leaving me for another and more lucrative post, or for an advantageous marriage or other less formal arrangement. The discord between us thus aroused caused us such embarrassment that we could no longer play cards of an evening and I had to fill the empty hours by reading the books I obtained from Mr. Lackington's bookshop in London.

Peaceful and comfortable though this life of mine appeared to be, I was yet aware that Melancholy was ever present at my shoulder and ever ready to engulph me in her drear embrace, and I sometimes wished that I could spend all twenty-four hours of the day engaged in profitable business. One evening, when I was sitting at the table after having supped even later than was my custom, and after having dismissed Jacques, I picked up the book which I had purposed to read, but before I could open it and find solace in its pages I was overwhelmed as if by a dark cloud, from which there seemed to be no escape; indeed, the harder I fought to evade it the darker and more stifling it became. I crossed my arms upon the table and laid my head upon them. After a while the cloud seemed to darken yet further and I wept — nay, I did not weep, for my Sorrow was too deep for tears. I mourned rather, silently and motionlessly, for my poor dead brother Henri, who had given my life a purpose through many of my emptiest days; and for Tony in her distant imprisonment (for I doubted not that she would never submit to Edward and that he would keep her locked up); and for unhappy Maman and the children she had lost; and even for Father, who had been so cruel to me in my childhood, but who had died loyal to his hopeless Cause. Most of my mourning, however, was for myself and my solitary and useless state — what purpose could my wealth serve if I had no one with whom to share it or to whom I could bequeath it, and if only the despicable Edward Rochester was left to inherit it through Tony? I contemplated putting an end to myself and my sorrows; my pistols, always well-oiled against the climate, were not far away.

I must have been thus confronting the great Void for an hour or more when there was borne to my nostrils on a gentle movement of the air the twin and inseparable scents of cocoa-nut oil and fresh-pressed linen. Madame Gilbert had approached stealthily on her bare feet and was standing close to me. What could my housekeeper want with me at this hour? Why was she breaking in so presumptuously upon my private misery? I had not summoned her.

I neither raised my head nor spoke and the silence was filled with the fluttering of insects round the lamp, the hum of the ever-wakeful town, and the ceaseless barking of near and distant dogs. When Madame Gilbert's voice came, it was but a whisper.

"Mr. Mason," she said in English, "I think that you are lonely."

I answered not, nor was I ready to admit to anyone the depths of Misery into which I had sunk. I hoped that my silence and immobility would drive her away, but no, she stood her ground.

"Mr. Mason," she said, and her words seemed but the faintest exhalation of her breath, "I too am lonely."

In the ensuing silence I could hear my heart beating faintly in my breast, but I was quite unable to speak and the onus of breaking the silence again fell to Madame Gilbert.

"Did we not agree," she said with her most precise delivery, "when we were young, that we would order our lives by the light of Reason?"

I half-lifted my head and half-nodded.

"Do you not think that we should still do so?"

I half-nodded again.

"Very well then, Mr. Mason. In the matter of our both being lonely — " she must have taken a step closer to me, for I could feel her warmth and proximity, "— does not Reason indicate that we should assuage our loneliness by obeying Nature's promptings?"

I dropped my head on to my arms again, for she was speaking in riddles which I was in no frame of mind to solve.

"We are both free persons and of independent mind, are we not?" As she spoke, Betsy (I can no longer call her Madame Gilbert) put her hand on the back of my neck and commenced the gentlest possible kneading of it. Instantly I recalled how Matti would comfort my childish sorrows by such means. "We need not let the prying world concern us, need we?" she continued, still intent on applying Reason to our predicament.

I began, rather belatedly as my readers will surely think, to be altogether certain of my housekeeper's drift, but I did not raise my head lest she stop her kneading of my neck, which had become a caress tenderer than I would have deemed possible, and which was telling me perhaps more clearly than her words that an end to loneliness was indeed within our grasp.

"Were you the mistress of M. le Capitaine d'Aumont?" The question leapt from my mouth unbidden; it had, I am now convinced, hovered between us, unasked and unanswered, since that blowy day on Fort de Castrie.

Betsy was neither surprised nor discomfitted. "I had no choice, as you know well."

"But you told me that he was a kind Master — "

"He was kind and very loving in the over-wrought French fashion — I was the light of his eyes, the companion of his soul, and so on. In Paris, if only he had had the money, I was to have been the first black woman to have a salon, in the *demi-monde* of course, where wits and *philosophes* and *Amis des Noirs* would have foregathered and intrigue would have been nurtured; in the Antilles, on the other hand, he talked of taking me away to a desert Isle where we could be alone and happy together — he even told me that he had found the Island and was preparing a boat to sail there. Luckily he was posted back to France before he could implement any of such foolishness and I was able to persuade him to put the interests of *la famille d'Aumont* first." Betsy sighed faintly. "I think his mind had been unhinged by his marriage to a woman of no understanding. I could never have been his Madame de Stael or his Woman Friday." She let her hand drop from my neck and spoke even more softly. "In any case, I was pledged to another, and am now free to offer myself to him."

"P-p-p-pledged?" I stammered, looking up into her eyes for confirmation of what she was saying; in the lamplight they were bent upon me with a glow of loving-kindness. I began to be afraid.

"We were nine years of age, or thereabouts, as you must remember, but I was a woman in my heart and in my understanding, if not in my person, when I pledged that I would be faithful." Betsy lifted the lamp from the table and took my hand in her own. "Come!" she said, "I have something to shew you."

She led me through the dark and silent house, down the rear steps and across the yard to the door of the large chamber which had been Henri's. Releasing my hand, she opened the door quietly and lifted the lamp high. "Behold!" she whispered, and I saw that Matti's handsome four-poster bed had been installed in place of Henri's narrow one. Its white curtains and bed-spread were without spot or blemish and — I could scarce believe my eyes! — a clean fresh-pressed nightshirt of mine own was laid out upon the near side, whilst on the far side there lay a lace-trimmed night-gown of a whiteness to match the bed-linen.

Had not Betsy resumed my hand most firmly into her own I would have turned away and withdrawn to my own chamber in the house, for I was still afraid — I was even trembling, knowing not why I trembled. Reason told me that the prying world would not blame me for taking a Negress for a mistress, but Fear reminded me that a black mistress was reputed to turn quite unbiddable unless her Master controlled her with his fists. Betsy, aware that my hand was trying to loosen itself from her grasp and attuned as always to the state of my feelings, whispered the only words which could have reassured me: "Dickie! You must be brave for me."

Oh, how I had been longing without knowing it, during all those years, for her to call me "Dickie" again, each syllable enunciated separately and affectionately! What else could I be but brave? I renewed my grip of her hand and we entered the chamber together. I decided that it was a precaution dictated by Reason to lock the door after us.

Thus was I admitted to the sweet comforts of Betsy's white bed and black person. As devotees of Reason and of Nature we determined to conduct our new conspiracy with the decorum appropriate to our years, for at thirty we were no longer in the first flush of our youth. Without delay we entered upon a regimen of such discretion, sobriety and regularity that it would have done credit to a couple who had been clandestine lovers for forty years. I made shift to return from the office at the same hour every evening so that my mistress and I could have time for a leisurely supper together, much intimate conversation and several games of cards before retiring to her bed. The servants knew of the new dispensation, of course, but only Jacques required reproof for familiarity of speech — he leeringly referred to Betsy as "Madame" instead of "Madame Gilbert", but only once.

My readers, my friends, and especially those who are female, steel yourselves for a shock! This humdrum, if comfortable, *ménage* of ours lasted for less than six weeks. Reason may be a fine reliable carriage-horse but Nature, seemingly, is not bred to run in the same harness. The end came with very little warning and in a manner which I cannot describe even now without embarrassment. It happened thus:

I was reading a business letter in my office on the first floor of the building in the Calle de Santa Ana when my mind wandered to the exceptional warmth of the kiss with which Betsy had released me from her bed that morning. I glanced idly out of the window but hardly saw the motley throng of Mulatto mashers in preposterous hats, foxy Spanish lawyers, free Negroes of varying degrees of raggedness, *marchandes* with baskets on their heads, and so on, all going about their business with a quietness and caution uncharacteristic of Trinidadians, for none knew how they stood with their new rulers, the British. I was about to resume reading my letter when my incredulous eye caught sight of my Sable Venus, the barefoot Goddess of Beauty and Love whom I had last seen on the night of the soldiers' mutiny in Tobago. She was on the other side of the street, walking toward my office with a lissom but stately grace; the kerchief on her head was as white as the wing of a *crabier bec*; and her neat grey dress, its skirt looped up at several points to shew the rows of lace upon the white petticoat underneath, seemed to reflect the sunlight like a rainbow. On her bosom she wore a posy of bright flowers tied with gay ribbons; in her left hand she carried a covered basket decorated with more flowers and ribbons; and in her right hand she held a letter. She smiled as she walked, her white teeth gleaming in her black face. I shall not describe her charms further, for my pen fails me, and in any case my readers will have recognized that this Goddess was that same Betsy who was my staid thirty-year-old housekeeper and discreet mistress.

I gazed upon Betsy with the awe due to a Goddess, yet with some puzzlement for I could not believe that she proposed to break our unspoken agreement that she should not come to the office, but lo! she looked up at my window and then seemed to be reconnoitring a path across the filth on the street. As she did so she was accosted by a corpulent and perspiring redcoat, somewhat the worse for rum, who saluted her and bowed stiffly (because of his thick uniform) and smiled and smirked and made eyes at her in the most insolent fashion, and then laid his gross red hand upon her sweet round black forearm. I saw not his rank nor anything else about him, for I was so filled with rage at his presumption that I ignored my pistols and seized the nearest weapon to hand, which was my umbrella, and charged hatless down the stairs, through my compting-house, and across the street. Before I could strike a blow Betsy's voice rang out, in the accents of an affronted English lady.

"Unhand me this instant, or I shall report you to your officer!"

The redcoat, quite dumbfounded, immediately released her and she backed away, giving me the chance to knock off his hat and beat him over the head and shoulders so heartily that he bawled for help from the lookers-on, who seemed more inclined to cheer my endeavours or to withdraw hastily than to save him from a beating.

The vigour of my attack was such that I broke my umbrella with a blow which also knocked down my adversary. From the corner of one eye I saw Mister O'Brien ushering Betsy into the safety of the compting-house and shutting the door (and I mentally wrote an *aide-memoire* to myself that I should warmly commend him, and possibly reward him, for this useful service); from the corner of the other eye I saw a group of redcoats trotting round the corner from the Plaza de la Marina with their muskets "at the port" and the street emptying ahead of them. My anger was assuaged to some degree, but I was out of breath and stood irresolute for a few moments. I was promptly seized by the redcoats, who were incensed by my treatment of their comrade and manhandled me down the street and into Government House on the Plaza, now Colonel Picton's headquarters. Here, considerably bruised, I was handed over to a phlegmatic sergeant, who shook his head sadly at the reports of my infamous behaviour and gave it as his opinion that the Colonel would let me cool my temper in jail for several weeks before dealing with me in his usual fashion, that is, harshly.

Drawing myself up to my full height, I demanded to be led into the Governor's presence forthwith, giving the names of the many well-to-do and respected citizens of Port-of-Spain who would vouch for me. The sergeant maintained his stolid front and informed me patiently that the Colonel was closetted with a local white gentleman who had a handsome Mulatto daughter to dispose of and would resent any interruption; and moreover that he, the sergeant, had yet to come across a miscreant who did not claim to have friends in high places. At this I demanded in a loud voice to see an officer. The sergeant sighed, but fetched an ensign who, upon hearing the charges against me, directed that I should be locked in the "waiting-room" until I could be escorted to the town jail and committed to the tender care of M. Vallot, the notorious jailer.

The "waiting-room" was in fact an exceedingly small and windowless apartment already crowded with perhaps a dozen people who had given offence to the military that morning. Most were surly Mulattoes and free Negroes who looked capable of revolutionary activities, but there were also two large Negresses who, they said, had provoked an officer with patois insults which he did not understand, but the tone of which he found objectionable — they were hoping in voluble fashion that their owners would soon come and pay to have them released, and were highly delighted that a gentleman such as I had to squeeze between them in order to find a seat upon the narrow bench provided. After an hour of this discomfort, during which I consoled myself by calling to mind the brilliant image of my Goddess, and tortured myself by wondering why she had decided to visit my office so enchantingly bedecked, the sergeant unlocked the door and beckoned to me.

"A lady to see you," he said, and there behind him was my Betsy, transformed. She was still carrying her letter but she had removed the flowers and ribbons from her bosom and from her basket; she had dropped her chin and rounded her shoulders; and she was rolling her eyes coquettishly at the sergeant. She curtsied to me with a giggling perfunctoriness nicely calculated to suggest that she was a privileged female servant of the looser sort.

"Massieu Mason," she said, emphasizing my name for the benefit of my companions in crime, "me bring you refreshments you order this morning; and this letter too, for you eyes only."

She held out the letter and as she did so I perceived that she had so subjugated the sergeant with her wiles (he had referred to a Negress as a lady, forsooth!) that he would make no objection if I read the letter there and then. I took the letter, opened it and found that it went thus:

> Beloved, when You hold me in your Arms and kiss me my Life
> is completed and I am indeed the happiest Woman in the World.

I cannot wait to see You again and am come to deliver this Letter
Myself. I need hardly sign My Name.

Below this was a postscript in boldly written capital letters: "PRAY
CONTINUE TO BE BRAVE FOR ME!"

I looked into Betsy's sliding eyes, well aware that the sergeant and the
roomful of offenders were watching and listening with great attention.

"Pray convey my heartfelt thanks to the author of this letter," I said,
using English for the benefit of the sergeant, "and would you request your
mistress to inform all the members of the Illustrious Cabildo that I am
locked up here on a trumpery charge."

"Pardon?" asked Betsy, pretending not to understand my English. I
therefore repeated the message in patois, at which my companions pricked
up their ears, as Betsy had intended they should. Betsy gave me the scantest
of curtsies to acknowledge that she understood, and handed me the basket.
Without thinking, I bowed my thanks, but stopped myself, just in time,
from taking her hand and kissing it.

"Massieu Mason, me pass you message," she said, and added with
studied insouciance: "but you go be free soon."

She turned away with a swing of most provocative skirts and must
have directed one of her sauciest smiles at the sergeant, for as he shut the
door his oafish countenance was as moony as a love-lorn boy's. I doubt if
she had needed to bribe him with actual cash.

My fellow-prisoners now regarded me with considerable interest; the
two Negresses because they had divined that Betsy was my mistress and
were lubriciously intent upon discovering all that they could about our
ménage; and the others because delightful odours were emanating from
Betsy's basket, reminding them that the lunch-hour had passed without any
food being offered to us. Having great faith in Betsy's word that I would
be free soon, I distributed the refreshments around the room, and though
no one had much, everyone had something to his or her taste, whether half
of a savoury pastel, or a small piece of fresh bread and a morsel of smoked
ham, or a little sugar-cake made with cocoa-nut, or a mango of the most
perfect ripeness. Even more welcome was the bottle of Madeira, which
was jealously watched as it went from mouth to mouth around the airless
and increasingly fetid room.

My faith in Betsy was not misplaced, for within half an hour the door
opened again and the sergeant crooked his finger at me. I followed him
and was quickly ushered into a room in which I had passed many pleasant
evenings with Don José. Colonel Picton was seated at a large table in the
centre, a drawn sword in front of him with its point towards me; alongside

the sword was my broken umbrella. I saw that the Governor's savage mien and choleric complexion accorded only too well with his reputation for violence and brutality and perceived that I would have to call upon all the strength bestowed upon me by the image of my Goddess and by the words of the note she had written to me. The Governor did not raise his eyes from the paper he was reading; instead, he kept me standing for a full five minutes as if I were an erring schoolboy, so that I was well able to take note of the quite extraordinary prominence of his nose, the conscious disorder of his hair, and the studied carelessness of his dress. When he did lay down his paper it was to inspect me from head to foot, slowly and not less than three times, in the most insulting manner — his grey eyes were so domineering and were surrounded by whites so biliously yellow that they alone would have caused me to fear for my life. His voice, when at last he spoke, was a military bark not unlike Father's, but his unfamiliar accent, as I learned later, was that of a Welsh country gentleman who had not troubled himself to learn the social graces.

"You are Jonas Mason, of this damned miserable and benighted town?"

"Jonas Mason was my father, recently deceased. I am Richard Mason, merchant, at your service, sir."

"Ah, Jonas was the old reprobate and unrepentant Jacobite, was he? So you will be the son, of a different kidney, for you are well-known, are you not, for your diabolical Jacobinical and Republican sympathies?" He spoke the polysyllabical words with such relish that his question became a most terrifying accusation. Again, I called up the image of Betsy and the words of her note.

"No sir, I attend to my business and do not involve myself in public affairs."

The Governor picked up another paper and tried my temper with a further and even longer silence, during which I wondered where he had obtained so much intelligence, and reflected that I would have to be more careful of my speech in future, even in front of friends. In the end, the Governor had to speak first.

"But my information is that you would shortly have been appointed to el Ilustre Cabildo, despite your youth."

"That hardly brands me as a Republican, sir."

"But if you are so loyal and well-intentioned a subject, why have you not been to see me on one of those tiresome deputations which I have to meet every day? Why have you been keeping your damned great carcase out of my sight, Mr. Mason?"

"My business has required all my attention, sir."

Yet another silence followed, but this time the Governor did not remove his grey-and-yellow gaze from my countenance. For the third time I countered his silence with my silence and he had to speak first.

"Worth a pretty penny, are you?"

I hesitated for he was, of course, giving me the opportunity to make him an offer, and I knew not what inducements he had already received that he should be seeing me so promptly; furthermore, I did not want to raise his expectations should it later be necessary to make him another offer in circumstances even less favourable to myself.

"I have recently had heavy losses," I temporized.

"How damned unfortunate for you! However, your losses have not included your friends, for some of them have been speaking to me in the language I understand, thus enabling me to deal with your offence in the speediest possible manner." Here the Governor leapt to his feet, seizing his sword in his right hand and my broken umbrella in his left. "Follow me!" he barked.

I did as he bade and we ascended to the upper galerie of Government House which commanded a prospect of the Plaza del Marina, the waterfront, and all the ships at anchor; it also commanded a view of the gallows in the centre of the Plaza, not too far from the west door of the Church of the Immaculate Conception. From the gibbet depended the bodies of two men, their faces so suffused that it was impossible to distinguish the colour of their skins — the inhabitants of la Trinidad had quickly learned that Picton was no respecter of hue, for he hanged black curfew-breakers, Mulatto upstarts and white deserters with equal alacrity and expedition. I called Betsy's image to mind and wondered if it were to be for the last time, but the Governor allowed me no time for regret.

"Mr. Richard Mason, merchant, of this town of Port-of-Spain," he bellowed, and so loudly that many passers-by in the street below stopped to listen, straining their necks to obtain a better view, and were held as though spellbound by a vituperative and oath-bespattered denunciation, of which I propose to report only the peroration: " — I understand that your dastardly crime of wantonly attacking a soldier under my command was probably out of character and provoked by the tender passion, and I propose to release you. However, Mr. Mason, I must warn you that any repetition of such infamous conduct will lead you there!" With a dramatic gesture he pointed his sword at the gallows and its ghastly burdens. He then raised his voice even further. "Begone! Out of my sight!" he cried, and commenced to beat me with the stump of my umbrella in full view of the considerable crowd which had gathered. Needless to say, I retreated with what little dignity I could muster.

(This incident did not incline me favourably to the Governor, and when he was later charged in London with authorizing illegal tortures, I was not amongst those who supported him; nor did I subscribe one penny to the fund raised for his defence; nor did I render him any assistance in his none-too-secret plans for interfering in the affairs of Spanish America.)

I walked the few steps to my office, followed by a crowd of little Negroes who were no doubt hoping to see me further discomfitted. Mister O'Brien informed me that Madame Gilbert had returned home, she having escorted him there personally. With further Irish obliquity he caused me to understand that the good lady would be overjoyed to see me at *her* earliest convenience. I therefore donned my pistols and my hat and set off for home, dispersing the little Negroes with a few threats.

As I trudged along I was hoping that I was about to be transported from Gehenna to the Garden of Eden or some blissful Arcadia. On mounting the front steps I fancied that I caught a glimpse of Betsy at the far end of the salon, but when I hurried through to embrace her she was not to be found; nor were any of the servants or the little boys. I was stricken with fearful doubt; I searched the whole house without success; I looked into the stables and the outhouses — they were empty; yet I knew that Betsy must be somewhere, for she would not have left the house completely unattended. Ultimately, and with uncertain step I entered her chamber, breaking another of our unspoken agreements that I should not do so in daylight, but she was not to be seen; I opened her press and found her sweet-smelling garments but not her person. However, as I turned to leave the room in chagrin my ankle was seized in a firm grip. I looked down and saw that a black hand had indeed fastened itself there and that it was attached to a rounded black arm which projected from under the bed — Betsy had been playing hide-and-seek with me! She giggled like a little girl as I pulled her out from under the bed and stood her on her feet to receive the shower of kisses which she so richly deserved.

In a lull in our embraces I asked the roguish creature how she had achieved my release.

"I laid out sums of money where they would exert most influence," she replied.

"Where?" I asked.

"I have good friends — we black mistresses have to stand by each other, since we none of us have the status of wife to protect us."

I allowed the reference to marriage to pass and queried: "You laid out your own money?"

"Of course, and I shall be submitting my bill in due course." She wound her arms so tightly round my neck that she caused me pain where I had been bruised by the redcoats, but also great joy that the bruises had been suffered in her defence. I did not let her know that she was hurting me.

"How much money did you pay?"

"Oh, my brave Dickie! I refuse to put a figure on your value to me after the way you battled for me today!"

"But you said you were going to submit a bill."

"The bill will require payment, but not necessarily in money," said the provoking female, breaking away from my encircling arms and running out of the room to hide herself again elsewhere. I set off in pursuit and we occupied ourselves happily thus for some time until Sam announced his imminent arrival with much overloud shouting at his horses and cracking of his whip and we had to resume our feigned sobriety.

Yes, we two devotees of Reason had abandoned our Guide and fallen most unreasonably and passionately in love, and this in our thirty-first year! Only rarely were we able to repeat our game of hide-and-seek, as it was not easy to find excuses to dismiss all the servants at one time, but when we did, how sweet a pleasure was it!

Needless to say, our passion found many other outlets and so enmeshed us that various unfortunate consequences followed. My attention to business, for instance, became more lax than at any other time in my life (except for the present, in my extreme old age, when I have decided that I must write my Life and Times, come what may, lest either or both be misunderstood). In the midst of grave negotiations over some important deal I would be so overcome by a desire to see and fondle my Beloved that I would settle for a profit much smaller than it need have been, just for the sake of rushing home to her.

All our lives our quarrels had been silent ones, and now, even under the influence of passion, they remained so; but how fraught with rage and despair is a lovers' quarrel which is confined to silence! There were times when I thought that I must kill myself, just because Betsy had refused to speak to me for a few desolate hours; and there were times, she informed me later, when she would cheerfully have killed me with a kitchen knife! Yet how honeyed were our reconciliations, sometimes silent too, when they came!

Our infatuation with each other also had untoward effects on the running of the household. Jacques, having been warned once, remained discreet in his speech, but Janga took the opportunity to have another of her affairs and to produce a coal-black sister for Earl. I need hardly describe at length what a less than well-ordered household is like — the linen that has been perfunctorily washed and pressed, the floors that have not been polished, the little boys running wild in the yard and making a

272

confounded noise, the irregular mealtimes and the uncertain quality of the cuisine, etc., etc.

Our passion, like our quarrels, could not maintain its *camboulay*-like conflagration for ever, and it died down somewhat, but it certainly did not die out; instead, it came to resemble the steadily glowing heat from the coals in a lovingly tended domestic coal-pot. Gradually our diurnal lives regained some calm — I found time to attend to business in a proper manner and with due attention to profit, while Betsy returned to the management of our household and of her own affairs; but every so often our passion flared up again, for example, when she welcomed me to the supper-table one evening wearing a magnificent low-cut robe of crimson and purple silk and a turban of what seemed to be cloth-of-gold. I had never before seen her in anything but plain grey and white and the effect of the colours upon my senses was overwhelming — I gaped at her like a boy for a full five minutes before being able to congratulate her. Two weeks later I requested that she wear the robe again and when she appeared in it I presented her with gold ornaments for her ears, neck, bosom and arms. They were worth a whole shipload of ironmongery, as she recognized immediately. She put them on in front of a looking-glass with great solemnity, then turned to reward me with a kiss, resembling the African Princess Imoinda, "fair Queen of Night", rather than my housekeeper.

"These are of such value that they frighten me," she said. "You had them from Caracas?"

"Yes, and I did not pay too much for them, as you are plainly suspecting. I bought them of an Israelite who owes me a favour and allowed me to beat him down; and even if I had paid the price which he jokingly asked first, it would have represented only a tiny fraction of your value to me."

My readers may ask: was I not ashamed to take a black woman for a mistress, and to indulge her thus lavishly? I do not think that I have the words to answer this question, although I must acknowledge my readers' right to ask it. Excuses which I concoct, whether for my own peace of mind or for that of others, appear nugatory when I commit them to paper. I cannot avoid the patent and painful truths that my mistress was an ex-slave and the daughter of slave parents, however chiefly her grandparents may have been; that her complexion was of the blackest and her features cast in Africa's mould; that she steadfastly refused to wear shoes, no matter how many pairs I bought for her; that she insisted upon wearing around her ankle one of the heaviest and most valuable of the gold bracelets which I had given her; that when she thought she was unobserved she would sometimes break into barbaric dance-steps at the sound of Negro music;

273

that she had a brother who, as a runaway slave, had been engaged in the slaughter of whites in St. Domingue; and that she was, finally, of an age when most white Créole men would have discarded her for some younger, fresher, and more amenable creature, whether Negress or Mulatta.

At the time of which I write the end of the eighteenth century was fast approaching and the nineteenth century was casting its shadow ahead, warning mankind that Reason could retreat as well as advance, as was shewn by the monstrous tyranny imposed upon great France by Bonaparte and upon poor little Trinidad by Picton (in concert with Begorrat and his like). I could not then be, and cannot be now, other than a man of the eighteenth century, and Reason, that century's mentor, tells me unequivocally that on the one hand I could not have lived with any other woman than Betsy and that on the other I could not have married her, even if it had been legal under the Spanish law still in force in la Trinidad, because of the disastrous effect such a step would have had upon my standing in society and consequently upon my business affairs. Betsy, as a woman of the eighteenth century with a firm grasp of the importance of commerce, knew all this as well as I did and her various references to marriage at that time were in the nature of teases, rather than hints with any hope or purpose behind them.

So it came about that I convinced myself that I was doing nothing of which to be ashamed, especially when I recalled that I had not "taken" Betsy as a mistress — she had freely offered herself to me in full knowledge of the circumstances and of the likely consequences — and that my love for her was indubitably the noblest part of my none-too-shining character (a point which I ask my readers to weigh with especial care).

For the next seven years or so we lived a life of considerable domestic happiness spiced, of course, with quarrels; it was also a time of steady progress in our business affairs. I was the envy of the few discreet and thoughtful bachelor friends whom I invited to intimate suppers with Betsy. (One of these friends was Father Étienne, a French priest who said he had a concern for our souls but seemed more interested in the delicate French dishes which Betsy had learned to prepare whilst in Paris.) These gentlemen could scarce comprehend that my handsome black mistress's skills in the kitchen were matched by her lively and well-informed conversation and by her no mean ability at the card-table. (Such supper-parties were, needless to say, held at the back of the house, out of sight of the crowds which now paraded up and down Frederick Street, as the Calle de San Carlos had been re-named, and invitations to them were highly prized.)

CHAPTER XXIII

A very short Chapter in which I have to refer to the unhappiest Year in the History of Trinidad and to its Consequences for Myself; I have a lucky Escape from an unfortunate Involvement

"Why has Sam stopped singing topical songs?" I asked of Betsy one evening, as we sat peaceably on the back galerie, "I hear nothing from him these days but the old love-songs he was singing when I bought him years ago; what is more, he no longer brings me news."

Betsy did not look up from the copy of the *Trinidad Courant* which she was perusing with her customary close attention — many a bargain had she found amongst the goods advertised for sale in that newspaper.

"Perhaps he does not wish to upset you," she said.

"What is that?" I queried, "Why should I be upset by Sam singing a song? I laughed as loud as anyone at 'Picton batt' Massa Mason'."

"Surely you know that the Negroes are restive?" said Betsy, as though she were reporting some misdemeanour by Merry and his two fellows.

I did not answer her straightaway, for I was somewhat nettled that I had not been aware that there were stirrings of revolt and had had to hear of them from Betsy. The year was 1805 and she and I were still living in the same house in Frederick Street. Our quiet love and amity were in marked contrast to the noisy conflicts then taking place between the different nationalities amongst the planters of Trinidad, and indeed between the nations of the world which calls itself civilized, who were at each others' throats like wild beasts. I prided myself upon having the earliest possible news of the progress of the various wars being waged, from my ever-widening network of correspondents along the trade-routes to Portugal and the United Kingdom, to the United States and Canada and

275

to all parts of Central and South America. Perhaps, to speak the truth I was rather more than "nettled" that my information about the mood of the local Negroes was not as up-to-date as my news from far places.

"Why have you remained silent upon this matter?" I demanded abruptly.

"Dickie," answered Betsy, shewing some surprise, "I was sure that you knew, and that it was you who were being silent."

Again I did not answer immediately, for I was mentally reviewing all the evidence of Negro unrest which had reached my ears and eyes but which I had chosen to ignore — the increasing numbers of runaway slaves advertised in the *Courant*; the many incidents of Negro insolence and curfew-breaking which, taken singly, did not amount to much, but taken together suggested that the Negroes might have been gaining confidence by banding together secretly with a view to an uprising on the lines of the bloody but successful one in St. Domingue (or Haiti, as it had been re-named by its "Emperor" Dessalines). I was able to persuade myself that Sam's uncharacteristic taciturnity in my presence was matched by a similar caution in the attitudes of Merry and his two companions, now approaching fifteen years of age and all stout young fellows — I recalled with some apprehension the comments Father had made about their soldierly qualities.

Alarmed by the confluence of all these pieces of evidence, and convinced that Betsy must know much more than I did, I determined to question her closely. I turned my head to look at her and she was still unconcernedly reading the *Courant*. My heart almost failed me, for I had thought that she and I shared our thoughts and read each other's minds without the need for interrogation and I had been discomposed by the discovery that she had kept silent because she thought I was withholding my thoughts from her. I chose my words carefully.

"Are the Negroes so restive that they are likely to revolt?" I asked.

"Dickie," replied Betsy, without looking up at me, "it is best if you do not ask me questions of that nature."

"But our lives may depend — "

"If I hear that our lives are at risk, I shall inform you."

"— and what of our warehouses?"

(I referred to "our" warehouses, for Betsy was now part-owner of one of them and used it for her own ventures.)

"If I hear that there is a threat to our warehouses, I shall inform you in good time. Pray question me no more."

"But should we not be taking steps — " I persisted.

"It is hard enough for me to discover what is happening, for as your mistress and business partner I am not trusted by anyone, black, white, or Mulatto. If I was suspected of giving you any kind of warning I would be cut off from the few sources from which I now obtain my intelligence."

"Betsy, my dear, this is unreasonable and absurd!"

Betsy stood up.

"Mr. Mason," she said, "there could be two notions as to what is reasonable and what unreasonable; and as to being absurd, I am absurd enough not to wish to speak on this matter again."

"But I must insist — "

" 'Insist', sir? I do not understand what you mean!"

"You *must* tell me what — "

"Mr. Mason, I am under no obligation whatsoever to tell you anything that does not concern the running of your household." Here she changed to patois. "Me go to my bed," she said and left me with my mouth agape.

I was astonished at this outcome, but could not help recalling our lovers' quarrels, how they originated in trifles and ended in caresses. However, my astonishment turned to dismay and then to anger when I discovered that the door of Betsy's chamber was locked against me and that she would not accede to my pleas to open it; indeed, she refused to answer me in speech at all, or to admit me to her bed, for a period which stretched from sad days into weeks and from dreary weeks into months and from empty months into longer than a year.

Thus it was that throughout the rumours and counter-rumours, the frights and alarms, and the dreadful events of the year 1805, I was deprived both of a vital source of intelligence and of those quasi-connubial comforts which I had come to regard as mine of right. Betsy spoke to me as rarely as she could and then only in patois; in consequence, I lost the benefit of her cool reasonableness and trenchant wit when the news broke that the Negroes had formed themselves into *bataillons* and had elected Kings and Queens as well as Generals, Treasurers and Grand Judges; I could not even have the reassurance of her night-time presence and her loving pillow-talk when the leaders of the various *bataillons* betrayed each other (as though they were European powers) and were barbarously put to death on the orders of Governor Hislop. Little wonder was it that we could not meet each other's eyes while Trinidad lived under the Terror which caused every white and Mulatto to look sidelong in fear at every Negro and Negress, wondering where their loyalties lay, while every Negro and Negress had to look askance at every white and Mulatto, remembering that they belonged to the race who could flog, hang, and decapitate with such ferocity. Every household which could afford servants was put in fear of even the most trusted, and every servant looked upon his or her owners in a new and terrible light.

What, then, of my own household? One day, at the height of the unrest, Sam, along with Merry and his two fellows, disappeared without warning. However, it was not more than two or three hours before I had information that they had been arrested and thrown into the already overcrowded jail. I secured their instant release by the outlay of quite small sums in gold and once I had them home again informed them that I would not inquire into what they had done, or had proposed to do, if they would promise to keep out of trouble in future. This they did in a surly manner; it was many months before Sam resumed his singing around the stables, and Merry lived up to his name again. Jacques, remained unswervingly loyal; he had mixed with some English servants and had heard the phrase "a gentleman's gentleman". He decided that it described him to a nicety and that "gentlemen" did not involve themselves in foolish conspiracies.

As to Betsy, words cannot describe the fears and wild fancies which were unleashed in my head by our being separated in body and mind while yet continuing to live in the same household. In truth, there came a time when my mind was so frenzied that I contemplated giving her a week's notice and sending her packing; I also contemplated acceding to a proposal from a penniless French Créole gentleman that I should marry his elder daughter Charmaine. (The news of my estrangement from Betsy must have reached him in some circuitous manner.) This charming and affectionate creature had been truly well-educated in Paris before the Revolution, and had written some passable verses and painted some delightful pictures. More important, she made no secret of her age, which was no less than seven-and-thirty, that is, very near to my own, and she had kept house for her father very capably for many years after the death of her mother. (The gentleman now found his daughter surplus to his requirements, as he proposed to marry again, the young lady in question boasting a dowry which, I quickly ascertained, was negligible.) Everything was in Charmaine's favour — I was of course in a position to overlook her lack of a dowry, and I had received no mysterious notes concerning her. There appeared to be no obstacle to our union. However, one day I came upon her sitting in the back galerie of her home when she was not expecting me, and behold! she had slipped off her shoes to reveal her mottled red and white feet. The toes were so crowded upon one another, and the rest so squashed and mis-shapen, no doubt by the wearing of tight shoes, that she appeared to be deformed and crippled. I was so disgusted that I immediately made my excuses and put the lady off with as much dispatch as *la politesse* permitted. My readers may deduce from all this that I was comparing the lady's feet to another pair of feet, and indeed they may be right, but at the time no such thought occurred to me.

In time the Negro unrest receded, although the manner of its suppression left behind much bitterness and the Negroes remained sullen for many years, not recovering their *joie-de-vivre* until it became clear to them that their friends in Parliament were gaining such strength that the Abolition of the Slave Trade was virtually a certainty and Emancipation a real, although distant, possibility.

CHAPTER XXIV

Following Debate with my Housekeeper, we go our separate Ways to seek our nearest Relations; on my Journey I meet with Hostility from the Climate but reach my Destination

The years after Edward took Tony away were clouded by my not knowing her fate; I wrote to her many times, but received not one reply. I did not even know whether she and Edward had reached England safely or had perished upon the ocean, the perils of which I knew only too well from the fate of some of my ventures. When the rift between Betsy and myself occurred I was driven by loneliness to be more active in the matter: I requested my London correspondent to institute discreet inquiries and to expend whatever monies were necessary. After the usual delays consequent upon naval warfare I received the report of the inquiry agent; stripped of much unnecessary verbiage, the gist of it was that there was no evidence that Edward Rochester, Esquire, was other than a single man who spent as much of his time as the activities of Napoleon Bonaparte would allow upon the Continent of Europe and whilst there favoured the company of ladies of pleasure, whose nationality appeared to be a matter of indifference to him; he was supporting at least one illegitimate child; of a wife there was no trace. The agent had been thorough, in keeping with the substantial size of his fee, and had gone to the trouble of examining the passenger-list of the vessel in which Edward had sailed from New York to Liverpool in 1797; he had found no Mrs. Rochester entered therein.

Unwilling to contemplate the possibility that Edward had incarcerated Tony in a mad-house in the United States, or had otherwise disposed of her in that uncivilized Republic, I wrote back instanter demanding that the agent copy out the whole of the passenger-list and forward it to me. After another long delay, rendered more disagreeable by my having no one to give me pillow-counsel on the matter, the copy of the list arrived, and on it, sure enough, there were entered "Miss Bertha — lunatic lady" and "Mistress Grace Poole — lunatic lady's attendant".

I had had this intelligence for only a few weeks and was pondering in dismal loneliness what action I should take next, when Madame Gilbert surprised me one evening by serving my supper herself, an action she had not performed since our quarrel. When I had finished and she had cleared the dishes etc. on to a tray she took up a stance with her hands crossed in front of her which plainly indicated that she wished to speak to me.

"Madame Gilbert," I said, "if you have something to say to me, pray proceed."

"Mr. Mason," she began, and I looked up at her sharply for she spoke to me in English only when she had something truly important to convey, "I would like permission to be absent for perhaps two or three months, if you would be so good as to keep my place here open for me. I would, of course, expect no wages."

"But the household —" I said, and found myself so flabbergasted that I could speak no further.

"Rest easy, Mr. Mason. I have in mind a person who would perform my duties in a satisfactory manner whilst I am away."

"But where on earth are you going?"

"I am not bound to offer you an explanation, Mr. Mason, when I could simply offer you a week's notice."

"Ah, but-but-but-but —" I could not stop myself from stammering like Henri, "M-M-M-Madame G-G-G-G —"

As though her heart-strings had been loosened by this echo of my poor brother, Madame Gilbert's voice softened.

"Master," she said, "I have not heard from M. le Capitaine for a twelvemonth now, and I fear that he may have been wounded again and be in need of my help. I am, of course, his only living relation."

"I had not heard that he had been wounded."

"Master, we have not exchanged any news about our respective families in recent times."

"That is entirely true, Madame Gilbert. Pray bring me up-to-date."

"I think you knew, did you not, Master, that Jéhu rose to be an aide to Toussaint l'Ouverture and was promoted to Capitaine?"

"Yes, indeed, I knew that."

"Well, he seemed to bear a charmed life, just like his Général, *le Centaure des Savanes*, and he escaped death by a hair's-breadth on innumerable occasions. However, as you may have heard, Toussaint was too trusting and was tricked into going to France and once there was starved and frozen to death on the express orders of Bonaparte. After that Jéhu seems to have lost heart, for he grew careless, he told me, and had an arm hacked off in an engagement with the French when it was he who should have been doing the hacking —" What a pang shot through my frame at the thought of Jéhu without one of his potent arms! "— and he had to hide in the mountains until the wound healed. When he was sufficiently recovered to ride and fight he joined Dessalines and was promoted to Colonel. I learned all this more than a year ago and I have heard nothing since, but I have a presentiment that M. le Capitaine needs me and that is why I propose to go to Haiti —"

"Madame Gilbert!" I interrupted, "Are you out of your mind? Such a voyage would be extremely foolhardy at this time. You know well what sums insurers are demanding!"

"Mr. Mason, sir, it is very kind of you to be so concerned for my safety but I am sure that I could make my way to Haiti and return without mishap. I have a sufficiency of money."

"A Negress with a sufficiency of money would be in greater danger than anyone!"

"But I would not draw attention to myself; I would travel as a plain *marchande*; and I would carry my pistols."

How my housekeeper proposed to disguise herself as a "plain" *marchande* defeated me, for at nearly forty years of age she was as handsome and elegant as ever, with a figure so youthful and movements so supple and sprightly that first-time visitors to my house often thought that she was a maid rather than my housekeeper. I tried to visualize her with a basket of provisions perched upon her head, and failed.

"You would need at least two stout young fellows to protect you; they could travel as your sons or nephews —"

Madame Gilbert's hand was resting upon the table not too far from me; without thinking I reached out and took it into my own.

"— I insist that you do not travel unprotected."

To my surprise, Madame Gilbert did not withdraw her hand; instead, she touched my face with the other and whispered: "Dickie!"

Quite overcome by hearing my name pronounced in the old familiar way, I burst into tears, kneeled down and grasped my house-keeper round her knees, mumbling "B-B-B-Betsy!" into her skirts.

Thus, allowing for my facility in telling nancy-stories, were Betsy and I reconciled. Aided by Dame Nature and her wayward handmaid Passion, we re-commenced our life together, a life which had, as I remember, an especial and fugitive sweetness since we had to spend most of our time making arrangements for parting again.

What a relief it was to be able to share my news, or rather lack of news, about Tony! When Betsy had heard me through, she looked at me steadily for a few moments and was about to speak, but before she could utter the words "stick-in-the-mud!" I told her of my decision, made that instant, that I would go to England and find out what had happened to my sister. I would leave, I announced, as soon after Betsy had left for Haiti as was possible.

An immediate consequence of this decision was that our passion became even more intense than before, as we contemplated being separated by the four thousand miles of the stormy Atlantic Ocean instead of the mere nine hundred of the familiar Caribbean Sea between Trinidad and Haiti.

After much confabulation we agreed that it would be best if Betsy left as quietly as possible in the middle of the night and that I would make no inquiries after her whereabouts until at least four months had passed. It was not long, then, before I woke to find my love's place in the bed beside me cold and only a trace of her fragrance lingering in her chamber.

Sadly I moved back to my own bleak chamber and sadly I gave my instructions to Madame du Vernay, the replacement house-keeper whom Betsy had found for me. She was a quiet, devout and almost mouse-like little Mulatto lady who had recently had the misfortune of being discarded by her white Master and rejected by their "pass-for-white" children after thirty years of faithful concubinage. Her spirit appeared to have been broken and while she knew how to run the household while I was present I was loath to leave her in charge for an absence the length of which I could not predict; I therefore promoted Jacques to butler, as he had proved himself loyal and not unproficient over the years, warning him to be tender of Madame du Vernay's feelings, as she was scarcely used to being second-in-command to a Negro.

I left my business in charge of Mister O'Brien. I had recently caught him peculating small sums (which was not surprising in that he now appeared to be the sole support of no less than three Mulatto ladies, each one plainer and more fecund than the next) and warned him that I would have him in jail on my return should there be any further instances. He nevertheless had the gall to ask me for an increase in his salary, which I countered with an offer of a percentage of any profits he might make whilst I was away; an offer which he was constrained to accept.

My extensive knowledge of shipping enabled me to select the most rapid passage to the United Kingdom. Since this involved landing at Greenock, I wrote to Mr. Tulloch, Father's lawyer in Edinburgh, to inform him that I hoped to call on him on my way southwards, and to hear whether there was any truth in Father's assertion that I might be heir to the chieftaincy of one of the Macdonald clans and to a fertile glen or two.

I shall not burden my readers with a long description of my dismal and lonely voyage, which seemed never-ending as I sailed from port to noisome port, first northwards through the Antilles and up the coast of America, and then eastwards across the Atlantic Ocean. It was unfortunate that I had chosen to travel in the early part of the year for the cold, taken together with the effects of *mal-de-mer*, forced me to stay in my bunk night and day, and my misery was not to be dispelled by thoughts of my beloved, for I knew that she was in far greater danger of her life than I was.

At Greenock, the ship's captain informed me, there would be a fine prospect of mountains and sea-lochs to admire. This was my first introduction to the nineteenth-century notion that the rockier and more deserted a landscape, the more romantic and interesting it is. However, when the anchor was dropped and I mounted to the deck I found that the ship was entirely enveloped in a fog so cold and dank that I marvelled that human life was being sustained, sometimes even cheerfully, in the midst of it. There were shouts of welcome from the crews of the small boats which were approaching the ship, and seemingly floating in mid-air rather than upon the water. The captain and the sailors shouted back in the broad Scots with which I was familiar from my days in Tobago, but which seemed to become even broader as they exchanged pleasantries with their fellow-countrymen.

The captain, seeing that I was looking about me in dejection, assured me that I could warm myself at a fire just as soon as I went ashore and found myself an inn. The boatmen who took my shivering person towards the quay seemed quite at home in a world where they could see nothing in any direction, and they barely looked over their shoulders as they pulled lustily at their oars.

At the inn, when I demanded a private room, the landlady said she would have to light a fire in it before I could occupy it, and would I mind waiting in the public room, where a fire was already burning. I approached it and discovered that while it warmed whichever aspect of my person I presented to it, it could not reach the other aspects, which were assailed by icy draughts rushing upon me from the doors and ill-fitting windows; but not only did the fire fail to warm me, it also emitted fumes from its coals which were so sulphureous that they were like to choke me. The crowding customers and scurrying servants of this popular hostelry were white-skinned in the extreme, and they took no notice of me at all. I found myself looking around for black or Mulatto faces, and the frank inquiring looks with which they would have met my eyes, but none, of course, were to be seen. When the landlady reappeared, it was to instruct a chamber-maid to shew the "foreign gentleman" to his room.

This my first meeting with "Caledonia stern and wild", the "land of the mountain and the flood", in which I should have been at home by right of inheritance and boyhood imaginings, was a disappointment which I have not yet overcome. I was as much a stranger there — a foreign gentleman — as I have been anywhere; except, as I was now recognizing, in my Betsy's arms — how my whole being ached for her black presence! How I longed to know that she was safe!

Failing to warm myself, even in the private room with the curtains drawn and the fire roaring in what the chamber-maid called the "lum", I determined to set out for Edinburgh as soon as possible, omitting even a courtesy call upon my correspondent in Glasgow. The post-chaise journey from Greenock to Edinburgh was the nearest approximation to the reputed torments of Hell which I had ever suffered — it was worse, far worse, than the night of the hurricano in Tobago. The fog persisted; there was nothing to warm me in the chaise; and the driver was a silent surly Scotsman whose only words to me were the scarcely encouraging: "If ye're cauld, man, ye'll jist have tae thole it."

The country roads were smoother than those of Trinidad, but when we passed through Glasgow, the iron-bound wheels of the chaise rattled abominably upon rough cobble-stones, adding their mite to the noise from a thousand other vehicles and their demented drivers, all trying to manage their huge horses in a fog so thick and yellow that it made noonday as dark as night. Leaving this dreadful city behind we made good speed to Edinburgh, where the fog shrouded the black crags and crag-like buildings of which the capital seemed to consist. In the falling darkness the driver had difficulty in finding the dwelling of Father's lawyer, so he called upon a "caddie" to help him. This gentleman, who spoke with a Highland accent which was identical to that used by Fergus and the other overseers, and by Father upon occasion, offered to be my guide, messenger and friend for the duration of my stay in Edinburgh. Since he named a sum for his services which was an affront to my business self, I assumed his own accent, told him my name was Macdonald, and beat him down in a satisfactory manner. I thought he was about to deceive me, and possibly rob me, for he led the chaise to the entrance of a dark alley-way and announced that Mr. Tulloch's house was reached by a narrow door opening off the alley. The driver, seeing my hesitation, opened his mouth to say: "He's no a robber, ye can gang wi' him." Thus it was that I was led up three flights of an exceedingly narrow stone staircase, through an even narrower door, and into an astonishingly warm and comfortable little salon.

Mr. Tulloch welcomed me hospitably and told me in a high old squeaky voice that it was the coldest April that he could remember in all of his eighty-seven years; he apologized that he could not induce the fire to burn any hotter for me.

I remember the warmth of Mr. Tulloch's room more than anything he said, for when, over a late supper, I asked him about my Highland relatives he launched into a confused and confusing genealogical dissertation.

None of it could I follow because the heat of the room and the effects of a large tumbler of hot whisky-and-water made me so drowsy that I fell asleep as he droned away about my "second cousin twice removed". I was wakened by a touch on my shoulder, which I thought for a moment was Betsy's, but which was that of Kirsty, Mr. Tulloch's housekeeper, inviting me to retire to the "spare room".

In the morning I discovered that whilst I was warm enough if I remained under the heavy bedclothes, yet when I arose to attend to Nature the cold was so biting that I trembled as though I had the ague. Washing my face perfunctorily in the scant pint of hot water which Kirsty brought to me, I determined that enough was enough; that my visit to the United Kingdom must be of the shortest possible duration and confined to checking on Tony's whereabouts and on her welfare. The matters of the Macdonald inheritance and possible chieftaincy could be pursued by correspondence from a warmer clime.

On learning of this decision and of the reasons for it, Mr. Tulloch expressed his disappointment and recommended me to a tailor who would provide me with warmer garments. The caddie was waiting outside Mr. Tulloch's door and conveyed me promptly to the tailor, of whom I bought a thick and extremely heavy fur-lined cloak, or *surtout*. Long before mid-day I had engaged a post-chaise, dismissed the caddie, and set off pell-mell for —shire, in the midlands of England, where lay Thornfield, Edward Rochester's ancestral home.

As the chaise left Edinburgh, the fog lifted, allowing the sun to shine, and to reveal a bare countryside with not a green bud visible on the few naked and twisted trees; the bare earth of the ploughed fields suggested no possibility of green growth; fields which I took to be pasture-land were dun-coloured and desolate. The sun gave forth no warmth and before we had travelled far the cold had penetrated my cloak — so much for the warmest garment that money could buy — and I was in danger of losing consciousness. However, the driver was a kindly and resourceful fellow, if a little slow of intellect. Upon grasping the origin of my discomfort, he stopped frequently at inns in order to revive me with hot drinks in front of coal-fires. At one place he was able to borrow a copper foot-warmer, which he re-filled with hot water at intervals, and which proved the most effective expedient of all. I shall pass over my experiences in the various inns where we had to change horses and spend uncomfortable nights.

Thus was I conveyed towards my meeting with Edward. The nearer I approached, the more clearly I recalled the violence of his nature and the more apprehensive I became. What would I do if he simply denied all knowledge of Tony and her whereabouts and denounced me as an impostor? Was he capable of seizing me and hiding me away, pretending I had never existed? Would I recognize Tony when I saw her? She might have changed out of recognition in the ten years since I had seen her. I almost called out to the driver to slow down, but a remnant of pride prevented me, and the chaise maintained its spanking pace towards Thornfield and my encounter with its inhabitants.

CHAPTER XXV

After some Delays, I meet Edward Rochester; I make my Way, without his Permission, to an unfrequented Part of his House, where I find a Prisoner

It was late afternoon when I reached Thornfield. As always, apprehension enhanced my powers of observation and I have a crystal memory of noting that the parkland round the house was of a fresher green than the fields of Scotland and that the elegantly spaced out old trees more like the trees in Trinidad. As I stepped from the chaise no more than two or three glances were sufficient for me to imprint upon the tablets of my memory the huge grey old pile that was Thornfield Hall; it was almost as forbidding as the cliff-like buildings of Edinburgh, and as I approached the massy oaken door I had intimations of the manifold forms and manifestations of evil which it was large enough to conceal. (My readers will note, once again, that the functioning of my faculty of Reason was dependent upon the presence or propinquity of Betsy and her cool intellect; four thousand miles away from her, I succumbed to Unreason.)

Upon passing through the door I did not need the footman to inform me that Mr. Rochester had company, for a babble of conversation could be heard from a doorway in the vast hall, and youthful chatter and laughter from an upstairs room. The footman — how strange that his face was white! — also informed me that Mr. Rochester had had to leave his guests on a matter of business and that the time of his return was uncertain. In Trinidad I would have acceded to his suggestion that I wait for Edward in the hall, but despite an enormous and fragrant wood-fire burning in the fireplace, the place was subject to a draught of air which seemed to have derived from the Pole. I therefore refused the footman's offer to help me off with my *surtout* and insisted that he conduct me to the salon, where I hoped the temperature would be more endurable; it proved to be a large room, as magnificent as the hall, but scarcely warmer. There were only a half-dozen richly dressed ladies present; I bowed to the one whom I deemed the eldest.

"Madame," I said, "it appears that I come at an inopportune time, when my friend, Mr. Rochester, is from home, but I arrive from a very long journey, and I think I may presume so far on old and intimate acquaintance as to install myself by the fire until he returns."

Without waiting for an answer I moved toward the fire and the lady accompanied me, adroitly introducing herself as Lady Ingram whilst making a pretence of conducting me warmthwards. We had exchanged a few pleasantries of the most perfunctory nature, and I had noted that the other ladies were not at all uninterested in my appearance, when my attention was caught by a woman in plain grey sitting in a window-recess and half-hidden by a crimson curtain. For a second or two I thought she was Betsy, miraculously transported over the ocean, for she was wearing the same kind of long-sleeved high-necked dress as had always been affected by my dear mistress in public; further glances revealed that, unlike Betsy, she was so thin as to be almost emaciated; that the complexion of her narrow face was even paler than those of the other ladies present; and that her colourless hair was parted in the middle and dragged tightly over her ears in a manner that seemed unnatural as well as unbecoming. It was her eyes, however, which added most to my unease, for they were as wan as the rest of her and they removed not their unwinking gaze from my face. I knew, after only a few moments, that she was like myself, an observer born, one who watched others from the shadows with an eye to profit. To add even further to my perturbation, she was attended by a female familiar, a little ringletted doll-like creature, neither child nor woman, or rather of the size of a little girl but got up like a lady of fashion, who ran up to me, made her inspection with knowing eyes and ran back to whisper her findings to her superior.

So agitated did my state of mind become that I fear Lady Ingram must have thought me insufferably dull, but she was excused my company when a bell rang loudly, apparently to warn Edward's guests that it was time to dress for dinner. In a short while I found myself alone in the salon, even the witch, as I now described her to myself, having vanished along with her acolyte. My spirits rose a little and when I had assured myself that I was unlikely to be espied, I approached the fire very close and turned myself round and round before it as though I were a carcase upon a spit. My spirits rose a little further still as I achieved some warmth.

When the guests had re-assembled in their evening finery I was approached by a bluff elderly gentleman who introduced himself as Lord Ingram and told me that he had taken the liberty of arranging a place for me at Mr. Rochester's table. Of the meal I recall only that my seat was at the greatest possible distance from the fire and that the food consisted of unseasoned and only partially cooked fishes and meats, served with vegetables boiled until there was no flavour left in them.

When the ladies and gentlemen returned to the salon, expressing some surprise that Mr. Rochester had not yet returned, I followed them and discovered that the woman in grey had resumed her seat in the window-recess and was gazing upon the company. On perceiving me, however, she transferred her baleful eyes to me and did not remove them, causing my depressed spirits to fall even further. I began to be certain that she was truly a witch — not one of the wretched old Obeah-women who pass for witches in Trinidad and other Islands in the West Indies, but an Old World sorceress of infinite power and wickedness, and of a kind which must surely exist, otherwise where would Shakespeare have found the means to raise the hairs on the back of my neck with his versions of their spells?

Kindly old Lord Ingram, seeing me shivering and shaking and thinking that it was only the cold that was troubling me, insisted that I return to the fireside and sit in a large armchair there. As luck would have it, this placed me out of sight of the witch and I was able to make some not altogether rambling replies to the gentlemen who now crowded around Lord Ingram and myself. (English gentlemen, I noticed, were not above excluding their ladies from the warmth of the fire, although those ladies' low-cut dresses must have rendered them most vulnerable to the boreal blasts which were so unmanning me.)

When one gentleman asked of me whence I came, I replied "the West Indies", and was straightway inundated with questions about Jamaica and the effects upon the planters of the Abolition of the slave trade, then very newly in force. Many of the gentlemen had interests there, or had friends or relations who were planters, and the talk became animated although not altogether well-informed. Some of the ladies, upon overhearing the topic, came to join in, anxious to learn from the "gentleman from Jamaica" about how "the poor darkies" were enjoying themselves now that slavery had been abolished. With the assistance of the better-informed gentlemen I did what I could to dispel this misapprehension by explaining that it was only the trade in African slaves which had been abolished and that the Negroes already in the West Indies had not been emancipated. When the lady-like little cries of disappointment at this news had subsided, I was about to correct the further misapprehension that I was from Jamaica, but my instinctive conspirator's caution came to my aid and I decided that it might be to my advantage to maintain the confusion, at least until after I had spoken to Edward. (Further experience has persuaded me that on this matter the inhabitants of the United Kingdom are invincibly ignorant; to them the West Indies is synomymous with Jamaica and Port-of-Spain merely another name for SpanishTown. Even the much publicized trials, for monstrous crimes, of my whilom adversary Governor Picton, which were being held at the time of which I write, failed to inscribe Trinidad on the national consciousness as a British Colony.)

The conversation had begun to flag, as conversations will, and most of the ladies and gentlemen had drifted away, when Lord Ingram announced that he had a diversion for the younger ladies — an old gypsy woman had arrived, had been installed in the library, and would tell their fortunes. I was standing up, out of politeness to the one lady who was still in converse with me, and at the moment Lord Ingram spoke saw that the witch was still at her post and had resumed her gaze at me. I became convinced, against all Reason, that she and the gypsy woman were in concert to some nefarious end, though what that end could be defeated even my heated fancy.

There was much talk and merriment as the young ladies went to have their fortunes told and returned to the salon, either dejected or delighted. Wine and glasses had been set out on a sideboard and I helped myself to more than I had ever drunk. Still the witch's eyes did not leave my face. Some of the gentlemen made jokes and laughed heartily, and with the help of the wine I managed to smile and laugh mirthlessly with them. Would Edward never come? Even the trouble I anticipated when I met him would be preferable to being subjected to the unblinking examination of the witch's eyes. Temporary relief came to me when the last of the young ladies returned to the salon to be quizzed by her friends, for a moment later I saw the footman enter and whisper to the witch, whereupon she rose to her feet and stole away with a strange gliding stride. I took refuge in the fireside chair again and sat there wondering why I had travelled four thousand miles only to over-indulge in wine, listen to meaningless babble, and be pursued by witches.

I must have been dozing in my chair, overcome by the wine and the weariness of too much travel, when there came a touch upon my arm and a grating whisper in my ear: "Sir, Mr. Rochester is coom and wishes to see thee." I opened my eyes and the witch's face was only inches from my own; it was more terrifying close to than it had been at a distance, for the eyelashes of her red-rimmed orbs were almost white, and her mouth was twisted into a sickly grin, showing irregular and ill-shaped teeth.

"Wilt' coom wi' me, sir?" came the grating voice again and, mesmerized, I followed the creature out of the salon and into a long corridor which, though lit by many lamps, was yet airless and cold. She stopped at a door, opened it and motioned me to pass through. When I had done so she closed the door silently behind me, leaving me alone in the near darkness of a room which I knew must be Edward's library, for bookshelves stretched from wall to wall and from floor to ceiling. As my eyes became accustomed to the dimness I discerned that I was not alone, for Edward was sitting bent over a low glowing fire. He held a heavy iron implement in his hand, hefting it as if he were about to use it to strike a blow. As I watched, he gripped it fiercely, raised it, and crashed it down upon a large coal in the centre of the fire, breaking it into many pieces. Flames leapt up and in their flickering light Edward's face was truly diabolical. He turned and looked at me from under his heavy brows for several minutes, then used the iron implement — a poker, I believe it is called — to point to the armchair on the other side of the fire. When I had sate myself on the edge of this, he cleared his throat raspingly and spoke in a low but sonorous voice.

"I suppose," he said, "that you have told my guests and my servants that you are, or were, my brother-in-law."

Deciding to match his bluntness with bluntness, I replied: "No, I have not, and they are all, without exception, under the impression that I am a planter from Jamaica."

"Then in the Devil's name, why have you come?"

"Edward," I said peaceably, "I have come to see my sister, who is my only living relative; or to have news of her, since she does not answer my letters."

Edward pondered this reply grimly for several minutes.

"So that complete dumb idiot of a brother of yours is dead, then?"

"You are well aware of that sad fact, Edward."

"And you have not yet sired a legitimate heir?"

I hesitated, but saw no advantage in concealing the truth, which Edward could easily ascertain from Trinidad, and shook my head.

Here there occurred another long silence during which, I was certain, Edward was considering the implications of my news; I, on the other hand, was prey to fear and uncertainty, for he was still hefting the poker as though he was barely in control of convulsive rage. At last he laid it down.

"So you wish to see Bertha?" he asked.

"I do," I answered.

"And what if she is dead?"

"Pray do not prolong these evasions, Edward. She is after all my sister, bound to me by the ties of blood and of a shared upbringing."

"Ha! What are such ties to me, or to Bertha in her present state?"

"She is alive?"

"Richard," he snarled, "Bertha is as good as dead. She is so demented that I have to keep her locked up and only three people besides myself know of her existence — and *they* are all under the impression that she is a cast mistress."

"— but as her brother I may see her? It is my right, I think."

"Richard," said Edward, throwing himself back in his chair. "I am willing to let you see her, for reasons of sentiment, but I am afraid I must impose certain conditions which you must accept or reject *in toto*."

At this point I should have denied Edward's right to impose conditions, but I am afraid that I began to succumb to his old power over me and I failed to do so. I was, if I may make excuses, in a precarious position, alone and friendless in the house of a ruthless man of considerable wealth and influence — his guests had spoken of him with respect and even awe; moreover, my resolve was weakened by the cold and by anxieties about Betsy — each minute which I spent away from her increased my desire to return "home" to Trinidad.

As if to emphasize the weakness of my situation, Edward picked up the poker again and calmly bent it almost double with his bare hands; then, without looking at me, he straightened it and spoke.

"My first condition is that you give me your word as a man of honour, as a Highland what-d'ye-call-it, that you will not reveal to anyone during my lifetime that your sister Bertha is still alive; my second condition is that you likewise give me your word that you will leave Thornfield tomorrow morning at first light and will not return during my lifetime."

I protested, I remonstrated, I made every representation short of actually begging, but Edward used the full force of his will to exploit my weakness so that I finally succumbed and gave my word.

"Dick," said Edward almost affably, having won his point, "I can now tell you that your sister is concealed in the same room in this very house where Jesuits and other priests were hidden during the centuries when we Rochesters were an Old Catholic family, and where your own father recuperated in secret from the wounds he received in the Rebellion of 1745."

"My father was here?" I exclaimed, making my astonishment somewhat too obvious.

Edward laughed. "I see that your father did not apprise you of the manner in which he came by his wounds. He was galloping most gallantly, carrying despatches from the Young Pretender to the English Jacobites who were to rise in support of the Stewart cause, but who preferred not to risk their necks, when some of our country-folk, loyal to King George, waylaid and unhorsed him — those honourable wounds of his were inflicted by pitchforks wielded by mere peasants. Oh, he put up a good fight — he wounded one of our tenants with a pistol shot; the fellow is an old man now but still takes pride in exhibiting the scar. Another had the tendons in both his wrists severed by your father's dirk and died many years later, still dependent upon my father's charity."

In other circumstances I might have been — nay, I would have been — interested to hear more of this history and to judge how much of it was truth and how much a nancy-story of Edward's, but I was impatient to see Tony before retiring, since I had undertaken to leave at first light. Edward, however, was adamant that he must see his guests before they retired, and that I should not think of seeing Tony except in the presence of himself and her attendant; she had, he averred, a madwoman's strength at the service of her preternatural cunning. He proposed, therefore, to call the attendant, Mistress Grace Poole, a most capable and phenomenally strong woman who belonged to these parts but whom he had recruited in America. Whilst waiting for this woman Edward began to shew signs of impatience. Jumping to his feet, he said: "I have been a poor host this evening and Lord Ingram must be thinking ill of me, which is something I cannot afford."

The footman announced the attendant (or nurse — I know not her proper title) and there entered a plain stout red-haired woman of the middle age and of respectful demeanour. She had a sympathetic eye, but carried with her the unmistakeable odour of Hollands Geneva, or "gin", as it is now nick-named.

"How is your charge this evening?" demanded Edward without preamble.

"Quiet, sir, or I would not have left her," replied Mistress Poole, with the confidence of one who knows her value. Her hands, I noticed, were as large as a man's.

"This gentleman," explained Edward, "is an old friend. He wishes to see Miss Bertha, but he is leaving early tomorrow so I will have to take him upstairs at about six o'clock. You will be so good as to have Miss Bertha dressed and ready for a visitor," — here Mistress Poole lifted her chin as if to express disagreement, but Edward was in too much haste to notice — "and you will inform the gentleman now of what he may expect in the way of behaviour from your charge." He turned to me. "You will not forget that I have your word?"

"No, Edward," I replied, "I shall not forget."

After Edward had hurried away, Mistress Poole stood patiently waiting for me to speak, not looking at me but at a point somewhere high above my head.

"Well," I asked eventually, "in what condition is Miss Bertha? You may speak freely to me."

With an unmistakeable gesture, Mistress Poole held out her right hand, but continued to look over my head. I took out my purse and put five guineas on her palm. After glancing at them briefly, she secreted them away with prodigious speed, then turned her eyes upon me for a second or two.

"I think," she said, "that the gentleman should judge for himself of the lady's condition."

"But Mr. Rochester has just instructed you to prepare me for what I may find."

"Yes, sir."

"Please speak out, then."

"I think that the gentleman should visit Miss Bertha without any other person being present."

"Not even yourself?"

"I should be happy to attend, or to wait within call, if the gentleman should ask me."

In brief, I arranged with Mistress Poole that after the household was asleep she would knock twice on my chamber door and conduct me to Tony's secret prison in the "priest's hole". As she left the library she gave me a barely perceptible curtsy and said: "I am sure, sir, that Mrs. Rochester will be right pleased to learn that her brother is come to see her; and I should perhaps warn you, sir, that she will not brush her hair, nor will she let me touch it, so that her appearance is summat wild."

This speech was a shock to me, for it made plain that I was being drawn into a welter of deceptions, in which I had no one to trust. Mistress Poole, it seemed, was privy to everything that Edward had sworn me to keep secret. Was she breaking an oath of silence, or was she unaware of the importance of what she knew? If she spread her knowledge abroad, perhaps even tonight, would Edward blame me and wreak some terrible vengeance?

Never have I felt so alone, so much a stranger, as in that vast mansion; my only possible allies were the enigmatic and mercenary Mistress Poole and her "charge", my ever unpredictable and irascible sister, whom Edward was convinced was a madwoman of superhuman strength. Sitting before the library fire and watching the glowing coals as they died into ashes, I gave myself up to yearning for Betsy and to fears for her safety, searching as she was in strife-torn Haiti for a brother who was most likely dead; even the uttering of his name might be dangerous. Oh, why did we part? Why did we not "take care of our garden" like Candide and his companions?

Before long Edward came to shew me to my chamber and I joined the guests who were repairing upstairs with the cheerful goodnights which betoken untroubled minds.

I shall not describe how I waited for Mistress Poole's double knock, for the interval is a blank page in my memory, but I can recall how she guided me with a small candle along silent passages and up flights of stairs — I know not how many. The higher we climbed the colder and more disagreeable became the air — how a breath of a tropical Trade Wind would have freshened that mansion's musty upper storeys! In a narrow passage, which must have been at the very top of the house, Mistress Poole opened an even narrower black door and led me into a surprisingly large chamber. Its floor and low ceiling were polished almost to blackness, as were the furnishings — a curtained bed and an enormous press; the walls were hung with what I recognized, from my reading of literature, to be dark old tapestries. In the feeble light of the candle, it was a room that inspired thoughts of plotting and murder — here might Rizzio have been done to death as Mary Stewart wept and called down curses upon his slayers.

Mistress Poole seemed oblivious to anything uncanny about the room and walked straight to a point where the tapestry was looped up to reveal the dark panelling of the walls; she pressed a carved roundel and a panel slid to one side to reveal an iron-studded door of massive construction; this she opened with a large key. Stepping aside, she gestured to me to pass through, but I hesitated and then whispered: "Pray announce me!" Shrugging her shoulders, she entered the room beyond the door and said in a quiet matter-of-fact tone: "Miss Bertha, here is your brother to see you."

As I followed Mistress Poole, I was aware of the room before I saw anyone in it. It was without a window, and although not near so large as the adjoining chamber it had yet something of the aspect of a chapel, with a vaulted roof from the peak of which there hung a lamp upon a chain; at the far end, where there might have been an altar, there was instead a fireplace enclosed in a high and strong iron cage (or fender, as I later learned to call it). Neither chair nor stool was to be seen; indeed, the only furnishings were a bed and, hanging from a hook upon the wall, a leather garment — was it a strait-jacket?

The occupant of the room was sitting on the floor with her back to the fire; she was a portly woman, her face almost concealed by grizzled locks which hung well below her shoulders. Upon seeing me she leapt to her feet with some agility and I perceived that much of her portliness was due to her being wrapped in many layers of clothing. She drew back her hair with both hands, looked into my face intently for a moment, and then shewed her teeth in the smile I had known from childhood; I needed no more convincing that this was indeed my unfortunate sister Tony.

"Dickie!" she said, and her husky voice had not changed, " 'tis you, 'tis truly you! and I had thought that old Pooley was telling me a nancy-story to quell my wrath," — here she gave Mistress Poole a most quizzical look — "and I was being very wrathful, Pooley, was I not? I was quite ready to set something alight or to burst into flames myself." She turned to gaze at me again, then stepped up to me and touched my face with fingers which were, for fingers belonging to Tony, of the gentlest. "Oh Dickie, you have not changed one whit! You are still the great lump that was once my little brother."

CHAPTER XXVI

My Visit to my unfortunate Sister is interrupted in a horrid Manner; I have further Meeting with Edward and his Witch-like associate; I leave the United Kingdom

"Come, great lump," said Tony, taking me by the hand, "let us sit on the bed with your rich man's cloak around us and you shall tell me all the news." When we had done as she suggested and she had rubbed the fur of the cloak against her cheek for a while, she called in a loud whisper: "Pooley, stay by the door and act as sentinel; we all know how distrustful a man is Edward and how sharp are his ears."

When I had seen that Mistress Poole was stationed where she could best listen for the approach of danger, yet was within call should I need help, I addressed myself to Tony.

"And how are you, Tony? I trust that I find you well."

"I?" said Tony, "I do not matter any more; I am a Nobody, shut away where none can see me. It is your news which is of consequence, Dickie, for you are a Somebody; this cloak is telling me that."

"Where shall I begin?"

"Is it true that Father and Henri died within minutes of each other?"

"Of course it is true. How could you doubt such news?"

Tony shivered and gripped my arm tightly.

"Oh Dickie, if you were living here with no one but Pooley to talk to for years on end, you would understand that I do not always know what is true and what is not true. Sometimes, but only rarely, Edward will keep his temper with me for long enough to tell me news, but how do I know if he is telling me the truth when he has told me so many lies? Sometimes I dream dreams, even when I am wide awake, about being back in Tobago and riding

Hector; sometimes I wake from the dreams and sometimes it seems that I do not. Pooley tries to help me to remember —" Here she called out to Mistress Poole: "You try to help me, do you not? Gin makes you kind." She turned to me again. "But she does not know what is true in my memories and what is not, for I have often told her lies. So Father and Henri are dead; yes, I knew that, for I remember weeping for Father and then cursing him for having me marry Edward; and as for Henri, I think I said to myself that he was happier dead and then I asked God to forgive me for the thought."

Tony was quiet for a few minutes and I was finding it in my heart to be truly sorry for her when she spoke again.

"What of my darling Betsy, whom you would not give back to me?" Her grip on my arm became even tighter. "Is she still your housekeeper?"

I nodded speechlessly, for we were on dangerous ground.

"And is she as beautiful as ever?"

I could make no response of any kind.

"Of course she is! I can see it in your eye! She will be beautiful when she is ninety! And you have summoned the courage to make her your mistress, have you not? I can see that in your eye too!"

What could I do but nod?

"And you have had children?"

I could only shake my head.

"But you will not care about that, so long as you have *her* and *all* the money — that is, everything you longed for, while I have nothing, not even my freedom. I might as well be a slave! I *am* a slave in all but name!" Here Tony's mind leapt from one topic to another in the manner I remembered from her childhood. "What of Jéhu? What news of him?" she demanded.

I hesitated, for Tony was becoming more and more excited and I dreaded what might happen if I excited her further, for had she not warned me almost as soon as she saw me that she was still capable of being "very wrathful"? She detected my hesitation; my weakness, perhaps.

"I shall set myself ablaze if you do not answer me and tell me the truth," she threatened. "What of Jéhu?"

"Betsy has gone to Haiti —"

"Haiti? Where is Haiti?"

"It is the new name which the Negroes have given to St. Domingue. Betsy has gone there to try to find Jéhu as she has not heard from him for a twelvemonth. He lost his right arm and —"

"Jéhu has lost an arm?" whispered Tony, "and now you know not where he is! And you have allowed sweet Betsy to go to that wild place! You did not let her go alone?" I feared that she would do me an injury, so fiercely did she dig her fingers into the flesh of my arm. "Pooley!" she called out in a voice that was a shade louder than was wise, "I want to shout and scream at all the dreadful news which Mr. Mason is giving me, but I am keeping quiet. Am I not being good?"

"Just you stay that way," answered Mistress Poole from her post at the door, "and we shall manage our trip to the stables after all."

At this, Tony let go of my arm, burst into tears and hid her face against my shoulder, her disordered hair almost covering the lower half of my face. She continued to sob quietly in heart-rending fashion while I pondered these words of Mistress Poole's. They had caused me to remark that Tony or at least her clothing, stank of the equine race; I had not been aware of the odour before, perhaps because my sister had never smelled of anything else in all the years I had known her.

Seeing her charge upset, Mistress Poole left the door and approached us, adding the pungency of Hollands to the stench of horses in my nostrils, but seemed satisfied that violent behaviour was not imminent and gave me a reassuring purse of her lips and nod of her head.

"Do I understand," I asked through the tangle of Tony's hair which covered my mouth, "that you take her to the stables?"

"Every night, when the lady's behaviour warrants it, and I deem it to be safe."

"Even with such precautions, is it wise?"

"Mr. Mason sir, if the lady could sleep in the hay-loft above the horses and ride them every day God gives, rain or shine, she would do very well and my services would not be required (except at the full moon, of course) but Mr. Rochester will not hear of it, so I take her when I can, mostly between two of the clock and five. Sometimes, if the lady has been outrageous, I have to withdraw the privilege, and I never let her ride, of course. I would be a right fool not to use this means of managing her."

Tony, who may or may not have been listening to this speech, now mumbled into my shoulder: "I do hope Betsy finds Jéhu — even with only one arm he would still be the finest man —" here her sobs became deeper, "— and he was not all hairy and brute-like, he was smooth and gentle — oh, how he could soothe a restive horse with one touch of his hand —" Suddenly, her mood changed again. "Take me home, Dickie!" she begged with extreme vehemence but without raising her voice, "take me home this instant!"

I did not respond, for what she asked was impossible, as well she knew, and she started to beat me with her fists, breathing loudly through her clenched teeth as though to stop herself from shouting. I was defending myself as best I could against these blows (which, and this is no nancy-story, were scarce as painful as the playful "Tobago love" punches which Betsy and I used to exchange in the early days of our passion) and Mistress Poole was

300

watching us with her hands outstretched ready to intervene, when there came the sound of the half-closed door being pushed fully open. Mistress Poole shouted "'Ware!" but could not stop Edward from entering the room and seeing what Tony was doing. He straightway raised a hunting-crop he was carrying and advanced upon us shouting: "Desist, madwoman, desist!"

What followed was a confused fracas in which I found myself trying to defend Tony from Edward (and taking some of the whip's blows upon my own shoulders) while Mistress Poole tried to use her strength and professional skills to restrain him from behind. Tony was the most agile of us all, despite her bulky clothing, and danced around us screaming and striking a blow where she could; she succeeded in seizing Edward's whip, wrenching it out of his hand and throwing it, with howls of glee, upon the fire. At that moment Edward broke free from Mistress Poole's restraining arms, seized me and flung me across the room toward the fire-place. The point of my shoulder, already bruised by his whipstock, struck a corner of the fender with such force that I was instantly knocked unconscious.

When I regained the use of my senses, with the searing vapours of a smelling-bottle in my nostrils, I was sitting in an easy-chair with Edward bending over me. The pain in my shoulder was agonizing; I was in my shirt-sleeves and rigid with cold; and Edward was sponging blood from my wound in a manner so brusque that it was causing me spasms of pain even more excruciating.

"I am not in immediate danger?" I asked in alarm.

"No — a mere scratch," answered Edward, and I groaned. "Bear up, man! I will fetch a surgeon for you now, myself. Jane!" he added, turning to a figure who was standing in the shadows, holding a candle, the only light (or heat) in the room.

"Sir?" a voice answered, and I recognized it as that of the witch of the window-recess; its thin harsh tone was anything but deferential.

Edward proceeded to give the witch instructions, to which I could not attend because of my condition and because he spake both fast and low; in concluding them, however, he said loud and clear: "You will not speak to him on any pretext."

"Yes, sir!" said she, as though she were a nurse calming a fractious child and reserving the right, as an old family retainer, to speak whenever she was so disposed, "not a word, Mr. Rochester, sir. Troost me!"

Edward then turned to me and said, with some emphasis; "Richard, it will be at the peril of your life if you speak to Miss Eyre: open your lips — agitate yourself — and I will not answer for the consequences."

Edward then left, and Miss Eyre laid down the candle and busied herself with a basin. I looked around and saw that I was in the dark chamber off which Tony's prison opened, and sitting facing the giant press which, by a trick of my disordered fancy or because the floor truly was uneven, seemed to be leaning forward and ready to topple over and crush me.

The hours which followed resembled nothing so much as a suffocating nightmare. In the absence of a fire, the cold alone would have congealed the blood in my veins, without the assistance of my injuries. The witch, presumably following Edward's instructions, bound up my shoulder with bandages, but so tightly that they were like to kill me; she constantly sponged away blood in a manner even more brusque than Edward's; she forced the smelling-bottle upon me so often that I feared for my nasal membrane, that it would be permanently damaged; and although she obeyed Edward's injunction against speaking to me, she neverthless muttered to herself in a rhythmical manner which suggested that she was casting spells. As though her activities were not enough, the monstrous press continued to loom darkly over me — in the flickering light of the candle the faces carved upon the door panels seemed — nay, certainly were! — those of witches and warlocks, satyrs and daemons, sphinxes and gargoyles, while the ebon crucifix which surmounted the whole with its tortured, emaciated, thorn-crowned Christ appeared altogether the most evil representation of sorcery and witchcraft which the human mind could devise.

I could, of course, shut my eyes and exclude the ominous press from my sight, and brush aside the witch's hand as she presented the smelling-bottle yet again, but I could not defend myself against the onslaughts of the icy air and of the grievous hurt in my shoulder except by losing consciousness, and this I did at intervals. I might never have regained my senses at all had not Betsy appeared to me in what must have been a dream — her dear black face came close to mine, she smiled her incomparable teasing smile and said: "Dickie!" — then, in a flash, her face was distorted by fear and she cried: "Oh Dickie, help me!" — I strained forward to reach out my hand to her, but she vanished. I was left strengthened, nevertheless, to hold on to life for Another's sake as well as for my own.

I was awakened by Edward drawing back the curtains and letting in the sun's earliest rays. He had brought with him a surgeon, a precise little man, who, once apprised of my condition, set about removing my bandages and dressing my wounds with a skill and gentleness which contrasted strongly with Miss Eyre's painful bungling. As he worked away assiduously, I observed the witch talking in an undertone to Edward while he listened respectfully — I was sure that she was urging him to some intervention.

"Carter," said Edward, while the witch grimaced horridly behind him, "assure Mr. Mason that there will be no danger from the bites of a madwoman."

"Bites, Mr. Rochester?" asked Mr. Carter, regarding my wounds doubtfully.

"Yes, yes," said Edward testily, the witch's face hanging in the air at his shoulder (or so it seemed), "You know your patient's capabilities when roused — she bit him several times and threatened to drain his heart."

Mr. Carter examined my wounds more carefully.

"I see contusions and lacerations consequent upon —" he began, but Edward interrupted.

"— consequent upon several bites from a frenzied madwoman," he said, with an unmistakable threat in his voice.

The little surgeon glanced at Edward's stern face, and at Miss Eyre's ghastly visage; then, calling to mind no doubt his fee and his dependency on the great landlord's goodwill, he gave way.

"Ah, yes, of course," he agreed, "a bite, or perhaps several bites, from a lunatic, the flesh being torn as well as contused and lacerated." Then, his conscience seeming to prick him, he said quietly into my ear: "But I can assure you that there is no danger whatsoever of contamination or morbific infection if you have the wound dressed regularly." With some dispatch he set about binding up my shoulder and arm, but not quickly enough for Edward.

"Hurry! — hurry!" he urged, "I must have him off."

Miss Eyre again whispered to Edward and he seemed to be even more deferential than before.

"Very well, Jane," he said like a complaisant husband, "I shall fetch him a clean shirt and neck-handkerchief." He hurried away.

On Edward's return with the clothing the witch asked: "Was anyone stirring below when you went down, sir?"

"No, Jane, all was very still; we shall get him off cannily. Here, Carter, help him on with his waistcoat. Dick, where did you leave your furred cloak? You cannot travel a mile without that, I know, in this damned cold climate."

I thought it probable that my cloak had been left in the secret room and the same thought must have occurred to Edward, for we both turned our eyes to the point where the door would have been visible, had not the tapestry there been released from the loop in order to conceal it again. Edward gave me a threatening glance from under his fierce brows and clenched a fist in front of his mouth, as though forbidding me to say a word. He then turned to the witch.

"Jane," he said, "will you be so good as to take this key and go down to the library — what a mercy you are shod with velvet, my dear! A clod-hopping messenger would never do at this juncture. In one of the drawers of my bureau, I know not which, you will find a little phial and a little glass; take them out, re-lock the drawer, and return here with them as softly as you went."

Miss Jane seemed a little put out by these instructions, even though they were couched in courteous terms and delivered in a tone which, emerging from Edward Rochester's lips, was little short of abject. She even pouted, and I was led to suspect that she might not be a witch after all; although if she was not, it was hard to account for her power over a man such as Edward for she was without feminine allurement of a kind that was plain to the eye.

"Aye, sir," she said sulkily, "I must do as I'm told, I s'pose." She then left the room with many hesitations and mistrustful backward glances. Edward quickly locked the door behind her, sped across the room, lifted the tapestry, slid back the panel to reveal the heavy door, and knocked upon it three times with a particular rhythm. Very shortly the key turned from the inside, bringing my heart into my mouth, I may say, for I knew I was in no condition to witness, let alone take part in, an exchange of fisticuffs, or even a mere altercation, between Edward and Tony. The door opened by a slit and Edward spoke in an urgent whisper; he was answered by Mistress Poole, whose voice was somewhat slurred but whether from sleep or gin, or perhaps both, it was hard to judge. My trepidation mounted as I waited for the kind of blast from Tony which would set off a counter-blast from Edward, but none came, and in a moment or two my cloak was handed over, the door closed and the tapestry dropped again. Edward carried the cloak to the window and examined it.

"Ha!" he exclaimed, "it seems to have escaped the blood which was being splashed around. On your feet, Dick!"

"Miss Bertha has not been injured?" I asked.

"No, man, no! The Devil looks after his own. She escaped injury entirely, and has now fallen into a deep sleep, assisted by a draught prescribed by Carter here and which Mistress Poole laces with some of her own peculiar cordial. On your feet!"

I rose, with some assistance from Mr. Carter, and just as soon as Edward had thrown the cloak over my shoulders, there was a knock on the chamber door. Edward made haste to admit Miss Eyre, who was panting in unladylike fashion, presumably from the speed with which she had run to perform her errand. The phial and glass passed quickly from her hand to Edward's, but not without a conspiratorial exchange of glances.

"Now, Dick," said Edward, emptying the phial into the glass, "I got this cordial in Rome — it is not a thing to be used indiscriminately, but it is good upon occasion: as now, for instance. Carter, I am administering it on my own responsibility." He held out the glass to me. "Drink!" he said.

Mr. Carter was sniffing the air in the direction of the phial and glass with an expression of alarm upon his countenance which, in happier circumstances, would have been comical. Seeing him thus, I mustered enough courage to ask of Edward: "Is it inflammatory to the blood?"

"Not a bit!" replied Edward. "It will stimulate all your vital functions for long enough to get you to Carter's house. Drink!"

Mr. Carter, who was standing timidly behind Edward and Miss Eyre, shook his head at me and my courage rose to the point of defiance.

"Edward," I said stoutly, "I am well able to travel to Mr. Carter's house without the aid of stimulants of unknown composition."

As Edward glowered and Miss Eyre shewed her teeth in a lop-sided grin, I took several steps; they were somewhat unsteady but firm enough to prove my point and Edward gave way, returning the cordial to the phial with an ill grace.

In quick time Edward hurried Carter and myself down to the fresh cold air out-of-doors, across the yard to a point beyond the stables, and into a post-chaise which was waiting there concealed from the house. As I leaned out of the window to say goodbye and saw Miss Eyre's slight figure standing in front of Edward's broad frame and illumined by the morning sun, she appeared much younger than I had thought her, perhaps no more than eighteen, though no less pasty of complexion and irregular of feature. I was inclined, yet again, to blame myself for branding her as a witch in my thoughts, but she promptly aroused my suspicions again, for when I asked Edward to take the greatest care of his unhappy and partially demented charge, and to treat her as tenderly as may be, Miss Eyre took it upon herself to answer for him.

"Mr. Rochester doos 'is best for Grace Poole," she said, and her quiet dialect words sounded far more fraught with menace than if they had been uttered by Edward at his most irate, "An' 'e 'as doon it, an' 'e will do it, as tha knows, or shud know."

I was astounded: firstly, that Edward had seemingly succeeded in concealing Tony's existence from Miss Eyre (unless, of course, she was merely pretending that she knew nothing of Tony); and secondly that, instead of taking her extraordinarily forward speech as an affront, Edward smiled down at the creature with every sign of infatuation, mesmerization, or bewitchment. I could no longer doubt that these two were engaged in conspiracy, but whether to the detriment of a third party such as my sister, or of each other, I could only guess. I determined there and then that I must somehow strengthen the hand of Mistress Poole if I were to help and defend poor Tony. How this end was to be achieved was not at all clear to me, the nature and purpose of the conspiracy being a mystery, but I knew that it had to be done, otherwise the enormous trouble and expense of my journey would have been in vain.

As we drove away from Thornfield the motion of the post-chaise jolted my shoulder but caused me far less pain than I had feared, so that I was able to persuade Mr. Carter that I was fit to travel on to London; he insisted, however, that I warm myself by his fire, eat a breakfast of bacon and eggs, grilled kidneys, etc., and swallow an analgetic draught. The effect of these three, and of my dreadful sleepless night, was that I fell into unconsciousness in the chaise without having debated with myself how I could most expeditiously ensure that Mistress Poole continued to attend Tony, did not succumb to over-indulgence in spirituous liquors, and was not dismissed out-of-hand by Edward if he discovered the nightly visits to the stables. I knew for a certainty that in the care of a less experienced and understanding nurse, Tony would become quite uncontrollable and might inflict great injury upon herself or others.

It was not until the following day, when approaching the pall of smoke which hung over London, that I became mentally alert enough to conclude that I must use the services of the inquiry agent to keep in touch with Mistress Poole and through her with Tony.

To be brief: within twenty-four hours I had visited the inquiry agent, apprised him of the situation, and engaged him to supervize Mistress Poole and to make whatever financial arrangement seemed consistent with not increasing her consumption of Hollands. He also accepted a down-payment and undertook to submit a note of his fees and expenses at three-monthly intervals. Within the same period I also visited my London correspondent and found to my dismay that there was no letter from Betsy awaiting me, although she had earnestly promised me that she would use every available means to have one or more of her discreet missives reach me in the United Kingdom. Filled with fear, I omitted the visit to Mr. Lackington's bookshop to which I had much looked forward and went straight to the West India Dock and by good fortune and the outlay of considerable sums of money succeeded in obtaining a cabin on a ship bound for Trinidad via Madeira.

In truth, 'tis an ill wind, I thought to myself as I laid my weary body upon the narrow bunk, for a call at Madeira would give me the opportunity to meet my correspondent there face-to-face and to confront him with some bills of long standing which he had failed to pay. By a coincidence he bore the same surname, Eyre, as did the pallid being who wielded such influence over Edward Rochester, a circumstance which may have prejudiced me against the young lady for, to judge by his dealings with me, the fellow was amongst the most unprincipled and grasping of my correspondents.

Within forty-eight hours, then, I had left the chill shores of the United Kingdom never, I fervently hoped, to return.

CHAPTER XXVII

I am delayed at Madeira; receive unwelcome News of two Kinds; and have Difficulty in deciding in which Direction I should travel

"Mr. Mason, sir," said Mr. Eyre, as we sate sipping tea on the airy galerie of his house in Funchal, "your ship proving unseaworthy is certainly the Lord's will and He may even intend the apparent misfortune as a blessing. If you would accept a sick old bachelor's hospitality for a while, the expense to yourself would be quite insignificant and you would recuperate your health very rapidly in this kindly climate; a climate which is to me, nevertheless, no more than the Vale of Sorrow from which I shall shortly depart, unmourned by any near or dear to me. Moreover, I might even be able to put one or two profitable ventures in your way, since I may not be spared to see them come to fruition."

From this I understood that Mr. Eyre could not bring himself to pay his debts in actual cash, but wished to satisfy me out of posthumous profits. However, I was only too willing to accept his invitation and to use my enforced stay in Madeira to allow the inflammation in my shoulder to subside, since it had been exacerbated by the motion of the ship and by the hardness of my bunk. As time went on I discovered that, in addition to his dilatoriness in paying his debts, Mr. Eyre had two other disagreeable propensities — the first, at which I have hinted above, was that for larding all his conversation most liberally with pious phrases and Biblical texts; and the second, that for attempting to convert me to his Methodistical beliefs. He did not cease from praising the Lord for enabling him to accumulate a fortune in the region of £20,000, mainly from trading in the miscellaneous goods which slave-trading captains need in order to barter for Negroes on the Guinea and other coasts. He told me that he had sometimes had to accept parcels of Negroes in settlement of debts and had found such transactions very profitable, considering the perishable nature of the goods and the great expense of shipping them, but that he had never been guided by the Lord to deal in Negroes and foresaw no diminution in his profits as a result of Abolition. He had also made profits from exporting wine, although he would have none in his house and instantly dismissed any servant so un-Christian as to be found drinking it.

As the weeks of my stay extended to more than a month and no ship bound for Trinidad appeared, Mr. Eyre and I perforce became quite intimate, although the unpaid bills precluded the development of any true friendship between us; I could not, of course, confide to him my great longing to see Betsy again — he would not have thought it the Lord's will that I should have a Negress for a mistress. On his side, he told me (while I dreamed of Betsy) that he had quarrelled with his sister and her husband over their slavish adherence to the Church of England and had wished to leave his fortune to his brother's orphan daughter, but had been informed that she was dead. He was therefore thinking of leaving his estate to a foundation devoted to converting the Catholic inhabitants of Madeira to Methodism.

My shoulder mended quickly — Mr. Eyre assuring me that this was due to the Mercy of the Lord even unto Sinners, as well as to my abstinence from wine — and I began to be impatient for a ship to carry me westwards, but the first ship to arrive was one bound for the East Indies. It brought a private letter for Mr. Eyre and a batch of the London newspapers to which he subscribed. While Mr. Eyre perused his letter I leafed rapidly through the newspapers looking for shipping news which might be of assistance to me in finding a ship for Trinidad but was stopped short by an item in an inconspicuous position at the bottom of a page; it stated baldly that a great part of the city of Port-of-Spain in the British Colony of Trinidad had been burned to the ground on the 24th of March, that is, seven or eight weeks before, and that one life had been lost. There were no details and a hasty but thorough search through all the other papers revealed no more than that Governor Hislop had appealed to the Government in London for aid. I hurried to the office of His Majesty's Consul and was informed that he had seen the newspaper report but could neither confirm nor deny it. I contemplated the awful possibility that Betsy had returned early from her trip and had perished; the one life lost might have been hers — on the other hand, Betsy being who she was, it was unlikely that she had willingly returned that early from her search for Jéhu.

On my return from the Consul's Mr. Eyre button-holed me; the letter he had received was from his orphan niece, now miraculously discovered to be alive. The old man was tremulous with joy — praising the Lord, wiping the tears from his eyes, and quite unable to apprehend my news of the disaster in Port-of-Spain. When he had collected himself, he insisted upon reading the letter aloud to me, although he had a struggle to decipher it, the hand being, he complained, neat in appearance but barely legible. His niece, she wrote, had been working as a governess and had had the great good fortune to engage the affections of her employer — here Mr. Eyre peered at the letter but could not decipher the gentleman's name — who had made an offer of marriage, which she had accepted. The wedding was to take place in four weeks' time.

"Here, Mason," said Mr. Eyre, handing me the letter, "perhaps your young eyes can make out the good man's name, God bless him!"

Taking the letter, I saw that it had come from "Thornfield Hall, —shire, England" and that the employer's name was "Mr. Edward Rochester". At the bottom, instead of a signature, there was inscribed in a plain script: "JANE EYRE".

I was astounded to the point of speechlessness at the coincidence that Miss Eyre was not only Mr. Eyre's namesake but also his niece; a coincidence which seemed to belong to the contrived world of novels rather than to the real world of affairs. Although my lips could form no words my mind was yet engaged in a review of all the implications of this truly extraordinary intelligence. Much that had perplexed me at Thornfield, and which must have puzzled my readers also, was now explained, yet the news brought new mysteries, for example, the dominion which Miss Jane exercised over Edward that he was prepared to commit bigamy in order to possess her paltry person. In my less rational moments (that is, when Betsy is absent) I am still inclined to attribute her power to witchcraft, for when I regained my power of speech I straightway informed Mr. Eyre that the name which he had been unable to decipher was that of Edward Rochester of Thornfield Hall and he shewed no sign of recognition whatsoever; it therefore seemed unlikely that Edward could have known of the relation between Jane and her uncle or of the possibility that she might become a wealthy heiress whom it would be worth his while to seduce.

I then apprised Mr. Eyre, in as kindly a manner as I could, of the fact that Edward was already married to my sister and that any marriage which Miss Eyre might contract with him would be a bigamous one. He was, as I need hardly tell my readers, as astonished and distressed as I, and bemoaned that his rapidly declining health prevented him from hastening to England to prevent the marriage; he pressed me, not without an old man's tears, to go to the defence of his innocent young orphan niece and of my poor sister before further wrong was done to them. "Further wrong" was indeed what I feared, for if Edward went through a form of marriage with Miss Eyre he would be under the necessity of concealing Tony's existence more completely than before; and I even wondered if he had not disposed of her already in some horrid manner.

I was thus placed in a quandary. Although I maintained some outward composure, I was hideously divided in my mind as I frequented the quayside, the shipping offices, and the inns where the ships' officers took their refreshment, anxiously seeking to meet a captain, mate or supercargo with further news of the conflagration in Port-of-Spain; or better with a vacant berth on a ship sailing to Trinidad or to one of the Windward Islands. At the same time I was hoping that I might find a berth on a fast ship back to England, for half of my divided mind wanted to prevent Edward's marriage to Jane Eyre, and to assure myself that Tony was not in any danger.

A few days later, though it seemed like much longer, Mr. Eyre told me of a ship due in from Liverpool on its way to the East Indies; the captain was an old and trusted friend of his with an interest in saving the souls of young people, and his cargo consisted of building hardware, tools, etc. As soon as this ship was sighted, I was out in a cutter to meet her and to climb quickly, if clumsily, aboard. Before the ship had anchored the captain had agreed to sell me his cargo and to take it to Trinidad. When I asked about a berth I found that I had rejoiced too soon, for I would have had to share the captain's cabin, no other being available, with himself and the ship's boy, whom he introduced as his nephew and a good clean-living God-fearing youngster, but whom I suspected, from his rolling eyes and insolent bearing, of being the captain's catamite. I went ashore and was debating with myself (and with the image of Betsy with whom I often had silent dialogue) whether to risk a voyage in such company when I learned that the fastest ship belonging to the East India Company had been sighted and that she was bound direct for London; she was so fast indeed that she could out-distance any French privateer or warship and sailed independently of the Company's leisurely convoys. A wealthy Nabob having disembarked at the Cape, his commodious cabin was available and I hesitated not at all, for I calculated that the speed of the ship would allow me to land at London, persuade Mr. Eyre's solicitor, Mr. Briggs, to accompany me, and arrive in Thornfield in time to stop the marriage.

Before I embarked I visited Mr. Eyre, who was now confined to his sick-bed, and he requested me not to inform Miss Eyre that she might inherit his fortune, for changing his will would take some time and he feared that he might "pass to the other side" before he could sign the new document. Despite his condition, he then presented me with a substantial bill for my accommodation.

Thus the morning of the wedding found me at Thornfield, Mr. Briggs at my side. On the journey northward in a rattling post-chaise I had informed the solicitor of Edward's violent nature and he decided that public intervention at the wedding-service would be more prudent than attempting to warn Miss Eyre beforehand.

When we drove up to the church, somewhat early, there was no one to be seen, nor was there any sign of preparations for a wedding, so Mr. Briggs and I had to wait in the churchyard to see what might transpire.

At the appointed hour we were treated to the strangest of spectacles — Edward Rochester and a veiled figure, which could only be that of Miss Eyre, marching hand-in-hand toward the church without a single attendant. Edward was most handsomely attired and clearly of this corporeal world, but his bride wore a filmy grey-white wedding-dress and veil which made her look like a daylight phantom, a wraith born of mist and presaging death or other evil. I would not have been surprised if the weak English sunshine had caused her to dissolve into the air and "leave not a wrack behind".

Mr. Briggs and I followed the couple into the small and damp-smelling church to find them already standing at the altar-rail, while the clergyman and his attendant were just taking up their places. The church was otherwise empty.

The clergyman commenced the service without any preamble whatsoever, mumbling away without looking up from his book and I was exceedingly glad to have Mr. Briggs present, for left to myself I would have missed the pause when we had to declare "the just cause why these persons might not lawfully be joined together". Mr. Briggs, fortunately, behaved as though he interrupted weddings every day.

"The marriage cannot go on," he said calmly. "I declare the existence of an impediment."

At these words Edward turned and saw me. He breathed deeply through clenched teeth, then started toward me with uplifted arm as though to strike me, but the clergyman exclaimed: "Sir! Remember that you are in a sacred place!" and he desisted.

I have wished, upon my honour, that Edward had indeed struck me, for I had proved in the secret room that I could give some account of myself in a bodily encounter; instead, he glared at me with such malevolent hatred in his eyes, while Miss Eyre lifted her veil to reveal a face so distorted with a passion which could only be evil, that my heart failed me and I passed into a stupor of abject fear in which I heard nothing of the subsequent proceedings until aroused by Edward shouting: "— if I am married, it is to a bad, mad, and embruted partner! Come, all of you, follow!"

Mr. Briggs kindly took my arm and he and I and the clergyman set off after Edward, who had Miss Eyre by the elbow in a fierce grip and was propelling her along at great speed. We followed him back to the Hall, up the three flights of stairs, through the low door and into the tapestried chamber. Lifting the tapestry, sliding back the panel, and unlocking the inner door with a master-key were the work of a moment.

"Be quiet, everyone!" whispered Edward savagely, "Mason, you know this place — this is where she bit you so grievously." He then opened the door cautiously and ushered us into the chapel-like secret room, whence we could hear a husky voice, it could only have been Tony's, rising and falling in a strange manner and every so often making a noise like a dog snarling and barking.

As I entered, Mistress Poole was standing by the fire and signalling to us urgently to be quiet. Tony was lying on the floor with her back to us near to her attendant and she appeared to be narrating a story with many gesticulations, a story so engrossing that she had not heard our arrival.

"— and then, Pooley," she was declaiming, "old Jupiter, what a horse he had been in his day, what a spirited darling of a horse, he decided that he had had enough of the stupid little cur barking at him: 'bow-wow-wow!' and he rose to his feet ever so slowly," — here Tony demonstrated the horse's actions by raising herself slowly on to all fours — "and he whinnied thus," — she gave a fair rendering of a horse's whinny — "and the nasty little dog would not stop barking 'bow-wow-wow!' and snapping at his feet so Jupiter reared up," — she rose to her feet and waved her arms in the air as though they were the front legs of a horse — "and still the damned dog went 'bow-wow-bow!' and Jupiter whinnied again like a yearling," — Tony whinnied even louder; and how strange the sound was in that dark secret chamber! — "and he brought his hooves down on that wretched dog like this," — and she suited the action to the words — "and then my lovely Jupiter fell over, dead!" — she fell over with great dramatic emphasis — "oh Pooley, I could not believe it but he had killed the dog and his old heart had just stopped. I wept and wept and wept and I had him buried — I would not permit Father to sell him for meat —"

Tony stopped, for upon arising to her feet again she had seen us standing in a solemn group by the door. She scanned our faces slowly and with ever-widening eyes, then cried out in patois: "Dickie, if you no come to take me home, me go give you such a —" She ran toward me, but whether to strike me, or to embrace me, or to grasp me around the knees in supplication I shall never know for she was intercepted by Edward seizing

312

her round the waist and carrying her back to the fireplace. Struggling convulsively to free herself from him she reverted to English and gave vent to a stream of foul cane-field abuse, so that the clergyman started back in horror and even man-of-the-world Mr. Briggs turned around to assure himself that his escape route was not obstructed.

"Edward!" I remonstrated, "we had better leave her. She will do me no harm."

"I know what I am doing," shouted Edward, wrestling poor Tony to the floor, though not before her face had become purple with the effort of resisting him. "Have I not had fifteen years of experience to guide me? Mistress Poole, the rope!"

I was about to intervene, though I knew too well that I was no match for Edward, but Mistress Poole dissuaded me with a quick gesture of her two hands. She then passed Edward a stout cord with which he tied Tony's wrists and ankles; as she continued to struggle, he tied her to the fender, at which she gave up and lay still, panting, but her wild eyes continuing to look out from the mass of her tangled hair, straying from Edward to me, then to the other two gentlemen, and finally to Miss Eyre. (She, still in her wedding-gown, resembled no one so much as a greedy little girl who, upon opening a box of sweetmeats to select the largest for her enjoyment, discovers that she is face-to-face with a live frog placed therein by a mischievous brother. I might have felt more pity for the young lady had I not known, as she did not, that another box of sweetmeats, in the form of her uncle's not inconsiderable fortune, would be at her disposal just as soon as his will was signed and he had "gone to meet his Maker". Moreover, since I had prevented her marriage to Edward Rochester, the sweetmeats would be all her very own.)

Edward seemed inclined to make a speech, but Tony regained her breath first and addressed herself to Miss Eyre.

"Ah, I gave you a fright the night before last, did I not, Miss Jane Upstart Eyre? You pretended to be asleep when I visited your chamber dressed as a ghost, all in white, but you were awake, you know, for your eyelids were pressed together much too tight when I held the candle to your face. Are you not lucky, that I set nothing afire with that candle? I should have done, for you have not heeded my warning at all. You wanted to be Mrs. Rochester in my place before I was dead, did you not?" She turned to the horror-stricken clergyman, still in his white surplice. "You have not married them, have you, Father?"

Mr. Wood shook his head and Tony gave a fierce yell such as my pen cannot describe, except to write that it mingled triumph and despair in a manner most chilling to the heart.

When Tony had done with her yelling, Edward pointed his finger at her. "That," he said in tones of disgust, "is my *wife*! What you have heard are the endearments which are to comfort me for better for worse, for richer for poorer, in sickness and in health, etcetera, etcetera. Off with you now, all of you! The raree-show is over for tonight."

In shepherding us out, Edward turned his back upon Mistress Poole. She caught my eye and indicated by a gesture towards Tony's bonds that she would untie them as soon as the door was locked, and I formed the impression that the agent had already been to see her; the gesture ended, however, with her putting a hand in the pocket of her apron, withdrawing a small flask and taking a quick pull of its contents.

In the one or two seconds left to me before I had to yield to Edward's brusque insistence that I quit the room I saw Tony's countenance; she had turned her eyes upon me and there was no triumph left in them, only a despairing appeal to me.

"Dickie!" she called softly, "oh, Dickie!"

Torn between grief that this might be the last time that I would see my sister and shame that I was truly glad not to be responsible for her, I heard not all the words which were passing between Mr. Briggs and Miss Eyre as we descended the stairs, only that he was advising her not to return with me to Madeira but to remain in England until she heard further, either from or of Mr. Eyre. When we reached the open air and the lawyer asked me: "Have we anything else to stay for?" I replied: "No, no — let us be gone!" for the cold was afflicting me and my thoughts had turned to the first ship out of West India Dock; to a warm climate; to the possibility that I had lost my home, all my business papers, and several warehouses full of goods in the fire at Port-of-Spain; and, most of all, to my beloved, of whose safety and whereabouts I knew nothing and to find whom I would have expended my substance, down to the last halfpenny.

CHAPTER XXVIII

I return to Trinidad to discover that two Surprises await me

"Welcome home, Mr. Mason," said Betsy as I climbed the steps to the front galerie at l'Orangerie. I had taken a hired carriage thence after landing from the ship and discovering that the only one of my warehouses to survive the fire was safe under Mister O'Brien's supervision. There was a constraint in Betsy's manner as she greeted me, which was not surprising, since we had not seen each other for almost a year and circumstances had vastly changed — our former home in Frederick Street was a heap of ashes, along with half of Port-of-Spain, as I had seen with some emotion from the carriage window, and the decrepit little estate-house could hardly be desribed as "home", although I could see familiar faces amongst the servants craning their necks to catch a glimpse of Massa on his return from his long absence.

"Thank you, Madame Gilbert," I replied with equal constraint, "it is indeed a pleasure to be home."

At this, Betsy was inclined to busy herself with offering me refreshments and calling Jacques to attend to a change of clothing for me and so on, but something conscious in her eye prompted me to speak.

"I think that you have news for me," I said.

"As you must have for me, sir," countered she.

"Pray tell me your news first. What of Jéhu?"

Betsy hesitated and pursed her lips, then ordered Jacques to ensure that the gaping servants returned to their work. When this had been achieved she beckoned me to follow her and led me through the house and past the servants' quarters to the outside room which had been Tony's prison. On the way she explained to me something which I already knew,

315

that the servants were so afraid to enter this room that it could not be used for anything except a store; they believed that Tony's spirit haunted it, and could be heard cursing and weeping on moonless nights. When we reached the door she stood aside and motioned me to open it and enter. I did so, and there, propped up on a simple bed, lay Jéhu; his hair was almost white, but I would have recognized his crooked face anywhere, but not his body, for there was not even a stump where his right arm should have been and only his right leg was stretched out footless upon the bed; the left was entirely missing. I was so horrified that I could not speak, but he was unperturbed.

"Me glad to see you, Massieu Mason," he said cheerfully in patois. "You only Massieu in Trinidad who own a colonel!"

"But how did-did-did —?" I stammered, "how did you come here?"

"The fewer people who know that the better," interposed Betsy in English. "In fact, the fewer people who know that M. le Capitaine is living here, the better."

"You right-right-right," said Jéhu, "but you wrong to call me Capitaine when me Colonel."

"Dessalines make you *acting* Colonel," said Betsy, "Toussaint make you *full* Capitaine. To me, you M. le Capitaine." She gave a mocking military salute.

They continued in this bantering vein for a time, but both were eyeing me with knowing half-smiles and I perceived that they were withholding further news from me, but of what nature I could not guess. When the bantering had finished Betsy made some excuse and left the room. I thereupon hastened to assure M. le Capitaine that I had no desire to own him, that indeed I respected him for his gallant deeds on behalf of his people and would arrange for his manumission as soon as I could. He replied earnestly that he wanted no public manumission at that time and would accept my word that he was free; he would also like to have my promise that I would not reveal his presence in Trinidad to anyone. I gave my word and made the promise and, to seal the bargain, held out my right hand as if to grasp his. He was quite unembarrassed and quickly took my hand in his left and shook it with a vigour which shewed that his remaining arm had lost little of its might.

(It has never ceased to amaze me how little bitterness Jéhu had in him; it was as though he had spent all his rage in Haiti and was now prepared to accept the world as it came. In only one particular did he show a sign of residual anger — he never spoke English in any form, nor would he speak metropolitan French; only patois, or Créole as it is known in Haiti, crossed his lips.)

Betsy now re-entered the room. To my surprise she was carrying an infant of a few months, a remarkably ill-favoured mid-brown Mulatto child, its round head already covered with tight black curls. I regarded it with considerable distaste, thinking that Janga had committed another of her indiscretions, but this time with some white man or light Mulatto, when I was startled by the tiny creature frowning and, in doing so, coming to resemble Father in no small degree — it had the same prominent eyes (but brown instead of Father's ferocious blue), early intimation of the same high beak-like nose (which was quite incongruous upon so small a face), the same straight lips, the same large domed forehead (now furrowed with the deep vertical clefts which I used to dread so much), and the same protruding ears.

I looked up from the child's face to Betsy's; she was smiling in her incomparable roguish fashion. She held the infant out to me as if she wished me to take it in my arms. I started back, but she still held it out insistently, and I yielded, mainly, as I told myself, to please her — if it was Janga's it was after all an addition to my stock of slaves and she would qualify for the bonus instituted by Father; it looked healthy enough, despite its extraordinary ugliness.

"Mr. Mason," said Betsy, as I held the brown mite in gingerly fashion, "will you not acknowledge your son?"

"B-B-B-Betsy —" I stammered, "I t-t-trust that this is one of your t-t-t-teases —"

The floor commenced to heave, as though it were the deck of a ship, and I wondered if I had failed to regain the "land-legs" of which seamen speak. Betsy quickly resumed the infant into her arms as I fell over in a dead faint.

When I recovered my senses, after I know not what interval, Betsy was fanning me vigorously. When I opened my eyes she stroked my face.

"Poor Father," she said, "the shock has been too much. I should have broken the news more gently."

"Betsy, why the man faint?" asked M. le Capitaine, who was holding the infant in the crook of his good arm. "Is *you* nearly dead making child for him when you old woman."

I sat up, fully conscious.

"What is this about 'nearly dead'?" I asked.

"Child have big head, *oui!*" pointed out M. le Capitaine. "Colt like that always trouble to mare. He go be big Chief, *oui*."

"Enough!" cried Betsy, "I want my child's father to acknowledge him."

I rose to my feet and accepted the infant into my arms. He was certainly a Mulatto according to Dr. Johnson's elegantly insulting definition — "one begot between a white and a black, as a mule between different species of animal" — as any child of mine and Betsy's had to be, yet I had fancied that Nature's laws would not apply to us and that if we had a son he would be white like me, while if we had a daughter she would have Betsy's (and Matti's) beloved black skin and bold-featured African beauty. The creature had fallen asleep and was not frowning, so his likeness to Father was not so apparent and I was assailed by doubts. I quickly calculated the months I had been away.

"How old is he?" I asked.

Betsy did not answer me directly; instead, she pointed her finger at the child's ankle, round which was a string of jumbie-beads. Whilst I was pondering the meaning of her gesture, she began to lose patience with me.

"These are not to ward off *mal yeux*," she said abruptly, "but to remind his father of certain undertakings, solemnly entered into and hitherto honoured."

I was about to yield, out of loyalty to Betsy rather than from conviction, when the infant frowned again, in his sleep this time, and I beheld Father's lineaments so clearly that I could resist certainty no longer.

"Betsy my dear," I said, aware that M. le Capitaine was watching and listening with close attention, "thank you for giving me a son."

"Oh Dickie!" she said, and I knew that my doubts were forgiven me, "it is my pleasure and my privilege!" She curtsied deeply, then embraced me with great warmth while M. le Capitaine made jocular hrrumphing noises in mock embarrassment. (Thus I learned that he bore me no ill-will for taking his sister as my mistress — perhaps she had informed him of the real nature of the arrangement!)

Our son decided at this point that he wished to take part in the proceedings and set up a howling which seemed likely to bring down the roof of even that solidly-built jail-room. Betsy took him from me and made off, presumably to allay his pangs at Dame Nature's founts.

We named this son of ours Anthony Roderick Gilbert. M. le Capitaine volunteered to act as unofficial (and ungodly) godfather and, since we produced no more children, Rory became the centre of all our affections. Whether he was the pride of our middle years and the solace of our old age my readers will discover if they care to persevere even further with my chronicle.

Later on that day of my return I commenced the process of recounting to Betsy and her brother (for Jéhu instantly became, and has remained, a loved and respected member of our little family) my various experiences in the United Kingdom and in Madeira. They were particularly interested in my account of Tony's unhappy circumstances, but were only moderately sympathetic, as was only natural, considering the wrong she had done them.

"Mamzelle Tony need bringing up sharp now and then," said M. le Capitaine, "but plenty gentling in between. She yoked to wrong man." He said no more, did not inquire after Tony again, and appeared completely indifferent to the further news of her which shortly arrived. Betsy, on the other hand, was more forgiving and remained willing to hear of the former mistress who had sold her for the price of a horse, which was fortunate for me, for I was shortly to need her never-failing good counsel.

In view of Betsy's statement that it was best if as few persons as possible knew about her trip to Haiti, I made only one inquiry of her, and that was, where had my son been born? The reply was that Rory had entered the world on board a schooner on the return journey and whilst it was hundreds of miles from land; the nationality of the schooner was a matter on which its captain refused to be explicit, so my son cannot claim to be a citizen of any country or territory by right of birth, a circumstance which appears not to have disadvantaged him.

Over the ensuing years Betsy and M. le Capitaine have let fall enough remarks for me to learn that Betsy had shown all the courage and resource I would have expected of her, searching a strange and troubled country for a lost brother whilst *enceinte*. M. le Capitaine for his part, has let it be known that he would not have abandoned the land of the victorious Negroes had he not been so severely disabled.

"If me have foot on end of this leg," he once said to me, "me stay in country me fight for."

CHAPTER XXIX

In the Midst of a busy Life I receive sad News

After the events described in the last chapter there commenced the busiest time of my life, made the busier by my having to waste valuable hours on the daily five-mile carriage journey from l'Orangerie to the blackened desert which was Port-of-Spain. (Every article which had survived the fire, down to the last hinge and copper shingle-nail, had been removed by its owner, or by thieves, so that the ashes of the town lay about in sifted heaps.) There was, however, one aspect of these tedious daily journeys from which I could profit. Sam had resumed his singing of topical songs and by careful listening I made myself *au fait* with the current sentiments of the Negroes. It seemed that they had entirely given up thoughts of rebellion and were now pinning their hopes to the efforts of their advocates in Parliament. (Upon hearing this news from me, M. le Capitaine snorted: "Trinidad Negroes *macommère*-men, oui! They *never* go fight.")

In the surviving warehouse Mister O'Brien had screened off one corner to accommodate his families, whilst in another corner he had set up a makeshift compting-house, where I had perforce to join him at a rough table, shutting my ears the while to the sounds of domestic life being lived with Hibernian Mulatto volubility.

That my affairs prospered again so quickly was due in no small measure to Mister O'Brien's devotion in saving my books from the flames and to the businesslike fashion in which he had disposed of the cargo of building hardware which I had sent from Madeira. His percentage of the profits was substantial enough, but was swallowed up in the cost of re-building the various shacks on the plot of land which he owned; his philoprogenitive propensities were such that he could never accumulate sufficient capital to start a business of his own.

In addition to re-establishing my trading-house, I was engaged in buying a lot for, and building, a new house facing northward over Paradise Estate on the edge of town, where some privacy and cool breezes might compensate for the unobstructed panorama of disagreeable mountains visible from the front galerie. (To our great good fortune, Paradise Estate was later purchased by the Cabildo and became the Savannah, or pasture for the citizen's animals, so that the breezes have never been shut off by buildings across the street.) I also had to spend time selling the lot on Frederick Street and making vastly expensive arrangements for the transfer of my family's remains to a proper burial ground in the new lot.

At home, of course, I was being introduced to the mixed blessings of fatherhood. Little Rory was a strong, healthy and thriving infant, but at the same time extremely noisy when balked (which, in the nature of things, he had to be from time to time) so that, in the crowded little estate house it was sometimes — nay, often — difficult to enjoy a whole night's repose. As my readers will imagine, I pressed ahead as fast as I could with the building of the new and more commodious house, with an adequate nursery, a fine chamber for Betsy, etc.

One day during this busy period, it must have been early in 1809, I received a packet from London at the warehouse. I opened it and saw that it was a report from the inquiry agent. The first few paragraphs were in his usual high-flown, hyperbolical and prolix style and promised nothing of moment, so when I was called away on an urgent matter of business I put the report in my pocket, determining to read it at home.

When I did take out the report to read it I was glad to to be at home and with Betsy close by. (I cannot give my readers even an approximation to the agent's literary style, for I have mislaid the report altogether.) After the first few paragraphs which, as I have said, were devoted to mere verbiage, the agent proceeded to this effect: Reading in the public prints of a disastrous fire and loss of life at Thornfield Hall, he had cancelled all his engagements and hastened to —shire to investigate. The Hall was entirely burned down and one life had been lost, that of Mrs. Rochester, who was suspected by local observers of having started the fire. Once the building was ablaze she had ascended to the roof and had apparently shouted, sung and danced until Mr. Rochester had approached her, when she had jumped from the roof, killing herself instantly.

"Betsy!" I cried, "Read this!"

Seeing that I was distressed, Betsy came and sat on my knee and read the report with dispatch. When she came to the news of Tony's death she sucked in her breath and said, with all the sincerity in the world: "Oh Dickie, to lose your sister in such a way, how terrible!" She put her arms round me and held me tightly, but I did not weep; instead, I asked Betsy to read aloud to me the rest of the report.

Mr. Rochester, continued the agent, had retreated with great speed but was still descending the stairs when the roof fell and trapped him; when rescued, it was found that he was grievously hurt; it later transpired that he had lost one hand and the sight of both eyes. The attendant Mistress Poole was known to have escaped but had brought suspicion upon herself by disappearing. The agent had, however, found her after much trouble and no little expense. She had testified that Mr. Rochester, in his frustration and grief at being prevented from marrying Miss Eyre, had broken off acquaintance with all the local gentry, dismissed all the servants except Mistress Poole herself, shut himself up like a hermit at the Hall, and sold almost all of his horses, the better at risible prices and the worn-out to the knacker. This last action, said Mistress Poole, had disturbed Miss Bertha, as she called her patient, to the extent that she became all but unmanageable; Mistress Poole had consequently been forced to ask Mr. Rochester for another attendant to relieve her on two days per week, so that she might have her sleep, but the gentleman was so unhinged that he refused to listen to her and so dangerous-seeming that she dared not press the matter; she could hardly be blamed if she nodded off when she had slept little for upwards of a fortnight, and her patient had stolen her keys and set fire to the house.

The report ended with the news that the whereabouts of Miss Eyre were not known to any of the servants or to the local villagers, nor, it seemed, to Mr. Rochester himself, for on the few occasions when he emerged from the Hall it was to inquire if anyone had seen her. The agent knew not if I wished him to find Miss Eyre, but would take no steps until he had received my instructions and my authorization for the expenditure involved.

(Needless to say, I expended none of my money upon discovering the fate of the scheming Miss Eyre who, I had now convinced myself, was not a witch at all but a calculating adventuress who, unaware of the possibility of an inheritance from her uncle, had set about ensnaring Edward Rochester with a shew of common schoolgirl pertness. He had a taste, as he had said himself, for ladies who were not too submissive, and might even have become infatuated. On the other hand it was not impossible that he had discovered that Miss Eyre might fall heir to £20,000 and had decided to risk a bigamous marriage in order to lay his hands upon it.)

"So that is that!" said Betsy, when she had finished reading.

I took her face between my hands and turned it toward me to obtain clarification of this ambiguous remark — I read in her eyes that she was concerned for me that I was now without any close legitimate family, but that she had long foreseen that Tony would come to a tragic end, probably of her own making, and that she, Betsy, could not find it in her heart to grieve over-much. As if to confirm the message in her eyes, Betsy kissed me tenderly and kneaded my neck in her most comforting manner.

"Would you be so good as to inform M. le Capitaine of the sad news?" I said, and Betsy nodded. We spake not of Tony again.

(My readers should know that She Who Looks Over My Shoulder As I Write — and who also has access, when I fall into an old man's doze, to the key of the strong-box in which I keep these ledgers — she insists that I inform them that I am telling a nancy-story when I write that I could read messages in my mistress's eyes; Betsy, she says, might well have been thinking thoughts altogether different.)

Though we spake not of Tony for many years, yet she lived on in my heart and mind; oft-times she would appear to my internal eye, sometimes when I was awake, sometimes in dreams; always she was amongst swirling smoke and flames on the battlemented roof of grey Thornfield Hall, crazily singing a Negro song (for I was sure it was a rude cane-field song about Camboulay which the onlookers had heard above the crackling and roaring of the conflagration) and dancing in that barbarous Negro manner of which she had always been mistress and which involved so much swaying of the body and wriggling of the shoulders as well as shuffling and stamping of the feet. Then I would see Edward approach her along the roof, his arm upraised — perhaps to lift her up in his arms, perhaps to knock her unconscious — whilst she howled abuse and defiance until he reached for her and she leapt upon the battlement, swayed outward for a moment as Edward lunged for her again, then slipped and fell down past the flames belching from the windows; I would run forward to save her, my dear turbulent hateful sister, but something would be stopping me, I was held fast by the ankles, or by a heavy weight pressing upon my shoulders, and her fall would continue until her blood and brains mingled upon the unyielding flagstones. Once this vision or dream had started I could find no way of stopping it; when I called upon Reason to release me, there was no answer, and the terrible dream would take its course.

CHAPTER XXX

Our Affairs prosper; but we encounter Difficulties in the Upbringing of our Son Rory

It is strange, is it not, my readers, that in my old age I remember the distant past more clearly than more recent times, so that the events of the first forty-two years of my life have filled twenty-nine chapters while those of the next forty years may fill only three or four — that is, if my hand retains enough strength to write even that small number. Yes, my pen is apt to fall from my fingers after the exertion of writing for an hour, or even less; and since I am no longer able to lift this ledger I have to rely on the strength of Mr. Merry's arm to return it to the strong-box. I could, it is true, dictate to an amanuensis (Mr. O'Brien's son Sylvester is quite competent in that sphere) but involving another person would endanger the excitingly secret and conspiratorial nature of these my memoirs, their contents known only to myself, to Her Who Looks Over My Shoulder, and to my readers of the twentieth century (for I have left strict instructions that after my death my strong-box is not to be opened until this sanctimonious and censorious century has met its end, and Reason and Enlightenment have re-asserted their sway, as I am confident they will).

Reason, since I have invoked her, tells me that the second four decades of my life were full of incidents and events, great and small, public and private, and insists, moreover, that I shall not satisfy the curiosity of my readers if I do not make an attempt to describe at least the more salient occurrences in the later lives of myself, Betsy, and our son Rory.

As to public events in Trinidad during this period, my readers, if they are interested, will have to consult history-books (if any have been written about such an out-of-the-way Island) to learn about the great public works of Governor Woodford (and also about his venomous and unreasonable persecution of the Mulattoes); about the campaign for the emancipation of the Negroes and its eventual success (if success it may truly be called); about the worldwide search for labour to replace the freed and now work-shy Africans and the eventual importation of thousands of coolies from Hindoostan. (New-landed groups of these last I have recently seen with my own eyes from my chair here on the front galerie, trailing along behind the bullock-carts carrying their pitiful baggage and their cooking pots, their shy wives and daughters pulling their sarees over their faces whenever they see bold Negro eyes regarding them, and their skeleton-like children fearfully holding on to their parents' clothing. I cannot believe that such scraggy creatures, however skilful, can do the work previously done by stalwart and muscular Negroes.)

My business affairs, to be as brief as possible, continued to prosper, as did Betsy's. We foresaw, much earlier than most, that Emancipation was inevitable and that after it Negro labour would be unreliable, if obtainable at all. I therefore sold both Sans Peur and l'Orangerie and invested the proceeds in manufacturing in the United Kingdom and in further developing trade with South America; I thus severed my last links with the sugar production which I had so loathed from boyhood — I even sold without regret the wildernesses that were Braemore and Craigellachie. Sans Peur went to Malcolm's son Alexander, who had been managing it for me since before Father died; he had learned from me how to accumulate a little capital but not, I am afraid, to keep abreast of world affairs. Our hardware business had its ups and downs — there were lean times when no one seemed to have the cash to buy even a hinge or a door-lock, yet as soon as some measure of prosperity returned people were crowding into our warehouses demanding our goods and willing to pay prices which gave us a fair profit and sometimes a much larger one.

(Mention of Alexander may prompt my readers to ask what became of the other Mulatto children of Father's loyal clansmen — it would seem that only he made a life for himself, marrying (yes, marrying!) the daughter of a small Mulatto proprietor and having his children educated; the rest found low-paid jobs of one kind or another in the countryside or drifted into Port-of-Spain, some answering to the name of Macdonald and some to that of Mason, and there kept (and still keep) themselves alive by means of the various savoury and less savoury expedients open to unlettered free coloured men and women.)

Our family life, which I shall describe at greater length, as I have promised, was largely devoted to the difficult task of rearing our only child, the egregious Rory. In infancy, as I have already put on paper, he was noisy and wilful in the extreme, and as soon as he could walk (or rather run, for Rory rarely walked) which was at an earlier age than any other child known to us, he shewed that he had a disposition which was bold, adventurous and contumacious; nothing in the house, the kitchen, or the yard was safe from his meddling explorations; trees, fences and buildings existed merely to be climbed and the higher they were the more irresistible the challenge they presented to him.

Horses were to Rory, as they were to Father, the means to adventurous or other ends rather than ends in themselves as they were to Tony, and as soon as he could ride, which was at the age of five (or was it four?), he would escape from whomever was supposed to be in charge of him, mount a pony, or an ass, or a mule, and then endeavour to discover how far the animal would carry him before it became exhausted. Within a year or two he was having to be fetched back from as far afield as St. Ann's, Maraval, or even Chaguaramas. In these escapades he was encouraged, I am afraid, by M. le Capitaine (whom he had nicknamed "Mi Capi"); it seemed that listening to Rory's accounts of his adventures consoled his uncle for his restricted and unadventurous life. Betsy, being Betsy, made valiant attempts to discipline her son; but in regard to Rory at least, did not appear to have inherited Matti's unquestionable authority.

Rory early revealed a talent for subduing the servants to his will and not one of them, from dignified butler Jacques to witless yard-boy Prince, could oppose him. Only poor little ineffectual Madame du Vernay, whom we had retained, out of charity and because of her skills as a sempstress, after Betsy's return from Haiti, could gently cajole him into a kind of submission; perhaps it was because she was a fellow-Mulatto that he seemed anxious to retain "Tantie Cécile's" regard and affection at all times. He even, as we learned later, submitted to being taught prayers by her.

As my readers will understand, Betsy and I had many discussions about Rory and how to control his behaviour.

"Betsy," I said on at least two occasions, "I am convinced that Tony's daemon did not die with her, but has taken flight over the Atlantic and entered into Rory. How else can you explain his misbehaviour?"

"I am not at all convinced," replied Betsy, "that there is such a thing as a daemon — if I were I would have to believe in spirits and jumbies and all the rest of that nonsense. Perhaps if you took more of a hand in admonishing and disciplining him he might remember to behave when out of our sight. It is wrong of you to leave it all to me."

To this I did not answer, for I could hardly tell Betsy that my previous admonishments had had little effect and that I was determined that I would not beat my son in the way that Father had beaten me. Yet when I was confronted by his defiance, by Father's face in a little brown version daring me to exert my authority, I was so tempted to follow Father's example and beat him unmercifully that I would withdraw and leave the fellow unreprimanded and unchastised.

Thus it was that by the time Rory was seven, which was in the year of Waterloo, we were constrained to employ a tutor for him, a young man new-landed from France with glowing recommendations. To be as brief as possible, within a week Rory had so scared the poor fellow out of his wits that he packed his bags in the night and sailed for Guadeloupe in a schooner which weighed anchor at dawn.

Thinking that someone with more experience of disciplining the young was required, we placed Rory with a retired British Army Major who had ambitions to set up an Academy for young gentlemen on military lines, and to whom I loaned money for that purpose. The Major's ambitions foundered on the rock of Rory's intractability and he contented himself with setting up a riding school for young ladies.

It occurred to us that Tony, when of Rory's age, had been at her happiest when galloping over Braemore Estate, acting as a kind of apprentice planter and learning to grow sugar. I therefore approached a Monsieur Noel, a Mulatto proprietor with an estate in the Naparimas, whom I had met in the way of business and who had often expressed his admiration for Rory's spirit (although I must admit that the more he lauded my son the more money he was wanting to borrow). He had three boys of his own, Anselm, Leonard and Claude, who were all older than Rory and capable of helping to control his wilder impulses. We agreed that he could share the lessons they were receiving from a private tutor in the morning, and their active outdoor pursuits in the afternoons. Rory was delighted with the plan and cantered off southwards on the Royal Road in the most carefree manner, with his hat on the back of his head and his groom, Duke, and three spare horses following him.

Our house was very quiet without Rory's antics; I was able to give my full attention to business, knowing that I would not be interrupted by urgent messages about his latest misdemeanour; whilst at home of an evening Betsy and I enjoyed the kind of peace which we liked best — we had reached, of course, fifty years of age. Although we did not say much to each other on the subject, yet we shared many poignant glances and each knew that the other was missing the boy keenly. As for M. le Capitaine, he was desolate, for Rory's visit to his room had been the high point of his day — there was no one else who would listen with such close attention to his tales of derring-do under Toussaint in Haiti. Tantie Cécile likewise fretted and listened avidly to any scrap of news.

M. Noel's reports on Rory's behaviour were excellent at first, although it was clear that he was not benefiting much from his morning lessons. After a month or two there were hints that despite his youth (he was now just short of eleven years of age) he was leading M. Noel's boys into ever more adventurous, though not actually wicked, escapades. Then, one Sunday morning, a month before the end of the six-month trial period upon which we had agreed, M. Noel arrived at our house on horseback, followed by Rory upon an ass, his hat tipped forward over his eyes. He was holding himself still in a manner with which I was all too familiar and which caused my heart to sink. He appeared to have grown much and could have passed for fourteen years of age.

M. Noel refused to dismount and insisted that he, Rory and I speak together in private. I therefore called for my umbrella and we crossed the road and entered the town pasture (or Savannah) through a gate in the fence, moving to a point where we could be seen from the house, but not overheard.

"Monsieur Mason," said my Mulatto friend, "this son of yours has taken it upon himself to put the world to rights and while I applaud his sentiments I cannot approve his actions; nor can I continue to carry the responsibility of restraining him."

We both looked at my son, who was sitting motionless upon his ass with his neck stiff; uncharacteristically, he neither spoke nor raised his eyes.

"M. Noel," I said, "pray enlighten me as to the nature of Rory's offence." As I spoke I saw Betsy emerge on to our galerie and shade her eyes to watch us; her presence, even at that distance, was both comfort and disturbance to me. I am sure that Rory saw her too, out of the corner of his downcast eye, and was wondering how she would respond to his apparent state of disgrace.

"Monsieur," replied M. Noel, "as you are well aware, free people of my colour, which is of course shared by your son, have to tread carefully these days, since we are not regarded with favour by Government House, or by its instruments the *Alcaldes* and the *Alguazils*." He spoke as though he was accustomed to making speeches on this topic to his sons and perhaps to other fellow-Mulattoes. "There was an instance of this only a fortnight ago when the twelve-year-old son of one of my neighbours was apprehended on a charge of petty theft, was roughly handled by the *Alguazils* and sentenced to fifty lashes by the Alcalde in Ordinary. I joined with all the other free coloured gentlemen of the Naparimas in protesting to the Governor that the sentence was cruelly severe and that the boy's father should have been left to punish him as he saw fit, but to no avail; in fact, we were dismissed with insults. If the boy had been white, even the bastard of some newly-landed riff-raff, such a sentence would have been unthinkable; if he had been a Negro slave he would have had some protection from the law; but as the legitimate son of a respectable free-coloured member of society he is at the mercy of a prejudiced and untrammelled *Alcalde*. It is insupportable that a personal disgust with our mixed origins on the part of the Governor should be elevated into a public policy."

M. Noel was speaking with ever-increasing passion, although he did not raise his voice, and I could see that Rory was listening to him with close attention, not lifting his eyes, but with his mouth set in an angry grimace.

"The boy John Lynch," continued M. Noel grimly, "was given the first twenty-five lashes ten days ago and was due for the rest the day before yesterday, but your son Rodrigue —"

Here I saw Rory's jaw tighten and his frown deepen and I marvelled that a boy of not quite eleven years of age could so resemble a grandfather whom he had never seen in every particular except the colour of his skin and the texture of his hair; he had even inherited Father's manner of indicating the state of his emotions by the angle of his hat-brim.

"— your son, M. Mason, inveigled my three sons into a secret plan to release the boy from confinement in the middle of the night. Having succeeded in this by a bold but extremely foolhardy stratagem, they intended to hide the boy in a cave deep in the forest, a place sometimes used by runaway slaves. Rodrigue is fortunate indeed that my eldest son inadvertently revealed the plot to me, so that I was able to return the young offender to custody before there was any hue-and-cry, for otherwise he, Rodrigue, would have received at least fifty lashes and would have been responsible for my own sons receiving similar or perhaps greater punishment; moreover, he would have provoked even more zealous persecution of the whole free-coloured population by the Governor and his minions. I hope that I have succeeded in having the whole affair hushed up — I have certainly expended enough money." He turned and addressed Rory directly, although my son did not lift the brim of his hat. "Much will depend, my friend, on whether you decide to hold your tongue; if you do not do so, word will spread around and be picked up by Governor Woodford's spies, who are everywhere. You must understand that the well-being and safety of the free-coloured people to whom you belong depend not upon individual actions, however gallant, praiseworthy and justified, but upon us *not* provoking the antagonism of the Governor and his fellow-whites and thus endangering the prodigious efforts we are making to induce our friends in London — and we do have friends in high places there — to have the laws changed and the Governor's hands tied."

I was much struck by M. Noel's manner of speaking to my son — more as though he were a recalcitrant young man than a young boy — and determined that I must emulate him.

"I am sure that Rory understands the need to hold his tongue, and will do so," I said; as I spoke, the boy jerked up his head so that his hat fell to the back of his neck, revealing his crisped hair, so unlike my father's but movingly resembling that of his other grandfather, the estimable Gilbert.

"Father!" he whispered passionately, "*you* did not see John Lynch's back and backside; they were all caked with blood and he screamed when we tried to wash them clean."

"But I saw the weals, Rodrigue," said M. Noel, "and I can assure your father that although they were an affront to any man of sensibility, yet I have seen worse, and John Lynch is a hardy young man who will accept his punishment quietly now, in the longer-term interests of himself and his fellow free-coloureds."

"Before God!" swore Rory, still in a whisper, "I would rather die than accept a flogging from anyone!"

"Rory —" I began, but he had not done and ignored me. His eyes were bulging and his face was flushed.

"What is more, if anyone tries to flog me, I shall kill him before he lays a lash on me; and if I am overcome by numbers and held down I shall not rest until I have killed the man who wielded the lash!"

M. Noel and I, two grown men, could only stare in amazement at this boy scarce out of the nursery, for he was speaking in deadly earnest and was neither comical nor ridiculous; when neither of us answered him Rory took a deep breath and glanced toward Betsy on the galerie.

"I would like to greet Maman," he said. "May I be excused?"

"No," I said, somewhat surprised at my own firmness, "not until you have given us your word of honour that you will remain silent about this affair."

"I may not even tell Maman?"

"Yes, you may tell Maman," I said, adding for the benefit of M. Noel: "She will help you to keep your mouth shut, having kept more secrets than anyone I know. May we have your word, Rory?"

"May I not tell M. le Capitaine Gilbert?"

"No, you may not tell M. le Capitaine. In fact, Rory, it will be the test of your word that he does not learn of this affair from you. Now, your word of honour, if you please."

Rory huffed and puffed a while, then looked to M. Noel for confirmation that that gentleman was in agreement with my demand; receiving a nod from him, my son sat up as straight as a ramrod upon the ass, pulled on his hat and straightened the brim, and then put his right hand over his heart.

"I give you my word of honour," he said in a low voice, "that I will tell no one but Maman of this affair, and that I will swear her to silence before I tell her; I also give you my word that I will kill any man, white, coloured or black, who offers to flog me, or succeeds by the use of *force majeure*. May I be excused now?"

I dismissed him and watched him ride the ass to the gate in the fence. I watched him with mingled pride and foreboding — pride in his prowess as a leader and in his daring to do what he thought was right; pride in his physique, for if he had Tony's daemonic energy and Jéhu's strength, agility and grace, he was also shewing signs that he would have my great size; pride in the manly way he had given his word of honour; but foreboding, for I could not imagine how I was to restrain him, even with Betsy's aid, if the experienced and thoughtful M. Noel, with three boys of his own to help him, had quailed at the prospect.

M. Noel took his leave, but not before expressing the hope that I would credit his account with the hundred sovereigns which he had expended in hushing up Rory's escapade; a suggestion to which I agreed immediately. I also told him to come to me for a subscription should the cause of the free-coloureds require substantial assistance for I was somewhat ashamed that I had not fully appreciated the severity of Governor Woodford's actions against a group to whom, of course, my only child belonged by right of his free birth and his brown skin.

And how did Betsy respond to the news of her son's latest and most alarming misconduct? She surrounded herself with a wall of silence so complete that I could not tell in what particular I had offended, no matter how hard I searched my conscience. Since Rory, doubtless impressed with his own manliness in having been party to great matters, was treating us to a period of extraordinarily good behaviour we had no need to consult each other about the restraint of him and the wall of silence continued unbreached except, of course, for the necessary minimum of household communications in patois. Although Betsy did not deny me her bed, yet her pillow-silence was unrelenting.

When, after an interval, Rory misbehaved again — ask me not what was his exact offence — Betsy and I had lost the will to consult with each other and I therefore admonished the boy myself. In the midst of doing so I let fall that he was so far behind in his studies that I might have to send him to Paris to be properly educated — I intended this as a serious threat at the time (oh, to be rid of the fellow!) but thought better of it afterwards and made no inquiries about schools in Paris. However, Rory must have informed his mother of what I had said, for on the first occasion when we were alone together and not liable to be overheard she gave vent to her feelings.

"What is this about my son going to school in France?" she demanded in English.

"Betsy, my dear, —" I began.

"I would like to inform you that Rory is my son and that I will not give my consent to any such course."

"I was, perhaps foolishly, using school in France as a threat —"

"Mr. Mason, you have hurt Rory's feelings very deeply in thus suggesting that he should be banished. He is under the impression that his colour is an embarrassment to you and that you desire to be rid of him for good."

"Betsy —"

"Mr. Mason, he is so distressed that I can only conclude that you did indeed suggest to him that he is unwanted. He informed me that he was much happier living with M. Noel, where he was a Mulatto amongst Mulattoes, than in this household where everyone but Tantie Cécile is either white or black."

"I can only suggest —"

"I hope that your suggestion, whatever it is, shews more regard for your son's feelings, and for mine, than your heartless threats."

"Betsy, what do you wish me to do?"

"What do I wish? When have my wishes been important?"

"Nevertheless, my dear, I will be only too happy to act in any way which would please you."

At this, Betsy laughed, but not altogether pleasantly.

"Perhaps, Mr. Mason," she said, "if you could stand up to me in a straightforward manner, instead of making arrangements behind my back, you could also stand up to Rory and restrain him."

(I am sure that at this point I remembered those stories about men who found it necessary to control their black mistresses with their fists; but I am also sure that I put the stories where they belonged, at the back of my mind.)

"Betsy," I argued, "it was I who made Rory give his word to be silent, word which he has kept."

"You acted with firmness on that occasion because you could hardly do otherwise in the presence of M. Noel; and Rory has kept his word for my sake, and for the sake of M. le Capitaine from whom he has learned what honour is, and for his own sake, because he respects himself —"

I remember that I was stung by the unsaid words and determined that I must convince my son that his white father was both interested in his welfare and worthy of respect, but how this disputation with Betsy ended I cannot for the life of me recall. My efforts to gain Rory's respect met with only a small degree of success and his behaviour continued to be wild, provoking and unpredictable. He steadfastly refused to attend to any lessons, whether taught by me or by Betsy, and it seemed likely that he would reach manhood as illiterate and ignorant as his Aunt Tony.

These efforts of mine brought about a gradual reconciliation with Betsy, but I must confess that I lost more of her respect over my dealings with Rory than I did over any other matter and, much to my distress, she ceased to call me "Dickie". However, I consoled myself that she rarely questioned my judgment on matters of business and allowed me to manage some of her investments for her — I am sure that many of the white gentlemen with whom I did deals for her would have been horrified to learn that I was acting on behalf of a Negress!

When Rory was twelve or thirteen years of age I received early intelligence from my whist-playing crony Father Étienne that a group of French Créole and other lily-white Catholic gentlemen were planning to persuade an order of French monks to set up a school or college in Trinidad and thus save themselves the trouble and expense of sending their sons to France or Ireland to be educated. After anxious and thorough consultations with Betsy, I made the monks an offer of a sum so generous that they could scarcely refuse Rory a place in the proposed College; but knowing the prejudice of white Christian gentlemen on the question of skin-colour, I also arranged that the monks take Rory as a private pupil before they had even found a building in which to set up their College.

The monks proved themselves to be of rare intelligence and accomplishments and, which is more to the point, able both to restrain Rory and to inspire him with interest in his studies. He made progress in all his subjects with such rapidity that we were confirmed in our belief that, as a son of ours, he was not at all stupid. When the College opened, after many delays, mainly due to the difficulty in finding an adequate building, Rory was of course the only boy of colour in attendance; he averred often enough that no other pupil would make friends with him, but that he did not care at all, so long as he was far ahead of them all in his studies, and well able to take care of himself with his fists when out of the classroom.

Betsy and I had only one quarrel with the monks — they insisted that Rory must be baptized and attend Mass regularly if he were to be admitted to the College. We were prepared to do battle on this issue, as true Voltaireans, or to increase our donation to an even greater size, but gave way when Rory announced that he had no objections to being baptized

333

or to saying his prayers. We detected in this victory of Unreason the hand of the devout Tantie Cécile.

Peace and harmony were restored to our household at long last. (Rory spent his vacations in the Naparimas with M. Noel and his sons, an arrangement made more agreeable to that gentleman by my not pressing for exact punctuality in his payments of interest on an outstanding loan.) To add to the general happiness, the political situation in Haiti had changed so much that M. le Capitaine was able to emerge from his self-imposed obscurity; in this he was helped by a young surgeon, new out from Edinburgh, who diagnosed his leg as now healed and hardened enough to take a wooden foot. When this had been fitted and M. le Capitaine, with Madame du Vernay's aid, had perfected himself in hopping about with the aid of a crutch, he undertook to supervize the care of the horses, to the immediate improvement of their health and efficiency, and presumably of their happiness also, if that is an emotion of which the equine is capable.

In time M. le Capitaine found that he could mount the steps of the back galerie without too much assistance, and many a pleasant evening we four spent there over our cards — Betsy, myself, M. le Capitaine and Madame du Vernay. Between the latter two there grew up a warm friendship which shewed signs of becoming even warmer. I think that I successfully concealed my surprise when I first noticed that their eyes were meeting frequently and their hands touching, but when I mentioned the affair to Betsy she smiled knowingly at me, shewing no signs of surprise at all.

"You seem to think it strange," she said.

"It is not usual for a Mulatto lady —" I began.

"— for a Mulatto lady to ally herself with a Negro?"

"I did not intend to say that."

"I think you did, Dickie, and also to doubt how any lady could attach herself to a man as crippled as my brother."

I was silent.

"She ministers to his wounded person while he ministers to her wounded heart. What could be more fitting or more in keeping with the principles of Reason?"

"But her children —"

"Her children will be confirmed in their belief that their dark brown mother is beneath contempt, and further confirmed therein when she marries Jéhu."

"But Jéhu has always said that, as a soldier, he does not believe in marriage."

"Wait and see."

334

I waited, and sure enough Betsy's words came true. The ceremony was of the simplest and the subsequent celebrations of the happiest I have seen, confined as they were to the few friends who knew the couple well enough to share their manifest joy.

As to our carefree evenings over cards, they continued unchanged, and were rendered the more carefree by our knowing that Rory was studying his books with all the passion which he had previously devoted to misbehaviour.

CHAPTER XXXI

An untoward Event brings Sadness into our Lives; we are condescended to by Persons in a high Position but are not much comforted

"Mr. Mason!" cried Betsy, omitting to give me the somewhat formal kiss to which I was now accustomed of an evening, "Rory has not yet come home from the College; it is not like him to cause me distress in this way."

This was one of the few occasions upon which my down-to-earth mistress was guilty of telling herself a nancy-story — only two years earlier it would have been *most* like Rory to be causing her distress.

"No doubt the brothers have detained him for some reason," I said. "Perhaps it is a saint's day and they are saying an extra Mass."

"That would scarcely account for his being nearly three hours late."

"He may have made a friend at last and have gone to his home."

"Do you know of a single French Créole family who would allow their son to bring home a Mulatto friend?"

"He may have taken a walk along the Quay to see what is going on, and to look at the ships."

"Mr. Mason, it has been dark for an hour and I have a presentiment that something is wrong. Rory is only fifteen."

"My dear, Rory is nearly sixteen and big for his age; he is well able to look after himself. I am sure that he will return soon with some simple explanation of his absence."

"But if the *Alguazils* once laid hands upon him and Governor Woodford heard of it —" Here Betsy lowered her voice to the level which, I knew from long experience, meant that she was about to berate me but did not wish the servants to overhear her. "Mr. Mason, you must steel yourself to act —"

At this point M. le Capitaine and his Madame arrived and Betsy forbore to continue berating me in their presence. However, their woebegone countenances persuaded me that Betsy was right and I sat down and wrote a note to the Father Superior and sent off Merry with it.

Whilst awaiting an answer Betsy and I scarcely touched a savourless supper, during which she remained silent and regarded me with a gaze that can only be described as baleful. Suspecting that I was to be blamed for Rory's absence as well as for infirmity of purpose, I searched my memory for any recent speech or action of mine which might have caused my son disquiet and could remember nothing of moment. We were still making a pretence of eating when Merry returned, escorting the Father Superior. That monk's countenance bore a most severe and accusatory expression, which may have been merely the mark of his profession but which was hardly reassuring to us. We both toppled our chairs in our haste to rise to our feet.

"What has happened?" demanded Betsy without ceremony, "Where is my son?"

She stood motionless while I offered the Father a chair; when I made to introduce her to him, for they had not met, she forestalled me.

"Where is my son?" she reiterated.

"Monsieur," said the Father, ignoring Betsy altogether, "I am come myself to inform you of a most regrettable incident at the College today, and which may have some bearing upon your son's failure to return home." He stopped, clearly to give me an opportunity to dismiss Betsy, having misread that lady's position and influence in the house.

"Proceed, Monsieur," she said.

"Monsieur Mason, I am afraid that the matter is of the most serious; during recess this afternoon your son Rodrigue attacked another boy, Godefroi de Champfleurs, who is the only surviving son of M. le Comte de Champfleurs, of whom you have no doubt heard. Godefroi is the oldest of our pupils and is something of a leader, as befits his age and his ancestry. Rodrigue not only bloodied his nose, he knocked him down and caused his head to come in violent contact with a corner of the building so that he was rendered unconscious and bled profusely. I was called to the scene immediately and my first impression was that Godefroi was dead — he was entirely motionless, his face was without any colour at all, and his head lay in a large pool of blood. However, I discovered that his heart was beating and the doctor (who arrived as soon as was humanly possible) staunched the flow of blood and declared that the boy was heavily concussed and would be considerably weakened by loss of blood, but was not in danger of his life."

337

"Rory was provoked," interposed Betsy.

"Monsieur," said the Father, "I have not been able to hear Rodrigue's account of the incident since he did not remain at the scene of the fight, nor did he return to the classroom after recess. However, one of the other boys, under close questioning, did agree that Godefroi had commented upon the colour of Rodrigue's skin and upon the texture of his hair —"

"I imagine," interrupted Betsy, "that these comments were derogatory and unkind, to say the least."

"— if I may continue, Monsieur, the one boy who admitted to hearing the remarks also insisted that they were no more than simple statements of fact and made in a Christian spirit —"

"I know that 'Christian spirit' only too well," said Betsy tartly, "and it is more wounding than the worst of insults — but where is Rory?"

"— moreover, Monsieur, I have to inform you that further inquiries amongst the boys revealed nothing at all regarding the whereabouts of your son — none of them saw him go and none knew where he had gone or might have planned to go. I had expected to find that he had returned to your protection."

"He is not here," I said.

"I would recommend that you search every nook and cranny of your premises, for after committing a grave crime a boy may be so overcome by shame and guilt, or by fear of punishment, that he wishes to hide his face whilst still being safe at home. Now I must leave you, for I have promised to visit poor suffering Godefroi and to reassure and pacify his irate parents. When you have found Rodrigue please let me know at once and we can then discuss plans for his education in surroundings more appropriate to his nature. I cannot express how grieved I am that our star pupil should have betrayed our belief in him in so barbarous a manner."

The Father Superior then took his leave with a promptitude which saved him from a tongue-lashing by Betsy, who was more agitated than I had ever seen her. I eventually calmed her by myself accepting a *sotto voce* tongue-lashing about my pusillanimity in face of the monk, my dilatoriness in not instantly initiating a search for Rory, and my general shortcomings as a father. When she had done we set about the search in earnest. When our son was not found on the premises we extended the search to all quarters of the town (including rum-shops and, at M. le Capitaine's suggestion, houses of ill-fame) and to all the *pirogues*, small boats and lighters drawn up upon the strand; I even sent a skiff around the ships anchored off-shore, but all to no avail. (In these, as in all our subsequent inquiries, we were considerably hampered by the need for extreme caution, for the outcome we least desired was that Rory should fall into the hands of Governor Woodford.) Before daybreak I dispatched Rory's groom Earl on a fast horse to Naparima, with a message apprising M. Noel of the circumstances and asking him whether Rory was with him, and if not whether he would be good enough to search the cave where John Lynch had been hidden and indeed any other hiding-places known to him. There was no need to warn M. Noel of the need for thoroughness and caution; yet again, no trace of our son was found.

After forty-eight hours had passed we began to fear that our son had left the Island altogether, for had he been hidden by friends they would surely have informed him that Godefroi de Champfleurs was still alive and would have arranged for a message to reach us. Away from Trinidad, however, it might be a very long time before he learned that he was not a Mulatto murderer who need expect no mercy from the white authorities. I perceived that I had been to blame for not myself going around the small boats and anchored ships and insisting upon the most thorough of searches. When I attempted to remedy this omission I discovered that even after so short an interval, several ships had sailed for distant ports, several schooners had left for neighbouring islands, and up to a score of small boats had departed for the fishing-grounds or with unspecified cargoes for unknown destinations; Mulatto youngsters of muscular build were two-a-penny along the shore and no one had noticed a strange one; so by then Rory might have been upon the high seas bound for North America or Europe, or could have already landed on the shores of the Republica de Gran Colombia (the creation of Bolivar and of which Venezuela was then a province). These shores were only a short distance across the Boca and abounded in bays and coves where he could have been landed secretly.

Not relishing further tongue-lashing from my mistress, I intensified my inquiries (and oh how discreet they had to be!) through all possible channels known and open to me — that is, amongst legitimate traders, amongst smugglers, and amongst those who, like myself, were something of both. Betsy similarly used the channels open to her but, as usual, did not confide to me what these channels were, only admitting after an interval that her inquiries had proved fruitless. We joined together to offer a substantial reward, sufficient to procure information but not so large as to arouse suspicion that Rory had a political price on his head; still no one came to us with authentic intelligence.

The affair did not die down quickly for the implacable M. le Compte de Champfleurs and the incorrigibly prejudiced Governor Woodford, although far from being allies, nevertheless joined forces to seek out Rory, M. le Comte summoning every French Créole to mount his horse and comb the Island for his son's assailant, and the Governor warning every *Alcalde*, *Commandante* and *Alguazil* of the need to apprehend the dangerous Mulatto miscreant.

As the weeks went by without any word of our son, the doubt and unease in our little household began to deepen.

"I am afraid," said Betsy one day, "that Rory has inherited our several talents for conspiracy and concealment and that he does not wish us to find him, perhaps because he is unsure whether he is truly wanted by us all."

"He did not conceal his antipathy to Godefroi de Champfleurs," I countered, not being anxious to discuss the latter part of Betsy's speech, "nor did he answer his insults with subterfuge or conspiracy —" Here I bit my tongue for I was about to add that I found it hard to believe that he was still alive; this doubt I was not yet ready to express publicly.

"Mr. Mason," answered Betsy, "it is possible, nay probable, that my son and M. le Capitaine's nephew is prepared both to defend to his honour openly and to use subterfuge when he judges it necessary — for example, when he wishes to prevent dishonour being brought upon his parents, however doubtful he may be as to whether they both love him without reserve."

"She right-right," said M. le Capitaine, interrupting our English conversation, as was his wont, with a remark in Patois which shewed that he had followed closely what we had been saying but had chosen to ignore Betsy's sharp thrusts at me as none of his business. "That boy want to fight, he fight and no one go stop him; he want to hide, he hide and no one go find him — he my nephew, and he have chief's blood!"

Shortly after this conversation I discovered that Madame Jéhu shared my lack of optimism and had arranged for Masses to be said for Rory's departed soul. I chided her half-heartedly and promised not to reveal her trespass to the more hopeful ones, Betsy and M. le Capitaine.

In the years which followed we continued to lavish considerable sums of money upon inquiries which proved fruitless; I shall not weary my readers by recounting the many false alarms and unfounded rumours which reached us from time to time, raising our hopes and dashing them again. Even now, it is my opinion that we might have found Rory if Governor Woodford had been on our side and had made official inquiries of other Governments as to whether a young Trinidadian Mulatto had come to their attention, perhaps by joining their armed forces; or had used his access to intelligence from British Government spies to discover who was fighting in the various rebellious armies and navies then bent on destroying the Spanish American empire. (By this time I had come round to the view first propounded by M. le Capitaine that my son had become a fighting soldier or sailor, a view which I adopted unwillingly.)

Despite the vigour with which I pursued my efforts to find Rory, and the liberality with which I expended my riches upon the quest, Betsy was less than her usual forgiving self and continued to address me as Mr. Mason, even during those pillow-talks when we debated where our son might be and achieved that intimacy which is the concomitant of a shared grief.

In 1828 Governor Woodford fell ill and died on the voyage home. His successor Major-General Sir Lewis Grant was a soldier of the highest principles, determined to ensure that the law and the instructions of the London Government were obeyed to the letter, as I learned when he summoned me to Government House for a personal and private consultation. During a most instructive hour alone with him, he requested of me "advice and intelligence corrective of that which he had received from French-speaking gentlemen currently holding office in the Colony and from other interested persons."

Having no reason, except my own judgment, to trust the new Governor, but being no friend of the haughty French Créole planters as a class (however much I might desire to maintain good relations with them as individual customers for hardware and loans) I tempted him with just enough of my information and my opinions as to apprise him of their quality and to ensure that he would have to see me again. This gambit was successful in a most unexpected manner for as I was taking my leave he clapped me on the shoulder and asked if he might call upon me and my "good lady" in the near future. I was hemming and hawing in the utmost astonishment and alarm when the Governor put me at my ease somewhat by saying that he was well aware of my domestic arrangements, would call the following week and would expect me to present Madame Gilbert to him. I continued to hesitate, thinking that, however well-informed he might be as to the nature of my *ménage*, he yet seemed unaware that colour barriers in Trinidad were as rigid as those reported from Hindoostan and that having Betsy presented to him would endear him to no one in white society. However, I did the Governor an injustice, for he took pains to assure me that his visit would be made incognito and that he would be dressed, not in his splendid uniform, but in what he jocularly called "mufti".

On the way home from Government House Sam sang a song in his now cracked old voice; a song which shewed that the Negroes were already rejoicing in the Governor's intention to enforce the London Government's policy of "ameliorating" their condition; a policy which they took to mean that Emancipation was not far away. Cognisant as I was of the planters' dependence on the labour of the Negroes if they were to maintain their wealth and position, and well-acquainted with the strength of the West Indian interest in Parliament, I could not share the optimism expressed in Sam's song.

Once at home, I lost no time in informing Betsy of the Governor's proposed visit.

"Oh, Dickie!" she whispered, when finally convinced that I was not retelling a nancy-story and that the interview had taken place exactly as I had described it, "Oh, Dickie, if we are careful and politic we may be able to re-commence our search for Rory with the Governor's help." She then kissed me warmly in her erstwhile affectionate manner, which I had all but forgotten. "I wonder what the Governor's preferences are; I must institute inquiries."

Thus it was that my mistress and I once again became true allies; once again we spoke of Rory as though we might be seeing him on the morrow; and once again my heart would jump as she spoke my name with the syllables provocatively separated: "Dick-ie!"

On the day of His Excellency's visit, when he and his Secretary were announced, having descended from a hired closed-carriage, Betsy appeared, not in her usual housekeeper's grey gown as I had feared she might, nor yet in her most elaborate and colourful new outfit and laden with gold ornaments, but in a plain high-necked dress cut from a rich dark-coloured stuff and with a matching kerchief, her sole ornament being a cameo upon a fine gold chain. Her dignified appearance (and remember that we were now over sixty years of age) made a great impression upon the gallant Major-General, for he bowed and kissed her black hand and pressed it as though it were lily-white; he even insisted that Betsy took her seat before he took his, much to the agitation of his Secretary. (As she composed herself upon her chair I noticed that she was wearing a handsome pair of satin shoes — she was leaving nothing to chance in the search for her son!)

After further compliments Betsy offered the Governor a glass of the ten-year-old Glenlivet which I still imported regularly from Father's suppliers in Scotland; he accepted with an alacrity which shewed that Betsy's inquires had been as thorough as ever. Having sipped it he announced reverently that it was the finest whisky he had tasted and that he would be obliged to have the name of our local importer.

These preliminaries over, the three of us commenced an exchange of views and information on a wide range of topics while the Secretary, poor young fellow, goggled and gaped. We touched upon the current state of the sugar and cocoa markets; the utility or otherwise of steam engines in grinding sugar-cane considering how often the engine of the San Fernando paddle-steamer broke down, leaving passengers stranded in the middle of the Gulf; the desirability or otherwise of entirely replacing Spanish with English law; the labour difficulties likely to follow upon Emancipation should Parliament pass the Bill shortly to be debated; etc., etc. On this first occasion Betsy and I did not broach the subject nearest to our hearts, but since all three protagonists were devotees of the pastime of trading intelligence we became so engrossed that the Governor overstayed his time with us by three-quarters of an hour, a condescension which caused further agitation on the part of his Secretary.

When the Governor rose to take his leave I thought for a moment that Betsy and I had failed to play our hand to the best advantage, for he was most formal in his farewells, but whilst Betsy was engaged in what seemed like deliberately prolonged parting speeches with his Secretary, he took me down the front steps out of earshot and, abandoning formality, assured me that he had much enjoyed our hospitality and our company and would certainly invite himself again but would not bring his Secretary in future; he also expressed his deep regret that he could not see his way to bringing Lady Grant to meet Madame Gilbert.

The Governor kept his word and called upon us occasionally of an evening, always incognito and alone. Even on the first of these visits, as the Governor sipped at a generous measure of Glenlivet, we exchanged worthwhile information, with the result that several planters were prosecuted for the illegal importation of Negro slaves, a trade which the Governor was intent upon putting down and which I had no interest in maintaining. In return, he promised to institute a search through semi-official channels for "a twenty-year-old Mulatto of over six feet in height who speaks English, French and Patois, each as though it were his mother-tongue, and Spanish with some fluency." If found, the young man was to be informed that the matter which had caused him to leave home was not as serious as he had imagined and that he should communicate with his parents as soon as possible.

Whilst we were awaiting the results of this search with what patience we could muster, Governor Grant's visits to our house were maliciously reported to Lady Grant as being venereal in intent; he therefore discontinued them, but in order to reassure his wife and maintain his acquaintance with us he regularly invited Betsy and myself to visit Government House in the discreetest possible manner after dark, and to play whist in his private quarters. On these visits we discovered why her Ladyship had not accompanied her husband to our house — she was the most garrulous woman it is possible to imagine and an insuperable barrier to confidential business. Her presence would have been very irksome indeed had not His Excellency, in concert with Betsy, invented adroit stratagems which left him alone with me for serious negotiations. (These stratagems usually involved Lady Grant being manoeuvred into asking Betsy's opinion as to the right clothes and toilette for the climate she was having to endure; the two ladies would then retire for further consultations.) Thus Sir Lewis achieved and maintained his deserved reputation as the best-informed of all Trinidad's Governors.

White society may have heard rumours about these visits to Government House but continued to act as though Betsy did not exist at all; on the other hand, our bachelor friends were duly impressed and Father Étienne, worldly and pragmatical as he was, used our acquaintance with the Governor to press upon us the advisability of marriage — it would be valid under the English law shortly to be introduced to the Colony; it would be a seal of at least some respectability upon our long and faithful association; it would improve his standing with his Bishop if he could point to one favourable result from his many visits to us; and finally, he would be prepared, for an appropriate fee, to conduct a very private ceremony himself. I may return to this matter later.

Each time that we returned from a visit to Government House we would find M. le Capitaine and his Madame waiting up for us, the latter close to the lamp and stitching away with unceasing industry, while the former sate where he could without difficulty take her hand away from her work for a moment and kiss it. In the early days they would greet us with one voice, asking: "What of Rory?" but as the months went past without any word, they would merely look at us with the question in their eyes and we would have to shake our heads. At length M. le Capitaine was moved to complain.

"Me think Governor move like morocoy," he said, "when he looking for Mulatto; for a béké, now, he move like lightning."

"Chéri," said Madame Jéhu, "you do the Governor an injustice. I am sure that he is doing what he can."

"Oh yes?" replied her husband, "then tell me why Monsieur and Madame play cards in *back* room at Government House! I tell you no black woman go play cards there on *front* galerie or even in front room. Not now! Not never!"

"It may yet happen," said Betsy, "for if I can rise from slavery, ignorance, poverty and ostracism to my present position in sixty years, surely some little black girl who is educating herself at this moment can rise to greater eminence than I in sixty years from now, and not be ostracized."

"No such thing happening," argued M. le Capitaine, "or go happen. Tell me name of one little black boy who educating himself — who *wanting* to educate himself — never mind one little black girl. Look at Merry's boy Michael now; he clever-clever and he speak French like a Frenchman but he done always be missing when it come to lesson time, for he afraid his friends go mock him and call him 'Professor'."

"But look at what you and your friends achieved in Haiti; you educated yourselves. You can read and speak French and you wrote it very well —"

"We took Haiti with gun and cutlass," interrupted M. le Capitaine, "and then we learn to read and write so we could govern country. Trinidad Negroes never go fight — me tell you again and again: they only *macommère* men, *oui*! — so they never take over country and never have to learn to read book and use pen."

"But when Emancipation comes," I interposed, "as I am now sure it will, everyone will be a free British subject —"

"You think Emancipation go make black people Mulatto?" inquired M. le Capitaine caustically, "or Mulatto people white? No, no, white Governor still move like morocoy to find Mulatto like Rory, even after Emancipation."

These debates, and as my readers will imagine they were not infrequent, most often ended in silence, while we contemplated a future in which we might never see Rory again and which held we knew not what calamities.

In 1833 Governor Grant was replaced by Governor Sir George F. Hill, a gentleman of weaker fibre who listened to the hostile views of the Colonial Secretary upon my character and opinions; I therefore lost the only influence I had had in Government House since the days of Don José and had perforce to pursue the now almost hopeless quest for Rory through my own agents and correspondents, not all of whom I could trust on such a delicate matter.

Governor Hill was charged, of course, with the implementation of the Emancipation Act which was due to come into force upon the first of August 1834 and by which all slaves were to become apprentices for six years before becoming fully free. Whilst all in our household were in agreement (for once) that Emancipation was both politic and right, we differed as to whether there would be disturbances and danger upon the day when it was due to take effect. Madame Jéhu, who since her marriage had taken to expressing her feelings freely, was certain that the horrors formerly committed in St. Domingue were about to be perpetrated once more in Trinidad and argued, not without tears, that we should lock ourselves into the house and prepare to defend our lives with our pistols. I was inclined to agree with her that due precautions should be taken but M. le Capitaine, holding the views which he did upon the lack of spirit of Trinidad Negroes, was in favour of carrying on as if the day were nothing unusual and Betsy took his part. I need hardly say that neither party to this disagreement was in favour of permitting any form of celebration on the part of the servants; indeed, we had not countenanced fêtes of any kind since Rory went missing; and in any case all our servants were already free wage-earners for we had been privily manumitting them and their children over the previous five years. Only Prince, our witless and easily-replaced yard-boy, and Michael, Merry's talented but unreliable son, had elected to leave us for paid work elsewhere. The two parties were united only in wishing that Rory was still with us, to act as our comfort and defender.

In the event, we did not lock ourselves into the house but spent the great day (and indeed the following week) in a state of alertness with the jalousies closed. The servants brought us news of a crowd of old Negroes and Negresses (accompanied by many children) who had assembled outside Government House and were vociferating "*pas de six ans, point de six ans*", that is, that they did not wish to serve six years' apprenticeship but to be entirely free at once. Peering through a half-opened jalousie I could see more old Negroes shuffling across the Grand Savannah in the direction of St. Ann's, no doubt intending to augment the crowd interrogating the Governor; they were not being deterred by torrents of rain which were falling. Later we were informed that the crowd were being assisted by a young Negro, French-speaking Michael Merry no less, who represented their case to His Excellency, saying in "an eloquent and respectful tone" that they had "toiled all their lives, had enriched their Masters by the sweat of their brow, and that King William was surely too good and noble to exact of them six years more servitude."

Upon hearing of this "eloquent and respectful tone", and of who had used it, and of the fact that not one of the crowd was armed even with a *bois*, M. le Capitaine exploded.

"If me young again," he declaimed, "and me have two leg, or just two arm, and me done find five hundred fighting men, then there go be no apprenticeship —"

"But I thought that you had given up all these bloodthirsty thoughts," said his lady-wife in a voice louder than I had previously heard from her, "I thought that you agree with me —"

"Cécile, Liberty is Liberty," said M. le Capitaine, breaking into the most elegant French, "and Equality is Equality, and Fraternity is Fraternity, and they are inseparable and indivisible, like your Trinity, and —"

"Jéhu!" warned Madame, "pray do not blaspheme in my presence —"

"It is a blasphemy to apprentice people to Liberty, which is an inalienable right —"

I report the commencement of this quarrel, not only because its content is interesting, but also because it demonstrated that attaining the status of legal wife had freed Madame Jéhu Gilbert from the shackles of dependency and enabled her to reveal her true character.

I remember not how the disagreement proceeded, only that it ended with M. le Capitaine hopping and stumping away to his chamber in dudgeon, while his Madame fell upon her knees, crossed herself repeatedly, and prayed aloud most fervently to her God, giving thanks that the day which she so dreaded had passed off peacefully so far and begging Him to forgive her husband for his wicked thoughts.

Within the hour, as my readers may have anticipated, the couple were reconciled, the first move having been made by M. le Capitaine; he called peremptorily from his chamber that he was in need of his wife's help as he had thrown away both crutch and foot in his wrath and was now quite unable to regain them. His Madame pretended not to hear him and he had to change his tone step by step until his military bark had become a wheedle; since he appeared sufficiently contrite the lady deigned to go to his assistance and was treated to the dulciloquy which so "ministered to her wounded heart", while she repaid him by "ministering to his wounded body".

Toward sunset of the great day I was still at my jalousie and espied through the narrow slit no less a person than Colonel Hardy, the Officer of His Majesty's Troops; he was driving past in a gig, with his aide-de-camp seated beside him. They were preceded and followed by groups of comely young Negresses who were jumping up joyously and singing songs about the goodness of King William in granting them freedom. The gallant Colonel seemed mightily pleased and was bowing and waving to the Negresses as though he were King William himself.

Later in the week we heard that a number of refractory local "apprentices" had had to be flogged to persuade them to return to their work and that an even greater number had been flogged at Naparima, but otherwise Emancipation proceeded peacefully, as Betsy and M. le Capitaine had predicted that it would. Its far-reaching consequences only gradually became apparent.

As to Betsy and myself, although we were on opposing sides in the disagreement about the danger to our personal safety, yet we were at one in making arrangements to protect our warehouses and, as I have explained already, in ensuring that we lost no money from the effects of Emancipation and that we made what profit we could, which was not insubstantial. Perhaps I should qualify that last statement, which borders on a nancy-story. Out of sentiment I loaned a considerable sum of money to Alexander Macdonald so that he could pay the unreasonably high wages demanded by his newly-freed Negroes and thus harvest and sell his sugar. As I write, more than ten years later, the whole of this debt is still outstanding and Alexander is hard put to pay me the interest; yet disliking sugar-estates as much as ever, I am unwilling to foreclose and encumber myself with one, as Betsy would have me do and the debt is such, I am afraid, that it cancels out the profit which I made from exporting to Brazil quantities of first-class American wrought-iron manacles, leg-irons, etc., most of them second-hand, which had become surplus to requirement in Trinidad after Emancipation. The Island was well rid of them.

At about this time Mister O'Brien died and I had to labour exceeding hard to keep the business going without his help. (I support his families as best I can by employing no less than four of his sons, although only Sylvester has inherited his father's equanimity, capability and devotion to my interests; the others co-mingle Irish irascibility with Mulatto torpor in a manner which justifies me in paying them only minimal wages.)

Betsy and I continued to be more or less at one in our hearts, but although she sometimes absently called me "Dickie" in the privacy of her chamber, she did not address me as anything but "Mr. Mason" in public and I knew that she had not ceased to blame me for the loss of Rory. Our life was of a uniform dullness and greyness and the next few years could best be represented by another succession of blank pages in this ledger in which I now write so laboriously. However, because of Betsy's company the dullness did not cause me to succumb to Melancholy; I was also cheered somewhat by the continuing success of our respective businesses.

(She Who Looks Over My Shoulder As I Write wishes me to inform my readers that she had no interest whatsoever in my exporting of that infamous hardware to Brazil and that had she known of it at the time would have made her views very clear indeed.)

CHAPTER XXXII

*My Mistress and I receive an unexpected Visitor late at Night; he presents us
with a Gift more precious than Rubies and takes his Leave*

I must now, I think, jump forward six years to 1840, when Betsy and I
were in our seventy-third year and still living quietly and monotonously
in our house overlooking the Grand Savannah. Late one evening, when
we had finished reading and were almost ready to retire, a young man
of soldierly bearing arrived bringing an unaddressed letter. Speaking
in English but with a Spanish accent, he insisted upon placing it in my
hands himself and left without waiting for an answer. Before opening the
letter I had already decided that it was from a business associate, a ship's
captain of many interests who performed certain services for me and whose
movements were not tied to night or day. However, the contents, which
were written in capital letters, were not from my captain friend at all;
indeed, they were so astounding that I could scarce believe the evidence of
my eyes. I can reproduce them from memory with great exactitude thus:

¡REVERED FATHER!

    IF YOU WOULD IMMEDIATELY DISMISS LOS CRIADOS:
LOCK ALL THE JALOUSIES IN THE SALON AND ALL THE
OUTSIDE DOORS SAVE THE ONE TO THE WEST: AND
EXTINGUISH ALL THE LAMPS EXCEPT ONE (WHICH
SHOULD BE DIMMED): THEN I SHALL, WITHIN THE
HOUR, BE KNEELING TO ASK FOR YOUR BLESSING AND
FOR THOSE OF MY BELOVED MOTHER, EL MUY
ESTIMABLE MI CAPI, AND TANTIE CÉCILE. INFELIZ-
MENTE, MY VISIT MUST BE OF THE MOST BRIEF,

BUT I BRING A GIFT WHICH WILL OFFER YOU MUCH
COMFORT.
    I REMAIN, DEAREST FATHER,
      YOUR MOST AFFECTIONATE SON Q.B.S.M.
PLEASE BURN THIS LETTER AS SOON AS YOU HAVE READ
AND COMPREHENDED IT.

Speechless, I handed the letter to Betsy and gazed at her while she
put on her spectacles and held it up to the lamp. As she scanned the lines
her eyes widened and her hands began to tremble.

"Rory is coming!" she whispered. "He is alive! After all those years!
You were wrong, Mr. Mason! I knew it! I knew it!"

As soon as she spoke I trembled too, for my melancholic nature saw
only trouble and danger ahead.

"It may be a trick," I said, hearing an old man's quaver in my voice
for the first time. "A robber might send such a letter so that he might
break in upon us unobserved."

"But what robber would know of the nick-name 'Mi Capi'? That is
Rory's authentication of the letter. Had we not better burn it right away,
as he asks?"

I therefore held the letter to the glass funnel of the lamp and we
watched it consume itself in flames. We dismissed the few servants who
were still on duty and quietly awoke M. le Capitaine and Tantie Cécile.

Upon hearing the import of the letter they became as excited as
we were, agreeing with Betsy that it was probably, but not certainly,
genuine. We all three set to and helped M. le Capitaine to dress and
fit on his wooden foot, which was normally a lengthy business; in doing
so we got in each other's way and made more noise than we should have
done — it was fortunate that the couple now lived in the main house, the
steps having become too much for the old soldier, otherwise we might
have let the servants know that something truly unusual was about to
happen.

M. le Capitaine, once dressed, assumed a very military demeanour
and brusquely informed us that we must fetch our pistols, which we did,
loading and priming them with trembling hands while Madame crossed
herself over and over again. M. le Capitaine then announced that we
must take further military precautions, and sat us all at the end of the
dining-table farthest from the west door, with the dimmed lamp stood
upon the table at the other end and shaded with a palmetto fan on the near
side so that we were all in darkness; needless to say, my white face had to
be in the darkest shadow of all.

We waited, we four ancients, for what seemed much longer than an hour, with our pistols laid on the table in front of us. We listened with strained attention to the noises of the night, which were more numerous, more various, and more inexplicable than any I had heard in peace-time. Suddenly our two yard-dogs barked furiously, as though they had detected an intruder; the neighbours' dogs on both sides answered just as furiously and the barking spread from yard to yard far into the distance in a manner which was all-too-familiar and yet, on that night, altogether fiendish. We heard Jacques sleepily ordering our dogs to be quiet and the creatures obeying at last, in their own time as was their habit. In the ensuing silence (or what passes for silence in Port-of-Spain) we saw the door cautiously opened and a huge dark figure enter — it was a man carrying what appeared to be a child. He closed the door as cautiously as he had opened it, shot the bolt and turned to face us. As though instantly understanding why we had disposed the lamp, the fan and ourselves in the manner which I have described, he stepped forward with a cat-like tread and turned up the wick of the lamp so that his face, and that of the little girl upon his arm, were clearly illumined. His resemblance to Father left me speechless and breathless with craven fear. Betsy, however, was more mettlesome.

"Rory!" she whispered, rising and moving toward him. Rory, for it was indubitably he, stood the child upon the floor and, putting his left arm around her, swept off his hat and dropped it upon the floor; the hair thus revealed was so straight that it emphasized the European cast of his dark features but could not have been other than a wig. He went down upon one knee and, whispering something to the bright-eyed but solemn little girl, induced her to kneel too. By this time I had moved forward and was standing beside Betsy, unsure as to Rory's intentions but no longer quite so fearful.

"Father!" he said, in a voice far deeper and more musical than I remembered, "I am come to ask for your forgiveness and for your blessing upon myself and upon your grand-daughter Francisca Maria."

Although English was manifestly not altogether familiar to him any more, he yet spoke with such force and authority that I was swept into acting as he desired, regardless of my confused feelings. I put my hand upon his bowed head and said: "Bless you, my son!"

Rory was not satisfied. "Pray say that you forgive me," he said, not raising his head.

"I forgive you," I said, not entirely sure, in my confused state, what it was that I had to forgive him for, but aware that my fear had abated almost to vanishing point.

351

Rory raised his face to mine and signalled that I should bless the little girl, so I placed my hand upon her head and did so. No sooner had I finished than Betsy spoke.

"Oh, Rory, I forgive you and I bless you!" she whispered and, turning to the child, added: "and I bless you too, my darling Francisca!" I could see that she was resisting two urges, the first to fling her arms around her son, and the second to pick up and fondle her grand-daughter.

"I thank you both for your forgiveness," said Rory, still kneeling, "and my daughter and I thank you for your blessings and pray that God will protect you both." He crossed himself, then helped the mite to cross herself too.

He stood up, lifted Francisca in his two arms and held her out to Betsy and myself in silence. In the light of the lamp we could see that the little creature was perhaps three years of age, of a dark olive complexion and with long glossy black hair which was not quite straight but was not crisped either. Her features did not closely resemble those of anyone in the family, but it was not hard to believe that she was Betsy's grand-daughter, so large and clear were her hazel eyes and so obviously lively the spirit and mind behind her solemn expression. I fell in love with her at that moment (and if any of my readers think that "fell in love" is too strong a phrase, please forgive an old man who, at seventy-two, had resigned himself to being without heirs of his body and who had suddenly had a son restored to him in most dramatic circumstances and then been presented with a beautiful little grand-daughter of whose existence he had had no inkling).

"*Mis padres*," said Rory, ending the short silence, "I would like to request that you assume the care and protection of Francisca Maria from this moment. Her mother, my wife, is dead and I must go where no child can accompany me."

I took Francisca from her father, but she struggled and held out her arms to him, crying: "Papaito!" I therefore handed her to Betsy, in whose arms she immediately quieted, while never removing those remarkable orbs from Rory's face.

"Of course we shall assume the care of Francisca," said Betsy, kissing the child's forehead, "but you will be staying here with us for a while, will you not, dearest Rory?"

"Maman, I thank you with all my heart," said Rory, stooping to embrace his mother warmly and to reassure his daughter in whispered Spanish. "However, I fear that I am under a strict obligation to leave again in an hour's time." He turned to me and kissed me upon both my cheeks. "Father! I thank you too!" He looked around. "Now! Where are Mi Capi and Tantie Cécile?"

At this question, I removed the fan which was shading the lamp and revealed Rory's Tantie helping M. le Capitaine to stand upright with the aid of his crutch. Rory moved quickly with his soft tread, kneeled down before his uncle and bowed his head to request a blessing.

"This not right!" exclaimed M. le Capitaine, with only a hint of an old man's quaver, "Général not kneel to Colonel!" He handed his crutch to his Madame, saluted briefly but smartly with a left hand which trembled only slightly, and reached for his crutch again.

Rory looked up in surprise. "Where you hear me have *graduación de General?*" he asked in a patois which, although as interspersed with Spanish words as his English, was just as forceful.

"Me not hear nothing! Me look at you and me *see!*"

"We not in same army *y eres mi tío.* Bless me, *por favor,* Mi Capi."

M. le Capitaine frowned in dubiety, then handed his crutch to his Madame, put his hand on Rory's head, and said: "Me cannot ask God that not exist to bless you, but me know you fighting for people to be free and me hope you go win."

Rory then kneeled to his beloved Tantie, who had been regarding him with a countenance which, I noticed, was becoming more and more agitated and distressed.

"*Non, non,* Rodrigue!" she whispered, "do not ask for my forgiveness, or for me to bless you, unless you have already asked *le Bon Dieu* to forgive you. Oh, you have been wicked, wicked, to run away and never tell us that you were still alive! Oh, the Masses I have had said in case you —" Here she burst into a sobbing, all the more heart-rending for being silent, which shook the whole of her tiny person and caused the rest of us to gaze at her in astonishment; when Rory rose to his feet and attempted to put his arm round her to comfort her she pushed him away angrily. "You do not seem to understand how cruel you have been. After all the trouble we had with your upbringing, surely we deserved better than to be subjected to years of pain and anguish." She turned to her husband and put her head upon his breast, but not without due and tender regard for his equilibrium. He, for his part, since he had no free arm to support her, kissed the top of her head in some embarrassment.

Rory kneeled to her again.

"Tantie!" he began, "I can assure you —"

"Have you been to confession?" she interrupted, without lifting her head from Jéhu's breast.

"But of course!"

"And you have confessed to grievously wounding those who loved you most?"

Rory hesitated.

"I can see that you have not," whispered Tantie Cécile, "and it would be presumptuous of me to forgive you or to give you my blessing before you have repented and received absolution. Rest assured, Rory, that I shall pray for you unceasingly night and day."

With these unyielding words Rory had to be satisfied, for his Tantie would say no more, no matter how he cajoled her, revealing that she knew that silence was a weapon as effective as speech.

By this time Francisca had fallen asleep in Betsy's arms and had not, fortunately, witnessed her father's discomfiture. After a long silence, during which none present seemed inclined to look at another, Rory commenced to speak in a low voice, evidently somewhat chastened and intent upon offering justification for his actions. He had run away, he said, certain that he had killed Godefroi de Champfleurs, convinced that he would have brought dishonour upon us if he had stayed, and determined to act honourably in an honourable cause, thus proving that the calumnies uttered by his schoolmate had been entirely undeserved. Within days of landing upon the coast of Gran Colombia he had joined the forces of el Libertador Simon Bolivar, giving a false age. He had served in various regiments, including the Legión Británica, and had been fortunate enough to earn rapid promotion. He had been taken on to General Bolivar's staff and had been required to undertake duties so clandestine that it was essential that his identity be concealed; from that point onward, it became quite impossible for him to communicate with us — his present visit was perilous in the extreme and made only because the preservation of Francisca's life was paramount.

Rory stopped his narrative at this point, as though he were expecting questions or comment, but we were all without words. He then went on to describe how he had been present on that saddest of days, the 17th of December 1830, when el Libertador had passed away, although still a young man. During his last illness the great man had confided to him, in a rare moment of intimacy, that his own blood was almost certainly mixed and that his only true "*padre*" had been his black nurse Hipolita, a slave valued at three hundred pesos whose milk had nourished his life. Rory stopped again, this time regarding his mother Betsy intently and in silence, a silence which not one of us was inclined to break, so charged with emotion was it.

When Rory resumed he told us that after General Bolivar's death he had joined a South American army which he did not propose to name, but in which he had no occasion to speak any other language than Spanish, hence his loss of fluency in other tongues. He had quickly risen to a rank equivalent to that of General but his personal and political circumstances were now of the utmost delicacy. His purpose in coming to la Trinidad was twofold — first, to convey to us in person his profoundest apologies for the wrong he had done us, a wrong which he would confess fully at the first opportunity (and here he bowed gravely to his Tantie); and second, to place Francisca Maria in our care in order to preserve her life and to enable him to avenge her mother's murder at the hands of a Royalist *cuadrilla* — it was a public as well as a private duty. Passions were such that his enemies, and he had many, would not hesitate to take his daughter hostage, or even to murder her outright, so that he would be obliged, since she did not bear a close resemblance to any one on our side of the family, if we would represent her not as our grand-daughter but as the daughter of friends who had died in most tragical circumstances. In the interests of secrecy he had even deemed it necessary to part his child from her Indian nurse, to whom she was devoted but who could not have been trusted to hold her tongue.

Rory then went on to relate how he had had to elope with his wife, who had been the prized and cosseted only daughter of an Hidalgo family so exalted that they scorned to make a secret of the Inca princess who had been transported to Spain to marry an ancestor, but so proud that they would never accept either himself or little Francisca — he had a suspicion that the angry Hidalgos had arranged for his wife's death to avenge the stain upon the family honour caused by her marriage to a *mestizo* and a Republican.

"Oh Rory!" said Betsy, the light of the single lamp reflected in the tears in her eyes, "that she should have died in such a way and left you alone with a motherless child! Was she as beautiful as her daughter?" She reached out and touched her son's cheek, then looked down into the perfect little face, as enchanting in repose as it was when illumined by those jewel-like eyes.

"My wife had *valentia y resistencia*," replied Rory, "and we loved each other dearly; it would have been tempting God to ask for more."

At this, Betsy very cautiously handed the sleeping Francisca to Madame Jéhu, went to Rory and put her arms around him; he returned her embrace while the rest of us could only look on or look away as our natures dictated. When enough comfort had been given and received between mother and son Betsy asked Rory whether he had dined and when he replied that he had not but was suffering no pangs, fetched Madeira and fruit-cake from the sideboard. When our son had made a pretence of partaking of these refreshments in silence, and had gazed long upon his daughter's face as though to impress its lineaments indelibly upon his memory, he turned to me and asked whether I could let him have a substantial sum of money, as he found himself in urgent need of it; the sum was so large that I cannot trust myself to name it upon paper.

"Rory!" I exclaimed, "I do not keep such sums by me and in any case if you are to leave within the hour —"

"Most esteemed Father," said my son, "where else would you keep *specie*, in view of your opinion of bankers, except hidden in this house? Even when I was a little boy I knew that you had a secret repository which you changed from time to time — I even fancied, in my childish way, that should the house burn down, a pool of shining molten gold would be found amongst the ashes!"

"Mr. Mason," interposed Betsy, "let Rory have the money. If you are unwilling to make him an outright gift of it, I will recompense you from my own resources."

"I could arrange for a generous monthly allowance," I said, ignoring Betsy's offer, "payable in gold in any country you care to name, but a sum of such magnitude —"

"It would be altogether too perilous for me to collect a sum at regular intervals, and from the one place. Moreover, I need the money for a particular purpose and I need it now! It is *un asunto de honor* — a matter of honour."

"If it a matter of a soldier's honour —" said M. le Capitaine, leaving the rest unsaid.

Rory was so Hispanized in his accent and manner, in the cast of his mind, and even in the cut of his sober clothes, that he seemed a stranger rather then the child of my loins. (The world, I reflected, was still full of strangers, speaking with accents: would it ever be otherwise?) However, stranger or not, he was still Betsy's son, as she was reminding me with daggers from her eyes, and these, together with his uncanny resemblance to Father, overcame any further resistance on my part.

"I take it," I said to my son, "that you will require the money so wrapped that it will not chink?"

Rory bowed solemnly as if in thanks and agreement, but spake not. I rose to my feet and made my way out of the salon, not failing to exaggerate somewhat the shuffling nature of my old man's gait. When I returned with the money securely and silently packed into a stout linen bag, Betsy had resumed her grand-daughter into her arms and was conversing easily with Rory; M. le Capitaine was listening attentively to them while Madame Jéhu seemed to be saying a rosary with her beads in one hand while the other rested upon her husband's bony knee.

Upon seeing me Rory leapt to his feet, seized the bag of money from me and picked up his hat; he was clearly impatient to go. We tried to delay him by asking what name he was using, in case we read about him in the South American papers, but he answered shortly that he would not burden us with that knowledge; he would not even reveal the name in which Francisca had been christened. He ended our attempts to detain him by kneeling to me to receive my blessing; he then did the same to Betsy and M. le Capitaine, who obliged him as before; Madame Jéhu, however, would only offer him her cheek for a farewell kiss, which he was able to give her from his kneeling position, such was the difference in their heights. Lastly, he looked at Francisca Maria.

"I wish that she could have kneeled to me," he said, "to receive my blessing in the proper form before I depart, for she may never see me again. I will not wake her lest she cry out." He placed his hand lightly upon the sleeping head. "*!Que Dios te bendiga y proteja!*" he said and, bending to kiss her forehead, added: "*!Adios, mi Princesa!*"

With a few lithe and wondrously silent strides he was at the door, the money-bag which had cost me such effort to lift and carry a mere featherweight to his arm; he listened for a moment, unbolted the door with great care, opened it and slipped out. Not a dog barked, nor did we hear any other untoward sound during the ten minutes which we spent motionless and hearkening. When I tiptoed cautiously out on to the galerie at Betsy's insistence only the customary night-time hum from the direction of the quay could be heard under the starlit sky which arched over Port-of-Spain; that Rory had chosen a moonless night for his visit was in keeping with what appeared to be his employment. Thus did our son disappear again into that so near and yet so mysterious and turbulent Continent upon which Trinidad and its inhabitants have for the most part turned their backs.

When I returned to the salon, Francisca was no longer to be seen and Betsy was giving Madame Jéhu a low-voiced tongue-lashing of the kind which she usually reserved for me; she was expatiating upon the nature of charity and the desirabilty of human beings forgiving each other, unfettered by the requirements of any Deity. Madame, for her part, was defending her religion and her actions with vigour and some asperity, not omitting to refer to her superior status as a married woman. Neither seemed to have noticed that poor M. le Capitaine was gasping in considerable distress and signalling that he needed help to return to his bed. I succeeded in bringing the two females to their senses by going to his assistance myself. When I had got him to his bed and his wife had taken charge of him, Betsy and I took up our pistols from the table and retired to her chamber; there Francisca was asleep and breathing quietly in the middle of the great bed. Since she had cast off the sheet I could see that she was clad only in her shift and that her little limbs matched her face in beauty. I was indeed glad of her presence, for my mistress had seemed intent, as she followed me into her chamber, upon voiding the residue of her anger upon me; catching sight of her grand-daughter, however, she stood still and regarded her with benevolent eyes.

"Oh Dickie!" she said (and how relieved I was that her benevolence extended to me!), "Rory was right — she is truly a gift who will bring us much comfort."

"Yes," I agreed, but not with my whole heart, for though I had fallen deeply in love with Francisca, doubts were assailing me, and as I composed myself to sleep beside Rory's warm little "gift" I was pondering, in my customary melancholic manner, whether she would not bring tribulation as well as comfort, for I could not call to mind a single child who had not caused anguish to its parents and we were not youthful and resilient, but grandparents who had exceeded threescore years and ten and as such were less able to withstand minor tribulations, let alone anguish.

CHAPTER XXXIII

Our Household suffers a Loss as well as a Gain; our Grand-Daughter proves herself to be the Comfort which her Father promised, but safeguarding her Future involves strange Ceremonies

My readers, I married Betsy. We were in our seventy-ninth year and she consented to the ceremony, not to promote her own interest, nor yet to please me, but as part of a plan (which bore enough resemblance to a conspiracy to re-kindle our erstwhile fervour) and which had to do with safeguarding the future of our beloved Francisca Maria. (Marriage, if I may digress, as indeed I must, has not altered the relations between us as I had feared it might after observing Madame Jéhu's changed behaviour. Betsy has certainly decreed firmly that wielding a pen is now detrimental to my health and that this must be the last chapter of "the melangery of truths, half-truths and nancy-stories which you describe as your 'Life and Times'" but, as my readers know well, she would have issued that decree with as much authority had she been no more than my mistress.)

However, I anticipate, and must attempt to tell my tale in due order, or at least such order as an old man is able to impose upon the various incoherent memories which keep occurring to him and vying for his attention.

Rory's clandestine visit had one unhappy consequence — the excitement of it, and of the quarrel between his wife and his sister, proved too much for M. le Capitaine, who was, of course, a very old man whose constitution had long been weakened by his wounds. On the following morning he did not arise from his bed and despite devoted nursing he weakened day by day until a morning came when he requested that Francisca be brought to him. He gazed upon her solemn beauty for a full three minutes, but when her face began to crumple at the sight of his less than prepossessing countenance he signalled to his Madame that the little creature should be taken away. He died within the hour, and at his wife's insistence, we gave him a Christian burial next to his mother Matti in the little graveyard at the end of our plot. At the end of the ceremony, remembering my gesture of respect to Father and Henri and deciding that I had respected Jéhu more than either of them, I instructed Merry to hold my umbrella over me while I seized a spade and made to wield it. However, Betsy, who was holding Francisca by the hand, was having none of such foolishness.

"Put down that spade, Mr. Mason!" she called out. "You will kill yourself!"

"Please desist!" added Madame Jéhu. "My dear husband would not have expected any such exertion of you."

"Tonton Dickie!" whimpered Francisca, using that affectionate name for the first time and joining in the tears being freely shed by all around, family and servants alike.

Yielding to these demands by Reason and Sentiment, I returned the spade to the gravedigger and we all watched him and his colleague as they completed their sad task.

This was the last occasion upon which Madame Jéhu asserted herself openly for she straightway resumed the character of a devout little sempstress; her only transgression was that of quite brazenly teaching Francisca to say her prayers. She became a staunch ally of Betsy's (for they had made up the quarrel which had contributed to Jéhu's last illness) and silently took my mistress's side in any disagreement.

As to Francisca Maria, the three of us who remained were made to feel twenty years younger, so delightful a child was she, combining Spanish gravity with an impish sense of fun. Under the loving care of "Tantie Betsy" and of her nurse (the late Janga's daughter Joséphine) she quickly became accustomed to her strange new surroundings. I also had a part to play, and insisted upon playing it to the full, for "Tonton Dickie" was the only one in the household who understood her plaintive questions in Spanish and could explain to her that Mama had gone to Jesus; that Papaito had gone to fight the bad men and would come back for her when she was a little bigger; and that Encarnación (whom she mentioned often and whom I took to be her Indian nurse) had had to go home to her village in the mountains. This last invention of mine got me into hot water, for one day the infant managed to escape from Joséphine, cross the road and the Pitch Walk, and set off across the Savannah toward the mountains "to find Encarnación".

"I trust," said Betsy to me sharply, after Francisca had been retrieved safely, "that you are not going to tell my grand-daughter nancy-stories, indulge her and then fail to control the impulsive behaviour which results from your folly. I need hardly remind you of your signal failure to control my son. I could not bear a repetition of his escapades on the part of his daughter!"

"My dear," I answered mildly, remembering how Father had indulged Merry, "surely a grandfather, an old man with only one grandchild —"

"A single grandchild without parents is at greater risk of over-indulgence than any other, especially if the child is female and the indulger is a grandfather approaching his dotage."

Thus spake Betsy, and decreed that Francisca would be brought to me for only half-an-hour each day in the evening after I had returned from my office and she was ready for her bed. My retort to this proclamation was to use the precious half-hour to converse in Spanish only, insisting that *my* grand-daughter speak the beautiful Castilian which she had acquired from her mother and forget the market Spanish which she had learned from her nurse. Thus did we share many little secrets, for no one else in the household could follow a word of the language of Madrid, not even Betsy, and we gleefully used it to deceive others when in company.

Fortunately for me, Francisca shewed no desire to wander off again, and indeed proved to be the best possible infant for a household of old people, distributing her favours amongst us with kindly condescension — not for nothing had her father addressed her as "*Princesa*".

She grew all too quickly, as children watched over by old people will, and soon revealed a passion for horses almost equal to that of her great-aunt Tony. The telescope which I had used for checking that my goods were being unloaded with due care from ship to lighter was mounted upon a stand on our front galerie so that I could supervize Francisca as she rode around the Grand Savannah of a cool morning followed by her groom Earl. As I watched thus, and I think she was happy that I did so, her growing beauty began to be a source of anxiety to me, for I knew that she had to learn a painful lesson — the colour of her skin, no matter how satin-smooth it might be, and the wave in her long black hair, no matter how it might resemble a starlit sea, both meant that French Créole and other "local-white" young men would consider her as beneath their notice (except for a purpose which I do not care to mention). Perhaps she was learning this lesson already, for other youngsters out riding with their grooms, and they were mostly white, never approached her or spoke to her — how can one warn a child on such a matter? I could not share this anxiety with Betsy, for she was convinced that Rory would return and resume the care of his daughter before she came of age; yet I knew that we should long ago have started to make plans to appoint a guardian and to arrange our affairs so that no Mulatto adventurer or new arrival (as yet unaware of the gradations and significance of hue and hair-texture) could lay his hands upon the fortune which would be Francisca's.

The sad example of Tony and her marriage was ever in my mind (as was guilt about my part in facilitating it), but I would often take comfort from the dainty yet firm manner in which Francisca rode side-saddle upon her pony and the gentle yet determined way in which she induced it to canter. Surely she would never think to ride a hog, even if she had the opportunity, or tease anyone as Tony had teased us all and then, so disastrously, Edward! Surely she would live her life according to the precepts of Reason and not be driven by a daemon as was Tony!

Putting Tony's name to paper reminds me that some months ago — nay, it was a year or two ago, or perhaps even three — pungent smoke from Camboulay drifted across the Savannah from an estate in St. Ann's, entered my nostrils and revived my dread daylight illusion that I was seeing and hearing my doomed sister dancing and singing and shrieking upon the roof of Thornfield Hall as the flames licked around her. When that dream or vision had run its irresistible and undeviating course I began to wonder if my poor sister's body had been decently interred and a proper memorial erected over her last resting-place. Calling for pen and paper, I straightway wrote to Edward in my own hand. I received a reply after an interval of many many months; the delay being explained by its having been wrongly addressed to Jamaica; it was headed "Ferndean Manor" and signed "JANE ROCHESTER" in plain script while the rest was written in the neat-seeming but barely legible hand complained of by Mr. John Eyre. The writer could not be other than the adventuress Jane Eyre. She stated curtly that she had not seen fit to read my letter to her poor blinded husband; that Bertha Mason or Rochester (1764–1808) had been commemorated in the inconspicuous manner appropriate to a suicide, just outside Thornfield churchyard; and that the writer would be obliged if she received no further communication from an Island, and a family, of which her dear husband had only unhappy memories.

I shewed this letter to Betsy; she took some time to find and put on her spectacles and then read it with an expression of mounting distaste.

"So she got him!" she exclaimed. "I wonder how any woman, even the Miss Jane Eyre whom you described to me, could bear to live with that man!"

"But he is blinded and crippled," I argued as old men do, merely for the sake of arguing.

"Neither of these conditions is likely to have improved his temper, even if he has laid his hands upon her £20,000 as a consolation."

"I have come to the conclusion," I said continuing to make an argument, "that Miss Eyre had a hold upon Edward's affections which Tony never had; she had only to lift her eyebrow and he jumped to do her bidding — it was as though he were bewitched — and if she is conducting all his business as this letter suggests, she may even have strengthened her power over him."

"Nevertheless, Dickie, I cannot find it in my heart to be sorry for either of them. From what you have told me of her, and from what I know of him, they would seem to deserve each other." Thus Betsy intimated that she would hear no more of the Rochesters.

More recently another letter arrived, this time from my Edinburgh lawyer, the deceased Mr. Tulloch's son, now an old man himself. He asked if he might be relieved of the long-drawn-out task of investigating my right, if right there was, to a Macdonald chieftaincy; he was fairly certain that I did have a claim of some sort but the Lord Lyon was not partial to claims originating furth of Scotland and since no heritable or moveable property attached he would advise, as a friend as well as a lawyer, against my proceeding further in the matter. As to legitimizing the natural son whom I had mentioned, it was indeed possible in Scots Law, but would be the subject of much sanctimonious and obnoxious comment in the Edinburgh newspapers. He remained, he concluded, my very humble and obedient servant.

This letter I had to read aloud to Betsy, for she had again mislaid her reading glasses; when I had finished she stood up and walked over to my chair. As I watched her approach I marvelled once again that Tony had been right — she was as handsome and elegant in her late seventies as she had been at any other age, her carriage as upright and her kerchief as proudly carried; there was no doubt in my mind that she would be beautiful at ninety. She took a hold of my ear-lobe between her thumb and forefinger and pinched it in a form of reproof which I knew well.

"It is high time you put this nonsense out of your head," she said. "What profit would there be in a clan chieftaincy for an old man such as you? In Trinidad of all places? As to legitimizing Rory, perhaps the Macdonald clan might not relish a Chief as dark-skinned as he!"

I shrugged my shoulders, for there was a "merciless Macdonwald" in me who would have liked to be a Chief, whether there was a profit in it or no, and in defiance of Reason.

"Moreover," continued Betsy, pinching my ear once again, but a little more tenderly this time, "how could you legitimize a son who has altogether disappeared, or a grand-daughter whom we know not whether to acknowledge as such, and for whom we have no documents whatsoever?"

This was the first occasion upon which my ever-hopeful mistress had acknowledged to me that our son might never return. (During the six or more years since he had left his "little Princesa" with us we had heard nothing from him or of him, for he had not visited any of my correspondents, nor had news of a Mulatto General appeared in any of the Spanish American newspapers which I perused so thoroughly.) I therefore seized this opportunity to broach with Betsy the subject of protecting Francisca's future and she agreed for the first time to debate it with me. Once we had made a start we soon regained the youthful conspiratorial fervour.

Firstly, we called upon Rory's boyhood friend, M. Noel's eldest son Anselm, who had inherited his father's estate and was now a Mulatto of some standing. We swore him to secrecy and revealed to him the truth about Francisca's parentage; he duly expressed his astonishment and delight, and declared himself honoured to act as her guardian and joint executor of our estate. We then inveigled our smart young English lawyer, Mr. Peter Robinson, into devising a cunningly intricate series of overlapping and interlocking trusts, wills, deeds, depositions, affidavits, bonds, recognizances, etc., which would ensure that Francisca's fortune would never be at the disposal of a husband, and could be used as security against a loan only with the greatest of difficulty.

We had almost completed these arrangements when the lawyer declared that he must have at least one document in reference to Francisca which would verify her identity unequivocally to any court, and that in the circumstances that document must be a baptismal certificate. We tried to argue, but Mr. Robinson could see no other way out of the difficulty.

We therefore approached Father Étienne, swore him to secrecy in a manner which was perhaps unnecessary for a priest, and explained our dilemma. After much hesitation, he agreed to sign the necessary certificate; but in return for this obligement the ever-alert priest made three demands (to salve what was left of his conscience, as he said ruefully): the first, that we pay him a large sum of money which would be devoted to re-furbishing a church in which he had an interest; the second, that he actually baptize Francisca in the "conditional" form, since we knew not if Rory had had her baptized; and the third, that the relatives presenting the child should be a respectable married couple, that is, that we must consent to be married by him. Upon hearing this Betsy spoke her mind with some force.

"Father Étienne," she said, "I have no intention of marrying Mr. Mason, since under these English laws which have been imposed upon Trinidad all my hard-won assets would come under his control. Moreover I would become no more than his chattel once again and who knows what advantage he might take — the older he becomes the more unreasonable are his actions. No, no, no, our present arrangements are entirely to my satisfaction. We must find some other means of protecting Francisca."

Since no arguments would convince Betsy, and Father Étienne refused to moderate his demands, we had to have further recourse to Mr. Robinson. He was naturally delighted to earn more fees and drew up a second set of trusts, deeds, etc. etc., which this time included a partnership agreement under which Betsy and I were to share the expenses, profits and losses on our joint affairs for as long as we both should live. Severe pangs troubled me when I contemplated the great concession which entering into this partnership involved but I eventually consented, won over by Betsy announcing that she too was now prepared to make a concession, and a much greater one, by giving up her hard-won freedom, marrying me and thus becoming my chattel again. (As I ponder the outcome of these negotiations, I absently reach across my desk for Father's silver snuff-box, the one with the stag's head embossed upon it; I open it and empty its contents on to this very page upon which I write. Carefully, and with fingers which tremble somewhat, I sort the black and scarlet seeds into thirteen groups of ten and one of seven; none are missing. Much relieved, I return the magic beads to the box.)

It must have been a consequence of my advancing years that when I was about to sign all the necessary documents with my usual "Richard Mason" I was struck by uncomfortable doubts — was I truly entitled to sign thus? Was not my real name Roderick Macdonald? Would not some trickster with a sharp lawyer be able to deprive Francisca of her fortune on the grounds that he was a Macdonald and the true heir? Would not this proposed marriage to Betsy be invalid if I had given a false name? And so forth. If I had confessed these misgivings to Betsy, or even to Mr. Robinson, I might well have been reassured, but I was ashamed to voice them and kept them to myself, so that they trouble me to this day. (Perhaps I should emulate Father who, in his old age, reverted to calling himself Hamish Macdonald without embarrassment — but no, what would my customers think of such a strange and sudden metamorphosis in their trusted hardware merchant?)

So it came about that I signed the documents, perhaps because Betsy was standing over me, redolent, as always, of cocoa-nut oil, fresh linen, and the merest tantalizing breath of French perfume.

The marriage ceremony took place very early one morning in a tumbledown country church (with a papaya-tree growing high up on a gable-end) which has since been completely re-furbished by Father Étienne, using the extortionate sum which he extracted from us. It was on an estate whence, after Emancipation, the owner had fled to Paris and the Negroes to wherever else they could scratch a living, either on illegal small holdings in the bush or in Port-of-Spain and its environs; there was therefore no local population to wonder what was happening, except for a toothless old Negress who lived in a lean-to and swept the church meticulously three times a day, mumbling to herself the while. She wore four or five hats piled on her head and, according to Betsy, was a superannuated Obeah-woman who had lost her "congregation".

Our only guests (and witnesses) were Madame Jéhu and Mr. Robinson, as we had judged it prudent not to inform our friends and to leave Francisca at home with her governess. I commenced the proceedings by falling over at the church door, rendered quite unconscious by the rays of the sun which had struck me as I emerged from the covered carriage hatless and without an umbrella. I was quickly brought round again by Betsy, who had her own views as to the cause of my seizure.

"Dickie, you old fool," she said, flicking holy water from the font over my face from the ends of her now shrivelled black fingers while Madame Jéhu assiduously wielded her fan, "I should not have to coax you to be brave; it is not as though you were marrying a stranger!"

(This falling unconscious was not the first attack from which I had suffered and my doctor had warned me of the serious consequences which would follow if I did not avoid undue exertion and excitement. This reminded me that Father — and I seem to be recalling Himself more and more often these days — on being similarly warned, had quipped: "When I have given up exciting myself, I shall be dead!")

When Betsy was satisfied that I had recovered my strength, she became exceedingly brusque. "On your feet, Dickie!" she said, and when I had complied, not without a groan or two, we made our way hand-in-hand and very slowly down the aisle to the tawdry little altar where Father Étienne was waiting.

The vows which my beloved and I exchanged in that deserted church seemed but faint echoes of those which we had made to each other with such emotion when we were children and which we had kept so faithfully for seventy-odd years. Nevertheless, they pleased Madame Jéhu so much that she indulged in a flood of tears — tears in which we joined for company's sake, while Mr. Robinson looked away in embarrassment and the old Obeah-woman turned aside from her sweeping to gabble wordlessly at us and then shout: "Help from the Sanctuary!" in an eerie screech.

When the final blessing had been pronounced over us, and we had composed ourselves somewhat, Father Étienne produced the mildewed parish register and it became clear why he had decided to use this particular church — the last entry in the register was dated some twelve years before, so that it was a simple matter to enter our nuptials as having taken place a few days later, Father Étienne's conscience thus being burdened with no more than two false figures. The entry duly made, signed and witnessed, the priest prosaically packed his accoutrements into a valise while the rest of us shuffled slowly back up the aisle and out to the waiting carriage where Sam Junior, the coachman, was already holding the door open for us. We bade farewell to Mr. Robinson, who straightway mounted his horse, and to Father Étienne, who had procured himself an ass for the day's journey.

There followed something of a contretemps. I handed Betsy into the carriage and she took her seat facing forward; I then handed in Madame Jéhu, confident that she would sit beside Betsy as she had done on the way to the church; however, she took the front seat, that is, facing Betsy. The two ladies then gave me significant looks, clearly expecting that I would sit in public view beside the one who was now my wife; this was something which I had never done before, and which I had not contemplated that I might have to do. (We had been accustomed to travelling together only after dark and even then I had sat facing forward as befitted the Master, while Betsy sat demurely opposite, as befitted a valued housekeeper.) I gestured to Madame Jéhu, with as much gallantry as I could muster, that she should take her place beside Betsy, but she did not offer to move.

"I am sure that Madame Mason would wish her husband to sit beside her," she simpered, and indeed Betsy was patting the leather of the seat beside her in a manner which was inviting, and not at all impatient. To conceal my confusion and uncertainty I feigned difficulty in climbing into the carriage; upon seeing this Sam Junior hoisted me in without any of the finesse which his father would have used, and willy-nilly there I was, seated beside my black wife in full view of whomsoever wished to look through the carriage window and to draw his or her own conclusions.

As we drove homeward Betsy held my hand in hers and I could convince myself that there were those amongst the curious Negroes in the villages through which we passed, and amongst the motley crowds in the streets of Port-of-Spain, who were astonished to see the strange ill-assorted old couple, but I am sure that the majority were quite unmoved (except perhaps by envy that we were travelling in some comfort while they had to trudge and perspire in the hot sun).

A week or so later we drove out at the same early hour to the same little church to have Francisca "conditionally" baptized and found the old Obeah-woman still sweeping away as industriously as before. Francisca's godparents were, of course, M. Anselm Noel and Madame Jéhu Gilbert and as she stood between them on the side of the font opposite to Betsy and myself I knew not whether she was truly conscious of the nature of the ceremony, but I was certain that she was well aware of the delightful picture she made. She was wearing a white silk dress, a joint creation by Betsy and Madame Jéhu, the simple elegance of which concealed the gawkiness of her ten-year-old limbs and emphasized her Hispanic solemnity as she bowed her head and joined her hands in front of her in a most creditable show of piety.

After some proceedings which were as incomprehensible to me as had been the marriage service, Father Étienne started to ask the godparents a series of questions about "renouncing Satan and all his works? And all his pomps?" During these Francisca raised her eyes to mine without lifting her head, smiled the demurest of smiles, and winked at me. I suppose that my more devout readers, if there are to be any, may be shocked at this; others may like to know that Francisca's wink was a skill which she had only recently acquired and which she used to inform me privily that other persons present were being hypocritical or altogether too scrupulous and exacting. I returned the wink as conspiratorially as I could and she then moved her hazel orbs to Betsy's face, opened them wider and made the slightest kissing motion with her lips. I experienced some dizziness at the sight of my grand-daughter's mingling of beauty, gravity, innocence and roguishness and rather more at the candid manner in which she was telling us that she loved and trusted us, but when the old Negress shouted out: "Satan!" in a loud clear voice I was immediately assailed by a tightness and pain in my breast of the kind with which I was becoming all too familiar. Resolving that, for Francisca's sake, I must not lose consciousness, I reached for Betsy's hand and pressed it; receiving a reassuring pressure in return I seemed to gain strength, for the pain and dizziness receded somewhat and I remained upright.

The rest of the ceremony passed me by, except for the actual baptism with holy water, for I continued to wrestle with painful and confused thoughts — this living creature who loved us both so much knew not that Betsy and I were her flesh and blood, her very own Grandpapa and Grandmaman rather then her honorary "Tonton" and "Tantie". Surely we could now, after all these years, consider ourselves released from our pledge to Rory that we would keep Francisca's parentage secret? Surely it was now time that we impressed upon her that it was no real shame to have a Negress for a grandmother or to have in her veins the blood of African Chiefs and an Inca Princess, as well as that of Highland Chieftains, French Seigneurs and Spanish grandees? Surely she would need all the pride gained from this knowledge to live happily in a Trinidad which, whilst beginning to proclaim tolerance as a virtue, nevertheless still valued a white skin above —

POSTSCRIPT

My husband went to his eternal rest before he could complete of his "Life and Times"; it will now be locked away in keeping with his wishes. I can confirm to his readers that his passing was hastened by morbid though well-founded foreboding about the future happiness and well-being of our grand-daughter Francisca Maria Mason, and about the fate of his fortune; they may also wish to be informed that he and I did tell Francisca of our relation to her and that she straightway replied that she had suspected as much and had been calling us Grandpapa and Grandmaman "inside her head" for some time previously. Since my husband's death, which occurred not long afterwards, the little minx has taken to stroking my face, especially if I have disturbed her feelings by weeping, and attempting to comfort me by talking nonsense, for example, by saying that she wishes that she was black too; or, contrariwise, that she does not blame me for the colour of her skin, but Grandpapa, on the grounds that he was looking down (that is, allying himself with a Negress) whilst I was looking up (that is, being the faithful concubine of a white man). Truly she is as antithetical as was her grandfather! I trust that she is still as enamoured of me in a few years' time when some handsome light Mulatto young-man comes a-wooing my hard-won fortune, and my husband's, under the guise of being infatuated with her pretty face and comely person.

Elizabeth Mason

APPENDICES

AUTHOR'S NOTES

I read *Wide Sargasso Sea*, Jean Rhys's story of the first Mrs. Rochester, in 1981 or thereabouts, some fifteen years after it was published. During those years I read many reviews of it, and references to it, and formed a mental picture of the kind of novel it must be. The real novel turned out to be entirely different — so different indeed that I was left with this other novel fermenting away and demanding to be written. I am beholden then, in no small measure, to the shade of Jean Rhys as well as to that of Charlotte Bronte.

The historical background to my story is as accurate as I, a very amateur historian, can make it. Wars, mutinies, the hurricane, fires, etc., are all from recorded history, and where I have introduced historical persons (for example, Captain John Paul (Jones), Count Arthur Dillon, Colonel Thomas Picton) I have tried to have them speak and act in keeping with what I have learned of their characters. It is, however, unlikely that there was a sugar estate like my fictitious "Braemore" on the deserted island of Tobago when the British occupied it in 1763. Craigellachie, Grant's Trace, Willow Trace, Sans Peur, and l'Orangerie are also fictitious. I have made other slight alterations to history for the sake of my story — for example, I have caused the College of the Immaculate Conception (St. Mary's) to be founded rather earlier than it actually was, and since there does not seem to have been a group of nuns in Trinidad before 1836, I have invented one.

Unlike Jean Rhys, who set her novel in post-Emancipation times (that is, after 1834) I have tried to make the dates of the events in mine coincide precisely with those in *Jane Eyre* by using the one clue provided by Charlotte Bronte. In Chapter XXXII St. John Rivers presents Jane with "a new publication, a poem". This turns out to be *Marmion*, which was published in 1808.

375

I am well aware that "Negro" and "Negress" have become derogatory terms, and found writing them an uncomfortable experience. However, I decided that they were a part of history with which I could not tamper.

ACKNOWLEDGMENTS

I would like to thank the Scottish Arts Council for giving me a Travel and Research Grant which enabled me to visit Trinidad and Tobago to research this novel.

I am particularly grateful to Mr. David Cowie of Trinidad for his generous help and criticism, and for suggesting books, providing French and Spanish phrases, and introducing me to the libraries and bookshops of Trinidad.

The following have offered me encouragement as well as giving me help and information of various kinds: Mr. Douglas Archibald, Trinidad; Mr. Friedwart Bock, Camphill Rudolf Steiner Schools, Aberdeen; Ms. Bridget Brereton, University of the West Indies, Trinidad; Dr. Thomas Crawford and his wife Jean, Aberdeen; Mr. Kevin McCarra, Glasgow; Mr. David Philips, Tobago; Mr. Thomas Summers, Edinburgh.

I have learned most of my history from:

Anthony, Michael, *First in Trinidad*, (1985) Paria Publishing Co., Trinidad.

Archibald, Douglas, *Tobago, Melancholy Isle*, Vol. I, (1987) Westindiana Ltd, Trinidad.

Brereton, Bridget, *A History of Modern Trinidad*, (1981) Heinemann International, Oxford.

Edwards, Bryan, *The History of the British Colonies in the West Indies* (1801).

James, C.L.R., *The Black Jacobins*, (1938, 1980) Allison and Busby, London.

Mavrogordato, Olga, *Voices in the Street*, (1977) Inprint, Trinidad.

Naipaul, V.S., *The Loss of Eldorado*, (1969) Penguin Books, London.

Philippe, J.B., *Free Mulatto*, (1824) reprinted 1987 Paria Publishing Co., Trinidad.

Williams, Eric, *History of the Peoples of Trinidad and Tobago*, (1962) Andre Deutsch, London.

Woodcock, Henry Iles, *A History of Tobago*, (1866) reprinted by Columbus Publishers, Trinidad.

GLOSSARY

Unless otherwise indicated, the words in this Glossary are of English, French or Patois origin, Patois being a French-based language spoken in the French West Indies, in Haiti and Louisiana (in both of which it is known as Créole), and in Trinidad until recently (although many of its words are still used in day-to-day Trinidadian English).

I have taken some definitions from *Cote ce Cote la*, a Trinidad and Tobago dictionary compiled by John Mendes and published in Trinidad in 1985. These entries are marked (CcC1).

Alcalde —	magistrate (Spanish)
Alguazil —	constable (Sp)
Amis des Noirs —	"Friends of the Blacks", a French anti-slavery group
bagasse —	"trash" left after the juice has been pressed from the sugar-cane; it was burned to boil the sugar
béké —	(derogatory) a white person, "whitey"
belvédère —	"A summer-house erected on an eminence, commanding a fine view." (OED)
boat-tail —	the Carib grackle or "black-bird"
bois —	stave, stick as used in stick-fighting
Cabildo —	the Cabildo of Port-of-Spain was a powerful Town Council, representing the merchants and the planters
cache-cache —	hide-and-seek
le calalou or *callaloo* —	a purée or soup made from dasheen or other leaves, ochroes, onions, coconut milk, etc. The recipe varies from island to island. "A slimy vegetable dish" — V.S. Naipaul

Camboulay —	see page 33
canaille —	the mob, riff-raff
cat-a-corner —	diagonally
chac-chac —	maracas, "rattle-like instrument made from the hollowed out calabash, containing a small quantity of seeds and fitted with a wooden handle." (CcC1)
Charaibe —	Carib, Amerindian tribe of the South Caribbean
clairin —	raw, or "puncheon", rum
coal —	charcoal
coal-pot —	small charcoal stove
coartación —	literally "limitation"; a *coartación* agreement put a limit on the amount a master could charge a slave for his or her freedom (usually paid by instalments) (Sp)
cocarde —	cockade
cocier broom —	broom made from the ribs of the coconut leaf
cocioco —	piggy-back
cocrico —	Rufous-vented Chachalaca; a medium-sized forest bird of Tobago with a raucous call
Code Noir —	the French legal code relating to the treatment of slaves
Commandante —	Spanish government official, roughly equivalent to "District Officer"
corbeau or *cobo* —	the Black Vulture, which resembles a large crow and is the commonest scavenging bird of Trinidad; not known in Tobago
crabier bec —	a white heron
crapaud —	(Patois) frog; (French) toad
Créole —	at the time of this novel *Créole* meant "born in, or native to, the West Indies" and applied to people of all colours, as well as to horses, the local cuisine, etc. In Trinidad the noun now means "a native, having mixed parentage of European and Negro blood" (CcC1) while the adjective still retains its older meaning
criado —	servant (Sp)
cromac —	roughly made walking-stick (Gaelic)
cuadrilla —	gang (Sp)
cutlass —	machete. ("Also cutlash, cutlish, guilpin, pouyant, or poor people gun", CcC1)

dasheen —	a plant with an edible root, the leaves being commonly used in *callaloo*
dot —	dowry
douche-en-pluie —	shower-bath
enceinte —	pregnant
epée —	sword used in duelling and fencing
Exclusif —	the policy by which French colonies could export their produce only to France, and in French ships, and could import only French manufactured goods. The British operated a similar system
friseur —	hairdresser
galerie —	verandah
gorge de pigeon —	shot silk, resembling a pigeon's throat
hidalgo —	Spanish nobleman
houragan —	hurricane
infelizmente —	unhappily (Sp)
Jacobin —	"an extreme radical in politics" (OED): from the name of a French political club established 1789
Jacobite —	an adherent of the Stewarts, especially of James II and of his son "Prince Charlie"
jalousie —	louvred shutter
jumbie —	"Spirit, ghost. Mischievous or malevolent spirit, creature or person. A night person." (CcC1)
jumbie-bead —	small scarlet-and-black seed of a trailing leguminous plant, believed to ward off jumbies and *mal yeux*
Legión Británica —	a unit composed of British volunteers and mercenaries who fought on the side of Bolivar and his Patriots for the liberation of South America from Spanish rule (Sp)
macommère —	a female friend, gossip
macommère-man —	a lazy or effeminate man who stays around the house
mal-d'estomac —	literally "evil of the stomach"; sometimes attributed to the eating of earth by slaves, but it may have been a stress condition, or brought on by inadequate diet
mal yeux —	evil eye
Mandingo —	a Muslim African from the area between the Senegal and Gambia rivers. Some of those who

	were brought across the Atlantic as slaves could read and write Arabic
marchandle —	street vendor or trader
"*Massa bull*,	
Massa cow" —	"everything belongs to the Master, so what's the difference?"
mestizo —	of mixed blood (Sp)
mocojumbie —	a man who walks on stilts on special occasions, formerly connected with Obeah
mook —	"a very stupid person" (CcC1)
morocoy —	a large land-turtle
Mulatto —	"one begot between a white and a black, as a mule between different species of animal." Dr. Samuel Johnson's Dictionary (1755)
Obeah —	"a kind of witchcraft or sorcery practised in the West Indies; a survival of African magical rites, specializing in poisons and the power of terror through charms and fetishes." (CcC1)
padre —	father *or* parent (Sp)
Paniol —	Spanish or Spaniard
pastel (Spanish),	
pastelle (Patois) —	"delicacy made from grated corn stuffed with meat, olives, raisins, etc., wrapped and tied in fig (banana) leaves and boiled." (CcC1)
pickney —	pickaninny, Negro baby or small child (now derogatory)
pirogue —	a dug-out canoe
po-cham —	*pot-de-chambre*, chamber pot
Q.B.S.M. —	literally "who kisses your hand"; a formal ending to a letter (Sp)
!Que Dios te bendiga y proteja! —	May God bless and protect you! (Sp)
resistencia —	endurance
Sambo —	the offspring of a black person and a Mulatto (now derogatory)
sucrier —	sugar-bird, bananaquite
tamboo-bamboo, *tambour-bamboo* or *bamboo-tamboo* —	percussion instruments made from bamboo-stems of various thicknesses. "In the 1930s bamboo bands underwent a transition to steel." (CcC1)

382

usine —	a sugar-works
usquebaugh —	whisky (Scots, from the Gaelic)
valentia —	courage (Sp)
"y eres mi tio" —	"and you are my uncle" (Sp)

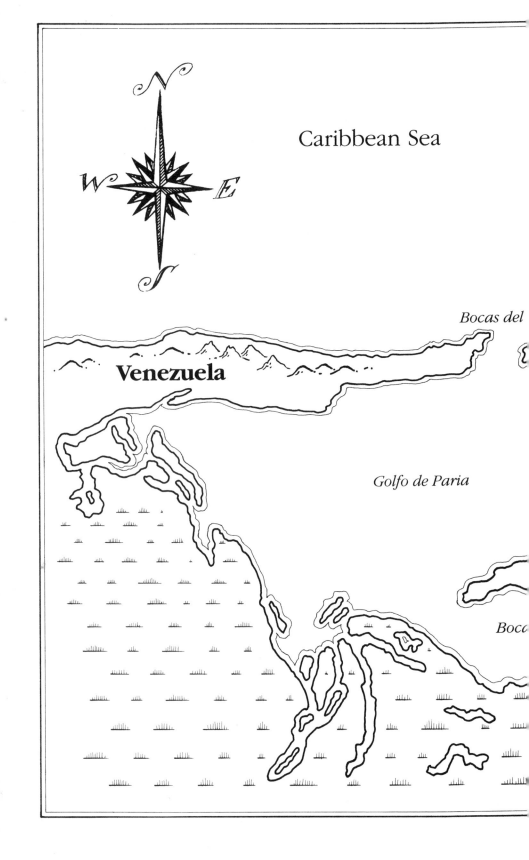

Caribbean Sea

Bocas del

Venezuela

Golfo de Paria

Boc